TIME'S PLAGUE

DREANA ELLIS

ISBN 979-8-218-49381-3

Isaiah—to the one who brings the constant balance to my life and has never
made me feel less than.
You make me feel loved, safe and beautiful.
I couldn't have written this love story without ours first.

To all those who always felt out of place and not good enough.
The world is meant to have you in it. Choose the people who choose you back.

CONTENT WARNING

This is a paranormal fantasy that does include some graphic or triggering scenes. This is a list of content in case any of it may be triggering for you

Pregnancy loss

Child loss

Blood

Suicide attempt

Stabbings

Murder

Nightmares

I

Every day, he loved more.
Through the changing of the seasons and altering lands, he loved.
With the constant sun, turning moon, and even beyond the death of stars, he loved.
Through blisses of sanity and in voids of desolation, he loved.
Final kisses before death came and tears forged when life gave, he loved. Every day,
he loved more.

SAVANNAH, GEORGIA JUNE 1902

Elric appreciated the summer breeze, the slight rustling of the leaves, and the fireflies dancing among them.

He felt so in love, but he felt so in love *every* time.

He heard her coming from a distance but didn't turn around until she was within reach.

Grabbing her quickly, he kissed her as if it were the last time, etching the moment into his mind.

She slapped him away, laughing, "How do you always know I'm coming?!"

He chuckled at her southern drawl; he was not entirely used to it yet.

"I just know. You look absolutely stunning tonight; turn around and let me see."

Holding out his arms wide, he waited for her to showcase.

She twirled while laughing. He loved that sound and was thankful she did it often.

The moon shone brightly on her lavender-colored gown embellished with shining gems reflecting the night sky. She wore her raven hair up with a few loose curls that framed her face.

He reached up to brush a curl off her forehead and traced her jaw before he cupped her chin and looked into her emerald eyes. "You're beautiful."

She grinned and grabbed him by the hand. "Keep talking to me like that, and I'll be stuck here all night, but we have a party to go to! Bonnie will be dreadfully ill-tempered with me tomorrow if I miss her engagement party."

"I feel like she will be ill-tempered because of how lovely you look. You'll be stealing all her attention away."

He winked at her as they walked down the road hand in hand.

They arrived at the party being held on one of the largest and most prestigious plantations in Savannah, renowned for its impressive stature and wealth. Handsome oak trees with delicately hanging Spanish moss made for a dreamy canopy walking up to the home. Guests walked between large white pillars wrapped in sculpted ivy, where they were greeted by servers with full platters of delicacies. A waiter approached, offering them each a flute of champagne. She accepted, and he declined. She, a bright socialite, and he an observant wallflower.

She looked into his eyes and smiled coyly. He leaned in and whispered, "I have fallen so deeply in love with-"

"Ava! You've made it!" A woman shrieked from across the room, interrupting the intimacy of their moment.

Before turning away from him, she held up a finger and sighed, "Don't lose that thought."

Ava let go of his hand to embrace her friend, a small blonde woman with a personality as loud as her bright red lips and rouged cheeks.

"Bonnie, I wouldn't have missed it for the world!"

"Ava, this is my Georgie! Have you seen my ring? I'm sure it cost a fortune! As did this party," she giggled. "Daddy and Georgie said I could have the absolute best; I only get married once, they say! Even though we know that's not true for Betsy Stevenson." Bonnie laughed, looking over her shoulder, "Sure, she marries more than a cat has lives, but she throws the best parties. Ava, bless your heart, did you finally bring your beau around? I am pleased to *finally* make your acquaintance." Shooting a glare at Ava, Bonnie held out her hand. "Bonnie Moore, soon to be Bonnie Grady." She batted her eyelashes at Elric.

Elric took her hand and lightly kissed the top of it. "Ms. Bonnie Moore, soon to be Grady. I am so pleased to meet you."

He held his hand out to George to shake it. "Elric Ferron, thank you for hosting us."

George looked at Elric curiously and smirked. "Elric? You sound like you come from across the great big blue with that fancy accent. What brings you here to America?"

Elric grinned back at him. "Came for business, stayed for love."

"And what kind of business are-"

Bonnie's shrill voice cut through the room, interrupting George's question. "Edith Montgomery, is that you?! Excuse us, please!"

George looked as though he'd like to continue, but Bonnie had already made it across the room, tapping her foot, displeased that George wasn't already at her side.

Ava looked at Elric and blew an exaggerated sigh of fatigue.

A waiter walked in front of Ava with more champagne. She proceeded to grab two flutes and beckoned Elric to come outside. He smiled at her, realizing again he'd follow her anywhere.

They made their way to the back porch, looking out onto a pond, where the frogs filled the night with croaking.

She handed him a glass and started on her second. "I hold my breath the whole time I'm around that girl. I love her to bits, but I never know what is going to come out of that mouth! Her tongue wags at both ends, I swear."

Ava laughed and put down her empty glass on the porch rail. She worked her hands up Elric's chest until her arms were linked around his neck.

"Dance with me."

"Always." He threw his champagne flute into the pond, where it splashed into the water, causing a momentary disruption in the song the frogs sang.

She laughed, and he closed his eyes, trying to capture it, transcribing the sound of his favorite melody in his heart.

They danced around the veranda, Elric twirling her every so often.

Ava looked at Elric, taking him in. Tall, lean, and handsome in a mysterious way. A straight nose set sharply on his face, and a deep cleft dimpled his chin covered by stubble. His dark brown hair was a stark contrast to his bright blue eyes. Eyes that seemed too old for his young face, which was always set in a permanent sort of calm.

She leaned her head against his chest, closing her eyes to listen for the thrumming of his heartbeat.

With her eyes still closed, she asked, "Now, what was it you were saying before we were interrupted?"

He placed his chin on the top of her head, captivated by the woman who held his heart. "How completely in love with you I am."

She raised her head, smiling, "And I with you."

Elric kissed her while holding his embrace. He could still feel her smile beneath his lips.

A flash went off inside the house, and Ava gasped. "A photographer! Bonnie's father spared no expense. Elric, we must have a photograph made!"

Ava pulled him inside, excitement written all over her face.

Elric walked up to the photographer. "Sir, how much for a photograph?"

The photographer smiled. "Nothing at all! This is a gift to the guests from the betrothed couple. Now you and your lady come up. Ma'am, sit in this seat and the gentleman, stand behind her – ah, yes, right there. Put your hand over her shoulder. Perfect!"

Ava looked up at Elric, tenderly kissing the top of his hand.

"I need you to be perfectly still for at least 15 minutes. As soon as the photo is taken, I must take it to the back and develop it immediately. It will take some time, but I will send someone for you as soon as it is ready."

While they waited for their photo to be developed, they made their rounds, drinking and dancing their way through the evening. As Ava socialized with some of her friends, Elric found himself drawn to a floral centerpiece, a clear vase full of vibrant red poppies. Just as he was about to reach out and touch a petal, the photographer's assistant interrupted his moment and handed him a metal plate.

Elric looked at the photo and smiled. He hadn't had a real still shot before, only drawings and paintings of her.

Although they had to stay still, light and warmth radiated from Ava's eyes, the same eyes he seemed to know so well. Elric traced the edge of the photo with his thumb and smiled, placing it in his breast pocket, feeling eager to add it to the collection.

BRISTOL, ENGLAND JUNE 1348

He walked into his home covered in soot, closing the door behind him. He looked at her sitting in a chair close to the hearth, a spoon in one hand stirring the contents of a pot above the fire and in the other her beloved copy of *The Iliad*, the book tattered from use. He stared at her until she noticed, and when she did, she quickly closed her book and laughed.

"No, I would not be able to tell you how many times I have read this. I no longer know that number."

He laughed as he walked up to her to brush a curl off her forehead, "How truly fortunate am I to have a wife who would know how to read."

She set down her book and her spoon to softly cradle his face.

"Surely you would be fortunate, even if I had been born of simple mind, Elric Ferron. I exceed in everything," she said with glee pulling at the corners of her lips.

"Why, but of course! And even if I was told the world would shatter if I loved you, surely, I would continue to do so, Ava Ferron. That is how beyond blessed I am."

Ava pulled his face close to hers and gently kissed him. She pulled away with soot on the end of her nose.

He tenderly rubbed it away. "I am famished."

"Good, the stew is almost finished," Ava said as she moved away.

He caught her and brought her back in, pushing his lips into her neck. "That isn't what I mean..."

They ended up lying on the floor with her head on his chest as they stared into the fire.

Her raven curls lay loose around her shoulders, her emerald eyes aglow in the flames.

She began to sing as she so often did, the harmonious and enchanting voice filling the small hovel. He closed his eyes and let the familiar song lull his spirit to an even more peaceful state.

I have loved all this past year
So that I may love no more;
I have sighed many a sigh,
Beloved, for thy pity,
My love is never thee nearer,
And that me grieveth sore;
Sweet loved-one, think on me,
I have loved thee long.
Sweet loved-one, I pray thee,
For one loving speech;

While I live in this wide world
None other will I seek.
With thy love, my sweet beloved,
My bliss though mightest increase;
A sweet kiss of thy mouth
Might be my cure.

Elric quickly got up. "Do not move."

He returned with one of the few pieces of paper he owned with charcoal in hand. He sat on the ground across from his muse and started to draw.

Ava propped herself up on one arm, lying on her side, "Now, what would your father have to say about you trading your work for *paper*." Saying the word paper with sarcastic disgust.

While crouching down his charcoal glided around the paper, Elric exhaled a long breathe and shook his head. "It does not matter. I would tell him before he could open his mouth that the drawings on these *papers* hold more value than any piece I could make for a knight."

She placed her other hand on her hip and furrowed her brow, making her voice deeper, "Elric, you were not a blacksmith's apprentice so you could trade your pieces for something that does not even give sustenance to you and your wife! You should be making armor for knights and lords, not pictures for handmaidens and Ladies!"

She guffawed at the sound of her imitation of Elric's father. She placed her hand back at her side and softened her expression.

"If an artist was what you chose to be, my only request is that I would forever be your muse."

He stopped drawing and looked up, "Until the end of my life."

They stayed quiet for a while as he drew, and she continued to stare into the fire, deep in thought. He focused, her jaw square and strong yet delicate on her face; her rose-colored lips, turned up slightly at the corners, always in a subtle, warm smile. Her rounded nose and a beauty mark right above her left eyebrow, another beneath her right eye.

7

"Would you like to see it now?" Elric asked as he put down his charcoal to dust off his hands.

She smiled and nodded her head before he turned it over to her. Ava quickly grabbed it from his hands, her eyes moved all across the page.

He watched her intently, "I hope it's to your liking. Your beauty is hardest to capture. It is the most divine. I wish I had colors to show the true beauty of your eyes, your lips, all of it. The charcoal captures your hair perfectly, though. Your curls cascade like water."

Ava put the paper down and wrapped a small, tattered sheet around herself. She crawled toward Elric and nestled herself in between his legs to take his hands in hers. They were rough and calloused from years of work, new wounds, and old scars.

"How do these hands, during the day, forge steel for cruel and heartless battles but at night create beautiful pieces like this? This is how I know that with strong hands you protect and with the same hands you love gently, and that this child in my womb will never lack."

Elric looked up at Ava, astonished. He placed a hand on her belly, tears pooling, "How long have you known?"

She laid her hands over his, "I have not bled for three months now. I had the need to be certain before I spoke to you. With all the other times, I could not bear another loss."

Elric took her into his arms and cradled his wife and unborn child. "I will love you and our child and any children that would follow. I will love you beyond life and any thereafter if I am able to do so."

Before Elric left the next morning, he kissed Ava while she slept. He leaned down and whispered to her belly. "Grow strong, sweet child."

She ran her hands through his hair before she turned back over to her side and swiftly fell back asleep.

On his way to the forge, Elric stopped at the monastery. A tranquil sanctuary nestled in the midst of rolling green hills and ancient trees. Although he didn't consider himself particularly spiritual, he had a fondness for the place of worship, but mostly for the people inside. He was admiring the old stone building when he spotted a brown robe knelt in a sea of red.

"Friar Geoffrey, what is it now you look for in a field of flowers?"

Geoffrey looked up and grinned. In his massive hand, he held a small, delicate red flower.

They mirrored in size, both towering above most men in height and both naturally strong, but Geoffrey's mind was made for science and his heart for people. The friar found solace in the priesthood, constantly trying to fix the ailments of this world. Where Elric was made to follow the life of a smith as his family had done for generations.

"With this poppy here, you are able to give relief from pain!" The friar called out.

Elric walked over, embraced his friend, and laughed, "You will cure us all, will you not?"

Geoffrey smiled and nodded, "What brings you here so early in the morning?"

Elric grabbed his friend by the shoulders and held tightly, "Ava is with child, longer than any of the others she has held."

Geoffrey beamed and they clasped in a warm embrace again, "My friend, God has blessed you. Let me walk with you to the forge. Tell me all Ava has said."

They arrived at the forge. Geoffrey held his hands together in front of him, "I will pray earnestly for your child throughout my day."

Elric grabbed his apron and began to tie it around his waist, "I am grateful; I have confidence God hears your prayers. Now go. I am certain there is someone in the monastery who needs your healing tonics."

He laughed and started to walk away but turned back to Elric, his face suddenly grim.

"Elric, watch for her. I have heard of terrible talk of a disease killing towns by the thousands. I have seen no signs of it here, but I heard it moves suddenly. Watch for her and pray."

Elric's hand rested on top of a hammer as he listened to his friend's warning.

"Geoffrey, what is it called?"

The friar looked at the flower in his hand, his eyes full of horrors not yet heard by the world, "The Black Death."

FOUR MONTHS LATER

A harsh and raspy noise pierced the air, echoing with discomfort. Elric sat in a chair, looking at Ava as she lay in bed. She stroked her growing belly, and he mumbled under his breath. The low glow of the hearth mostly shrouded the coldness of the small room.

"Husband, the concern is written on your face as if I am already on death's doorstep. And the way you normally talk to yourself puts me at ease, but for now, it is more stress-inducing. Geoffrey told me to rest and drink water. He gave me some sort of tonic. You will worry yourself sick as well. This fever will pass."

He forced a comforting expression, looking into her eyes that seemed less bright. Sweat had broken on her brow, and she had not been able to eat much.

"Ava, the black—"

"Has not been seen in this town, and was heard of miles from here," she interrupted. "You need to stop worrying—"

She started to cough, and Elric got up, but she waved him off. He was going to sit back down when he noticed the blood in her hand. Without hesitation, he picked her up, her frail body much lighter than it should be with her accompanying stomach, and started for the monastery.

"Elric, pleas-" Ava's words are cut short by another coughing fit.

"Hush, my love. This is the 'in sickness' part of our vows."

Geoffrey was startled when Elric pushed open the door, lying Ava on one of the nearest tables.

"Elric! What has happened?"

II

PARIS, FRANCE MAY 1822
He sat on the bridge and painted a distant memory. A sea of red flowers, a large man in brown robes gathering them. He liked painting here; there weren't as many people around since the merchants set up on the main road. He also liked it because *she* walked across the bridge every day. A little past midday, he saw her cross the bridge to deliver bread to the merchants and the people who lived in the city. She always gave a polite nod when she passed by, pushing her cart along the way. That raven-colored hair swayed as she moved, and a few loose curls settled on her forehead. But whenever he caught a glimpse of her eyes, his world stopped. Her eyes—always emerald green.

MODERN-DAY ARCATA, CALIFORNIA

The air is crisp and cool. A dense fog settles onto the ground, shrouding the forest in an ethereal haze. Jogging past the giant redwoods, no matter how many times he has seen them, he is always left in awe.

Just a true magnificence, he thinks as he goes past one with a small burrow at the base.

He backtracks, pulls his earbuds out to pause the music on his phone, and settles in against a log across from the burrow. The clock reads 6:42 a.m. There are only a few other people out this early in the morning: some runners and a couple of tourists, but mainly just him and the trees. He pulls a tattered moleskin journal from the pocket of his joggers and a wooden pencil with barely two inches of length left. He starts to sketch the tree and the surroundings, as well as the large and small ferns that take up most of the foliage. The moss around him is so vibrantly green, blanketing the trees and the ground. He can't wait to get home to put this sketch on a larger scale, using colors to bring it to life. He draws continuously and, after a while, glances at his clock, 7:36 a.m., noting that the little creature who made the burrow still hasn't surfaced. Stretching his arms above his head while twisting his back he wonders how much longer he could stay waiting for it to emerge to add to the sketch.

He rattles off his day out loud but quietly. "Consult at 10 a.m. It will take me about 50 minutes to run back home. If I leave at eight, I can be home right before nine, shower, dress, eat quickly, and be on the road by 9:30. And, traffic? Eh, they can wait for me. Five minutes won't make a difference."

Looking up he sees a woman with a white ball cap slowing her jog down, eyes wide and nervous, slowly turning around. He looks behind him to see if there is some sort of danger that would make her look so concerned.

He stands up, shoving his things in his pockets. "Miss, are you okay?"

She doesn't answer, quickening her pace.

He matches her speed. She seems afraid, and his concern is growing; he just wants to help her.

"Hey? Hey!" He shouts so he can get her attention.

13

She turns around, her eyes frenzied with alarm, and a pink can of pepper spray is gripped tightly in her hands.

"Please, I don't want trouble. I just want to go back home. I can give you some cash; it's only a couple of dollars, but that should buy you something? Please don't come closer. I will spray you."

Turning around, wildly confused, he looks for someone else. Then it dawns on him.

"Oh-oh no. I'm not crazy!"

She nervously forces out a giggle. "Okay, of course. I'm going to go..."

"I was just– Wait, look!" He goes into his pocket to pull out his sketchbook, and before he can finish his sentence proving his sanity, a burst of pepper spray smothers his face. His eyes burn immediately, and the skin around it stings with irritation. The moleskin falls to the ground.

The coughing is forceful and hard, "My drawing," he tries to say in between chokes, "showing you."

He bends down, placing his hands on his knees, just letting his nose run and snot hit the ground, each cough spewing out more. With tears streaming down his face, he's trying to resist the urge to rub his eyes, fearing it'll make it worse, but the knee-jerk reaction wants to win.

"Oh, crap. It looked like you were pulling out a weapon!" She yells angrily, "I am so sorry. Here, look up, look up!"

He feels an aggressive grasp on his jaw, pointing his face up.

Her tone softens. "It's just water, don't freak out."

The cool sensation of water covers his eyes and trickles down his face.

"Is that helping?"

"No," he laughs.

"I'm so sorry. I'm out here by myself jogging, and my family warned me not to because of 'the crazies' out here. I didn't care. It's the freaking forest, and aren't murderers in the city? But I think I also freaked myself out thinking of murderers and just really expected to run into one," she pulls a tissue out of a fanny pack and gently pats his eyes.

He stands straight up, taking the tissue from her hands. "Thank you, but actually, your family is right. More people go missing in national parks."

"I'll pepper spray you again," she says dryly.

"Noted. Just a joke," he replies with an innocent smile.

She lets out a sigh and an actual laugh this time, "What the hell were you doing, then?"

"Well," he waved his hand around, "If you grab my sketchbook that is somewhere on the ground, I can show you. I can't see well enough to find it at the moment."

She picks up the notebook off the ground right by his feet, "Where do you want me to go in the book?"

He dabs his eyes again with the tissue, blinking rapidly, hoping his vision will become less blurry, "Start from the last page and go back to whatever the last drawing is. Just to prove I'm drawing inspiration, not victims."

He can hear the book's pages whirring as she flips through them.

"Wow. This is that little animal cubby right there, right? This is beautiful. Are you an artist by hobby or trade?" She continues to flip through the pages, "Wow, I am so sorry. You were just enjoying your morning."

Even in his immense pain, he can't help but feel amused by this situation.

"Mostly hobby," he replies. "So, at this point, I don't mean to be more of a bother, but I can't see the trail well enough to make it back without tripping and injuring myself more. Could you just help me back to the main path?"

She snickers, and he's relieved she also feels the humor in this situation, not sensing any more tension.

"Yes, absolutely. It's my fault you're temporarily blind anyway. But it's your fault for getting temporarily blinded. Who talks to themselves out loud? Alone? In the middle of the forest... Do you need to take my arm?"

She hands back his sketchbook, and he puts it back in his pocket, then pulls out his phone, "If you don't mind. Just one moment."

Speaking to his phone, he begins dictating a message. "Text Anita 'Sorry running rather late PERIOD. Push the meeting to twelve PERIOD. Tell Mr. Kershaw I'll treat him to lunch for the inconvenience PERIOD. Thank you, Anita PERIOD. Please buy yourself coffee and lunch on me this morning to make up for having to deal with him PERIOD."

The woman stares at him, waiting. "You don't have to say period so aggressively; it can hear just fine. I swear you voice text like my dad. You ready?"

He puts out his hand, gesturing for her to lead the way. "Yes, quite ready. To answer your question, I was trying to figure out how long I could wait for whatever animal lives in that burrow to come out so I could sketch it. I don't like just filling in the blanks. I want to know what's happened. So, I was talking about my day aloud, seeing if I could wait it out a little longer. Just helps me process. I've done it for," he stops mid-sentence to think and changes the ending, "for my whole life."

He can tell she is listening attentively, still unable to make out her distinct features. He knows she wears the white ball cap; he can feel the familiar material of an athletic jacket where he's holding her arm and can make out that it is black. He gazes toward her face and can see an auburn ponytail coming out of the hat.

"Well, now that we've gotten more personal," he taps her arm to show the physical touch, "it is probably only right that we properly introduce ourselves. Elric Ferron."

"You are right. Robyn Renata. Again, sorry for assaulting you."

He grins, "No, no, you're quite alright. I'm sure I did seem somewhat alarming."

"I noticed you have an accent; what part of the UK are you from?"

"Ah, just somewhere small in England. You wouldn't know of it."

They continued walking, talking, and laughing for the next hour and a half as they made their way back to the main path, easily falling into conversation.

Robyn, a 25-year-old nurse who works the night shift, has three sisters. She is the second oldest and lives with her parents, and the two younger sisters. She had broken up with her longtime boyfriend last year and moved back in with her parents "temporarily" until she found a place of her own. Robyn admitted it was easier to live with them since she worked such long hours, and it was nice not to come home to an empty house. Her two younger teenage sisters, Kylie and

Keira, love having her at home while her older sister is abroad teaching English to children in China.

As he listens to her speak about her life and family, Elric is intrigued by the passion intricately laced in each sentence of either sorrow or joy.

Elric's vision cleared up just enough to make it home safely as soon as they reached the road. He pulls out his phone to check the time. Squinting, he could make out the 11:06 a.m. and four notifications from Anita at the top of his screen.

"That took a bit longer than I had thought, but I had a lovely time," he said and felt that he truly meant it.

Elric learned long ago it was better to distance himself from the human population, never wanting to get too close to anyone who couldn't last. He couldn't make out much more of Robyn's features but did notice her smile underneath the shadow of her hat.

"I did, too, after I found out you weren't a murderer. My car is parked this way." She motions behind her.

With a slight turn of his heel, Elric points in the opposite direction, "I live just up this way, a few blocks down. I can certainly make it on my own from here. I appreciate you escorting me."

Robyn's shoulders drop slightly, "Okay, well, it was nice meeting you, Elric."

"Likewise, Miss Renata."

She starts to walk in the direction of her car but suddenly turns around, taking off her ball cap and wringing it in her hands.

"See, I don't normally do this, and you could still be a psychopath, but I had a really great conversation with you, and I haven't had a great conversation with a man, like, ever. I'd like to see you again, to, you know, conversate or whatever, so maybe we could..."

He cuts her off smoothly, "Robyn, I'd like to converse with you again," he smirks, "or whatever."

With vision that's still blurry, he can make out a smile and notices a few auburn curls around her face.

Exchanging numbers, he promises her he will be in contact.

Elric walks into a little art studio downtown and greets the young woman at the front desk in a space that is warm and inviting. She has glowing dark skin and matlocks down to her waist, with gold ornamental cuffs through her hair, held back by a boho-chic headband. Thick, round, black-framed glasses overtake a small face, magnifying her dark brown eyes.

She jumps up from her desk. "Mr. Ferron! Your face is all blotchy! Are you okay?! What happened?" She squints. "Are your eyes okay?!" she asks, panicked.

"Anita, I'm alright. Just a little pepper spray to the face." He gives her a cheeky grin before continuing, "I promise I am quite fine. Funny story actually, I was assaulted, *and* I met a lovely woman. Is Mr. Kershaw waiting in my office? Did he express his interest?" He picks up a folder off of her desk counter, rifling through the pages.

Anita begins to answer with an anxious biting of her lip, "Uhm, y-yes. He picked the *Sea of Red*. He insisted on it." She grimaces. "I tried telling him, Mr. Ferron, he just wouldn't listen. "

Suddenly, Elric responds sternly. "That's okay, Anita, I'll handle that one."

He starts walking towards his office and hears Anita behind him. "You picked up a woman?"

Elric waves the folder over his head and without turning around, laughs. "Did you miss the part where I said I was assaulted?"

"Mr. Kershaw, so nice to meet you. I appreciate you working with me on my schedule this morning. Ran into quite the mishap."

Elric reaches out his hand to the man sitting in the chair. Mr. Kershaw takes it and stands up while shaking it. He releases Elric's hand to reach down to straighten out his jacket and smooth a pleat in his pants. Elric noted that Mr. Peter Kershaw is a well-dressed man, wearing only designer clothes down to his socks. A plum-colored suit with a chartreuse shirt and black silk tie sits tailored to his body. Not Elric's style, and he can't help but think he looks like a superhero's archnemesis. His platinum blonde hair and purple lensed glasses don't help stray away from the thought. Elric is the polar opposite in his simple beige henley shirt and jeans with some sort of stain on them from graphite or paint, or God knows what other material; his pants can never escape the mess. His dark mid-length hair often seems messy to some and free-spirited to others. Peter had sent his assistants like bloodhounds out to Elric's studio in an attempt to buy a piece of art. After a year of hounding, Elric finally decided to sit and discuss the possibility of selling one to Peter.

Elric, for the most part, painted out of the love of art and generosity to others. He would find ways to display it simply to share what he found beautiful with the world. He didn't need the money and didn't want the notoriety. Staying under the radar is what suited *his* lifestyle the best. Elric painted under corporations and nonprofits, never his own name, so he wasn't entirely sure how Kershaw even found out who he was. He made prints of his various works of art but always favored the name of anonymity. The only reason he has a studio is for temperature control to keep his work in a prime environment. He hired Anita after she watched him painting for three hours straight in a park and begged to be his apprentice as a 19-year-old woman trying to find her place in the art world. He finally agreed but wanted her to be able to make money while learning. She answers the odd phone call here and there and helps maintain the studio, but Elric has truly enjoyed being able just to teach her. He would be lying if he didn't admit that sometimes in his life, it's nice to have a small constant for a time before leaving again. Anita gives him that little piece of consistency.

"Is your face alright?" A voice deeper than Elric imagined bellowed out of the tall, thin man.

Elric runs his hands through his slightly damp hair, "Ah, yes, quite alright, just a misunderstanding. Now then, Mr. Kershaw, let's discuss what brings you here today. You flew all the way in from New York, correct?"

"Please call me Peter – all my friends and business partners do – and correct." Peter took his seat across from Elric's desk as Elric sat down behind it.

Peter crosses his legs and sits back in a very lax manner. Elric doesn't like it and has already determined he doesn't like Peter Kershaw.

"Oh no, that's okay. How was it that you found my studio?" Elric asks while trying to remain polite, but with an air of "you are not welcome here."

Peter clears his throat, "Ha, small details. Do you know what I do for a living?" Peter pretends like he is going to give Elric a chance to respond but swiftly answers his own rhetorical question: "Many things."

Elric tries not to roll his eyes and stifles a laugh. He settles back into his chair, crossing his arms, preparing for a ramble sprinkled with boastful comments throughout.

"I started in stock trading, following in my father's footsteps. I made so much money that I took my money and invested it into the best choice possible: myself. My ambitions, franchises, and properties among different investment opportunities. I became filthy rich, and do you know what I wanted to do with that success?"

Peter pauses to stare, and Elric gestures for him to continue with a flick of his wrist.

With a confident gaze and raised chin Peter settles in before starting his second spiel of the meeting, "I became a collector. A collector of the invaluable, the priceless, the *unobtainable*. I get what it is that everyone else cannot. And do you know why, Elric? Because *I can*."

Elric uncrosses his arm, sits up, and stares at Peter Kershaw. He runs through a couple of scenarios in his head of how he can handle this. He doesn't know if it's still the remnants of the pepper spray from this morning, but he chooses to be a little spicy.

"Mr. Kershaw, I'd love to show you something. Please follow me."

He stands up, and Peter follows with a victory gleaming in his eyes.

They walk past Anita as she watches intently.

"Anita, could you please hand my guest and me each a pair of gloves? Thank you so much."

With a baffled look, she hands a pair of white cotton gloves to each of the men.

"Mr. Kershaw, if you would please put the gloves on while I unlock this door."
Elric walks up to a door opposite his office. A fingerprint deadbolt is installed
on this door, the only one in the studio. Anita is well aware that no one goes
into that room, which explains the confusion on her face.

"Mr. Kershaw, if you will follow me."

Peter earnestly follows, ready for his dreams of collecting one of these works of
art to come true. As soon as he walks through the door, his eyes widen, and he
is not prepared for the amount of artwork stored there. The room holds large
crates with different sizes of canvases, charcoal and pencil drawings, and finished and unfinished sketches, all with protective layers in between each work.
There are so many more mediums than Peter expected: watercolor, acrylic, oil,
gouache, and ink paintings. Artwork is all over the walls and stored in different
shelving systems.

Kershaw sees the *Sea of Red* hung on the wall and makes a beeline for it. It's an
oil painting depicting a monastery in a large field of red poppies, with a figure
in brown robes bent over picking the flowers.

Taking off his glasses, Peter rubs his eyes as if his vision deceives him. "This
is more exquisite in person. You captured the Romanticism art movement
tremendously. My god, it looks like this was plucked straight from the 1800s.
What was your inspiration?"

Walking up behind him, Elric keeps his hands locked behind his back. "Thank
you. I appreciate your enthusiasm and knowledge. This is just an image I remember from my youth."

"Tremendous, truly. You seem to be no older than thirty, but I can count at least
six different styles of paintings in this room that are perfect—*impeccable*. And
that is only what I can see! What is this—"

Peter pauses mid-step and walks towards a wall with at least a dozen different
pieces, all of different styles. At the center is a charcoal drawing on parchment,
protected behind glass. Every piece of work contains the same subject. A woman
with dark curly hair, soft expressions, and bright eyes that even showed through
pieces that were black and gray. In pieces with color, those bright eyes were an

emerald green, framed with strong, dark features.

Peter gasps as he studies each piece, "This charcoal one, how old is this? It looks to be, it has to be, hundreds of years old! How do you have this? Who is this woman? You painted the rest of these? All of them?"

Elric chuckles, "You can make any piece of paper look old. Different effects and such."

"And the woman?" Peter insists.

Standing in front of the piece he has stared at a million times, if not more, his heart aches. It has for the last six hundred years. All the pictures of her have a different ache attached to them.

"She is a dream," Elric says, closing his eyes.

"She is the perfect dream then. How much for the Red Sea and one of these of the dream girl." Peter asks, almost drooling, waving his finger and pointing at the hanging portraits.

Opening his eyes Elric stiffly turns toward Peter, "Well, Mr. Kershaw, this is why I have brought you back here. Although your persistence and your investigative skills are somewhat impressive, I'm not even sure how you located me, but the *Sea of Red* and all the other pieces you see here are not for sale. Not for you anyway."

Peter's jaw drops briefly, but he quickly collects himself, smoothing over his suit jacket, "Now, Elric, everything has a price. People will always sell something for the right amount. I could make your wildest dreams come true."

"I'm doubtful of that. I am going to say something I know you are not used to hearing," Elric removes his gloves and smiles. "No."

He walks towards the door and doesn't turn around to face Peter until he reaches the threshold. He holds open his arm and inclines his head towards the exit, all while maintaining a charmingly polite grin.

Peter's face red with chagrin stumbles over his words, "I-I-I have neve- Are you kidding- Do you know who I- People don't tell me no! I tell people- I flew out here for you to be a complete douche?"

Peter stomps past Elric and Anita to storm out the door. Elric follows him out and stands in the doorway of his building, watching Peter's driver lean against the wall, smoking a cigarette. As soon as he sees his obviously angry employer, he throws it on the ground and runs to open the back door. Before the driver closes it, Peter Kershaw pretentiously flips off Elric.

Elric laughs and waves goodbye as Anita approaches from behind, waving vigorously.

"What an ass hat." Anita laughs.

Elric walks over to the driver's still-glowing cigarette, stomps it out, and throws it away.

"Yes. What an ass hat," he agrees.

III

BRISTOL, ENGLAND OCTOBER 1348
"Geoffrey, what can I do? I cannot lose her," Elric buried his face in his hands, trying to keep his sobs quiet as Ava slept in the next room.

Her fever had worsened, causing her body to shiver violently, sweat soaking her clothes. Her nose was bleeding often, and she continued to cough up more and more blood as time passed.

Geoffrey sat next to Elric and placed a hand on his shoulder, hanging his head low.

Elric looked up, eyes red and swollen from crying. "Is it the black de-?" he choked on his words, unable or unwilling to say it out loud.

"I believe it to be so," Geoffrey replied, never raising his gaze to meet Elric's.

The friar cleared his throat. "When I examined her, I noticed she had blackening on her toes. My dearest friend... I fear she only has a few days left."

Elric stood up and walked out the front doors of the monastery, heading to the poppy field and falling once he reached it. He lay in the dirt on his belly and cried harsh and painfully, chest-rattling, moaning sobs that heaved his whole body forward. He did not care who heard them; he cried with no shame.

After a while, he rolled over, the right side of his face caked with dirt. Gritty, gravel-mixed tears marked his face with the distress of the night. Dehydrated and exhausted, his body felt dry, as did his soul. He looked up to see Geoffrey standing at the edge of the field waiting. Straining to focus, Elric heard the friar's mumbled prayers in the distance.

He stood up and walked towards his friend, who was looking at him with devastated conviction written on his face. With every beat of Elric's heart, a snapshot of a memory flashed in his mind. The laugh he heard for the first time in the market, and turning his head to this mesmerizing woman. Their first embrace and a passionate first kiss. Running away for a secret midnight nuptial. Knowing her family would never approve, though, she could care less. As he carried her over the threshold of a starved-looking hovel, he was ashamed, knowing she deserved more. She told him love would keep them warm and their bellies full as she took delight in their new home. That's when he believed he would never be good enough for a heart as pure as hers. Ava was the grace, hope, and optimism he so desperately needed in his life.

His breath caught in his chest, bringing him back to the present. He did not think death could even save him from this misery.

"I may have a way you can save her," Geoffrey spoke barely above a whisper, his eyes never leaving the ground.

Elric stared at his dirt-stained, calloused hands before the pressure in his soul exploded into rage. He grabbed his friend violently by the collar of his robes, the fabric balling in his fist. "Why did you not say something sooner?!" he screamed, gritting his teeth to the point of pain, but none that could compare to what he felt inside at the thought of her leaving him forever.

With tears streaming down Geoffrey's face, he answered. "I fear it will damn your soul."

"And that is my decision to make! Not yours!" His anger and desperation tightened his grip on the friar's robes, turning his knuckles white. Once he noticed, he immediately released his friend.

25

"Geoffrey," Elric hung his head and began to weep, "I am so sorry. I am terrified of losing her. Please, I cannot find it in myself to care what happens to my soul. My wife... my child. Please."

Geoffrey embraced Elric and then held him at arm's length by his shoulders. "Come with me."

The two men walked to the back of the monastery, where a pile of hay lay in a heap. Geoffrey grabbed a pitchfork lying against the wall, easily picking up the pile of hay with it, then threw it to the side before dropping down to his knees and digging into the earth. Elric knelt beside him and began to dig with no clue what it was that they were trying to unearth.

About a foot down, Elric scraped a solid surface, bending his fingernails back. Geoffrey shoved his hand into the dirt and pulled out a wooden box. The box was square and smelled of pine, with burnt symbols on the top that were unrecognizable to Elric. Geoffrey shoved the box into his hands before covering them with his own.

"You are my friend. You are my brother. And I love Ava, but this..." Geoffrey said, shaking his hands over the box, "This is dark. A woman brought this to me after her daughter died from the Black Death. She said when she finally got it to save her daughter it was too late, but she could not bear to keep this in her house. A reminder of her failure, she said, but she begged me to destroy it. She tried and could not. I tried too, but to no avail. Fire did nothing, so I tossed it into the sea. I found it on my bed upon returning, dry as a bone. So, I hid it somewhere I would always know where it was and could easily tell if it had ever been moved."

Elric took the box and clutched it to his chest. "Thank you. I'm going to go see Ava before I take this to my home to open it. I will be back within the hour."

He turned to go but felt Geoffrey grab his sleeve to stop him.

"I implore you. Think about this before you do it. There are things worse than death."

Elric jerked his arm from his friend's grasp.

"I assure you, there is nothing worse than a life without her."

He ran back to Ava without giving the friar another look.

When he made his way back to her, she was shivering violently in her troubled sleep. He ran his hand across her forehead and felt that she was burning hotter than before. Elric knelt beside her to take her hand in his.

Ava opened her eyes slightly to mumble to him. "My love. I'm so cold. I'm so tired."

He choked back any tears fighting to flow. "It will be alright. Rest. I just needed to tell you I have to go back to our home, but I will be back before the hour is up. Geoffrey will be here to take care of you."

As if on cue, Geoffrey walked through the doors and stood on her other side, placing a gentle hand on her arm.

Ava's eyes welled up as she began to cough while holding a cloth up to her mouth, easily staining it with blood.

"Elric, please do not leave me. I am so afraid," she begged as her silent tears turned into sobs. "I do not want to die; I want to hold our baby. I want to love you and grow old. I want to watch our child grow. Please. I want to live the lives we are meant to."

He picked her up and held her on his lap with her face to his chest, cradling her as easily as a small child. "Shhh, shhh, shhh. It will be alright, my love. I will not leave, and you will not die."

Elric gave a pleading look to Geoffrey, and he nodded his head before he disappeared into another room and returned with a vial.

Ava calmed down, and Geoffrey tenderly touched her back. "Ava, take this. It will help calm your fever."

Elric grabbed it and held it to her lips to tilt it back into her feeble mouth. She swallowed it, weakly and willingly, while looking into Elric's eyes.

"Do not leave me."

"My soul is tied to yours. I could never." He offered her a smile, hoping to calm her nerves.

"I love you." Her speech was soft, her body relaxed.

He stifled a cry, wanting her to rest. "I will love you beyond this life and any thereafter."

She smiled, placing her hand on his cheek. He studied her face, not wanting to miss one detail in case he was never to see her again. Her hand slowly dropped before her body completely relaxed into his.

"It is a sleeping tonic. She will have a restful sleep for a few hours," Geoffrey told him as he took a seat next to Ava. "I promise I will not leave her side. Please make haste." Geoffrey looked at Ava sorrowfully and then turned his attention back. "And Elric, throw the box into the hearth. It must be in a place where you find peace, and *it* will come to you."

Elric nodded and softly laid her back down, struggling to leave her. He kissed the top of her head and left before he lost the will to.

Elric raced home, bursting through their house and leaving the door wide open behind him. The only place he ever found peace was the place he called home with Ava. Without another thought, he threw the box into the hearth, stoking the blinking embers. The glow pulsed like a heartbeat but wasn't quite strong enough to emit flames. He hurriedly moved outside to a small covering to grab a couple of dry logs and some kindling to build the fire back up. Rushing back inside, he added his elements, and in a few moments, the flames began to grow.

A dull red ember sparked in the groove of a marking and began to travel on the roadway of symbols until the whole box was aglow. Elric leaned in closer to get a better look, and tiny little pulses of bright light moved throughout the markings like water in a river. The box began to groan as if the wood was protesting. Then the box exploded and splintered violently, causing him to raise his arm to protect his face while he was knocked backward from the blast. A wind rushed into the house, striking out the flames and slamming the door shut. Silence and darkness enveloped Elric, and dread settled over him. Out of nowhere, a small cinder lit in the air at the center of the room. Floating around, it flickered again and again. Unsure of what to do, Elric hastily scooted back until he found his back pressed against a wall. The flame finally came to a dead stop in the air, giving a constant, steady light as it began to grow. The light stretched out like the roots of a tree, weaving together in different directions. Elric's face burned from the heat, but he could not look away. It was a beautiful and mesmerizing sight. The weaving roots started to take shape, allowing him to make out what was most certainly a body, legs, torso, and arms. A sudden eruption in a flash of bright white left Elric momentarily in blackness when the hearth lit on its own, brightening the whole room again. He looked up to see a child standing in the middle of the room.

An unnerving laugh filled the space, but the young girl's face remained blank. "Hello, Elric."

Elric stared at her in disbelief. She was surely no more than eight years old and stared back at him. Her skin was ghostly pale, and she had white hair down to her waist. She was marred from her feet to the top of her neck, with the same markings from the box seemingly etched into her skin. The marks were bright red, deep, and terrifying. Her eyes seemed to have no pupil or iris, just a pale white. Underneath her eyes were tear-stained patterns, but it seemed to be from ash rather than tears.

He hadn't been able to move, let alone speak, as he grabbed at his own body, wondering if this was a delusion from his recent lack of sleep.

The girl slowly approached him, crouching and tilting her head. Her gaze moved all around his face. Feeling violated by terror and this child's demonic stare, he had to force himself to keep breathing.

She stood back up to hover over him. "I'm sure this *form*," she gestured over her body, "is alarming for one reason or more." She smiled and stepped backward. "I can put you more at ease."

She raised her arms above her head and clapped, causing her to instantly transform into a woman. She became tall, thick, and strong in stature. Draped in a gray, sheer, and tattered peplos dress that was blackened around the hem, she reminded Elric of the Greek goddesses Ava described to him from her books. The woman's eyes didn't change, though–still void and chilling.

Thinking of Ava, Elric found his voice, "I need your help. My wife is dying."

The woman circled around Elric's home, examining different articles and running her fingers over the rough stone on the fireplace. She picked up Ava's book, turned a few pages, and set it back down. She moved elegantly but with too much speed to be of human nature. One of Elric's smithing works, an incomplete knife, was on the table next to a stale loaf of bread. She pressed her finger deep into the blade until the metal bit her skin. Where the mark should have welled up with blood, a dark black liquid seeped out. She stuck her finger in her mouth, sucking at the liquid. When she pulled it out, she held it up to Elric, smirking while she drew attention to the fact that the wound was gone. She stopped at the piece of parchment lying on the table.

"This is the one you aim to save? Are you sure you are ready for the commitment I ask for?" she asked, her eyes scanning the intimate drawing.

Elric crawled over to her out of desperation, looking up at desolate eyes, grabbing at her tattered garment.

"Anything you ask, it's yours. I just ask to be able to live my life with Ava."

An eerie laugh startled him from behind. The dress in his hands vanished along with the woman. He stood up and frantically spun around to find her sitting on his and Ava's bed. Her legs were crossed as she leaned back on her arms.

"This is uncommon. You have no knowledge of what I am or what you may be bartering with, but you are willing? Despite all the unknowns." She leaned forward, lacing her fingers together. "Is your life so inconsequential?"

Elric gathered himself and made sure his voice was steady and strong. "Certainly, you are a demon, are you not? Whether my life is significant or not has no meaning to you."

She offered a smug smirk and leaned back on the bed onto her elbows once again.

"A demon or an angel? I am answering your prayer, *am I not?*"

"What are you called?"

"Faye."

"And what are you then?"

Seemingly out of nowhere, Elric and Faye suddenly stood face to face. She lifted a hand to stroke his cheek, but he stepped back out of reach, leaving her hand hanging in the air.

She licked her lips. "Truly, it does not matter. Witch, demon, sorceress, fairy, or angel. Your beloved is running out of time, is she not?"

Fury rose in Elric, causing him to yell. "Then do not play games with me! Tell me what I must do and make haste!"

"Tsk, tsk," she clicked, "You are a brave one getting so testy with *something* you know nothing of."

She put her hand around his throat before he could react, lifting him off the floor as if his large, muscled body weighed nothing. Elric, for the first time tonight, was scared for his own life, pleading with his eyes, unable to rely on his voice.

Faye dropped him to the ground with a loud thud, lifting his chin to meet her eyes.

"I am quite taken with pity for the lesser being tonight. You are most fortunate. I feel so *gracious*." She said the last word with a hiss as if it stung her lips.

She sauntered back over to the table and waved her hand two inches above it. Black smoke emitted from underneath her hand and grew into a dense fog onto the surface of the table. She removed her hand, and the smoke evaporated. In its place lay a black leather-bound book.

Elric walked over with his hand out to touch it, but a second before he reached the book, he pulled back.

A pale hand ran across his chest, and she stood close behind him.

She whispered seductively in his ear, "All I need is a little blood, your vow, and your soul."

Elric didn't move and kept his eyes on the book. "Why do you need my soul? What use is it to you?"

Faye circled back around to face him. "My sustenance is the thing you people barely give any thought to. You vow it to God, but do you ever really think about what your soul can do beyond that? No. Small-minded imbeciles. I have figured it out, though, and have made it work to my advantage. The blood magic I have invested my being into has given me what I desire, but I have to keep it fed."

He knew it never mattered what it would take to save Ava, but a small twinge of worry made him wonder what it meant to lose his soul. The twinge quickly evaporated as he glanced at the parchment on the table.

"Tell me what I need to do."

Faye grabbed Elric's hand, picked up the unfinished knife, and placed it in his open palm.

"This must be all your decision. It only works if it is your doing and yours alone. Score your palm and make a mark of your flesh in the book." Faye released his hand and leaned against the wall.

"It's your choice, dearest, Elric. Live a life with or without her," she laughed mockingly.

He stared intently at her. "And explain to me what it is I am trading my soul for. What does life after this trade look like?"

"You live your life with your wife. The consequences of tonight will not concern you until death comes. Well, verily, until *I* come." Faye stated matter of fact.

"Let it be so then." Elric picked up the knife, ready to cut his palm. But before pressing the blade in, he asked one more question. "And Ava? Untouched by all of this?"

"Untouched by all of it. It is not she who makes the sacrifice."

He scored his palm with the blade and dragged the dagger across it. Immediately, a pool of blood welled from the gash. He opened the book and turned the pages until he found a blank one. As he flipped through the book, he saw hundreds of handprints of all different sizes. He could recognize men's and women's prints alike. What froze him in place was the handprint of a very small child. He looked up at Faye in silent questioning. She glared at him and shrugged.

"There are children who need to come to me for help as well. Who am I to turn them away?" she said.

His stomach churned, but he shook his head and found a clean page. Without wasting any more time, he turned his hand over and laid his palm down on the paper. Blood spilled onto the floor and table, seeping onto the edges of the drawing of Ava. He pressed long and hard with Ava at the forefront of his mind. Pulling his hand away, he saw the handprint starting to glow a fiery red.

Everywhere else the blood landed glowed as well, illuminating the parchment paper, table, and ground. He looked up at Faye as she smiled with delight, a look of insatiable hunger in her eyes, but then, her expression changed to confusion. Elric looked back down at the book and saw the glowing red imprint had changed to a black iridescent mark with brilliant colors, shimmering from different angles. Elric walked away and quickly ripped part of the tattered bed sheet to wrap his wounded hand. It was not so long ago that Ava wrapped herself in that same sheet while telling Elric she was with child.

For the first time that night, Faye sounded insecure, unsure even. "Your souls are so intertwined. I have never seen this with my own eyes. My marks stay red but this, *this* has not happened."

"What does it mean then?! Have we not made the deal?" he asked, distraught with concern, a crack in his voice giving it away.

"Nay, the deal has been made, the exchange complete." Faye tilted her head, listening for something. "Aye, the deal has been made, different than what is customary, and just barely too late."

His eyes widened with terror, and he lunged towards Faye, but she and the book vanished. Elric landed on the floor with a hard thump, grabbing onto the empty air. As he looked into the hearth, he saw the box had vanished, too. Pushing himself up, he stumbled out the door and ran to Ava, praying the urgency he felt in his soul was one of hope and not despair.

IV

MODERN- DAY ARCATA, CALIFORNIA

Elric sits at his desk, opens a drawer, and pulls out a leather case. He unlatches it and takes out a piece of metal from a cardboard slip. He stares at it, and it feels as though his heart physically seizes, remembering that night perfectly. He looks out the window, begging the tears to dry up.

Anita walks in, looking at her phone and paraphrasing an email aloud. "Mr. Ferron, the executive director of Art Across Arcata, Charles Hanover, emailed and," she looks up, "Oh, I'm so sorry, I didn't mean to intrude."

Elric coughs and wipes his eyes, putting his photo away. "No, not an intrusion. You know how I get lost sometimes."

His lips lift, but the emotion of the gesture doesn't reach his eyes. "What did Charles need?"

Anita looks at Elric with concern as he hopes she doesn't pry.

"He said the mural 'The Studio,'" she says with air quotes, knowing Elric never paints anything under his real name, "painted in the city square this past spring, was vandalized over the weekend. They said they would pay the studio to fix it.

I guess the damage was pretty extensive."

He pushes his chair back from his desk and walks over to Anita, "No, it was a donation in the first place. If you could email Charles, coordinate with him, and let him know *we* will be fixing it free of charge."

She beams. "*We?*"

Elric gives a genuine smile this time.

"Yes, *we*. Anita, you have so much talent in you. So much natural ability. Such promising talent that people should be able to see and enjoy for themselves."

She looks down and shifts her feet, and he hears a sniff.

"Thank you, Mr. Ferron. Truly. I've never had someone believe in me like you. I just…" She lifts her sweater sleeve and wipes her cheeks. "I'm really grateful for you."

Elric pulls her into a gentle, one-armed hug. "I believe in you and your talents so strongly."

He lets go of her and reaches into his pocket, grabbing his wallet and opening the money clip. He takes some cash out and puts it into Anita's hand. "Alright, go home. Buy yourself some dinner on me."

Anita grins and laughs, pushing the money away. "Mr. Ferron. This is the 3rd time this week you've bought me dinner. You often get lunch 'on you' and buy me enough coffee that I could paint three city murals in a week. The lines might be shaky but they would be painted."

He puts it back in her hand and closes it. "What's the point of having money if I'm not taking care of those I care about."

"Thanks, Mr. Ferron." Anita walks to her desk to grab her bag, waving to him as she walks out.

Elric goes back to his office and lays on a dark green velvet tufted couch that sits beside his desk. He grabs an old tennis ball that he keeps in the back of the cushion and throws it straight in the air. Toss and repeat. He thinks about Robyn and how much he enjoyed his walk with her. He couldn't help but feel guilty about it, though. He knew *she* was out there and hadn't found her yet. No matter how much he yearned to be with whatever form of herself she was, he wasn't sure he wanted to deal with the thought of the imminent loss that would undoubtedly occur. But it had to. It was the arrangement he found himself in. The gong of an old grandfather clock rings out as it reaches the top of the hour. He stops throwing the ball and shakes himself free of the trance of distant memories and future fears. He found resolve in the fact that sometimes it was nice to pretend he was living a normal life.

Elric moves to his desk in search of his phone. Once in his hand, he dials the number Robyn had entered. It rings once, twice, then to voicemail.

"Good evening, Robyn, this is Elric. I'd love to see you again tomorrow night if you're free. Give me a call back if you'd like."

Elric hangs up the phone and grabs his keys off the desk to head for the door when his phone starts to ring with Robyn's name lighting up the screen.

Lighting up he taps the green button to answer. "Hi, I'm really glad to hear from you."

Robyn replies, "Likewise."

Elric locks the doors to the studio and walks home, talking to Robyn for the entirety of his walk.

"That sounds perfect. I'll meet you there at 8 then." He hangs up the phone as he walks inside his home, greeted by a small black and brown mutt. As the dog jumps at Elric's legs, he bends down to pick him up, immediately recoiling as the dog licks his lips.

"If I have told you once," Elric says, gently cupping the dog's snout, "I have told you a thousand times. *STOP* licking my mouth."

The dog looks up at Elric and licks him again on the lips.

"Okay, Geoffrey. You can go now," he says, recoiling and putting him down.

The dog circles around his feet and follows him around the house as he puts away his things. He goes into the kitchen, gives Geoffrey some dinner, and scratches his head while he eats, happily wagging his tail.

Elric turns on the kettle and prepares himself a cup of tea. While waiting for the kettle to whistle he reads a note left by his dog walker, who takes care of Geoffrey twice a day. With Elric's schedule being so erratic he wanted to make sure his

36

small companion was well cared for.

He rents a small furnished house from a sweet old lady, Flora, who doesn't bother with contracts and doesn't mind him hanging his own decor. Trying to leave as little paper trail behind him as possible, this home has worked well for him. He rarely spends time at home even when he settles in one place long-term, but this house, by the forest and not far from his studio, has everything he needs and nothing tying him to it. It is simple and bare, besides a couple of portraits from his catalog and a few works of art by others. None of the art has the same style or subject content. He relates to the many different pieces making up his home as they reflect the many pieces that make up who he is.

"Come on, Geoffrey," he whistles. The dog gets up from where he was lying at Elric's feet as Elric had prepared his tea. The two move outside to the veranda. He sits down on patio furniture, left by Flora, and Geoffrey jumps onto his lap to settle in while Elric rhythmically strokes his back.

As they sit, Elric notices the sound of rain beginning to pitter-patter on the roof above them. He stares into it, reminiscing of one of the times he held *her* in the rain. He closes his eyes and can see her face standing beneath a pink magnolia tree in full bloom in the Tuileries Garden, laughing in the rain.

He had gotten her to ask her little brother to do the bread deliveries for her that day so that they could spend time together. Smiling, he thinks about the convincing it took day after day. Finally, when she agreed, Elric had the perfect day planned: a picnic in the gardens. She said she had never been there, and he knew she would fall in love with the flowers. She loved the flowers every time. She was dressed in a simple white shirt and sky-blue skirt. Her hair was tied up with a blue ribbon that matched her skirt, stray black curls framing her face. They started to walk with a basket that Elric had packed, and it began to pour as soon as they got there. They ran to the nearest tree for cover, and she laughed, always able to find delight in every situation. He remembered gently pulling her in, threading his fingers in her hair, and tenderly guiding her face closer to his. That's where he kissed her for the first time when he knew her in Paris. Underneath the pink magnolias. That became their spot, a place to sneak away to steal time and kisses.

He opens his eyes, and he's touching his lips as if the memory of her kiss was enough to bring warmth to his skin. Elric stands up and gently sits Geoffrey down in his seat, placing a blanket over him. He goes to retrieve an easel and a case of oil pastels, most of them barely enough to grip onto from being worked down to the very last bits. He finishes setting up on the veranda and begins to draw. The melodic rhythm of the rain blocks out the rest of the world. The familiar pinpricks of tears continue to threaten, and he doesn't stop them from flowing. Here in his solitude, where he is free to feel the heartstrings of his complex and damning life, where he owes no one an explanation as to what ails him, he feels deep until the sorrow is just a small murmur in his heart. Hours pass by, and the sun begins to shine through the raindrops that are still falling steadily. When he is finished drawing, he steps back and looks at the easel. He lightly touches the canvas, fingers settling on the petal of a pink magnolia.

SAVANNAH, GEORGIA JUNE 1902

Ava sat barefoot on the stairs of the white porch, fanning herself and reading a book. Elric walked up the dirt pathway to her family home, where he called on her each afternoon. He stopped for a moment before reaching her, already knowing what book would be in her hand. *The Iliad,* he shook his head and silently laughed.

This magic, curse, plague; whatever one wishes to call it, he thinks to himself, *has a cruel sense of humor.*

He decided to push his limits and his heart. He always chose to.

"How truly fortunate I am to have a lover who appreciates the classics?" He yelled as he continued to make his way to her.

Ava looked up from her book and smiled, warmth radiating from her and her eyes beaming. She gently set down her book and took off, running into his arms. He lifted her off the ground, embracing her. She grabbed his face firmly, bringing her lips to his while laughing.

"Surely you would've been fortunate, even if I had been born simple-minded Elric Ferron. I excel in everything."

His heart was arrested momentarily at the bittersweet sentence, which was familiar but also unknown today.

He cleared his throat, setting her down and holding her face in between his hands. "Of course, and even if I was told the world would shatter if I loved you, surely I would continue to do so."

Ava's eyes crinkled around the edges before shooting Elric a puzzled look. She laughed. "That was odd.... I felt like I had heard you say that before."

"Déjà vu," he said.

"Ah yes, that's what it is. I swear I dreamt about that conversation before. Maybe it was another life." Ava elbows him in the side, jesting.

Elric held her hand and walked towards the porch.

"Quite possibly." Raising his eyebrows at the naïve truth in her statement.

A whirring engine drew Elric's attention behind them. A young boy, no more than fourteen, riding a small motorcycle, pulled up to the dirt road along Ava's home. Attached to the bike was a sidecar packed tightly with a crate filled with glass bottles of milk. As he slowed down to a complete stop, the glass rattled against each other.

"Afternoon, Miss Novak! Your momma told us she'd be needin' more milk this week!" The boy said as he got off of his motorcycle, grabbing four bottles from the crate.

"Ivan! Yes, thank you so much! If you wouldn't mind taking it inside to her, I would be much obliged!" Ava said as waved.

"Yes, ma'am." Ivan walked past the couple, tipping his head to Elric. "Mr. Ferron. Will you be needing anything this week?"

Elric gave a kind look and patted Ivan softly on the back, "No, thank you, Ivan."

He looked down at the boy's shoes, noticing his soles barely hanging on by threads and his big toe threatening to make an appearance out of a hole on top. Elric reached into his pocket, pulling out a leather billfold. He took out a one hundred dollar note, looked at Ivan's full hands, and placed the bill in the breast pocket of his shirt, knowing how long this could take care of him and his family for months to come.

"But please take this."

Ivan's jaw dropped. "Mr. Ferron, my family can't take this. It's too much. We haven't even delivered milk. We definitely have not delivered this amount of milk. I don't know if our cow can even make this much milk. And Pa' well, he ain't much one for charity," he rambled.

"I insist. This is for a job always well done. Not Charity."

"Th-thank you, Mr. Ferron. Thank you." A crooked smile grew on the boy's face.

Quickly, he ran inside and dropped the milk off. When he came back outside, his smile was wider than before.

"Have a great day, Miss Novak, Mr. Ferron. A great day." Ivan said as he climbed on his motorbike.

He revved the engine once and waved before taking off down the road.

"You know I'd like to get me one of those," Elric said as he craned his neck watching Ivan and his motorcycle disappear.

"A delivery route for milk?" Ava asked sarcastically.

"Yes, exactly," Elric chuckled as he rolled his eyes. "No, a motorcycle."

He leaned forward, hoping to catch one last glimpse of the back, but it was too far off in the distance.

"Going that fast, with the wind in your hair just seems fun."

"No, it seems dangerous. Want to go fast with wind in your hair? Hop on a horse. I don't love Ivan on that thing, either. You could die," she sternly replied.

He laughed. "That's not likely."

Ava shook her head as they sat down on the porch, leaving no space between them.

"My birthday is tomorrow," she eagerly said, her voice brimming with excitement.

"Really? I hope there are people to celebrate it." Elric said, tucking her in closer to his body.

"Quit," she giggled. "Are we doing somethin'? Do I need to be ready for anything? Wear anything special?"

Leaning back on his elbows, he devoured her with his eyes.

"Well, you could wear one of your evening gowns, or something more casual, or..." he shrugged, looking over at her coyly and ran a finger sensually down her arm. "Nothing. Your choice."

Her face turned beet red, and she smacked him playfully on his arm. "My mama is inside! And if Daddy heard you! You'd be in for a good lickin'."

Elric gave a hard belly laugh. "Americans in the South. I prefer not to be licked; it seems rather personal."

Playfully she pushed his face away from her. "Elric, you know what I mean."

He looked at her and felt that familiar warmth in his chest. He leaned over, cradled her face, and kissed her. He could do that time and time again. Elric shook his head, knowing he *would* do it time and time again.

Ava placed her hands on his. "What's the matter? Sometimes, it seems like you're a hundred miles away from me."

He pulled his hands away from her face and rested them on her leg.

"Sometimes I feel like I am hundreds of years away," he looked at her, anguish in his eyes. "My head is just so full all at once—of everything that was, is, and yet to be. I replay all of it in my head, trying to figure out how to keep my *right now*. How to change my now to keep it my forever."

He rubbed his eyes, ran his hands through his hair, and looked up at her. Her expression was a mix of confusion and concern, like someone looking at a child who had been separated from their mother in a busy area.

"Elric, I do not know exactly what that means. But I do know this," resting her hand on his knee, "We do have right now, in this life, and when you are ready to tell me what it is that keeps you away up here," she gently tapped the side of his head, "I'm ready to hear it. I want our now to be our forever, too."

That tender and empathetic heart was a constant. Elric was forever grateful that even though the times and settings changed, who *she* was at her core was forever. That had never wavered.

"You are too good to me, Ava."

"You know what? You are right Mr. Ferron. I am." She leaned into him. "But in all seriousness, what are we doing for my birthday? I am going to be twenty-eight!"

"Everything and anything you want, my love."

He laid his head on hers, weeping where she could not see, mourning what she didn't know. His gut churned to hear it aloud while he tried to avoid thinking about when she turned twenty-eight.

Her twenty-eighth is the year when his heart breaks.

Twenty-eight is the year when he is lost again.

Twenty-eight is the year when he wishes he could cease to exist.

Because twenty-eight is the year she always dies.

V

TRIORA, LIGURIA ITALY 1588

Elric walked through narrow cobblestone streets, buildings bathed in the final warm glow of a setting sun as the darkness of night settled in. He pulled his hood up and gathered his cloak around himself to conceal his coin and his intentions. He had recently heard of a group of women responsible for calling down acid rain, killing cattle, and unleashing curses on men. In his years of searching for answers, he learned that the people with the information he sought would be the less fortunate or the disgustingly rich. It seemed they always had a run-in with a demon as well, for better or worse. But access to the poor was always easier than the rich. Elric stepped over piles of vomit on the road and walked by prostitutes calling out to him in an eager seduction. Beggars with hands out waited to receive, and pickpockets with hands hidden were ready to take. The stale air mixed with the pungent odor of bodily fluids made him draw his cloak over his nose and mouth. He saw a woman sitting on a step while she breastfed her child, a bright red scar running up her arm and across her shoulder, reminding him of scars from many years ago. It caused him to wonder what her affiliation might be.

Elric walked up to her and said the only word in Latin he learned to get his point across: "*Malefica?*" Witch.

She looked at him, her eyes widened.

"*Malefica?*" He repeated, pointing to the scar on her arm.

She glared at him, lifting the hand not holding the child, ready to strike. She rose to her feet and spat at him. She kept shouting at him, forcing him to reconsider his thoughts about her scar. Elric, unable to interpret what she said, held up his hands in surrender. Thankfully, he learned another phrase to get him out of trouble.

"*Mea culpa, mea culpa.*" My fault.

She opened a door behind her and slammed it shut. He could still hear her yelling from the inside. He walked away quickly from the interaction, not wanting to call unnecessary attention to himself, when he heard a raspy, low voice from the shadows.

"*Quid queris?*"

He turned and squinted into an alley, "Apologies. I do not know more than a few words in the Latin tongue."

There was no answer to his call, and the silence made him wary. Still, he took a chance and spoke barely above a whisper into the alley, "*Malefica?*"

A burst of white light filled the atmosphere above, and Elric looked up. As if the sky were a page in a book, the lightning moved like a threatening tear on the paper. The street illuminated for a few moments, and all the different faces in the street were highlighted. He looked down the alleyway and saw no inhabitants. The light dissipated, and the world went dark again. Elric felt the light touch of hot breath against his neck. A throaty gurgle accompanied the breathing.

It caused his skin to prickle. He whipped around and there was no one behind him. His eyes swept the people, all of them unbothered and carrying on with the night.

"*Veni. Come,*" The voice called for him once more from the alley.

Elric took a step into the darkness, "Who are you?" he asked.

"Your soul is in two. Both *partssss* are trapped," a second voice spoke in a whispered hiss that rattled Elric's bones.

"Come forth. Are you friend or foe?" He said aggressively, broadening his stance, readying for a fight.

He heard the sound of many footsteps closing in on him, causing his anxiety to rise.

Abruptly, a light shone on his face. He raised his hand to shield his eyes from the too-bright flame. Elric could see he stood in a circle of five women in black *Gonnella* dresses, but he was unable to make out their features.

"Lower the lamp so I may look upon your faces. If your plan is to rob me and kill me, please have at it and let me carry on with my night," Elric spoke harshly to the whole group.

The lamp was lowered, and he saw a woman with long, straight, cedar-colored hair partially covering her disfigured face. A large scar marred her face from temple to jaw, creating a permanent snarl in her lip. Another woman's eyes were covered with a dirty cloth, and tears of blood streamed down her cheeks from beneath it. The third had a deep mark across her throat. When she caught Elric's eyes on it, she reached up to touch it and averted her gaze. The scar seemed to remain as painful as the day it was made. The fourth and fifth women were identical twins as far as Elric could tell. They stood with their hands interlocked; one with burns scarring down the right side of her body, the other a perfect mirror on her left.

The woman with the cloth over her eyes dug her fingers into Elric's chest and spoke in the hiss-like voice from before. "Your soul is *sssssplit.*"

He took a step forward, letting her finger press in harder. "What do you know?"

The five women lifted up the sleeves of their dresses, unveiling red runes embedded in their forearms that seemed to pulse with pain.

The marks were the same as on the box from Geoffrey. Before he realized what was happening, the women grasped each other's arms, pressing the marks against one another, chanting in an unknown language. Rhythmic moans with raucous rasps of breaths accompanied the strange words. Had it not terrified him to his core, the sounds would have been hauntingly melodic.

Elric panicked and looked around for a way to escape. A black cloud of smoke quickly enveloped him, clouding his vision, but as quickly as the smoke came, it went. When he could see again, he stood in a single room still in the circle the women had created. The room had no windows or doors, but it held a single staircase leading up. The walls were lined with the markings of the cursed paper that called on Faye. The floors were covered in purple wax from the dozens of lavender-colored candles burning around the room. A single black candle sat lit on a table.

"What are your intentions?" Elric asked, keeping his voice even.

The woman with the scar across her throat broke out of the circle and drifted up to Elric, picking up his hand in hers.

With her free hand, she pressed down on the old wound, and only a hoarse breath came out.

She closed her eyes and began again. "To help."

MODERN-DAY ARCATA, CALIFORNIA

Elric stands on the sidewalk, hands in pockets, waiting for Robyn to show up for their date. He chose his favorite taco stand that sits on the road across from the beach. It's small and cheap but has been around for many years, easily becoming his most favored place to eat in this century. He eases himself down to sit on the curb, tossing away pieces of decaying pavement when that familiar guilt washes over him.

"What are you doing?" Elric mumbles quietly to himself.

He knows Robyn is a way to pass the time. She could turn out to be incredible and someone he could enjoy, but it's not like they could grow old together. It's not like he is doing this because he can really settle down and build a life. It's only a matter of time before he finds *her*, and he always wants to find *her*.

"Elric?" He hears Robyn's voice behind him and stands up, brushing off his pants.

He looks up and is met with golden-brown eyes that melt into an olive-toned complexion. Long auburn hair in loose waves cascades down, framing her heart-shaped face.

"Wow, you are beautiful. I've never seen you with clear, un-assaulted eyes before," he grins at her.

Robyn tucks a loose strand of hair behind her ear, slightly embarrassed but trying to keep herself composed.

"Thanks. You look great. I wasn't sure what to wear? We never really talked about it, so I threw this on, hoping it would be okay."

She opens her arms, exposing a simple ruby-red cotton dress with capped sleeves and sandals.

"Don't worry, I'll call and cancel the rock-climbing excursion," Elric jokes.

Robyn chuckles, "Oh, thank you, you're too kind."

"For tonight I have only planned tacos on the beach." He holds up a quilted blanket tucked under his arm and gestures toward the taco cart.

With an approving look, Robyn gestures with a wave of her hand, "Please lead the way."

They stand in line, exchanging the expected pleasantries. *How was your day? Was traffic bad? Have you ever eaten here before? The weather is nice.*

It's their turn, and Elric turns to the man running the taco cart.

"*Diego! Hola como esta y su familia?*" Elric says, slapping the man on the back. A middle-aged man with silver hair, dark skin worn by the sun, and deep wrinkles on his face smiles broadly at Elric. "*El-reek! Muy muy bien! Y cómo estás?*"

"*Maravillosa! Un momento por favor.*"

Elric turns back to Robyn. "Do you know what you would like? If not, I would be more than glad to order for you."

"It seems like you come here often enough. You can go ahead and just get me whatever you're getting."

Elric rubs his hands together. "Alright then," he beams at Diego. "*Dos elotes, cuatro carne asada tacos, cuatro pollo, y, tu tienes buñuelos? Entonces si, gracias Diego. Oh, y dos Jarritos.*"

It doesn't take long before Diego has their order. "*Listo, Señor Ferron!*"

"*Gracias Diego. Buenas noches.*" Elric hands him folded bills, noticing Robyn's eyes flicker to the two one-hundred-dollar bills.

Diego starts to speak, but Elric cuts him off with a nod and a kind tone. "*Gracias, Diego.*"

Elric, arms full for a Mexican food picnic, gestures with his shoulder. "Shall we?"

Robyn gives off a light laugh, filling the salty air, and she takes the blanket and drinks from Elric. "Let's go."

"You did not paint the mural downtown! It's so good! You painted the Redwoods in all those beautiful colors of teals and purples!" Robyn exclaims in between a bite of *carne asada*, "Oh my god, this is so good. I cannot eat another bite." She takes the last bite of taco and crumples the foil, setting it down on the blanket next to her. She grabs one of the orange Jarritos, takes a long sip, and then eats a *bunuelo* out of the shared bag.

Elric covers his mouth, swallowing his food, impressed by her appetite.

"Yes, I did. You said you couldn't eat another bite, and yet, you proceeded to finish the taco and then some," he quips.

"Yes, I did," she mimics jokingly, but then places her hand over her stomach. "Honestly, I should have stopped, but it was so good. Thank you so much. How long did the mural take you to complete?"

He scratches his head. "I think somewhere around four or six weeks? I'm not sure. I don't pay attention to time. Art takes as long as it is going to take."

"Hm. Well, tell me more about yourself. I talked your ear off the other day, I'm sure. Where'd you study? Is your family still in England? Siblings? How'd you end up in California?" She digs her toes into the cool sand, settling in.

Setting down his trash and drink, he turns his body slightly towards her, but leaving ample room.

"I am an only child. My parents died long ago. I never formally studied. The Redwoods drew me here."

She scoffs. "Those are terribly generic answers. I mean, I'm sorry your parents passed, but that's all the insight into yourself you can offer?"

He throws his head back and laughs. "Miss Renata, did you just call me generic? No, what is the term I see on the internet? Basic?"

"Are you 90 years old? No, you're not basic." Grinning, she rolls her eyes. "I just feel like those are answers you would give someone at a job interview, not a date. Give me more than the surface."

"Alright," Elric clasps his hands. "My father didn't want me to be an artist. He was very traditional, and it was expected, where I am from, to follow in his footsteps. It was a very medieval way of thinking."

He laughs at his own personal joke. Running his hands through his hair, he looks up at the sky, pausing momentarily.

"This time of day, twilight, it has such finesse to it. It is my favorite. Day and night seamlessly blend with no distinct tone of either one. To be able to recreate it, to be able to recreate different beauties of this world that I see... It makes my heart sing. I get to create and keep memories—moments in time. People in different places in time—I get to keep with me. Keep with me, created by me. My own emotions, beautiful or ugly, are poured into them. My pieces speak to me, recounting what it was that was in my soul at that moment. I couldn't do that with anything else. I don't take the ability to do what I do lightly. Frankly, my heart and soul belong to the craft. Sometimes, it feels like it is all I have to grasp onto."

Elric looks back down into Robyn's eyes. They are wide and attentive.

"That's all I really have, honestly. There is no family, there is no education I owe my life to. There is just my art and me."

"It sounds lonely." She looks up, gazing at the sky. "You are certainly a tortured artist... But your passion is wonderful. I wish I could see things the way you do. I think very few are gifted with a mind that can do that naturally."

Elric scoots in closer to Robyn, her shoulder nestled under his arm as he wraps it around her. With his other arm in front of her, he points toward the horizon over the ocean.

"Do you see the small lip of color separating the ocean and sky? It's a soft blush pink. Below it, dark ripples and slight reflections dance on the water. Above the pink, it blends with an indigo color palette. Most people would just say 'blue,' but you have to look past the basics to see the details."

She nods, and Elric gently nudges her chin with his knuckle to shift her head up.

"See the few pale twinkles starting to show up? Not enough to call it a night sky, but just enough to see little clusters of spotlights giving different dimensions to their area. And they don't just rest against a black canvas. They're different hues of a galaxy."

He softly turns her head one more time towards a pier. "And right there," lifting her hand and folding her fingers until only her index is out, "a couple walking hand in hand, you can barely see them. They are shadows, and the sky behind them is not yet illuminated. You just have to be aware of the universe around you. Your eyes alone can't see it. You have to see with your soul."

Elric drops her hand and scoots back to his original spot.

Robyn looks at him disappointed, her smile fading, but she quickly masks it by putting it back into place.

"I would have never seen it that way."

They sit for a while longer as the twilight turns into night and the stars settle into the sky. They laugh, and he asks more about Robyn and her life. He divulges a few details here and there, but only pertaining to the last five years or so—the least amount to satisfy her curiosity without giving away that his life is kept distant in details.

A text notification goes off on Robyn's phone, interrupting Elric's vague insight into his life.

"Oh, of course. It's my sister, Kylie, wondering where I am. She is worse than my actual mother. Oh my gosh, I didn't even realize it's almost midnight!" She exclaims. "Time flies, right?"

"Hmph," he raises his shoulders. "Sometimes. Let's get you back home before we worry your family. You did decide to meet a crazy man, after all."

They stand up, gather the blanket, dispose of the trash, and dust off the sand before walking across the beach back to their cars.

"Can I ask you something?" Robyn asks, looking down at her feet as she walks, stepping in footprints left by others along the way.

"Sure."

"Why did you leave Diego a $200 tip?"

"Why not?" Elric raises his eyebrows.

"That seems like a lot for a taco tip?" She shrugs.

"Life is long, and what is the point if you don't do something good with it?"

Robyn glances at him. "The saying is 'life is short'."

"It is," he says, "but that's just introspection on my part."

They arrive at Robyn's car, and she very clearly gives him a once over, "You are an interesting man, Elric."

A corner of his mouth lifts. "In a good way, I hope."

"In a very good way," she says coyly, playing with the ends of her hair. "Thank you for tonight."

He can tell by her body language she expects more before ending the night, but Elric refuses to follow her cue. He opens the door for her, bidding her a good night before, softly closing it and tapping on the roof. Robyn sheepishly waves as she drives away.

He walks to his car, a black 1967 Ford Mustang. Elric didn't care much for material possessions, but he enjoyed the invention and evolution of the car and decided this could be one of the few things he indulged in. Between the classic look of a Mustang, the unnecessary luxury of the Aston Martin DB11 parked in the garage, and his Triumph motorcycle covered in his drive, he appreciated all his indulgences. Opening the door, he slides into the driver seat, and lets a diminutive smile cross his face. He had a great time and felt at ease with Robyn. He never looked for more than that in people. Feeling peaceful around someone was enough for him, but with her, he felt a little more.

Elric leans his head against the window and closes his eyes, and those familiar emerald eyes flash through his mind. He jolts straight up, rubbing his face.

Erupting from a deep place of pain, he slams both hands down on the steering wheel and screams. A brazen, aggressive scream from deep within his gut. It leaves his throat burning and his eyes flooding with tears. They begin to fall unabashedly. At this point, he couldn't care less if someone saw or heard him.

It isn't memories of her or knowing she is out there in this time that holds him back or keeps him from living his life. It's quite the opposite.

It feels like a phantom pain in his being, a longing for them to be whole again. He misses her, has missed her for hundreds of years and there is a healing that happens when they are together.

Elric pulls out of the parking lot and drives aimlessly. He drives up a small ridge dotted with various homes and continues until he finds a lookout point. He parks and doesn't even bother to turn off the engine or shut his door properly. Rage builds inside him, never understanding why this is what his life had to become.

Ava is never aware of it, and for her, they are falling in love for the first time, but for him, it is all-consuming. Hundreds of lifetimes trying to solve a curse that keeps their souls in limbo.

He waits for the day they will be free, but fear lingers behind the idea of freedom, not knowing what that would look like. Would their lives immediately end? Would they be able to grow old together? Would he die, and she would live whatever life she was in, never knowing him?

Ava wasn't this hanging guillotine that was waiting to drop and kill whatever it was he was trying to build. The guillotine was fate waiting to split his soul from hers again and again.

Elric steps over the safety railing near the cliff's edge, ignoring a Do-Not-Cross sign hanging over it, but it is late, and there is no one to stop him from doing otherwise. He reaches the edge and hangs the tips of his shoes off. He looks up and sees two stars twinkling like heartbeats next to each other. From his viewpoint, they seem to be almost directly next to each other, but he knows that those two are millions of miles apart, and one of the stars is most likely already dead. He grimaces at the cruel comparison nature throws at him.

Elric spreads his arms out and lets the breeze caress his hair back; he feels unhinged and lets it out in a manic laugh before throwing himself over the edge.

VI

BRISTOL, ENGLAND October 1348

Elric burst through the doors of the monastery.

Overwrought, he yelled, "Ava!"

She was no longer lying on the table he originally set her on.

"Ava!"

He felt his heart being gripped by fear.

"Ava!"

Geoffrey ran out from the back room, and the grief on his face was palpable.

He grabbed at Geoffrey's chest, ripping at his tunic.

"Take me to her *now*," he growled through clenched teeth.

His friend nodded his head in heavy grief, his face already stained with tears as more began to fall onto his robes.

He led Elric to the back of the building as they passed rooms he never knew existed. Most of them were empty, just with a few friars either sleeping or sitting at tables hunched over books. Geoffrey walked him to the last room on the right, allowing Elric to step inside first.

A nun, whom Elric had seen a few times during the day at the markets, was sitting by Ava's bedside. She had a sponge in her hand and a bowl of water by her side, and she gently ran the wet sponge down Ava's arms.

Geoffrey cleared his throat. His voice was hoarse. "Sister, you may go. Thank you."

Elric stood at the foot of the bed and stared at Ava. The nun bowed her head, gathered her things, and walked behind them to exit the room. Before she reached the door, Elric grabbed her by the wrist. When he opened his mouth to speak, nothing came out, but the tears continued to drop, and all he could do was nod his head at her to show his gratitude. She nodded back, resting a hand on his shoulder, not saying anything. He released her, and she quietly left, looking at Geoffrey on her way out the door.

Elric moved over to Ava's bedside, raising the back of his hand to her cheek, letting it hover over her face for a moment. When his skin met hers, his sobs were explosive and painful. He dropped to his knees, laying his head on her stomach. His chest heaved, feeling as though he couldn't draw enough air into his lungs. He cradled her womb, whispering. "I did not know you yet."

Sweet loved-one, I pray thee,
For one loving speech;
While I live in this wide world
None other will I seek.
With thy love, my sweet beloved,
My bliss though mightest increase;
A sweet kiss of thy mouth
Might be my cure.

He sang quietly to his wife and child, hoping to comfort them in the afterlife, but truly, he sang it to comfort himself.

He kissed her belly and then turned his face towards hers. She reminded him of one of his drawings. She was just an essence of herself, a replica of the woman he loved, not actually her. Elric sat up, sliding his arm underneath her back and his other under her legs, gently rocking her in the bed.

He brushed her hair off her face. "I am-" his voice cut off by his groan, delicately placing his lips on her forehead.

Without lifting his mouth off her face, he spoke with his eyes tightly shut. "I am s-so sorry, my love. I tried."

After many hours, he placed her gently back on the bed and covered her with the sheet before kneeling on the floor and clasping her hand in his.

"I will love you beyond life."

Elric stayed like that until morning. Watching her, willing her to wake up from this eternal sleep.

Geoffrey stayed, leaning against a wall, never moving.

When morning finally came, and the sun crept in through the single window in the room, it illuminated Ava's face. Elric simply stared at her. His crying never ceased through the night. Only now was it just silent. His throat was raw, and he wasn't even sure he could make a sound if he wanted to.

He was startled when Geoffrey laid his hand on his back. "Elric, I am so sorry. The sisters must come in and start to prep—to take care of her."

Elric nodded and tried to stand, but his legs gave out underneath him. The friar caught him quickly, kneeling to wrap his arm under his and around his back. He stood up, lifting Elric with him.

"Are you ready?" Geoffrey asked, his face covered in lament.

"Wait," Elric rasped.

He bent down, kissing Ava's forehead one last time before his friend carried him out. He glanced back at her one more time before leaving the room.

Geoffrey walked him a few rooms down the way they came, almost having to pick Elric up to lay him in a bed.

"Rest here. At least try. No one will come in. I will bring you food and water." Geoffrey kept his voice even, but Elric could hear the cracks in its depths.

The world around Elric was breaking. He just wished it would demolish faster.

"Don't," he groaned, turning onto his side away from Geoffrey.

Geoffrey placed a hand on his head. Elric heard the friar draw in a breath to speak but must have thought better of it. He listened to the friar walk out of the room before the rough sound of the door grating into its threshold filled the air.

Elric stared blankly at the wall, never moving. There weren't any more tears as he continued to mourn silently. His spirit had nothing left to offer this plane of existence. The silence roared back at him, though, causing all his thoughts, memories, and anger to surface.

Was Faye real, or was it all a figment of his imagination? He brought up his palm to his face, looking at the soiled fabric tied around his palm. He turned over on his back and closed his eyes. Elric's body began to drift. It was so worn that it could do nothing else but shut down. He could hear Ava's laugh, light and melodic, a sound and song of its own. It would carry through the room, always lightening his mood.

His eyes sprung open, and he threw himself out of the bed onto the floor. Covering his ears and frantically looking around before he remembered she wasn't there. He brought his knees up to his chest, running his hands through his hair and pulling, burying his face in the tops of his knees, finding remnants of his voice and screaming. The screams choked him. His body rattled through the moans. Geoffrey rushed into the room, swinging open the door. Without hesitation, he put himself on the floor beside Elric, throwing his arms around him tightly until his body calmed.

It reminded Elric of a time when he was a boy. A raging storm blew through their tiny cottage, ripping off parts of the roof. He was terrified, and his mother had held him so tightly to protect him, but he could vividly remember that the tightness of her grasp gave him insight into her fear as well. The grip with which Geoffrey held Elric now gave insight into the friar's own pain.

He glanced up and saw his friend crying quietly beside him. His friend, always making room for everyone else's emotions, sometimes neglecting his own.

"Time?" He croaked.

Geoffrey, surprised, looked up and cleared his throat. "Past midday. Let me bring you some water."

Ready to wave him off, Elric is stopped by his dearest friends' desperation to help.

"Elric, please."

Elric dropped his head and nodded. Geoffrey disappeared for a few minutes and then returned with a wooden pitcher and cup in hand.

He lifted the cup to Elric's lips, leaning his head back. Elric grasped desperately for the cup, finishing off the water. Dropping the cup onto the floor, he crawled over to the bed, lifting himself to sit on its edge.

Geoffrey stood up, collecting the cup. "I know Ava's parents have passed, and she had no siblings. Are there other people you would want to tell before her ceremony? Your family?"

Elric shook his head solemnly. "Is she ready?"

"Yes. Have you thought about where you would like to lay her to rest?" Geoffrey turned the cup over in his hands, not making eye contact.

Elric stared out the window and saw a dry, dead field where a sea of red lay not too many months ago.

"Would you do it in the poppy fields? If that isn't too much to ask." He requested, never removing his gaze from the view outside the small window.

"You could never ask too much, my brother." Geoffrey walked over to Elric and sat beside him. The bed groaned underneath the weight of both men.

"Elric, you know I loved Ava as my own blood. I am so sorry that what I gave you did nothing."

He grabbed Geoffrey hard by his shoulders and shook him. "Do not ever apologize for trying to help us."

Releasing his friend he hauled him into an embrace.

"I was too late," said Elric.

The friar pulled away from him with lines of confusion, making a home on his brow. He sat quietly, waiting for Elric to explain.

"I met a demon and struck a deal of sorts."

He held up his hand for Geoffrey to examine, explaining the details of the night.

"It seems that as I began to solidify the bargain, Ava..."

Elric closed his eyes and laid straight back, leaning against the wall.

Geoffrey, understanding his inability to finish the sentence, picked up the conversation. "If the bargain was still made, what does that mean? Even though Ava..." his voice trailed off, realizing he had no more strength than Elric to finish the statement.

Elric raised his shoulders at the question. "That I do not know. And the demon had no knowledge either. She was distressed, it seemed."

"And the box I gave you? Where is it? We could possibly summon her again."

"Gone. She vanished with it," he rubbed the skin around the wound on his hand, "the book had so many hands, so many souls in it."

"Then we will find them. If others could know what this means, they may be able to lead us to this *demon*," Geoffrey said with disgust.

"Geoffrey," Elric spoke softly, "I do not want to li-"

A soft knock at the door interrupted them, and the nun from before walked in, her expression unreadable. "She is ready, Brother Geoffrey. Has the place for burial been deemed? So that I may let them know where to prepare."

"Sister, please let Altun know Elric has picked the poppy fields. Please, the west sides of the fields, under the large oak. Thank you."

The nun walked out of the room and gave Elric a caring smile. The sympathy in her eyes was almost too overwhelming for him.

He had failed his wife; he deserved none. Geoffrey turned his attention back to Elric. "The sun sets beautifully behind the hills of the oak. Ava should be one of the last things to be touched by the sun on earth for the day."

His heart squeezed tightly for a moment. "Thank you."

"We can do the service tomorrow morning if you wish," Geoffrey offered as he stood up.

Elric rose with him, his hand pressed against the wall for support. He felt as though all energy had leached out of his body.

"No, I'd like to do it this evening as the sun sets."

"Elric... there is no rush."

He looked straight into Geoffrey's eyes, his mouth in a hard line. "Please."

"As you wish. I'll bring you food, allow you to do what you need, and come back for you when it is time."

Elric nodded as he watched the friar leave the room. He did feel the need to rush despite the friar's advice. The quicker he gave Ava a proper burial, making sure her soul and her being were honored, the quicker he could join her in the afterlife. Because for Elric, there was no life without her.

Geoffrey walked Elric back to the room where he last saw Ava. There, Ava's body lay flat on the bed, covered in a thin, sheer shroud. Inside the delicate fabric, haloed around her body, were dried lavender sprigs and red poppy petals. In one hand, she held *The Iliad*. The other held her womb.

Elric took a deep breath and moved towards her, shedding tears. "She looks so lovely. You knew to get her book," he stopped to clear his throat, "thank you. She would have loved the flowers."

Their friend smiled and stood still in the doorway.

"There was not a day I did not see her within arm's length of that book. And Sister Margaret, the nun who has been tending to her, wanted to adorn her with beauty as lovely as she is."

Elric covered his mouth, unwilling to wail at her bedside again. "Are they ready for her?"

Geoffrey nodded, and Elric traced his fingers down the side of her face. "Soon, my love."

Elric tenderly cradled Ava to carry her outside. Walking towards the oak in the field, he could see a few other friars and nuns, some of whom he knew by name and others he did not. He noticed the one called Sister Margaret standing nearest to the grave, silently crying. They each held a lit candle, the soft glow of a beacon calling Elric to them.

As soon as they noticed him approach, they stood, bowing their heads in solemn condolences as he passed their places in the field. Ava was known around the monastery to frequently help with the sick, the children, and the hungry. There was not a soul who could say Ava was not a pure person inside and out. Elric reached the grave and began to shake, his knees nearing buckling. He did not have the will to put her in the ground and never see her face again. He felt an arm wrap around his waist and looked up to his right to see Sister Margaret holding him.

"It will be alright," she whispered tenderly and with compassion.

The smell of the freshly turned earth made him feel nauseous.

"I cannot put her on the dirt," he whispered back, tears leaving spots on her shroud.

Behind him, he heard heavy footsteps running back toward the monastery. As the nun continued to try and coax Elric, he heard the footsteps returning.

Geoffrey jumped into the grave, holding a long white silk cloth in his arms.

Elric yelled for him, distraught with insurmountable grief and gratitude. "I cannot let you do that. It was your mother's."

The friends shared a look of sorrow and tacit solidarity before the friar proceeded to lay the silk onto the dirt.

"My friend, my brother. This is your wife and child," said Geoffrey as he held out his arms, ready to receive Ava.

Elric looked at her, and a soft, almost peaceful expression looked back at him. He placed one final kiss on her lips through the shroud, then handed her into his best friend's arms, forcing himself to let go.

Geoffrey laid her down gently on the bed of silk, whispering a small goodbye to his friend before climbing back out.

The nuns began singing a mourning song, and Geoffrey started a prayer, but Elric could not hear it. Blood rushed to his ears, and his vision fogged. He looked up, directing his gaze toward the twilight sky, tears sliding down his cheeks. They began to cover her with dirt, sealing her inside the grave.

As they finished, Elric turned his head back to the grave, seeing nothing but the upturned dirt. He looked around and noticed Geoffrey still at his side, but the rest of the congregants started walking away. One of the members, a nun he hadn't noticed before, broke off from the group, not entering the monastery with the rest. He watched her walk down the dirt path in the darkness, abruptly stopping in the middle of the road. She raised her hands high above her head just before quickly sweeping them down, the moonlight making her white hair shine. The nun changed form, and he swore he could see her smiling at him.

Elric took off towards her, faintly acknowledging Geoffrey calling his name, but it did not matter.

He must reach Faye before she disappears. A deep force pushed him as he watched her move about a quarter of a mile past the monastery. He caught up to her quickly.

She danced barefoot, twirling down the path, singing in a hauntingly beautiful tone.

Her voice sounded like crystal ringing through the air.

I have loved all this past year
So that I may love no more;
I have sighed many a sigh,
Beloved, for thy pity,
My love is never thee nearer,
And that me grieveth sore;
Sweet loved-one, think on me,
I have loved thee long.
Sweet loved-one, I pray thee,
For one loving speech;
While I live in this wide world
None other will I seek.
With thy love, my sweet beloved,
My bliss though mightest increase;
A sweet kiss of thy mouth
Might be my cure.

Elric finally reached her near the end of her song. The lyrics caused a new fuel to the fire raging inside.

"Is my life a game to you?!" He roared, eyes narrowed, and fists balled.

Faye spun with her arms stretched out, eyes gleaming. She laughed boisterously, taking long strides toward Elric. When she reached him, she raised a hand to touch his cheek. He stepped back, repulsed, before she could reach him.

"I give you my soul, demon, and it does nothing. Now you show up at her burial? To mock me?"

He lunged at her throat but only grabbed air. Elric spun around, looking for Faye. He heard a wicked giggle above him. Faye was perched on a branch like a vulture, her back arched, and her arms spread out as if she were about to take off into flight.

When their eyes met, she relaxed, straightening out her spine, resting her elbows on her knees, and cradling her face in her hands.

"I came to pay my respects," she pouted. "Do you protest, dearest Elric?"

"Demon!" He spat. "Respect! What more do you want from me? I have nothing left to give, and what I do have, you already own."

Faye jumped down from the branch, landing behind Elric so softly that she didn't make a sound when she hit the ground. She stroked his back as she circled around him.

"Nay, you are right. I have no respect to pay, except to my own curiosity. Every man, woman, boy, or girl who marks my book gives me a tie to them until their last dying breath. I know where you are at a moment's notice. I wanted to see where you were after last night's precarious event."

She stopped circling and stood directly before him, almost frustrated.

"I do not know what any of this means, but I do know I did not get one soul last night. I received two. And when I thought I was only going to feel one, I felt two on this plane of existence." She glanced around her, waving her hand.

Elric's eyes widened, looking at the oak tree in the distance.

"Ava is alive?" he whispered, starting to move back towards the grave.

Faye grabbed his wrist tightly. "Not as you think. *That* Ava," she motioned her head towards the gravesite, "is gone. She is dead."

She released him, turning away. "Her soul is somewhere on Earth. I do not know how; I do not know where. But it won't be like you knew."

"I do not understand," Elric cried, his eyebrows drawing together.

"Neither do I." She stroked his arm gracefully. "Our paths will cross again, Elric Ferron. You are too interesting for me not to watch."

Her mouth curved into a smile, and then she was gone.

Elric was left with more questions than answers, but his resolve was the same. If his Ava wasn't in his world, he wouldn't be in it much longer, either. He decided that night he would take his own life.

Elric arrived at his front door, still ajar from the night before. He pushed it open all the way, and the memory of Ava lying on the floor posing for him flooded his mind. The night she told him she was pregnant with their child. The times they sat and shared a meal, made each other laugh, argued, complained, cried, made love. All of it moved in his mind, too much to bear. Shaking his head, he refused to be in the house longer than necessary. He slammed his hand down on the knife still on the table, crusted with blood. The fury residing in him guided him as if it had a life of its own. He turned to leave but stopped at the threshold.

A fleeting thought passed. *Ava wouldn't want this.*

He rubbed his hands up his face, lacing his fingers behind his head, knife still in hand. Elric looked over his shoulder and winced, dropping his hands, but then he caught the eye of her portrait, and it gave him the final push he needed to follow through.

Elric stomped through the untilled ground, resting for winter. Heading to the very back, he found a lone Ash tree and threw himself down at the base.

"No more thoughts, Elric," he said to himself.

With his eyes welled up with tears, he looked at his wrist through blurred vision. He raised his blade and pressed it to his wrist. The bite of the metal was hard and sharp. Elric bared his teeth, sucking in air as the wound began to weep. He repeated it on the other side, then dropped the knife on the dirt with a quiet thud. Resting his head against the bark, he stared at the night sky through the bare branches. The tears came freely and gently, cascading down to mix with the blood that began to stain the earth. He slowly blinked at the stars, and they seemed to blink back at him. A smile spread across his face as he began to sing.

While I live in this wide world, none other will I seek.

Elric's breaths began to slow and became shallower, vision ebbing in and out.

His head dropped, allowing his chin to tuck into his chest.

His breathing rattled.

"Ava."

His vision completely was dark, his control over his limbs was absent. A manic laugh tried to push it's way out of his throat, but nothing came of it. The air in his lungs almost ceasing to be.

Not too much longer, my love, he thought to himself.

His body eventually went completely slack, and a cold crept over him. He began to hear something; it seemed as though it was coming from miles away. No, not miles away. It was right next to him. What is it? The Angel of Death coming to collect? Faye to reap her reward?

"Damn you, Elric!" The voice was gruff, and he sensed his body being lifted off the ground.

It matters not, he thought. *The deed is done.*

Elric felt a warmth on his face and a bed beneath him. He turned over on his side, only to be met by familiar green eyes.

"What are we to do? Lie in bed all day? How slothful." Ava laughed, poking his nose.

Elric wrapped his arms around her before burying his face in her neck.

She laughed again, the sound comforting to Elric.

"Oh, is *that* what you were planning for the day? Elric Ferron." She chastised playfully.

The scent of the hearth she had stood over while cooking invaded his senses, burying himself deeper.

Ava's laugh started to lose its lightness as it morphed into something gravelly. Guttural moaning erupted in its stead, the skin on Ava's neck suddenly cold against Elric's face. Pushing himself off Ava, he focused on her face. It was no longer Ava, but instead, a full embrace with Faye, her marred skin leaving blood on Elric and her face contorted with a croaking laugh that came through closed lips.

The dream released its hold on him, and Elric's eyes flew open, his heart pounding in his rapidly moving chest. Clutching the sheets he was lying on, his knuckles were white and on fire from the tension. Relief washed over him as he realized he was back in the monastery. He relaxed his grip and looked to his side to see Geoffrey asleep in a chair. Elric made a motion to try and sit up, the shift of his weight causing the wood to creak. Geoffrey immediately woke and stood up, rushing to his side.

"Elric," Geoffrey called out, pain evident in his voice.

"You ruined my plan," he smirked.

The friar's face paled. "Do not ever make light of that." His voice was hard and grave. "I watched as Ava took her last breath, and I thought I would have to do the same with you, not even a full night passing between."

"I am regretful you were the one to find me," he said as his lip quivered. "Truly I am. I would not want to cause you any more pain. But I do not know how to live with mine."

Geoffrey hung his head before responding. "You learn to grow around the pain, not let the pain grow around you."

Elric turned his head away from his friend. "It seems, Friar, your ability to save is miraculous."

Lifting his arms, Elric inspected his skin for wounds, his voice trailing off. He turned his wrists over, and there was not one single mark or a sign there ever was one. He lifted the other arm, and it was the same. He was healed and with no sign of injury or scar.

He looked up at Geoffrey, eyes wide in confusion. "Did I not?"

Elric inspected Geoffrey's robes and saw blood-splattered and stained, his hands red and fingernails dirty.

Geoffrey's forehead furrowed. "You did. I found you, the wounds gaping and bleeding. I rushed you over, hoping to pack it—to save you. I laid you down upon the bed, no longer a breath or beating of a heart left inside you. I feared I was too late. I would not have believed it had my own eyes not witnessed it."

The Friar rubbed his eyes, sitting back down and throwing his hands into the air.

"Your wounds healed. I watched them heal by the grace of God. Color returned to your face. Your heart began to beat. Air moved through your body again. Your skin just weaved itself together. Elric, you were dead."

The color drained from Elric's face, the realization hitting him.

"This was not by God's grace, and I do not believe I will ever meet him."

VII

MODERN-DAY ARCATA, CALIFORNIA
"Hey man! Are you okay? Oh my god, Todd, call 911!"

"Does he have a pulse?"

"Holy crap, Jack, there is so much blood."

"Don't move him! Hi, yes, we found a man unconscious on the trail we are out at..."

Elric wakes to a commotion of voices above him. He opens his eyes, but the sun is too bright to leave them that way. He feels dirt and spit caked across his lips. The taste of metal sits on his tongue, and grit sits in his molars. He grinds his teeth, the cracking of the gravel sounding off beneath him.

He flips himself over on his back and lets out a moan. "Hang up the phone."

"Hey! Don't move! I'm on the phone, help is on the way." A young man with bright red hair stands above him, dressed in a simple t-shirt and gym shorts, talking on his phone.

"He's trying to get up. What should I do?" He says to the operator on the line.

"Hey man, she says you really shouldn't get up; you could have a broken spine or something!"

Elric sits up and rotates his neck, waving his arms up and down.

He holds up his hands over his eyes to block the light. "I am quite alright, as you can see. Please hang up the phone."

"Y-You have blood all over you, dude. I think you need medical attention. Seriously," the other man speaks up for the first time. He stands with a slicked-back ponytail, Pit Viper sunglasses, and gold chains hanging from his neck.

Elric forces courtesy and wishing to just move on with his day. Standing up, he holds out his hand and motions to hand the phone to him.

The redhead stares at him wide-eyed and hands over the phone.

"Much obliged."

Elric lets out an exasperated breath and puts the phone up to his ear. "Hello. With whom do I have the pleasure of speaking?"

Taking a few steps forward he rubs his sore chest. "Jen? Well, Jen, I am the gentleman these fine young men stumbled upon... No, no, I am completely fine."

Turning back toward the two men, he notices them watching intently. "It was all just a misunderstanding. Well, yes, just a little blood after a little tumble... Yes, I am completely capable and of sound mind... Right. Alright, well, thank you so much, Jen. Have a wonderful day."

Elric hangs up the phone, handing it back to the redhead.

He reaches into his back pocket and pulls out his wallet and hands them each 50 dollars.

"I am so sorry if I put a damper on your day, boys. I am perfectly fine. Thank you for your concern." Elric gives a two-finger salute and makes the trek up the trail back to the overlook, where he hopes his car has remained.

He reaches the top of the path to find his car idle, the engine still murmuring. "Oh, thank God." He gets in, making his way back home.

Walking into his front door, he is eagerly welcomed by his four-legged friend.

"Oh Geoffrey, I am so sorry," he says, wincing, picking up the small dog.

Geoffrey whines while licking his face. "Yes, yes, okay. Please stop, go use the restroom. I'm sure you're bursting."

Elric sets him back down, the dog dancing in circles at his feet until the back door opens, and the dog darts out.

Making his way to the bathroom he needs to assess what state of fright he must have had those boys in. He flips on the switch, the incandescent lights flickering to life. Dry streaks of blood run horizontally across his cheekbones from the way he landed face down. Having been laid out in the sun like a reptile bathing in the heat, his cheeks are flush, and his lips cracked and dry. Sweat runs across the road map of blood on his face, distorting the paths. He rubs his neck and winces. Turning his back to the mirror, he looks over his shoulder and sees a bright red sunburn marking him.

"Seems as though you flew too close to the sun, Icarus." He says to himself.

He laughs, pitying the boys finding him in such a state. He traces his fingers up the route of blood to find the starting point, arriving at a hard, sharp, and jagged edge at his temple. He pushes it, flinching at the touch, deciding he'll come back to it in a moment. His shirt, a simple white cotton button-up, is not only covered in dirt but soiled from an expansive blood stain. He turns around in front of the mirror, seeing that the mark goes from belly to back. He lifts his shirt and only sees faint yellow bruising as if the wounds had been weeks old. Taking off the shirt completely, he throws it onto the floor. He liked that shirt and was disappointed to dispose of it. His jeans were split up the side and splattered with blood.

"Wasteful," he mutters to himself.

He walks out of the bathroom and heads toward an art supply room at the back of the house to grab a palette knife out of a drawer.

Elric hears whining at the back door and goes to open it. "Not a good time, Geoffrey."

Geoffrey yips at him and follows him to the bathroom, stopping and sitting in the hallway to watch attentively.

"I do not love an audience," Elric sighs. He takes a deep breath. "Just do it."

He takes the tip of the palette knife and drives it into his temple, digging his way underneath the object embedded in his skin. Clenching his jaw, he sucks in his breath, sweat beading on his forehead. He doesn't stop pushing the palette knife in until he feels a pop then hears the *clink* of ceramic when the object hits the basin. Blood begins to slowly trickle down his face at the absence of the piece, now lying in the sink. Reaching up, he feels the hole left behind but remains unbothered because he knows it won't be there in the next hour. A bloodied rock the size of a quarter and about half an inch thick sits in the sink.

He picks it up and looks it over. "You little bastard."

Elric takes off the remainder of his clothes, piling them on the floor, and walks out into his kitchen, with Geoffrey following behind.

He pours the dog a bowl of food and gets him fresh water. Grabbing a bottle of wine from a rack on his counter, he pours himself a large glass. Feeling emotionally hungover from the night before, and unfortunately, the beating his body took didn't knock it out of him. For Elric, sometimes, the physical pain is the only thing to take his mind momentarily off hundreds of years of crushing emotion.

He stands naked in the middle of his hallway and takes a long gulp. The feelings of last night do not seem to be suppressed well enough with wine, and so Elric decides to head back into the kitchen for something stronger. Grabbing a bottle half full of whiskey from the top shelf, he heads for the cabinet. Elric shakes his head, deciding against cleaning more glasses. He pops the top of the bottle and throws the lid onto the floor. Chugging from the bottle, he walks into the bathroom and starts the shower. Hot air fills the room. It immediately reminds him of the thick air in Savannah.

He puts down the bottle at his side and stares at a fog-covered mirror. Inhaling sharply, he lets the steam fill his lungs. He wishes it would burn, again begging for the physicality of pain to replace the one in his soul. He can't see past the fog and wipes the mirror. As soon as he does, the clean spots are covered by the steam, creating a cloudy image. The distorted picture in front of him is just a reminder of the impossibly endless future and a fog he can't see through.

Stepping into the shower, he finishes off the drink and drops the bottle, letting it shatter onto the shower pan. He walks back into the falling water, fresh broken glass crunching beneath his feet, red pooling in the basin. He flinches at the sharp pains but doesn't stop it from happening. His body tenses as the biting prickles of heat hit his back. Taking a deep breath, he fully submerges himself, not releasing his breath until his body feels like it is floating. Releasing his breath, air comes crashing back heavily, knocking him off balance. His shoulder hits the shower wall with a loud thud, causing bottles lining the niche to fall onto the floor. He laughs, and it sounds slightly deranged. Picking himself back up, he hangs his head. The water flows downward, taking all the dirt and blood of the night with it. The wound on his head stings, but he doesn't move. He endures the pain. After a while, the water starts to run cold. Pinching the bridge of his nose, he lets out a long sigh and turns off the shower.

Elric steps out, not bothering to grab a towel, and heads into his room, hearing a low growl from Geoffrey as he enters.

He rolls his eyes in annoyance, knowing exactly who would elicit that response, as he was expecting the guest sooner rather than later.

A woman lays on his bed in a seductive pose—a silver silk dress clings to her body, leaving no room for imagination. White hair lay spread across his pillow.

"Honestly, Elric, you don't even have the decency to cover up in the presence of a lady?" she snickers.

"Faye, what the hell are you doing here? I'm tired," he grunts, reaching into the middle drawer of his dresser to find his black joggers.

Elric falls onto the bed beside Faye, slightly bouncing her and laying his arm over his eyes. He calls for Geoffrey and pats the empty spot next to him. The small dog jumps up, tense and never moving his eyes off her.

Faye turns over onto her stomach, kicking her legs in the air.

"Oh silly, you know I love to check in. Especially when you do things like this." She pokes the wound in his head.

He winces. "You know how I love being your favorite mystery, but not today," he says sarcastically.

"Fine, I know when I'm not wanted." Faye sticks out her lip in a fake pout.

She sits up and crosses her legs, lacing her fingers behind her head. Closing her eyes, she leans against Elric's headboard.

"I guess I'll just keep what I know about Ava to myself."

He promptly sits up, disturbing Geoffrey. "What is it?"

Faye opens one eye and looks at Elric. "No 'please?'"

"Faye," he snarls.

"Alright, alright. Sheesh. You're becoming so touchy in your old age," she smirks.

She raises her hand in front of her, subtly wiggling her fingers in a wave motion. A dark fog appears on his bed, no bigger than a golf ball. She continues to move her fingers, expanding the fog until it is three times its original size. Suddenly, she closes her fist, and the fog disappears. In its stead two lit candles appear: one white candle and one black, about six inches in length. A circlet of twine bands them together resting around the wicks.

Faye's face becomes serious as she furrows her brow. "You're right. You are my favorite mystery and even after almost seven-hundred years, I still can't figure it out. You gave up your soul, hers with it, but I can't lay claim to either. She's stuck in this loop, and you're stuck without an end."

She points to the candles. "Those are you two, the cord is your link."

Faye leans in closer, glaring at the flames. "Some cords burn and break, either due to death or the end of a relationship... Or the candles melt down while the cord remains fully intact, meaning you die with your linked one."

Waving her hands directly in the flames, she moves them back and forth. "Now your cord rests directly on the fire. It is constantly burning yet never breaking. Your candles never move, either. Same size always. The only change is that her candle flickers when she dies. It never goes out, just merely flickers."

Elric bends over to get a closer look, watching the embers in the twine moving like termites through wood.

"What does it mean?"

Faye rotates her wrists, waving her fingers, and the candles are swallowed up in a fog. She lays down her hand, and the fog disappears as well.

Elric sits stiffly, looking at Faye and waiting for an answer.

"I'm not sure," she responds with a shrug.

He stands up in irritation. "You come to torture me then? You said you had information on Ava. My mistake in thinking you would be helpful."

Faye appears beside him in a flash, their faces only inches apart. Geoffrey goes into a frenzy, barking at Faye from on top of the bed.

"You've upset Geoffrey," Elric says, picking up his companion and quietly shushing him, unintimated by her.

Faye laughs. "That friar meant so much to you. He was with you until the very end of his life, trying to help you. Did he ever meet an Ava?"

Geoffrey looks up, and Elric looks into his eyes.

"He did. It was in Ireland, 1373. We went to the Hill of Tara. We heard legends of witches there, and we tried to find answers or solutions to why I couldn't die. Obviously, you were no help," casting a glare at her. "We never found a witch, but we found Ava for the first time. Geoffrey and she became good friends. Again," he snickered. "Then we had to live through her death again. I would have gone mad had he not been by my side. He helped me piece together what our lives had turned into before he passed."

The familiar sting of tears hits Elric's eyes, but a different sort of sting hits his heart.

He rubs his tears away with his thumb before continuing. "He was and is the most important friend I've ever had in my life."

A quick look of grief passes over Faye's face but is gone as swiftly as it appeared. She huffs and turns her back to Elric, rummaging through a sketchbook kept on his desk.

"You'll meet Ava soon. You have the right time and place. I don't know when, but soon," she says, keeping her back to him.

He laughs. "Is that humanity I'm sensing in you?"

Faye turns around, disgusted. "Never. Just a morbid curiosity in time's plague."

Before he can respond, she is gone. He crawls under the covers of his bed, holding them up for Geoffrey to settle in next to him. He stares up at the ceiling, and his heart skips a beat.

"Soon," he murmurs before he drifts off to sleep.

FIVE MONTHS LATER

"Anita, could you come in here for a sec?" Elric yells from his desk.

"Yes, Mr. Ferron?" Anita walks in, wearing paint-stained overalls, hair high on her head held in place by two jade hair sticks. "I almost have that back room organized. I found your muller by the way," holding it out for him.

"Oh well, forget that project- my muller!" He takes the handheld tool, remnants of the last pigmentation mix still on the base, and steadies it on the palm of his hand. "Thank you! I know I could buy another, but I just really prefer this one."

"But the real reason I called you in," he rubs his hands together, his eyes gleaming, "Come sit."

Anita stares at him, waiting in anticipation.

"Mr. Hanover came in earlier today wanting another mural done. They are reconstructing the library and want a fresh new look."

She claps her hands and grins. "Another mural! Do I get to work on this one with you as well?"

He leans back. "Anita. You are taking over this project completely."

Her jaw drops, eyes wide. "I'm sorry, what?"

"He saw your landscape of the valley hanging on the wall," he points in the direction of her piece. "It stopped him dead in his tracks. He is expecting your call so you can go over the details."

He beams at her over the news, knowing what this could mean for her career.

"Mr. Ferron... are you freaking kidding me? I can't. This is a joke."

"You *can*." Elric stands up with a smirk and shakes Anita's hand, her face awe-struck. "Congratulations!"

Anita jumps up and throws her arms around him. "Thank you! I'm going to go call him now."

She walks out of the office, stopping in the doorframe, glowing. "Thank you again."

Elric smirks. "I didn't do anything Anita. It was on your own merit." He held so much pride for her and her talent.

"But still," her gratitude is apparent.

She grins at Elric and raises her eyebrows. "By the way, how do you feel about meeting the girlfriend's family tonight?"

Elric laughs. "I feel fine, thanks for asking."

"Just checking! You better get going! Aren't you supposed to be there at 6?" She calls over her shoulder as she walks out the door.

Panicked, he looks down at his watch. 5:36 p.m. "Oh crap."

Grabbing his phone, he rushes out the door, waving to Anita, who sits on the phone with a wide grin plastered on her face.

Elric arrives at the black door of a white craftsman-style home, holding a bouquet of white lilies and a bottle of Bowmore 25 scotch. He knocks and smooths out his shirt before the door can swing open. Not wanting to over-dress, he shows up in navy chinos, a white knit button up, and black sneakers.

Robyn answers the door in a light pink dress embellished with small red flowers.

She smiles through clenched teeth. "I thought you were going to be late."

"Never." His lips curl into a tender smile before he lightly kisses her on the cheek.

She lets out a slow breath and gives a genuine smile. "Okay, let's do this."

Robyn grabs his hand and leads him into a large, open kitchen. A barefoot woman wearing a simple yellow dress, her auburn hair in a messy bun, dances while chopping vegetables at a white kitchen island. A man with dark hair in a plaid shirt, cargo shorts, and glasses stands behind her, stirring a pot. Two teenage girls – with hair like Robyn's – sit at the counter on barstools, silently looking at their phones.

Robyn clears her throat. "Guys, Elric's here."

Everyone simultaneously looks up at Elric, and Robyn's mother shrieks.

"Robyn, he's so handsome! Come over here so I can get a look at you! You brought flowers!? *And* a gentleman? Maybe I should go jogging in the woods alone." She laughs and winks at her husband.

"Mom," Robyn groans.

Elric walks over to her mother, handing her the bouquet. "It's a pleasure to meet you, Mrs. Renata."

"The accent! So sexy! Robyn, you never mentioned how sexy he sounded. Oh honey, these are gorgeous." She hands the bouquet to one of the younger girls at the counter. "Kylie, go put these in water, please. Come over here, we hug in this house."

She grabs Elric and embraces him. "Please call me Brooke."

"Brooke." He smiles.

Elric turns his attention to her husband, who is standing at her side.

"James," firmly grasping Elric's hand. "No dead fish handshake here! *Ha,* and a scotch man! When are you marrying my daughter? Hand that over here, son!" His face lit up.

Robyn covers her face with her hands. "Dad. Please. Give the man a break."

"What?" Tilting his head down, he reads the label. "Bowmore 25! Expensive!" Robyn looks at Elric. "I'm sorry I thought they would be more chill."

Elric settles the tension in the air with his charm. "No need to apologize. Robyn told me you were a scotch enthusiast."

James waves the bottle at Brooke. "Sweetie, tell him it's on my bucket list to go to the distilleries in Scotland."

Brooke rolls her eyes, going back to chopping tomatoes and onions.

"Yes, it's on his list, and he talks about it *often*. You'd think at the top of his bucket list was to annoy me." She chortles, hip-checking James.

James laughs and goes back to tending to whatever is in the pot.

"Okay, anyway," Robyn says, pulling Elric toward the two girls. "Elric, this is Kylie, this is Kiera."

They momentarily look up from their phones, wave, and look back down.

"It's nice to meet both of you. I've heard great things."

"So have we," Kiera says, raising her eyebrows at Kylie.

The girls erupt into laughter.

"You two quit it," Brooke directs, pointing her knife at them. "Go set the table. Go now."

The girls leave the room, giggling to each other.

Elric looks at Robyn, her face flush. "I am going to kill them," she mutters.

Laughing, he wraps his arm around her waist, pulling her in as he lands a kiss on top of her head.

"Don't worry about it." He then brushes his lips over Robyn's ear to whisper, "but you'll have to tell me later what you told them." Pulling back, he wiggles his eyebrows at her. She playfully slaps him in the chest.

Still holding her around the waist, Elric looks back towards Brooke. "The red hair runs in the family? It is quite lovely."

Brooke places a hand on her chest, and the other one lightly touches her bun. "Oh yes, my mother, my grandmother, my great-great-grandmother, and grandmothers generations back all had the hair! Then I married that fox over there, and almost all my girls got it. Speaking of—Robyn, have you heard from your sister? Is she making it? I know she was still so jet lagged. Poor baby."

"Yep, she just said she would probably be running a little late, as usual. Mom, is there anything I can help you do?" Robyn asks.

"Oh, of course. I apologize. Brooke, James, is there anything I can help with?" Elric follows.

"No, you kids go on and head into the living room. We are almost done here," Brooke replies.

James turns around and stands at attention. "I'm just here to take orders." He erupts in his own amusement, "Go relax! We will call for you when it's done, and Elric, you can tell me more about your work and your wonderful taste in scotch."

They sit on a leather loveseat in the living room, her arms draped around his neck.

"That was embarrassing," she says, throwing her head back.

Placing his hand on the back of her head, he lifts it back up.

"No," he laughs, "I think they are genuine and sweet. And quite enthusiastic."

She guffaws. "Yeah, enthusiastic. We'll just go with that. Thank you for coming. It means a lot."

"Of course. I wouldn't have missed it," he responds.

She leans in and kisses him aggressively, gripping the collars of his shirt as she pulls him in.

He pulls away amused at her candor. "Your parents aren't the only enthusiastic ones. Maybe not on your parent's couch, though. I'm trying to make a good impression."

Tugging at the edges of his shirt, he straightens it from her flirtatious pull.

Robyn giggles and nestles into his side; he lifts his arm, draping it around her shoulders.

Twenty minutes go by before Robyn's mother calls for them to come to the dining room. Robyn looks at Elric's face and snickers.

"Go to the bathroom. I've left some lipstick on your face, and that is not coming off without soap," she says, rubbing at his mouth and then pushing him away. "Down the hall, the first door on the right."

Elric walks down to the bathroom and hears the front door open. A myriad of greetings are exchanged, and he safely assumes it's the other sister joining them. Elric scrubs his mouth, where bright red smudges leave a stain. Running his fingers through his hair to lay down flyaways, he looks at himself one final time in the mirror before exiting.

Exiting the bathroom, the smile is still sitting on his face. He rounds the corner into the dining room and sees Robyn seated at a long oak table. She looks up at him with the word *smitten* all but written on her face. There sit two empty chairs directly across from each other, one of them next to Robyn. The twins are sitting across from Robyn and her parents at both ends. He glides over, taking the vacant seat beside her.

Robyn places her hand on Elric's thigh and shouts into the kitchen. "Hey, grab the pitcher of lemonade! Mom forgot it!"

Brooke playfully scolds. "I believe I asked you to grab it, missy."

"I do not believe you did, mother," Robyn teases.

"Alright, you two, that's enough. I've brought the lemonade."

The bright voice renders Elric motionless. The familiarity of the sound freezes his gaze onto the tweed placemat in front of him and makes the edges of his vision fuzzy. Memories come crashing into his mind all at once. He hears the thud of the pitcher being set down on the table and feels the presence of another body next to him.

"Hi, I'm Ava."

Elric is certain the earth has stopped turning. It always does.

VIII

"Elric." Geoffrey stopped walking down the village's main road. He grabbed the back of Elric's tunic, forcefully halting him. Elric tripped over his own feet but caught himself before hitting the ground.

"Geoffrey, what could-" his words were cut short, along with his breath. She sat in front of a small home, children running in the grass around her. They watched her dote on a child in her arms. She twirled the girl's soft golden curls around her fingers as she cooed to make the little girl laugh. As Ava and Elric's eyes met, she tilted her head, and a look of confusion crossed her face. Her attention was brought back to the giggling girl in her arms.

Elric stumbled backward, catching himself on a tree. Geoffrey promptly captured him by the arm and pulled him behind one of the small village homes. As soon as Elric was out of sight, he retched beside a trough. His stomach twisted, betraying anything he had eaten. A cold sweat broke out over his body. His mind felt like it was underwater, with reality distorting what were logical thoughts. Geoffrey leaned against the home, rapidly muttering prayers as he rocked back

81

and forth.

"Geoffrey," Elric rasped.

The friar didn't move or acknowledge him at all.

"Geoffrey!" He yelled.

Finally, he looked up and stopped his frantic movements. His eyes were filled with turmoil. Elric could see Geoffrey's whole belief system being questioned in the friar's mind.

"That was Ava? Was that Ava? That was Ava." Elric wasn't sure if he had asked questions or made declarations. He couldn't even tell if his feet were still touching the ground by that time.

"Brother... I just do not know how it could be," Geoffrey said, never meeting Elric's eyes. "But it seemed like she recognized you."

He stood up straight and wiped his mouth with the back of his hand. Taking the bottom of his tunic, he lifted it up to wipe his face, which was covered in perspiration. Holding on to the outer walls, he walked around the corner, barely sticking his head out. He searched for those deep black curls, but she was no longer sitting in the yard with all the children he could see.

Elric felt like he was standing on top of the ocean's wave in the middle of a storm, his legs threatening to lose their footing at any moment, casting him down into the imaginative sea below him. Slowly he made his way out back to the path with Geoffrey following close behind, rubbing a small wooden cross in between his fingers. They could hear children laughing and screaming nearby. Not too far ahead, he noticed a small group with three women leading and rounding up the children. He saw the small golden-haired child first, toddling behind, and then he saw *her*.

Elric's pace quickened as he faintly heard his friend call for him. Elric caught up with the group until he was only a couple of feet away. He tried to catch their conversation, but there was too much commotion, and, anyway, his heart was beating in his ears. The group of women erupted into laughter, and his ears caught her sound quickly. Elric closed his eyes and could see Ava in their home. Laughing in front of their fireplace or while she cooked supper. He opened his eyes and stared at her intently, willing her to turn and look at him. As if she could feel his energy, she turned. He felt the air go thin as he stared into Ava's eyes.

"Ava." His voice was hoarse and feeble. His hands shook uncontrollably behind him.

She looked up, and the corners of her mouth lifted. Her eyebrows drew together, and she stared at him for a moment. Elric thought she was going to ignore him as she picked up the child and turned around, but he watched as she handed her off to one of the other women. She began to walk toward Elric, and he felt his stomach threaten him in the same way it had when he first saw her moments ago. He breathed in slowly, praying his body would calm.

She waved as she approached, her demeanor friendly.

"Good Morrow. Forgive me, have we met before?"

Elric almost pulled back at the unknown accent coming from her. He looked her over, and there wasn't a doubt in his mind that this was Ava.

"Ava." He reached out to her, and she took a step back, shaking her head.

"I'm so sorry. I do not recall meeting. Where would I know you?"

Shock recoiled through Elric as he heard the hard Irish dialect coming from her lips.

How could this be his Ava?

"Apologies," Elric stuttered, walking away. This couldn't be her.

She died.

He buried her.

He watched the earth cover her.

Closing his eyes tightly, all his senses were flooded by the memories of that night. The loose dirt that covered her body. The nuns singing and Geoffrey's prayers. His heart felt as though it was splitting inside of him.

"Wait," she called.

The accent was unknown, but the tone seemed so familiar. Elric stopped and fidgeted with his clothing.

A ghost. He thought. *I've gone mad. But madness gives me a chance with my beloved. Sanity does not.*

Elric decided to lean into the lunacy of the situation, walking back to the stranger he knew all too well.

MODERN-DAY ARCATA, CALIFORNIA

Elric forces himself to stand up and take the hand in front of him.

He looks up to see a woman with raven-colored hair and emerald-green eyes. Her smile rests softly on her face like water lilies on the pond. Elric tries to take her all in without seeming inappropriate. Long, loose curls that he has become so familiar with flow down to the middle of her back. This time, there are purple streaks hiding underneath. She is dressed simply in black yoga pants, an oversized band tee, and sandals. Simple makeup on her face, and a few gold rings adorn her fingers.

Elric holds her hand and shakes it, noticing a small script tattoo on the inside of her forearm.

He composes himself, masking all his emotions and putting them away to sort out later.

After clearing his throat, he finally greets her. "I'm Elric, pleased to meet you."

Slightly raising her arm, he reads her tattoo aloud.

"*Everything is more beautiful because we are doomed,*" he smiles. "*The Iliad.*"

A smile lights up her face, and her eyes sparkle.

"No one ever knows! They all just think I am dramatic! I'm impressed."

Elric recites the quote from memory. "*Any moment might be our last. Everything is more beautiful because we are doomed. You will never be lovelier than you are now. We will never be here again.*"

That well-known melodic laugh carries through the room, easing the weight on Elric's heart.

"Jimmy, look at that. Someone else who is obsessed with that old book. Good.

She can rattle off about the book to someone other than me!" Brooke jokes.

Robyn clears her throat and Elric looks back at her while noticing he is still holding Ava's hand.

"Oh, excuse me." He drops her hand and takes his seat. "That book is very close to my heart."

Ava walks around to the other side of the table and sits down. "Mine too."

She gives that captivating look, and he stares for far too long.

"Okay, we've established we like old books," Robyn says, annoyed and clearly ready to move on.

Robyn raises an eyebrow, and Elric turns his attention to her mother.

"Brooke," he says, "this looks absolutely delicious. I haven't had a home-cooked paella in quite some time," he adds, trying to swiftly divert the focus away from the awkward moment.

"Oh, you know paella! This is a family recipe. Where have you had it?"

"I traveled in Spain for quite some time, so, different local places."

"You'll have to tell me how mine compares," Brooke responds, impressed. "You're so well-traveled! Tell me more."

The conversation drifts from travel to art to food and to childhood stories. Elric tries to keep himself from looking in Ava's direction, but he can't help but steal a glance every so often. When he does, Elric catches Ava doing the same. Their gazes meet and then quickly break away.

Likewise, he tries to keep himself from looking at Robyn but can feel the holes she's drilling into the side of his head with her eyes. Keeping the conversation going with each family member, with the exception of Ava, Elric just tries to get through the night.

At a lull in the lively conversation, James speaks up.

"So, Elric, tell me, why haven't you painted my little pumpkin right there? I hear you're an amazing artist, and there's a beautiful subject. Where's the art?" He bursts out, "I joke! But seriously, she's gorgeous, why wouldn't you?"

"Dad!" Robyn speaks sternly. "You do not just ask that. Elric, ignore him, seriously."

Elric feigns a state of ease, wiping his mouth before answering.

"I don't do many portraits," he lies. "Mainly big projects, landscape painting. Really, I focus on working with non-profits. It takes certain circumstances for me to paint portraits, and I'm not as well trained in them, so I don't do them."

"Well, I'm sure the right circumstances will come along then!" James jests.

"That's enough, Jimmy." Brooke interjects, "Elric, would you like anything else?"

He pats his stomach, "No, thank you, I am quite pleasantly full. This was delicious. Just as good as in Spain, if I say so myself!"

Brooke waves her hand at Elric, "Oh, stop!"

"No, I am quite serious! I'll have to get your recipe." Elric flatters.

"Like I said, it is a family recipe, so when you become family, you can have it."

Brooke looks back and forth between Elric and Robyn.

Elric steals a glance at Ava, catching her glimpse just before she directs her attention back to the plate in front of her.

Robyn sets her elbows on the table and covers her eyes, "Mom. Please."

"I'm kidding! Kiera, Kylie, help me clean up, girls. The rest of you go relax!" Brooke says as she stands up, picking up plates.

Ava and Elric stand up at the same time while reaching for the platter of paella, which is set in the middle of the table. Their fingers graze each other, and they both quickly draw their hands back.

"I'm sorry," Elric says, rubbing his fingers together.

"No, you're a guest. You shouldn't be cleaning up." The simple sentence uttered from her lips enchants him.

Oh, how I have waited to hear your voice again, he thinks, wishing he could close his eyes and delight in it.

He clears his throat instead. "Thank you, but I-"

Robyn rapidly stands up from the table, the chair loudly scraping back.

"Elric. She has it. Come on." She aggressively grabs his hand and pulls him away from the table.

"Dad, did you know Elric has an old Mustang? Let's go check it out."

"Hot damn. Let's go, what year?" James stands up from the table, making his way out of the dining room.

As Robyn pulls Elric behind her, he glances back at Ava and notices her gaze fixed on him.

Elric looks away and shouts over Robyn's head, "It's a '67, sir."

Everything in his being begs him to turn back around towards her, but he refuses the temptation. He knows if he does, he will never leave, so he follows Robyn and James out the door.

"Thank you again so much. I had a great time," Elric says as he hugs Brooke at the door.

Robyn's parents wave goodbye as Elric walks with her out to his car parked on the street.

Robyn leans against his driver-side door and crosses her arms.

"Your parents are lovely," he says, pulling out his keys. He begins to fidget with them, the jingle an uncomfortable sound in the tense silence.

"Mmhm. Ava, too?" Robyn retorts.

"All your sisters were great," he says, forcing a smile and looking into her eyes to challenge the remark.

"Do you know her? Have you met her before? That all seemed so familiar. I felt like I was intruding," she scrutinizes, looking down at her fingernails, chipping away at the pink polish.

Elric puts his hand over hers. "I haven't been in Arcata that long, and I wasn't in China while she was."

She rips her hands away from him. "I know you weren't in China. Don't talk to me like I'm a psycho."

Elric drops his hands to his sides.

Robyn looks up, speaking softly under her breath. "I'm sorry. I'm not trying to be crazy; it just was an important night to me, and it felt ruined."

"It wasn't ruined. And it was a great night." Elric fiddles with his keys more; it was a great night for all the reasons she's worried about.

"And then, I don't know. You know how in movies when the romantic interests meet? I don't know. I guess I'm just feeling insecure. I'm blowing it out of proportion. Whatever, it doesn't matter."

She shakes it off and wraps herself around him. "Elric, thank you so much for coming and meeting my crazy family."

"I'm glad I met them." He pulls away and kisses her on the cheek, feeling like, for the first time tonight, he wasn't lying to her.

He gets into his car and rolls down his window. "I'll call you tomorrow," he says, mustering some sort of pleasing expression.

Her expression sours at what Elric can only assume is his hurried farewell and lackluster kiss.

Again, she rallies. Looking down, a flush creeps up on her face.

"Elric? There is something I've been wanting to say to you for a little while now. Something I've been feeling for a while..."

Oh no, he thinks. *Not now. Not tonight. I shouldn't have carried this on. This wasn't ever the plan. Love is never the plan.*

He calms his thoughts and places his hand on Robyn's cheek.

"Robyn, I don't want to kill your momentum but I had a set of different circumstances in mind for *that*."

Elric, you liar. His voice rattles in his head.

Obviously let down, Robyn's excited disposition vanishes.

"Okay, but—"

He gives a half smile and cuts her off.

"I'll call you tomorrow," he reiterates.

Elric drives away, his head feeling like a windmill and the wind just never seems to slow down.

Early the next morning, Elric walks into his art studio, still reeling from the night before. He passes Anita's desk, deep in thought.

"Good morning, Mr. Ferron! How'd last night go?" Anita asks, eagerly waiting to hear the details.

He continues past her, into his office, not registering that she is speaking.

"Mr. Ferron?"

Elric halts abruptly and turns around to her.

"Anita, I am so sorry. I was lost in thought. It was fine." He puts last night's event at the back of his mind and walks up to her desk.

"Tell me what you and Charles discussed?" He asks, quickly changing the subject and happy to focus on the world of art.

Anita forgets about her question and becomes giddy with excitement. "Oh, Mr. Ferron! It's going to be wonderful. We discussed doing a beachscape where the seafoam hits the shoreline that'll morph into the city skyline." Anita dances in places while discussing all her ideas and color schemes. Elric gets lost in hearing the details and is truly overjoyed to see Anita tackle such a project, her fervent passion setting her aglow.

"It's going to be magnificent. No one better to create it. If you need anything at all, don't hesitate to ask. And Anita?"

"Yes, Mr. Ferron?"

"My colleagues call me Elric."

Her lips go into a tight line trying to stifle her embarrassment at the social "promotion". "Well, okay then, *Elric.*"

"Much better," he says, giving smile in reassurance.

He steps into his office and closes the door behind him. Dropping down on the couch, he digs for his tennis ball in the cushion and starts to throw it in the air almost violently.

"What the hell are you going to do, Elric?" He asks out loud.

The last thing he wants to do is hurt Robyn. He never aims to hurt anyone, but at this point, it's inevitable.

He will not pursue Ava.

As much as it pains him, Elric will have to wait until the next cycle. Never has he been in this situation.

He could wait.

He's met her when she was as young as twenty-five, a mere blink in his immortal life. He's also met her closer to twenty-eight in which he only gets a few months with her.

No matter the facts, no matter the wait, he couldn't do this. Leaving painful marks across his timeline was not something he signed up for. He felt that the only pain that needed to exist was his own, as part of his penance.

He won't cause pain for Robyn by trying to pursue Ava, and a continued relationship with Robyn, realistically, was never an option and is definitely not one now. It is human nature to desire to have a connection with others, and he always tries to time the ending right with the least amount of emotional casualties. This time, it just got away from him, and unforeseen circumstances hit. He also knew he couldn't stay with Robyn, knowing Ava was right there. He would never be invested in Robyn as she desired and deserved.

Elric stuffs the ball back into its grave in the couch cushions. Pulling out his phone, he opens up a message thread with Robyn.

Can we get together tonight?

Robyn's reply was instant. *I thought you had to work late planning a mural? It's covered. Gold Bluffs Beach? 4 pm?*
Sure! That works! See you then :)

He lays down his phone on the floor, closes his eyes, and wishes he could just remain celibate. He wishes that he had seen Ava first, reflecting on the countless wishes he has made over hundreds of years.

He gets off the couch and walks out of his office. As he passes Anita, he yells over his shoulder. "I'm going to go into the back room. If anyone comes looking for me, tell them I don't exist."

"Gotcha," she says without looking up, sketching out plans in her notebook.

Elric grabs a large blank canvas, a jar of brushes, and a pan of watercolor paints. He grabs an old MP3 player connected to a Bluetooth speaker that remains in this room. He hits play, and a song by Max Richter fills the room.

Elric's mood matches the deepening of the music, his strokes broadening across the canvas. Deep blues and brilliant yellows fill the background of the cloth. An image of a woman starts to emerge. She has long dark curls with hidden purple strands and olive skin with light black script inside the arm. Sharp green eyes stand out as if they are staring right back at him. Elric paints red flowers in a halo around her body.

He steps back and looks at his work, crossing his arm and holding his chin.

"Red poppies," he says to himself.

They always seem to symbolize an end.

"An end before there was even a beginning."

Throwing the paintbrush at the canvas, red scores the subject's face.

Crumpling on the floor, he begins to cry, with the blaring music drowning out his sobs.

Elric waits in the parking lot, hands shoved in his pockets. The ocean's breeze is strong today. The wind is whipping his eyes, roaring in his ears, making it barely tolerable to be outside. Dark, angry clouds loom above, threatening at any moment to burst with rain.

"Fitting," Elric says to himself, looking up at the vengeful sky.

As soon as Robyn's car pulls up and parks next to him the thunder booms, and rain begins to pour in a torrential downfall. She smiles at him and motions for him to get in. He hurries over and climbs in before shutting the door quickly, the interior already soaked from the few seconds of rain.

He's ready to get this over with. Robyn is now a cruel reminder that he can't be with Ava in this time.

"Hey, how are you!" She leans over to kiss him, a familiar greeting.

He turns his head, cutting her off before she reaches his lips. "Robyn."

"What is it?" She pulls back, her brow furrowed. There isn't a hint of inquisition in her voice. She can feel what's coming.

Elric takes a breath. "Robyn, I have sincerely enjoyed getting to know you. You are beautiful and wonderful. And-"

Shaking her head, her eyes begin to glisten. "No. What are you doing? What is happening?"

Attempting to put a comforting hand on her, she swiftly withdraws, placing her hands in her lap far from reach.

"Robyn, I just can't do-"

She cuts him off again, her expression hardened, but tears still fall.

"You met my family last night. What changed in the last 24 hours? Elric, I love you. That's what I was going to tell you. You can't break up with someone who was about to say, 'I love you.'" She speaks quickly as if saying the words faster could stop the swing of the pendulum.

Robyn loses her poker face, her eyebrows drawing together, her lips quivering. A hopeless sadness clouds her face.

The sound of raindrops heavily hitting the car fills the void Elric can't.

He keeps his gaze forward through the windshield, watching the drops of water merge and overtake the glass.

"Oh my God, Elric! You have nothing to say?!" She shouts.

"Robyn," he says, hanging his head.

"I swear to God if you say my name one more time." Her anger escalates. "Then do it already. You've wasted enough of my time. Just freaking do it." When he doesn't respond, she glares at him. "Look at me!"

Elric picks up his head, meeting her gaze. He would have never ended it like this.

"In another life, this could have worked. And it not working—it has nothing to do with you. You have to believe me. I just have a demon you don't know about. I'm really sorry, I am. God, I wish you knew how sorry I am, but I can't do this anymore."

Robyn wipes her face with the back of her sleeve. "What demon? What could be so bad? Elric, I'll help. I can stay by your side. We can face it together. Please, I love you."

He looks away. "Please stop saying that. I'm sorry. You deserve an amazing love story. I was never meant to be written into yours."

He gets out of the car and hears her call for him before he closes the door and cuts off her cry. As Elric walks in front of her car to get to his own, he can see Robyn's forehead resting against the steering through the rain-streaked windshield. He gets in his car and drives off, resolved not to look back.

IX

SAVANNAH, GEORGIA OCTOBER 1902

"Oh, this weather is absolutely gorgeous. Did I tell you Bonnie thought about getting married in July!" Ava threw her head back and fanned herself. "July of all months! That girl would be sweatin' worse than a whore in church as she actually stands at the front of a church! Imagine that," she laughed.

Elric pulled Ava in as they walked through the doors of the chapel.

"Maybe don't compare the bride to a whore *as* we walk in the doors of the church?" He whispered.

She looked around and wrinkled her nose at Elric. "Oops."

They made their way to a row with a couple of empty spaces and politely nodded and smiled at other guests.

As they were seated, Elric leaned into Ava, "How am I supposed to look at the bride when you're sitting here looking as beautiful as you do?"

Ava gazed up, her eyes bright as she brushed her fingers against his jaw. The wedding march began, and all the guests stood and faced the back of the chapel. Bonnie walked in, escorted by her father. She wore an intricately beaded white dress with a 6-foot-long cathedral lace train. Bonnie walked by Ava and made eye contact, raising her shoulders in excitement.

"I'm getting married!" Bonnie nearly shouted.

Ava sniffled as she looked at her friend with deep affection and admiration. She mouthed back to her, "You look beautiful."

Bonnie fanned her eyes, smiling, and continued down the aisle to her betrothed.

Ava linked her arms with Elric and dabbed at her cheeks with the back of her hand. He reached into his pocket, pulled out a handkerchief, and placed it into Ava's hand.

She looked up at him with nothing but engrossed love in her eyes.

"One day, that'll be us."

Elric nodded and forced a smile as he watched countless friends over the centuries have what Ava and he never could—a happy beginning and end.

"That is my dream, my love."

They danced in the back gardens of Bonnie's family estate turned reception.

"Elric, have you ever seen anything so magnificent? There must be hundreds of flowers here!" Ava gushed, soaking in the event around her.

He glanced around at the hanging candles in white lanterns illuminating the gardens. White drapery hung over a large ivory pergola. Pink and purple roses, calla lilies, and dahlias filled vases on white draped tables. Waiters in tuxedos passed out endless glasses of champagne. Bonnie and her newly vowed husband, George, danced and laughed while mingling with guests. As Bonnie walked from guest to guest, George followed, fussing with her train as it caught on chairs, tables, and other people, apologizing as he moved.

Elric watched Ava, beaming as she danced around. Her hair was left loose, with just a few pins keeping strands out of her face. She wore a dark navy gown embellished under the bust with silver gems. Black lace draped over her shoulders and chest. She wore a diamond fringe necklace and a ruby ring on her left hand. Both were gifts from Elric for her birthday.

"I am looking at something even more magnificent." His gaze never left her face. Elric marveled at her beauty.

She looked around to see what was catching his attention before she realized he was looking at her.

Her cheeks turned pink as she bit on her lower lip to hold back a giggle.

They danced and drank late into the night under the covering of white drapes and bright stars.

"She'll be comin' round the mountain when she comes! She'll be comin' round the mountain when she comes! There's something about horses I think. Why does she have so many horses?" Ava cackled, grabbing Elric for support as they left the reception.

"I think you've had too much to drink."

"Do you think you've had too much to drink?" She loudly burst into another round of laughter.

She stopped laughing and looked around, almost falling over. "Elric?"

"Yes, my drunk love?"

"I've forgotten my shoes." She leaned against a stone wall fence, raising her foot, and wiggling her toes.

"Oh, my word." Elric picked her up and playfully buried his face in her neck. He sat her on top of the stone. "Do not move a muscle."

Ava froze in place, not moving a muscle, taking the command literally. Elric shook his head in amusement.

He held her face and kissed her, holding the position in place while he spoke. "I love you so much, Ava Novak. I'll be right back"

Elric turned to leave but she held onto him for one more kiss before releasing him once satisfied.

"Hurry back!"

Elric jogged back to the reception, where very few still remained. A few men were passed out, slumped over in their chairs. The bride and groom had already retreated to their room for what was left of the night.

He found her shoes on the lawn, where he remembered her throwing them while saying, *I'm cuttin' rug, and I can't do it with these darn things on.*

He grabbed them and hastily made his way back to her, not wanting to miss another moment with her.

As the stone wall came into view, he no longer saw Ava on top of it.

Anxiety settled into his chest, and a sweat broke out on the nape of his neck. He took off down the walkway and around the corner of the hedge. Ava sat on the ground against the stone, holding her stomach, blood running through her fingers.

He hurled himself to the ground and swept her up into his arms, taking off at a run back into the estate. The familiarity of her death had never stopped him from trying to save her. No matter how imminent.

"Ava, hold on. Do not die. Please! I am begging you to just hold on!" He yelled, mad with sorrow. He knew the wheels of fate had started turning, and no matter how hard he tried, there was no stopping them.

"Elric," Her voice was weak. She lay limp in his arms.

"Yes, my love." He kept the tears at bay.

He refused for her last moments to be filled with his fear.

"One of the waiters... stole my necklace and my ring. I wouldn't give it willingly." Blood stained her lips, trickling out the side of her mouth.

"We are going to find Bonnie's father. It's alright." Elric kept his voice steady and strong. Pretending like there was hope.

"Do. Not. Leave me." She went white. A single tear fell from her eye, her words broken with gasping breaths.

He contrived a smile for her. "I could never. My soul is tied to yours."

Elric burst through the doors of the manor, shouting, waking the whole house. The sound of doors opening echoed through quiet hallways.

"Dr. Moore! Get Dr. Moore! Someone get him now!" He shouted furiously. Elric knew there was no hope, but he would never let Ava think he didn't try every single time.

Dr. Moore came running down the hallway in only a maroon robe and socks.

Without hesitation, he yelled. "Get her in my study. Tabitha my bag now!"

Someone went in before Elric and cleared the doctor's desk. Elric laid her down, taking off his coat and laying it under her head.

All color gone from her face, she whispered, "I love you."

Elric could no longer keep the pain from registering on his face.

"I will love you beyond this life. And any thereafter."

MODERN-DAY ARCATA, CALIFORNIA

Elric opens his eyes and looks at the clock on the wall. 5:42 p.m. In front of him is an oil painting of a couple dancing under white drapery and an open night sky. The man's back is toward the viewer, but over his shoulder is a full view of Ava's face, laughter lighting up the portrait. He painted this not long after it happened. Elric used to wonder why he would paint memories with such pain in them, but he learned after many years that his most painful memories, more often than not, held hands with his most joyous ones. He places the tissue paper back over the canvas and gently tucks it back into its spot, hidden away with other memories.

He locks up his private room and closes the studio for the night as he walks by Anita's empty desk. It has been a month since she started working on the mural for the library. She only stopped by to pick up and drop off supplies, so their paths rarely crossed. The unveiling is next week and the pride he feels when thinking of her accomplishment is more than he can put into words. He hasn't seen the mural yet, but he knows he will be the one cheering the loudest for her debut.

His stomach soon calls for food, and he ventures into the city to see what will satisfy his hunger. As he walks, he pulls out his phone and reads a text from Charles Hanover, relaying how overjoyed he is with Anita's work.

Stowing his phone away, a smile of pride spreads across Elric's face as he thinks of his protege. The grin soon fades as a thought of Robyn enters his mind. It has been a couple of weeks since she last contacted him. After the breakup, she would frequently text him, asking to talk. He ignored the notifications when they came, and eventually, they stopped after a week or so. Elric sincerely hoped that she was doing okay and that someone would come in and sweep her off her feet, moving her on quickly from the heartache she felt.

The restaurants he passes are not piquing his interest, so he walks into a supermarket to sweep the aisles for something calling his name. After perusing aisles for food, he settles in the wine section, scanning for something new. He steps back to get a broader view of the shelves and shuffles his way into another body. "Oh, excuse me." He looks up and finds himself standing inches away from those damn emerald eyes.

His face brightens momentarily before returning to a more reserved expression.

"Ava," he reaches out to her before quickly pulling his hand back and nervously running it through his hair, "Have a good night."

Elric grabs a random bottle of wine off the shelf and turns to go.

"Elric, wait," that voice ceases his steps forward. It always will. "How are you?" Slowly turning on his heel, he knows he should just leave, but being able to be in her presence is something he cannot resist.

"I'm doing well. How are you?"

The corner of her mouth lifted. "I'm pretty good, just grabbing some wine. I wasn't sure what to get. What do you have?" She asks, grabbing the bottle from his hands.

"Chocolate wine?" Her face twists in disgust. "I mean to each their own, I guess." She hands the bottle back.

He rubs the nape of his neck, giving an awkward smile. "Ah, I didn't mean to grab that. Truthfully, I was just trying to get out of here. Didn't want to make things uncomfortable."

"I'm not uncomfortable. Unless you try to make me drink that. Then I will be," she jests. That face he knows all too well puts him at ease.

Elric puts the bottle of wine back. "Have you adjusted back to the states fine?"

"Oh yeah! Took a second to get the internal clock ticking right again, but it wasn't so bad." She says tapping the side of her head.

"That's great."

There's an awkward silence, and neither one of them knows what to fill it with. A few moments go by, and then they both speak at the same time,

"Have you found a job?"

"I guess I should get going."

"I'm sorry, go ahead." Elric runs his hand through his hair.

"No, no, you go." Ava's eyebrows perk up, her voice empathetic.

He hopes she attributes his awkwardness to the breakup with her sister.

His eyes crinkled at the corners, letting himself relax around her. "You're here for a wine. Let me help."

"Okay," she says, raising her eyebrow once again.

"Alright." He scans the bottles for a moment, picking some up and then putting them back until he lands on one, his eyes flashing with excitement. "Here, try this rosé and there is an exquisite goat gouda here. And rosemary crackers are a couple aisles over."

Her eyes are wide, her mouth slightly agape in a small smile. "Gouda is my favorite cheese. And I'd die for good rosé." She holds her fingers together, kissing the tips and then opening her hand.

"You basically planned my perfect wine meal."

Her smile is warm, like the sun rays slipping through a storm cloud. He feels his clouds start to fade, a glimmer of hope in the storm through that smile.

No. He thinks. *I can't cause more damage.*

"Ah. Yes. I hope you have a great rest of your evening."

Walking away before she could say goodbye, he took one last glance back and watched the smile fade from her lips.

ONE WEEK LATER

Anita stands in his office as Elric adjusts his tie in the bathroom mirror. Anita paces the room, wringing her hands, a beautiful gold-to-blue ombré gown flowing behind her. The boned bodice fitted to her perfectly with a slit up to the middle of her thigh. Her locks are worn half up, her signature gold coils and rings throughout. She wears a light gold shimmer on her eyes and a nude lip, complimenting her skin tone beautifully. Elric wears an all-black suit and a black silk tie. He moves his shoulders uncomfortably, feeling stiff, preferring to be in casual clothes. In conjunction with Art Across Arcata, Charles's company planned a black-tie event for all the donors and volunteers. The library was to be turned into a gala ballroom for the night.

Elric grabs Anita by the hand, tugging her to a stop. Squaring her up in front of him, he rests his hands on her shoulders.

"What if no one likes it?" Her voice shakes.

"Impossible. I haven't seen it, and I already know it's going to be magnificent." She looks away, and he gently picks up her chin, focusing her gaze on him.

Talking to her with the gentleness of a father encouraging his daughter. "I wouldn't have released you into the den of lions if you weren't a lioness yourself."

She takes a deep breath and embraces Elric. Their relationship is so different, but it is an emotional echo of a friendship he had long ago.

He looks at a gold watch on his wrist and taps on it. "Are you ready to go?"

Anita takes a step back and shakes her shoulders out. "Okay. Let's do this!"

Suddenly, his face lights up, and he snaps his fingers. "Oh, I almost forgot!"

He runs out, past Anita's desk, and into his private room. Anita follows but waits by her desk, eager to see what he is enthralled about.

Elric walks back out. In one arm, he carries a large canvas wrapped in white tissue, and in the other, a smaller package wrapped in navy blue paper. He tries to catch the door with his foot to close it behind him, but the door sets on the latch without ever catching and slowly pushes back open without Elric noticing.

"Big or little first?" he asks, animated.

"Elric, you did not have to-"

He cuts her off. "Big or little first?"

She playfully rubs her hands together. "Little."

Elric hands over the book-shaped gift, and she sets it on the counter of her desk, gently unwrapping it.

She pulls out a handmade leather sketchbook. Noticing an engraving at the bottom, she runs her fingers over it.

Anita Galdur

Opening up the sketchbook, she caresses the ridges of fresh pages. On the inside of the front cover is a pocket full of sketching and graphite pencils.

Anita gives Elric a gentle smile that reads just as well in her eyes, the gratitude overflowing in them.

"Thank you, thank you so much."

Elric holds out the canvas to her, "It is completely deserved, and that's not all."

She lets out a huff and takes the canvas, "I am not good at receiving gifts."

"But you deserve them."

Anita carefully takes the tissue off the canvas and sees a brilliantly colored painting of herself in the act of painting the mural she had been working so hard on. On the canvas, she holds a paintbrush up to the wall while looking over her shoulder and laughing. A bright orange stroke of paint is on her cheek and her arms.

Beside him now, Anita sheds a tear, making a pathway down her cheek for others to follow.

"How did you get this?" She laughs and presses the back of her hand delicately to her cheeks, "My makeup is going to be messed up."

"No, you look beautiful, it's not messing up." Elric takes a handkerchief out of his breast pocket and tucks it in her hand. "I wanted to see the artist at work, and I took a picture, wanting to immortalize your accomplishment."

"People beg for your work, and here you are spending time making me a one-of-a-kind. This is too much."

"I disagree. But we will be late to your unveiling if I do not get you out that door right now."

Anita gently sets down the canvas against her desk and wraps her arms around Elric. Though the brunt of his immortality has been spent under tragedy, relationships like these keep the rolling waves of madness at bay.

Elric and Anita walk out onto an outdoor stage with Charles. Behind them, a large sheet hangs, covering the mural. Charles gives a short speech on "the beacon of creativity this library will be in this city" and compares Anita's work to that of a lighthouse keeper. "The mural calling all artists home." On that cue, the sheet is dropped, revealing a beautiful artwork. Oceans and skyline meeting and melting into one cohesive thought.

Elric stands up and cheers loudly, causing all the other guests to give a standing ovation as well. Anita stays in her seat, tears of joy flowing down her face. He pulls a handkerchief from inside his breast pocket and places it in her palm. With her free hand, he pulls her to the center of the stage, and when she reaches it, the crowd explodes, encompassing Anita with joy.

Elric stays off to the sidelines for the rest of the event. He watches people swarm Anita, asking where she gets her inspiration, if she is available in the future, and where her assistant is so they can set up a meeting. He watches her shine brightly in that room and knows that when he moves on from Arcata, he will leave the studio and non-profit in great hands.

Walking around the room with his hands behind his back, he admires the different art they've collected from local artists hanging on the walls. Stopping, he intently studies a recreation of *The Hand of God* by Michelangelo; the hands are similar, but the background is covered in different words in different languages in graffiti.

"I've never tried that style before. I'd like to," he mumbles.

"Elric! This is wild." Anita is beaming as she taps his shoulder. "I have someone I want you to meet!"

They walk through the crowd, and she tells him how her new friend is a volunteer here and helped set up the decor inside. They ate lunch together or hung out at the mural while she painted daily.

Anita waves vigorously at someone over the crowd.

Seeing her in any life always catches his breath—no matter how much of a stone facade he tries to keep, it will inevitably crumble at her feet.

He watches as Ava makes her way through the crowd, their eyes locking.

She wears a blush pink gown, capped chiffon sleeves hanging from her shoulders. The bottom of the dress is embroidered with ivy leaves. Her hair is braided and twisted into a bun at the nape of her neck.

He feels warmth crawl through his chest. His eyes focus on her, and no matter how much he feels like he should avert them and walk away, he just can't fight it anymore.

"Elric!" Anita's voice is bubblier than ever, "This is-"

"Ava," Elric finishes, the smile finally reaching his eyes as he reaches out to take her hand.

"It's nice to see you again, Elric," Ava responds, shaking her head and laughing, grasping his hand.

They don't formally shake hands in greeting, but they hold each other with a magnetic pulse, keeping them linked.

Anita looks at their hands and then back and forth between the two. "When did you two meet?" she asks, confused and mesmerized by the interaction.

They drop hands, and by the looks on their faces, Anita can tell the answer is better left unsaid.

She claps once loudly. "It doesn't matter. My two favorite people! I'm ready to go. Let's go get some drinks!" Anita almost dances out the door to head to the nearest bar while still high from the excitement of the night.

Elric gives a hopeful smile and a slight bow, then extends his arm to Ava. "Shall we?"

Ava looks up as if searching his face for an answer and smirks at him. "This is probably not a good idea."

"Probably not," he replies, holding out his hand.

Ava takes it, and suddenly, Elric's universe has its Northern Star back.

"No! You did not!" Anita howls.

"I swear on my life I did. I was quite inebriated and thought I was in my hostel in Scotland on the warmest bed ever. When, in fact, I was in a sheep pen, and the lot I was traveling with found me covered in muck, sleeping on a sheep. Never slept better, though."

Elric waves his arms, laughing to the point of tears as he tells the story with Ava and Anita.

"If you got a few more shots in me I'd be that drunk again. So, I am going to cap it here; I smelled like mutton for weeks," he says, finishing off his drink and pushing the glass away.

"Alright, Ava," Anita says, tossing another shot back. "What have you done?"

"Oh gosh." Ava taps her chin in thought.

Elric smacks his forehead sarcastically. "You have *that* many instances?!"

"No! Just none are sleeping-with-sheep worthy." Ava pauses for a moment to think before speaking again. "Okay, once I told my friends I could climb a tree and I did climb it, really high actually, but then I was too afraid to come down and they had to call 9-1-1."

They all erupt again, Ava placing her hand on Elric's knee. The night continues with stories filled with laughter, joy, and celebration.

Ava and Anita are in a battle of complimenting each other when the bartender shouts out, *last call*.

"It's 2 a.m.?! I have to take my cat to pee." Anita jumps down from a barstool, heels in hand.

"Your cat doesn't pee in a litter box?" asks Ava.

"It's a long story," Anita replies and falls into another fit of giggling.

Elric, more sober than both women, holds Anita by her arm. He looks at the bartender and asks for two glasses of water.

Placing one in each of the women's hands, he taps the bottom of the glasses in unison. "Drink, please."

"Okay, Dad," Anita says, rolling her eyes dramatically while giggling.

The three of them walk out of the bar, Elric holding Anita up for support.

"Good thing I have to make sure you aren't too drunk, "she slurs.

"Yes, good thing," he agrees, knowing there would be no point in convincing her otherwise.

"I don't live super-duper far. I can do it. I bid you adieu." Anita curtsies and immediately starts to stumble.

Elric catches her on her way to the ground. "How about I walk you anyway? I just enjoy your company and being in the presence of such a great, soon-to-be-famous artist."

Anita has a broad, dimpled smile. "I am a great artist, aren't I? Fine, walk with me, common folk."

Ava covers her mouth to hide a laugh, walking on Anita's other side to act as a bumper. Elric promptly moves Ava to the inner side of the sidewalk, assuming the position closest to the road as he is the most sober.

Anita starts to sing loudly as they walk.

Elric futilely tries to shush her as they walk up the stairs of her building. Finally reaching the door, Anita unlocks it with a surprising amount of ease.

She kicks off her shoes and yells, "Ava! Can you unzip me? Thenyouguyscango." Her words all run into one another.

Ava disappears with Anita into her apartment, but Elric can still hear Anita's voice, which is now rapping.

He leans against a wall in the hallway, waiting for Ava to help Anita, his smile wide as he listens to Anita rap battle with herself.

When Ava reemerges, she gently closes the door behind her. Elric hears Anita yell, "Behave!" before the door shuts completely.

He pinches the bridge of his nose and looks up to find Ava simply watching him.

"Are you staying with your parents, or do you live around here?" He asks as they make the trek back out to the street.

She pulls pins out of her hair and throws them in a clutch. Shaking out her hair, she combs her fingers through it.

"I was getting such a headache. I got my own apartment not too long ago, but I live on the other side of town."

Elric pulls out his phone. "You can't drive, and neither can I. Want me to call you a taxi? I'll pay for it."

Ava put her hand over the phone. "No, I don't like taking taxis this late. It's creepy."

"I understand. I can ride with you and then just come back on my own?"

Ava shakes her head. "That's too much. I can call my dad. Wait, it's three in the morning. He'll be so mad. Parents will always make you feel like you're sixteen and doing something illegal. Am I right?"

With a sleepy nod, he lets out a yawn and tries to hide it behind his hand.

"My studio is only a couple blocks from here. I have a couple of comfortable sofas in my office. My plan was to pass out on one of those. Does that sound like the safer bet?"

She looks down at her feet with apparent hesitation before looking up and answering, "At this point, yes."

They walk in the silence of the night, the occasional whir of a car disrupting the quiet until they reach the studio.

Elric unlocks the front doors and leaves the lights off in the main room as they wander through it. He takes off his jacket and throws it onto Anita's desk. Without reservation, he takes Ava by the hand and leads her to his office.

He fumbles over his keyring, trying to find the right one for his office.

Elric drops the keys onto the floor, "For crying out loud."

He and Ava both bend down to pick it up, knocking their heads together in the dark. Giggles and groans echo in the quiet studio.

"Hang on. We have technology." He pulls his phone from his pocket and turns on the flashlight, holding it under his chin, he wiggles his eyebrows, succeeding in another chorus of giggles from her. Finding his keys, he instantly pulls the correct one out and opens his door.

Turning back toward Ava, the light illuminates her face, revealing the only beacon he ever needs, calling him home.

Elric drops his phone, and it lands with the light up, creating a spotlight in between them. All hesitation left back at the bar, he reaches up, threading his fingers through her hair, his hand cupping the back of her neck. He doesn't pull them any closer but instead looks into her eyes, searching for sureness.

She doesn't speak. Looking over his face, she bites the inside of her lower lip, nodding gently.

Wrapping his other arm around her waist, he draws her body tight against his. Their lips meet, and an explosion hits Elric in the chest. She holds him, clinging onto his shirt. Their kiss is tender, but behind it, a strong, steady passion stirs like the ocean current pushing and pulling with the tide. She pushes him into his office, the kisses becoming more powerful and urgent with each step. Heat breaks out over their bodies, and Ava pushes him against a wall. He traces her body, gliding his fingers over the smooth fabric of her dress while hers reciprocate the gesture.

Laying a hand on his chest, she kisses him forcefully before breaking them apart. Placing the back of her hand on her forehead, she turns around and steps away. He remains against the wall, his breathing heavy, chest heaving, habitually running his hands through his hair. She nervously toys with the material of her dress, twisting it in her hands, turning back to Elric after a few moments of catching breaths.

"You know, since that night we met, I haven't stopped thinking about you, and I don't know why." She huffs in annoyance.

Elric straightens himself out and walks over to the couch. He throws himself in the corner, stretching his arms over the back of the couch and the armrest.

"I haven't stopped thinking of you," he replies, adding *ever* to the end of that sentence in his mind.

She moves to the couch on the other side of the office, sitting opposite of him, taking a deep breath.

"If I had met you before you met Robyn, there would be no question of," she looks at him, waving her finger back and forth between them, "*this*."

"I know." He closes his eyes. "When I saw you in the market, I didn't act on what I wanted to do because I don't want to hurt her. I was never going to pursue you. I was never going to hurt her."

He sits up quickly, placing his arms on his knees and interlacing his fingers together, "But then you were there tonight, and I'm just not the one to keep fighting fate."

"Ha!" She barks. "Listen, I think we are both a little too drunk right now. Can we table this for tomorrow? We are on the same page, but I can't sort out all the thoughts and feelings being thrown around in my head. And I can't think anymore with this dress on."

She grabs the top layer skirt, throwing it into the air.

He picks his phone back up, hoping to hide his disappointment from the only person who could always recognize it.

"I can fix one of those problems." He moves across the room and opens the doors of an armoire in the corner. Pulling open a drawer, he takes out gym shorts and a t-shirt and hands them to Ava.

"I spend a lot of time here." He opens another door flipping on a switch, lighting up a bathroom.

Ava grabs the clothes and walks into the bathroom. "Thank you."

She closes the door, and Elric is left in the dark. The pieces of his heart seem never to remain intact. Dropping back down onto the couch, he lays his arm over his eyes and sighs.

Ava returns from the bathroom in shorts and the baggy shirt and breathes in relief, "I love dressing up, but nothing feels better than taking it off."

He smirks but keeps his arm over his eyes. As he hears her moving around the room until she finally settles on the couch and seeks a comfortable spot. He knows the exact position she will be in.

"Elric?" She calls out in the dark.

"Yes?"

"Can you just come over here for a minute until I fall asleep? I hate sleeping in unknown places."

Elric gets off the couch, never having to think twice about her requests. He sees her lying on her stomach, her knee bent up. She sleeps like that in every cycle. The little constants make him feel grounded.

He lays down on his back on the floor next to the couch, placing his arm back over his eyes. "How long did it take you to get settled in Beijing?"

"Pfft. Forever. I probably didn't start sleeping without a light on until two months in."

"I don't like sleeping alone either." He wishes he could say *without you*.

He hears a rustling on the couch and feels her fingertips graze his.

"Why can't I stop thinking about you?" She whispers.

Elric grieves the idea of being able to share the truth.

Catching her fingers, he holds onto them, rubbing his thumb back and forth over them.

They fall asleep, their fingers woven together.

X

MADRID, SPAIN 1778
"Could you please sit still?" His voice was light and playful as he dodged a cherry that was thrown his way.

"What will you give me if I do as you say?" Ava batted her eyelashes at him

"I cannot say, all these people around us... It would not be honorable." His eyes lingered, moving down the length of her body before putting his attention back to his drawing.

She sat in the city square. A fair in the Plaza de la Cebada served as her backdrop. A basket of cherries was at her side. Her dress was bright orange, a standout color against the scenery behind her. A short, slender man with dark brown curls that barely rested above his ears walked by, holding an easel, a canvas, and some tools.

"Gabriel!" Elric waved. "Still working on your masterpiece?"

Gabriel lifted his hand as best he could with his arms full and relied on a nodded greeting instead. "Elric, Ava! Yes! My dream is for it to be a series of story-like paintings. This is number four in a plan for six."

"I look forward to seeing them." Elric let Gabriel go on his way and he set up a ways down the road.

Elric smiled at Ava. "Now, back to my very own living masterpiece in front of me."

Ava stood up, excitement spreading across her face. "No!" She laughed. "You stay over there!"

He set down his brushes and palette gently. He rushed over to catch her, but she began to run away.

The word of a Spanish art movement brought him to Madrid, but of course, he stayed for her.

MODERN-DAY ARCATA, CALIFORNIA

Disoriented and stiff, Elric begins to wake up. Slowly rubbing his eyes, he wonders why he is on the floor. The events of the night come back to him, and he sits up quickly to look at the couch. Ava isn't there. He looks in the direction of the bathroom and sees the door open and the light off, her dress still lying on the floor.

He stands up to stretch his back. "You're not a 300-year-old man anymore, Elric."

He laughs out loud at his own joke. Elric always did think he was the funniest person he knew. Ava, in every lifetime, would strongly disagree and argue *she* was, in fact, the funniest person either of them knew. Elric walks out of his office, stretching his arms, and his stomach churns. The door to his private room is wide open, and he mentally kicks himself, knowing that it's his fault the room was left open. Ava stands in the center of it, her back to the entrance. Elric hastens his pace, not wanting to alarm her by running. He prays she doesn't notice a room full of her face, but he doesn't see how she can not.

He enters the room and tries to sound casual. "Good morning. How did you sleep?"

She turns around to show her face covered in confusion and a little bit of fear. The epicenter of her emotions is an earthquake waiting to shatter his world.

"What the hell is this?" Her voice is hard. "Have you been stalking me?"

Taking a step forward, he extends a hand foolishly hoping to diffuse the bomb that has already gone off. "Ava, it's not what you think."

She takes a step back at his advancement.

"Tell me. What am I supposed to think? I met you a month ago, and my face is plastered all over this room—everywhere."

Ava moves over to the right and points aggressively at a canvas tucked in the corner. "*This!* This is from the night we met."

Her face is closed off to her emotions, but anger saturates her voice. Whatever fear she feels is tucked away in an effort to be strong. Whatever traces of passion last night held, are gone as well.

"Did you break up with Robyn because of me? Did you use Robyn to get to me?!"

Defeated, Elric drops his shoulders. "It's not that simple. It is not simple at all. Even if I explained it, it wouldn't matter. You wouldn't believe me."

Ava wraps her arms around herself, keeping her voice stern. "I don't see how there is any understanding this."

She turns back, looks at the wall of hanging art, and shakes her head. "I'm going to go now. Move out of my way."

Elric steps aside, giving her full access to the exit and making sure she won't so much as graze him.

She walks forward, bumping into a worktable covered in sketches and materials, but one canvas catches her eye. It holds the image of a pink magnolia tree with a couple kissing beneath the flowers in the middle of a rainstorm. She walks around the table to stand in front of it; her eyebrows are drawn down, and her mouth tight. A range of emotions registers on her face; the one Elric recognizes the most is familiarity. Ava reaches out and delicately rests her fingers on it. Immediately, her face goes completely blank. Her eyelids flutter rapidly, her body stills and her jaw grows slack. Her fingers twitch on top of the painting. "Ava?" Elric leans forward. "Ava?" He says a little louder.

He walks up to her, and right before reaching her, she doubles over and lands on her knees. She begins to claw at her throat, gasping for air. Elric closes the distance between them, holding her up while she catches her breath.

The panic inside him doesn't match the steady tone of his voice, "It's okay, relax. Relax, yeah, just like that. Breathe slow. Take your time."

Her face is covered in a cold sweat, which causes rouge strands of hair to stick to her skin. Ava pushes away from him, scrambling backward until her back hits the leg of the work table. She stares at him, her eyes wild, and she grabs a fistful of her hair.

"I saw us." She reaches for his face but quickly pulls back, retreating into herself, "I felt it, I *lived* it. You packed us a picnic, and it started to rain. I had a brother? I begged him the night before to make my deliveries so I could go with you."

Elric feels his heart about to burst through his chest, the pounding rattling him. His hands tremble as he attempts to lay one on her shoulder. He makes contact and she doesn't pull away.

"Ava," he says shakily, trying to clear the tremor in his voice. "You remember?"

She makes a hysterical-sounding cry. "*Remember?!* What the hell am I remembering?"

He looks at the painting and then back to Ava. "What happened after it started raining?"

"You took my hand, and we ran under the tree. That was the first time we kissed. That was our spot. But I also felt myself..." She looks down at her hands as if they aren't really hers, turning them over.

She begins to shed tears for memories so familiar but also wildly unknown.

He collapses down next to her and holds her face in his hands. "You felt yourself what?"

"Elric, I died. I drowned. You were there trying to revive me, but it was too late."

Her body begins to shake, her sobs growing more intense.

Elric tries to soothe her by holding her and trying to keep himself sane. This has never happened in any of the cycles before, and he has no idea how to navigate it. He can't help but think about what this could mean for them.

He gives her silence to ground herself. Knowing her so well, he knows that's exactly what she needs. Her crying slows, allowing her body to become more controlled again. Elric hasn't let her go, his mind drifting away from the moment.

"Tell me what this means," she demands, waving at the art on the wall.

"Ava, I don't know if right now is a good idea. Maybe when you- when we have had time to sit on this-"

"Tell me what this means. *Now.*"

He knows that tone, and it isn't one to test.

Taking a deep breath, he nudges away from her so he can look at her head-on. She clutches his hand firmly to keep him from retreating any further.

"We've known each other a long time."

"What does that mean?" She asks sharply.

He exhales and hopes the fear that suddenly fills him will allow him to go with it—unsure of how to tell her the truth he's been desperate to tell her for years.

"We were married long ago. We were in love. We've-"

Raking his fingers through his hair, he laughs at the absurdity of the words, "We've been in love numerous times."

He pauses momentarily, studying her, unwilling to go on if she looks like she will break. Her eyes stay unwavering and hold a surprising calmness to them. He just isn't sure if it is the calm before or after the storm. Elric goes into detail about when she got sick and about Faye. That neither he nor Faye knew what it meant when she died, even though he had made the deal. He explained who Geoffrey was, how he was there for him until the very end, and when Elric met the first reincarnation of her. He explains he had been to shamans, priests, and everything in between around the world to stop the cycle, but no one knew anything. Ever since then, he's lived dozens of lives with her. The whirlwind of their lives stuck in a loop of the beginnings of fathomless love to an inevitably bitter, painful end—all for it to begin again.

Ava watches intently, nodding occasionally, never removing her gaze from Elric.

His eyes flicker over to Ava's stomach, his shirt too big on her.

His voice breaks. "We were having a child. That child was lost as well. And it's something that's never happened again."

Ava grips her shirt and looks down, her body trembling.

"This is so much. I don't even know if I believe it, but that was all too real." Her head snaps back up. "Did you know Robyn was my sister? Did you know you would meet me here? In this... this life?"

She buries her face in her hands, seeming embarrassed of the question, the tense of lives past and present not falling naturally in her mouth as she speaks.

"No, I swear I didn't. I would have never done that. It was happenstance I met Robyn in the woods that day, and I didn't know you were her sister or that you were here in this city until the night we met."

Elric grips a metal bar running along the table, hoping it'll steady him. He is still waiting for his world to stop spinning.

"So, it's just chance for us to meet?"

"Yes."

"Is it every fifty years or something?"

"No, it's random. I think sometimes I miss a cycle if I'm not in the right place at the right time. I've had to wait longer times than others."

"Am I ever a child when we meet?!" She asks disgustedly.

"Oh God no," he exclaims, "Youngest I've met you is twenty-five."

Ava's eyes narrow in on him, "But in this whole giant world, we keep running into each other? How is that possible?"

Elric scratches at the stubble growing in.

"Fate's design? Really, I don't know."

"You don't die?"

"No. I can't. Even if I get injured, it heals supernaturally."

"You've been alive this entire time?"

"Yes."

"So that makes you hundreds of years old."

He nods.

Her tone grows somber. "I die every time? I was twenty-eight in that memory."

"Yes." He looks away.

She grabs his hand and shakes it, but he refuses to look at her. "What's the oldest I've lived to, with you?"

He focuses on the first artwork in his collection—the charcoal drawing of her in front of the fire.

"Elric."

"You never make it past twenty-eight. It's always sometime in your twenty-eighth year of life. That's how old you were the first time." His grief is evident on his face.

"I turn twenty-eight next month. Am I going to die sometime in the next year?" She clenches her jaw, panic rising in her.

"Ava, I-"

She releases him, burying her face in her hands, and stays silent for a few moments. Once again, he gives her quiet so she can contemplate. There are no words to make this better.

Lifting her head up she stares at the wall, "If I touch another one of those, will I remember? Could I- could we figure this out somehow?"

"I don't know. This is the first time this has happened."

Standing, she marches towards the wall. Elric jumps up and comes in close to her.

"Ava, if it does happen again, just like with the magnolias, you'll experience dying again. Do you want that? Because I've experienced it time and time again, and it will break you."

Ava raises her hand, looking over her shoulder. "Which is the first one?"

"Ava."

She abruptly turns around, squaring up with him and looking him dead in the eyes.

Ava takes another step towards him and shoves him hard in the chest. "I don't know what the hell any of this is. It's terrifying. I'm still not entirely convinced you didn't drug me at some point, and I just had an intense hallucination. If it is real, I also don't want to die. That is scarier than anything else."

Her expression softens, and she begins to pick at the skin around her nails. "But I do know this. I have never felt my heart beat as hard and fast as it did that night at my parents' house when I met you. And somehow, I felt it again through that painting. I don't know how real all of this is, but I do know that feeling was real. There's no certainty in anything else as of right now except that, so that is what I am choosing to go off of."

Elric stares at her, still in shock. Standing in a pool of uncertainty, choices not yet made.

Her voice goes hard with determination, "I don't even feel like I have the time to process what is happening if I'm a ticking time bomb. So, I'm going to touch one anyway, and you might as well be helpful. Elric, I don't want to die."

He drops his shoulders in defeat and walks up to the charcoal on parchment, placing his hand at the edge where blood stained it hundreds of years ago. "My entire existence has been about keeping you alive."

Ava comes up from behind and slips her hand underneath his. Keeping their hands interlocked, she moves it to the center of the drawing and rests her fingers there. Elric feels energy pulses through Ava, and her body threatens to fall. He holds her by the waist to keep her steady as the memories reclaim their territory.

Hours go by, and Elric has taken out every piece of Ava stored in his studio. Canvases, sketches, and a few photographs are scattered across the room, resting on drop cloths to protect them. Sitting on the floor, Ava holds a metal plate with a photo of them printed on it, studying it intensely. He brings in a bottle of water and sits beside her, putting the bottle in her hand. She closes the booklet of the picture and sets it down next to her. Opening her water, she takes long, deep gulps, causing the water to run down the sides of her mouth.

The collar of her shirt is stained with sweat, and last night's makeup is smeared under her eyes. The last few hours were excruciating, but they gave Ava a more complete understanding of who the woman was that lay beneath the surface of her soul. Her past selves and present self finally fused into one. She finally finds all the pieces of herself resting in one soul.

Elric stares at her as she finishes her water, wondering why he ever doubted her endurance to handle the situation. Ava rests her head on his shoulder and grasps his hand. She takes a deep breath, letting it out slowly.

"This was a fun night," she says, picking the picture back up. "Bonnie... Did she and George have a good life?"

"Bonnie and George had six daughters," he laughs. "They all talked as much as Bonnie. They were wonderful parents. She named her first daughter after you."

Ava rests her hand on her chest. "She was a good friend. So many friends, so many families, so many lives. I don't know how you do this every time. Why do you go through it? Just leave me even if you meet me. Go live a life not centered around me."

He softly laughs. "I do it because my life is not lived without you."

"I will love you beyond this life and any thereafter. You keep your promise. You keep keeping your promise," she says.

"I'll never stop," he says, stroking the back of her arm.

Ava turns to face him as he stares into her emerald eyes. He feels unequivocally at home for the first time. The pieces of her soul forge a person he no longer has to pretend to be in order to protect. He doesn't have to omit any information or keep his secrets hidden. She can know him without barriers. He feels at peace.

Her fingers slide up his neck and into his hair, pulling him in to kiss him unapologetically. The Ava who *is* giving way to the Avas that *were* – the Avas that have known him. She explores him for the first time but also knows exactly where she is. Elric brushes the hair from her face, and they share a smile, their lips barely touching. He pulls her on top of him, and she naturally rests her legs around his hips, straddling him. Grasping the back of her neck, he pulls her in for a deeper kiss. Running his fingers under her shirt and across her back, he feels Ava let out a gasp. Tugging the shirt over her head, he lays back on the drop cloth, and she drives her body into his.

And for once, Elric forgets that fate has him under its thumb.

Ava lies on his chest, running her fingers down his ribs. Elric twitches, letting out a forced giggle.

She removes her hand as her cheeks flush. "Sorry, I know you're ticklish there." He shakes his head and kisses the top of hers.

Ava sits up, pointing to a mark on the right side of her rib cage. "I was shot right here where this birthmark is. That's not just a coincidence, right?"

He feels the grip of peace and panic coincide and grimaces. "I'm not sure, I'm guessing not."

"Sorry, I don't mean to treat it casually."

"It's alright."

They lay there in silence–Ava deep in thought and Elric relishing the moment before the predicaments of their plague inescapably come to take it from them.

All of a sudden, they hear the front door of the studio rasp open slowly, causing Elric and Ava to sit frozen in place.

Anita's voice fills the front room. "Elric? Are you here? Your phone is dead, and I was worried when I saw your car at the library still."

The footsteps approach the room, and they both frantically stand up. Ava quickly grabs the shirt balled up on the floor, yanking it over her head and tugging it down to cover her bare butt. Elric, unable to find his pants, has only his hands to shield himself.

Anita enters the room, and her mouth falls open and she immediately averts her eyes before holding her hand over them.

"Uhm," She raises an eyebrow, "I told you two to behave," she nervously laughs. "I'm going to go grab coffee and lunch. Give you two time to collect yourselves. Text me if you want something," she walks out of the room throwing a *tsk tsk* over her shoulder.

Ava looks at Elric, her face crimson, a smile beneath the chagrin.

He hands her her shorts while reaching for his pants, which are suddenly easily spotted.

"Well, then," a sheepish grin tugs at his lips.

XI

Elric texts Anita, letting her know they've left the studio for the day and to enjoy her weekend, hoping to bypass the awkward encounter. He parks the car in his driveway and looks at his passenger, grateful and bewildered over the events of the last few hours. Catching his glance, she traces her fingertips over his morning stubble and holds his jaw tenderly. Her expression is soft in adoration. As they walk up the driveway of Elric's house, Ava's attention is drawn to a tan cloth covering a large object in the carport.

Ava breaks off from Elric, walking to the cover and lifting it up.

"Oh, my god. You didn't," she gasps as she completely lifts the cover off of a Triumph motorcycle.

Elric buckles over entertained by the woman who will never change. "No matter the life, you still feel the same way about motorcycles, I guess."

Ava places a hand on her hip. "What, you're some kind of badass now?"

Elric walks over to her and grasps her arm, pulling her in close.

"I always have been, baby," he says, wiggling his eyebrows. "Always will be."

"Oh, god," she playfully shoves him aside.

They make their way to the front door, smiling, hand in hand, doing what feels perfectly natural. As he unlocks his front door, his phone goes off.

Glad you two hit it off.

Only Anita would be so brazen.

As soon as he opens the door, Geoffrey immediately jumps at him, barking with excitement. The small dog stops when he notices Ava standing quietly behind Elric. She stays there, her dress tucked under her arm, not wanting to alarm the small dog. He slowly approaches her, sniffing the air. Ava kneels, gently holding out the back of her hand to him. He sniffs it for a moment before wagging his tail and jumping at her. Knocking her off balance, when her body meets the ground, Geoffrey takes advantage, climbing up her body to get to her face.

"Geoffrey, no!" Elric picks him up, while extending a hand. "I'm so sorry."

She takes it, picking herself up. "No, it's fine!"

Ava throws down her dress onto the floor, and it lands with a feathery thud. She reaches for Geoffrey, taking him out of Elric's arms.

Geoffrey licks her face, and she giggles with delight, switching into a baby-like voice. "You're just a good baby who loves kisses, huh? Why won't that mean man let you give kisses?"

Elric laughs at the jab and strokes the dog's back.

She scratches behind his ears, her voice is much quieter as she speaks to Elric. "You named him after our friend," her eyes well as she connects the dots, and she kisses the top of the dog's head. "How did he die?"

"From a long life. Thankfully."

He sets his keys and phone down in a silver bowl sitting on his entry table and then closes the front door behind them.

"You were together the whole time?"

"'til his last breath."

The bittersweet mention of his friend reminds Elric of everyone he goes through time without, trying to remain grateful for what seems like a too-short presence in his life.

Leading Ava into the living room while she still holds the small dog, he puts his hands on her shoulders and pivots her focus to a hanging portrait. Ava takes a step forward, her eyes filling with grief and joy. She buries her chin on top of the dog's head, and he settles on her shoulder.

An oil painting of a vast landscape hangs with brilliant hues of rolling green, marking the canvas that blends into soft-spoken blues. In the right corner of the portrait sits an elderly man, the smile wrinkles around his eyes and mouth deep. The friar's tonsure hair sits with streaks of white and gray running throughout the once-all-chestnut brown in the painting. In the moment captured, he laughs heartily, hand on his belly. He is surrounded by children at his feet, all of them with looks of delight as they watch the man.

Ava grasps Elric's hand tighter without removing her eyes, and he stands next to her silently in a grief that's lasted centuries.

"Is this how he looked before he died? Happy? Helping people?" Her voice is tight.

Elric releases her hand to put his arms around her shoulders, bringing her in close. "Yes. He lived his life with so much joy and empathy. His only regret was not being able to save you. Geoffrey helped me to try and find a way to break whatever curse this is. We found little information here and there but nothing substantial."

Ava closes her eyes. "I met him here. Skryne. Hill of Tara."

"Yes, the hill brought us there. Those children were part of an orphanage you helped build before you died."

Elric points to the bottom of the canvas. A profile of a woman with raven curls sits with a golden-haired sleeping child in her arms.

Ava sets Geoffrey down on the floor. She looks down and places a hand over her stomach.

Her voice aches with sorrow. "Our baby."

The emotions behind remembrance and realization are palpable in the room. Many lives crash into her, their weight crushing on a weary, long-lived soul.

Elric wraps her in his arms and lets her fall apart. In all the fleeting times of the centuries, she's never known the grief of the loss of a child that almost was. He had never given room in himself to grieve the loss either, never wanting to open that door alone.

They stand holding each other with Geoffrey quietly curled up at their feet. The emotional wound opens and allows some of the pain to seep out. The silence in the air is comforting, words never needing to be passed between them for consolation. The physical touch speaks a thousand words neither one of them can properly express anyway.

Ava wipes her face with the collar of her shirt and Elric cleans himself up with his sleeves. He rubs his forehead back and forth with his middle finger, not realizing until this moment how exhausted he is. He cradles Ava's jaw in the palm of his hand and caringly places a kiss on each side of her face before leaving one on her lips.

"Come on. We need fluids and food." Taking her hand, he leads her to the kitchen, pulling out a barstool at the counter.

"Can I have a phone charger? I know someone in my family is going to be freaking out. I've been MIA for the last, what, like, almost 24 hours," she says.

He pulls out a cord and plugs it into the wall while she plugs her phone into the other end. He takes bottles of water out of the fridge and places them next to Ava. She grabs one and chugs it, smashing the bottle flat.

He rummages through the contents of his fridge. "Ah, uh... I have some bagels in the cabinet. Oh, here we go."

Pulling out a container of cherries, Elric gleefully puts them in front of her. One bright side to an immortal life is being able to bring out physical timestamps of their lives with things as simple as cherries.

Her eyes grow wide as she licks her lips. "Oh, my god, my favorite."

Winking, he takes out some cream cheese and throws the bagels in the toaster. Leaning over the counter, he watches Ava. She slowly bites into the cherries and then quickly smacks her lips together a few times to savor the taste.

Elric can feel his eyelids weighing him down with fatigue. He turns on his kettle, hoping a cup of tea will give him the little jolt of caffeine he needs.

"So, what do we do?" Ava asks.

"About what?" He replies.

"How-" her voice catches in her throat, giving away her fear.

She quickly clears it, regaining her composure, "How do we stop me from dying?"

The kettle whistles impatiently, waiting for Elric to remove it. "I don't know."

"What have you tried?" She asks as she pops the last cherry into her mouth and pushes the empty container away.

With his back to Ava, he squeezes his eyes shut tight and presses his palms into the countertop. "I'm not sure. A lot."

She gets off the barstool and walks around the counter to open cabinets in search of cups. She settles on two jade coffee mugs, pouring the tea and adding milk and sugar. Ava hands the cup to Elric, and he stares into the milky drink.

"You made it just how I like it," he says without looking up.

"Of course I did. I'm your wife," she smiles and pours her own cup, fixing it while continuing the conversation. "Well, where have you found the most information?"

Elric sets down his cup with a hard clank, splashing tea on the countertop.

He tries to stay calm, though the fear and anger in his voice betray him, layering his tone with a heavy uncertainty.

"You have just found all this out so for you to speak nonchalant about it is easy. For you to be ready to buckle down and figure it out is just an easy, logical choice at this moment. But for me, this is terrifying."

"I know it is for you. I can't begin to imagine how it is for you, but it's just not the same for you as it is for me. I am scared to death, and that says a lot, considering death does nothing to me. I don't know what to do. I've never experienced this before. I could take solace in the fact that at least I would get to love you again, even after a death. I would still get to love a version of you. But it wouldn't be *you*. Now, all the pieces of you are put together, and my best friend is here, standing in front of me. There is not one barrier between us, so the stakes seem even higher."

Thunder crashes as a prelude to the rain that begins to fall. Elric looks out the sliding glass door as it fills with water drops, the outside world becoming distorted. He can't decide if the distortion to the physical world is just a pathetic comparison to his own at this moment or just nature's cruel coincidence. Walking past Ava, he goes straight out that back door into his backyard and lets the rain fall on him. He looks up into the sky at the gray clouds floating above. He feels like his existence is just a slow-filling rain cloud. A darkened, moisture-laden thunderstorm of clouds, ready to burst. The extreme highs of love pack him with memories of laughter and joy, and the utmost lows of his soulmate dying, again and again, leak into his cloud as well. His life has just been packing everything in, creating what will be the torrential downpour of his remaining stability. He takes a deep breath, the smell of fresh rain hitting the pavement, grounding him to reality, as it always does.

Elric turns back to the house and sees Ava standing in the alcove holding Geoffrey. She looks at him, her eyebrows knitted in concern, and he feels guilty, knowing that he is the source of such worry.

Walking back to Ava, he takes Geoffrey from her arm, setting him inside the house. He takes both her hands in his apologetically, placing his lips on them.

"I am so sorry. I'm worrying you and I shouldn't be," he says, closing his eyes and speaking into her hands.

"Elric... Elric Ferron, look at me."

He raises his eyes to meet hers.

She releases his grip with one hand and traces her finger around his jaw before resting it on his cheek. "You haven't worried me. My heart breaks with all this pain you've endured for hundreds of years. I know I didn't know, I couldn't have known, but now you don't have to face it alone."

He pulls away from her, giving a cynical chuckle, "I do!"

Ava takes a step toward him, placing herself in the rain, and he retreats further. She crosses her arms over her chest, the rain soaking her.

"I am here now," she says, the optimism in her voice trying to burrow its way into Elric.

Anger crashes into him like a landslide, the boulders of fury gaining momentum. Finally, he has the pieces of his wife back together, but here he stands with her a foot away, reluctant to take her into his arms. The idea of losing her this time is just as painful as the first, if not more.

His voice raises over the beating rain. "No! You have no idea what I have been through! What I have endured!"

Thunder crashes giving emphasis to his words.

Ava reaches for him again, but he marches past her, grabbing his motorcycle helmet that is sitting on the patio table, and hurls it at the sliding glass door. Covering her head, she crouches for protection. The glass fractures and explodes, covering the ground in shards. The sound is more jarring than the thunderstorm looming overhead.

Elric yells, "I have tried everything! All these years! You think I just stood idly by killing time with you, waiting for you to die?"

As Ava stands back up, he opens his arms wide and takes a step toward the house. The glass crunches beneath his feet.

"You think I like collecting all these different versions of you?! I want one version. One that I live the rest of my life out with. I want the life back where we were happy in Bristol with a child on the way. A life where our friend got to see our family grow and thrive, and I haven't named a dog after him! Instead, my life has been full of trying to stop myself from going insane. Experiencing you die over and over and over... it creates all these cracks in my mind, and my sanity falls through those cracks. Fate is cruel, and we are damned! There is nothing that can be done."

A corner of the glass in the sliding door remains intact, but not for long, as Elric walks up to throw his fist into it. The rest of it shatters, falling to the ground along with the conversation. Blood runs through gashes on his knuckles, and droplets of red steadily hit the ground in rhythm with the rain. He presses his back to the wall of the house and slides down it, resting on top of the broken pane. Elric looks at Ava. She is drenched in the downpour, and her face is blotchy. He catches her eyes, discovering that they are red and glistening.

"Ava," he calls out to her.

She walks past him into the house, wiping her face free of rain and tears. Setting his head back, he looks out into the yard, defeatedly, knowing that the battle and the feeling of loss are all caused by his own words.

"You fool," he says aloud, berating himself.

After a few moments, Ava returns from the kitchen with a towel in her hands.

"Get up." Her tone is hard and unyielding.

He doesn't move. Just simply stares at her, unable to read the look in her bloodshot eyes.

"I said. Get. Up. Come on." She holds out her hand, motioning for him to take it.

He clutches it like it's the most important thing he'll ever hold. She pulls him inside, sitting with him on the couch and wrapping his knuckles in the towel as they both soak the cushions beneath them.

He looks at his wrapped wounds and wonders if she could so easily wrap the wounds in his heart.

They sit in silence for a while as she picks out tiny fragments of glass from his wound. From the night before and the shower of rain, her hair lays messily around her face, tangles resting on her shoulders. Little smudges of black messily line her eyes, and her lips are left with the remnants of blush lipstick stains. He notices for the first time a small, thin white scar on her jawline. He brushes the mark with his free hand and her eyes flicker towards him and then back to her task.

"You're so beautiful." He drops his hand back to his side. "How'd you get this?"

"Stop it." She says flatly, concentrating on her work, "I'm not in the mood for flattery. I was on a rope swing as a kid, fell, and caught my chin on a rock."

"It's strange. There's just parts of your lives I don't know."

Her demeanor becomes more gentle, "It's strange that there's huge gaps in your life that I don't know either."

"Ouch. Are you mining for gold?" He winces, tugging his hand back from her.

Ava pulls his hand back into her lap and continues to remove tiny pieces of glass.

"Man up. I'm almost finished anyway."

After another minute, she sets down her tools and leans back on the sofa next to him. A few inches separate them.

"Your anger is still explosive, I see. You let it build up to the extreme, and then it just boils over."

He shrugs his shoulders, refusing to meet her gaze. Lying his head on the back of the couch, he just stares at the ceiling. Ava doesn't push the subject of his anger any further, letting out a sigh, and sitting up.

"I can't imagine how hard it's been. I basically got this hard reset every time, and you just gathered all these memories. Some beautiful and amazing, but also just traumatic."

Elric opens his house mouth to speak, and she holds up her hand. "I'm not done. You had your monologue outside."

Smiling, he lifts a hand to run it through his hair but stops himself. Ava stands, pacing the living room as she speaks.

"We are going to figure this out. We have to. I turn twenty-eight next month, and from there, it's basically a ticking time bomb. As much as you don't want me to die, I don't want to either. There has to be people like us, at least someone like you."

She stops moving, standing directly in front of him.

"Look at me, please. Please."

Elric shifts his gaze towards her, finally making eye contact.

"I am not giving up until I absolutely stop breathing. I can't, not at this point. We are going to figure this out. I feel like I am finally me. My life has always felt empty. I could have the most amazing experiences, travel to the most beautiful places, feel like the most loved woman, but I felt empty."

She runs her hands over her eyes. "You know that time of day where it's not daytime anymore, but it's not nighttime yet. There's no celestial counterpart to the sky. That's how I have felt—like an empty sky. Life was still beautiful, but my sun or my moon was missing."

The corners of his mouth lift, his eyes crinkling in the corners. He picks his head up and stares at her with admiration. Her determination always impressed him, but her balance to his life is what kept him tethered to the feeling of wholeness no matter what life cycle they were in. In the areas where he felt like he failed or just couldn't keep calm, she would come in and fill the voids and vice versa. Their personalities together were what made him feel like they could conquer the world. He hoped that this time, their relationship was truly the conquering type.

"Could you say something? I don't always know what's going on in your head," Ava says, frustrated.

"You know. I think the twilight sky is more beautiful because of the absence of a moon or sun."

"And what does that mean?" She asks, moving away from him.

He scratches at the scruff starting to grow on his neck, hesitating to let her know his thoughts, knowing how she'll react.

"You don't need a moon or a sun. You can live a life without me. A good one. You have been." He knows what he says is true but wishes it wasn't.

Her eyes narrow at him before looking up and blinking away tears.

"That is not a life I am willing to live. You are right. My life was good before I remembered who I was–who I *am.*" She bit out her sentence. "Why am I going to settle for a life that is merely good when I could share an extraordinary one with you."

Elric never questioned whether she loved him enough, but he always questioned whether he loved her as deeply and wonderfully as she deserved. However, at that moment, he knew he'd never wonder again.

He beckons for her, his eyes soft and full of warmth. "Come here."

"No." She crosses her arms over her body.

"Come here," he says, reaching out for her further.

"Elric."

"Please." His voice is delicate and soothing.

She drops her arms and walks over to him. Ava crawls into his lap, and he wraps her in a tight embrace. He kisses the top of her head and rests his cheek on it.

"Tell me what's in your head," she says quietly against his chest.

"Can we just enjoy this moment?"

She rocks into him with her shoulder, hard. "No."

Ava laughs lightly, and the sound warms Elric.

He sighs deeply. "*Any moment might be our last. Everything is more beautiful because we are doomed. You will never be lovelier than you are right now. We will never be here again.*"

With the broken door, there is no barrier to keep the soundscape of rainfall from penetrating the room. The storm now lulls into a gentle shower. They sit encompassed in each other, letting the steady resonance of the earth fill the space where words are absent. The hours go by as twilight seeps into the room, sleep coming to claim them both. Neither of them loosen their hold on the other.

XII

Ava and Elric both wake up to a phone's ringtone chiming off. She jumps up in a frenzy and runs to the counter where her phone is plugged in.

"Ouch, crap." She catches her little toe on the leg of the barstool, knocking it a couple of inches off its original placement.

"Hello?" She answers the phone, wincing and bending over to rub the injured digit.

Elric stands up and stretches before heading into the kitchen to get a glass of water and rummage through the fridge. Opening the toaster oven, he sees the stale bagels sitting in there unclaimed. He wrinkles his nose and quietly closes the door, leaving the bagels in their final resting place. A draft rolls through his home, causing him to shiver and remember the shattered door. He rubs his eyebrows, irritated by his outburst. Picking up his own phone from the countertop, he texts Anita, asking her to find someone to replace the French doors immediately.

She texts back promptly, *On it*.

"No, Rob, I'm good. My phone died. Yeah, I know. Let Mom know I'm okay. I know it's been a couple days. Dude, I'm almost 30 years old. When I go AWOL for more than a few days, *then* you can get concerned. What if I was just sick of you guys? I'm joking."

Ava goes silent on the phone as Robyn goes off on the other end. She rolls her eyes at Elric and mouths a quick *sorry*. He shakes his head silently, laughing. Elric points to his stomach, signaling for hunger and she nods vigorously before turning her attention back to the phone.

"Yes, I understand why you were worried, but you guys remember I lived across the world on my own, right? Okay, sure. Tell Mom I'll call her later. What? Where am I?"

She looks at Elric in a panic before responding, "Uh. Remember that friend Anita I told you about? Just crashed with her. Yup. Well... she doesn't have the same phone charger as me. Yes, I will. Okay, Rob. Okay, love you too. Bye."

Ava hangs up her phone and looks at the screen. "There are 43 missed calls and... Jesus, 84 text messages."

Ava locks her phone and sets it back on the counter. "But to answer your question," she saunters over to Elric and snakes her arms around his waist, "Yes, I'm starving. But I absolutely stink."

Lifting her arm, she takes a deep whiff and feigns a gag.

He grins. "Well, before we go eat, let's take care of that."

Picking her up, he roughly tosses her over his shoulder before marching down the hallway to his room. She kicks her legs and laughs, hitting him on the back, pretending to try and get away. He stands her up on the tiled bathroom floor, and she immediately pushes him into a wall, an urgency taking over. Her lips search his body as she starts to pull his shirt up. His body responds to her call, and he quickly removes his shirt and throws it into the sink on accident as Ava's hands slide down his chest and abs before beginning to work at the button of his pants. She gets it undone and grabs at his face, bringing his lips to hers. Ava gently bites at his bottom lip before pulling off. She works on undressing as Elric rotates to turn the shower on, filling the bathroom with steam. Turning his attention back towards Ava, he looks at her naked body and revels in the beauty that is graciously given to him.

He lets out a low groan and closes the gap between them. Elric sets his hand on the front of her throat, closing his fingers around it. He could feel her swallow beneath his grasp. Without lifting his hand, he slides it up until he is holding her jaw and draws her into him. A slight gasp leaves her lips, and Elric smiles. Weaving his hands into her hair, he connects his mouth to hers and leads them backward into the shower. She shivers as her back hits the cold tile, and he buries his lips onto her neck, relishing the taste of her skin.

Breathing heavily, she digs her nails into his back, then hikes her knee up as she lets his hands flow down her body with the water.

"Your pants," she says with her voice barely above a whisper.

"What?" He mumbles into her skin.

Releasing her neck, he briskly pins her arms above her head, holding both her delicate wrists in one of his hands. With his other hand, he glides across her body like silk. Her skin rises in small prickles, a ripple of energy moving through her, causing her to tremble.

She clears her throat and speaks louder. "Your pants are still on."

Elric lifts his head and looks into Ava's glazed-over eyes. Her cheeks flush. He licks his lips and looks down at his open-button water-soaked pants. He gives a throaty laugh and nestles back into her neck.

She moves her mouth close to his ear and whispers. "Let's take care of that."

Elric rummages through his drawers and tosses a fresh pair of his clothes at Ava while she sits on the bed, wrapped in a towel and brushing her hair. He takes another pair of clean shorts out of the drawer for himself and puts them on before collapsing on his bed. Ava gets dressed and nestles herself in the crook of his arm. He wraps around her, taking a moment just to breathe her in.

"I'm going to need to go to my place. As much as I'd love to live in your oversized t-shirts and shorts, I'd like to grab some of my own stuff and my own toothbrush," she tells him.

"No problem. I'll call us a ride. Let's grab breakfast, and then we will figure out musical cars. Both of ours are still at the library. Sound good?" Elric says.

"Love it, let's go." She pops up and slides into a pair of flip-flops he has lying next to his door.

She holds out her arms. "How do I look?"

"More beautiful than ever," He replies, crawling over the bed to her and kissing her, truly meaning the sentiment.

Ava pushes him off playfully. "No. I'm starving. Let's go."

"I love you," Elric tells her.

Her eyebrows drop, and she blinks a few times, smiling at him. "That's the first time you've actually said it this- this life?"

He nods his head. "I will love you beyond this life."

"And any thereafter," she finishes.

He pulls her into another embrace before leaving the room.

They leave the house, and he locks the door behind them as the taxi pulls into the driveway.

Elric gives the name of a small bakery, and the driver nods while starting the meter. His phone chimes with a text from Anita, letting him know someone will be there to replace the doors within the hour.

Replying with a quick *Thanks,* he tucks his phone away. They sink into the back seat and enjoy the ride in silence.

They arrive at a cafe with large display cases full of colorful pastries, the strong aroma of coffee beans hitting them in the face as they walk inside.

Ava's mouth begins to water. "Oh my god. I didn't realize how hungry I was until this moment. I'm ready to order *now.*"

Elric smiles and runs his hand up and down her spine as she speaks to the person behind the counter. He has always enjoyed the sound of her voice, whether she is doing something meaningful or as simple as ordering baked goods.

"Elric?" She says, bringing him back out of his thoughts.

He stops moving his hand but leaves it on her and orders a breakfast sandwich, pavlova, and coffee. The girl behind the counter smiles and hands him a tray of assorted pastries as Ava grabs two full cups of coffee off the counter.

Looking over the tray, he laughs. "You almost ordered one of everything."

She walks to a table in the corner of the cafe and lifts her shoulders into a slight shrug while sliding into a booth.

"I didn't know what to get, so I wanted to try a little bit of everything."

He kisses the top of her head and sits in the chair across from her. The table is soon littered with sugar packets and creamer cups. Ava starts in on a small pastry filled with berries and cream, drizzled with icing.

"Please, you have to try this," she begs with a full mouth, offering it up to him.

Taking a bite, he nods his head sarcastically. "Wow, the best thing I've ever had."

"Whatever. I'll just enjoy all of it."

He watches her as she eats–leaving his food untouched. He has never taken these moments for granted, only looking upon them with pure reverence because he knows each one is fleeting. These are the moments he lived for. These are the moments that he would die for—if he could.

Ava goes to grab her coffee cup and he places his hand on hers before she reaches it. She looks up and into his eyes.

"I love you," he says.

"I love you, too," she replies without hesitation.

Ava looks at him for a moment longer. "What are you thinking?

"Nothing," he replies.

"I know you too well for that. I can see the gears in your brain turning."

He laughs and runs his hands through his hair. "I know we have to talk about the important things, but I'm enjoying this moment."

Ava takes a napkin and wipes her mouth. Setting the napkin back down, she replaces it with a coffee cup, holding it firmly between both her hands. She positions it underneath her nose and inhales.

"I know. I've been thinking, though," she takes a sip and repositions herself. "I don't know how we don't hurt Robyn in this. It's important that we don't hurt her."

Elric rubs his lips together and tries to keep his face as serious as possible. He hasn't expected that to be her foremost thought, but he isn't surprised that she's already caring for someone else's emotions.

"No, I know. And I didn't- I don't want to hurt your sister either," he replies. He loses his poker face, and his chest moves as he tries to stifle a chuckle.

"Elric!" Ava's eyebrows come down as she crosses her arms.

"Listen." He leans in across the table, no longer trying to hide his grin. "There is an actual impending death happening with an actual demon witch, and you're still worried about someone else's feelings above that. I love that. I wouldn't expect anything different from you." He shrugs. "But some would say it's lacking perspective."

She smiles and playfully slaps his hands. "I understand, but here in this time, it's my family, and the last thing I want to do is devastate someone, especially my sister. I love her, too."

He kisses her hands. "I understand. As we figure everything out, we just keep those halves of our lives separate until we solve the bigger part. Family dynamics can be tackled later."

"Okay," Ava agrees, nodding her head. "So, the impending doom?"

Elric releases the hold on her hands and leans back, the chair making a creaking noise as he shifts his weight.

He looks past Ava at the wall. It's a peachy pastel color with intricately detailed crown molding. Bright floral decals border the walls, and in the center, six black and white photographs sit in two rows of three.

From left to right, the top three photos depict a field of wildflowers in bloom, a skeleton lying in a grave, and a large outdoor fountain with women lying around it and children playing in the water. In the same order, the bottom three photos are a field on fire, a woman smiling at a small infant in her arms, and a collapsed building with people standing in a panic out front, covered in dust and rubble. A small label beneath the photographs reads *Revolution of Joy & Pain*.

Elric sighs and looks back at Ava. "This is what I have put together on my own." He pauses as a server comes up to their table to clear away empty plates. They exchange thank yous, and Ava continues to eat what's still in front of her.

"As I was saying, what I have put together on my own."

A different server comes up, interrupting the conversation. "Would you like some more coffee?"

Getting frustrated, Elric tries to remain polite and smiles patiently at the server. Ava looks up at him. "Yes. For both of us, thank you."

The server refills their coffees and walks away.

She continues eating with her mouth full again. She holds out a small pastry with light, fluffy cream and peaches.

"You've got to try this one. It's so good."

"Okay, I will but first," as soon as he leans forward again, a third person comes up to the table interrupting him again.

With a loud clunk a plate of bright red macarons are aggressively set on the table.

Elric looks down and pinches the bridge of his nose. Ava touches his free hand for a reassuring calm.

"Thank you, but I'm sorry, this must be another table's. We have all our food," she says.

"Oh, no. These are from me. A little introductory gift, so to speak. I've been dying to meet you, Ava. Well, I guess you've actually been the one dying."

Elric's skin crawls at the familiar voice. His gaze hikes up to find Faye standing over them. She gives a vicious grin, baring all her teeth as if she is ready to bite. Her hair is in a loose braid, and she wears a long-sleeved floor-length black dress. It has a deep plunge in the front, baring almost all of her breasts, too much for this setting and time of day.

Elric stands up, shoving his chair back, causing it to fall to the ground with a loud crash. The chatter in the bakery from other patrons has momentarily ceased, and all attention is on him. After a few silent seconds and no show to see, everyone turns their focus back to their own tables. But at the moment, Elric could not care less about whether everyone is watching him or not. He moves over to Ava, blocking her from Faye's sight.

139

"You're Faye." Ava says, gripping the back of his shirt.

Faye licks her teeth and clicks her tongue. "The one and only."

She glides over to Elric's fallen chair, picking it up and sitting down. Crossing her legs, she leans back and moves her eyes up and down over Ava.

"Oh, Elric. You hurt my feelings," Faye pouts. "You act like I'm a rabid animal!"

"I can shoot and kill an animal. I haven't been so lucky with you," he says through clenched teeth.

Faye leans back and takes a pastry from a small plate, a malice-soaked laugh leaving her lips. "Please, sit down. You're going to draw attention to yourself. I'm acting civil. Why shouldn't you?"

She takes a bite and looks at Ava, pointing to the pastry in her hand.

"This is good! You have great taste! Hope you don't mind." Faye takes another bite, licking her lips clean while staring at Ava.

Ava pulls on Elric's shirt. "It's okay. Sit down."

Elric doesn't make a move. His eyes are trained on Faye.

Ava's voice stays calm. "Elric..."

He looks down at her. She hasn't moved from her seat. He nods at her and slides into the booth beside her.

Placing his hand under the table, he reaches for Ava, needing to touch her to assure himself that she is safe. She sets her hand on top of his and methodically runs her thumb back and forth over it. It helps to soothe him.

"Aw, you guys are so cute. Ain't love a bitch, though?" Faye says, smiling as she takes another bite of pastry.

"Faye," he says, his jaw tensing.

She finishes the pastry and brushes her fingertips against one another to remove the glaze residue. Faye picks up Elric's coffee cup and holds it up.

"You were finished, right?" She sneers.

He glares at her as she drinks, obviously not caring for an answer.

"Ahhh, you know I just love a good cup of coffee. But nothing beats real coffee in Colombia. Am I right, Elric? When was that? 1974?"

"Faye, enough," he growls.

Faye holds up her hands in a mocking defense. "Okay, okay. So testy."

Laughing, she shifts her sight and targets Ava.

"Well, you are beautiful. No wonder this guy is obsessed. I've never had the pleasure of meeting you. I was always a little too late, and it's hard to meet someone six feet under, ya know?"

Faye crosses her thumb over her neck in a line, closing her eyes and sticking out her tongue. Elric lurches forward, but Ava holds him back. She all but places her body on top of his.

Faye lets out a wicked giggle and holds out her hand for Ava. Staring at it, Ava looks back at Elric, but his eyes remain unwavering from his objective.

"Oh, come on. Truce. I just want to give a proper greeting to the famous Ava," she says with a soft smile on her face.

Ava lets go of his hand and grabs Faye's for a firm handshake. Suddenly, Faye jerks Ava closer and sniffs up the length of her forearm like a wolf on the hunt. Elric clutches at Ava's arm, but Faye's grip is impossibly strong.

She looks up at Ava, her face serious. "No, but something is different this time. I never sense you until your soul leaves a body, but yesterday it was like fireworks went off. Why is that? What has changed?"

Faye lets go, and Ava recoils against the cushion of the booth. She sinks into Elric, and they swap positions, his body back on top of hers. Faye leans back and circles her bottom lip with her middle finger as she glares at the couple across from her.

"You have more knowledge, I see. I'm not sure to what extent, though," Faye says.

"How did you know something was different?" Ava asks.

"Your candle burned brighter. Brighter than it ever has. I was *intrigued*," Faye replies.

"Candle?"

"Part of her magic," Elric interjects. "There's two candles representing us, a cord linking them. Ours are different from everyone else's, though."

"Okay, whatever. So, are you here to play games?" Ava asks, annoyed.

"She's not here to help," Elric points out.

"Oh, Elric, after all this time, I thought we had become friends." Faye reaches towards him.

Ava knocks her hand away before she can touch Elric. Faye cackles and carelessly leans back in her chair.

"We bother you. Don't we?" Ava asks, glaring.

Faye's lips tighten, and she forces a smile. "Why would a couple of scummy *humans* bother me?"

The word humans leaves her mouth in a stiff hiss.

"I can tell you are angry, but I'm not sure why. You act like this is just a game to pass the time, but it's not just a game. And even if it was, it doesn't seem to be one you're winning." Ava keeps her voice steady, her burning stare locked on Faye's, never wavering.

Faye slams her fists on the table and once again draws the other patrons' attention. She releases her hands and flattens them out, sliding them against the hard surface.

Distress is starting to reveal itself in Faye's expression, something Elric has only seen on her once before, and that was the night they met.

"What is it about us that drives you mad? If we are stuck in this loop, why does it bother you so much?" Ava unburies herself from Elric and leans forward. "You wouldn't be watching us if you didn't care, but you are obsessed enough to come here and bother us? Why would meeting me make any sort of difference to you?"

Suddenly, it dawns on Elric. "The witches I met in Triora. They couldn't even speak of you? Why?"

"Their souls belong to me." Faye picks at her nails, trying to seem bored. "I can't have people spilling all my secrets. Especially if they want revenge. And let's face it, most people do."

"So, they made deals just like I did, and their souls were traded to you, but they weren't just witches that joined a coven. You tricked them, and they became enslaved," Elric says.

Faye takes an exasperated breath and tilts her head. "And what of it?"

"All this time... Wow. I don't know how I never realized it." Elric sits back and stares at her in disbelief.

Faye leans back, exaggerating a pouty lip and whine. "Oh no, did you figure out that the witch lies?"

"You made a deal to save a loved one, and they pledged their soul to you. You, of course, made it sound like I didn't have to worry until I was dead, but you collect immediately as long as the deal goes according to plan? The person who makes the deal is in eternal servitude, and their loved one is saved. Am I right?"

"Yes and no, I have to wait until they're dead. But there is no clause saying how long I have to wait until they die. Or how." She stares at Ava coldly.

"You kill them?" A shiver goes down Ava's spine and her stomach goes sour.

"I kill them. I influence others to kill. I drive them mad until they take their own life. To-may-to, to-mah-to." Faye shrugs.

"But you couldn't collect my soul. Or hers. You still can't."

"And that's how you're losing," Ava interjects.

Faye grits her teeth. "I am *not* losing. I am just playing the long game."

"To what end, Faye? We are stuck, and you could help us break this curse. We could all stop this torture." Elric tries to plead with her, hoping for a sliver of humanity.

"You're so smart, Elric," she smirks. "You're right. I can't collect either of you. And frankly, it has to do with this one," she says, pointing to Ava, "dying before the contract was sealed. I didn't deliver on my part."

Faye stands up and crouches over the table, inches from Elric's face.

"But you know why it's okay?" Faye's eyes dart back and forth between the two lovers. "Because watching you break every time she dies is so worth it. I have centuries of you going mad." A cruel smile forms on her lips. "I always hope they're more gruesome than the last." She laughs.

Without thinking, Elric grabs a knife on the table and shouts, driving it right into her chest.

She raises an eyebrow, unphased, and stares at Elric for an unnerving amount of time.

Finally, she looks down at her chest and snickers. "Oh, honey. You'll have to do better than that."

Faye blows them a kiss, then she raises her arms over her head and quickly brings them back down, disappearing in the transition. The knife lands on the floor, the reverb of metal bouncing on the ground sounding off. Before Elric has time to speak a word, a loud shriek cuts through the room. Their attention is drawn to a woman backing away from her table and screaming at the scene she just witnessed.

"We have to go. Right now," Ava says, holding Elric's hand to pull him away from the table and out the cafe door. Outside, they break into a run as soon as their feet hit the sidewalk.

They don't stop until they are well out of range of the commotion, hiding in the backlot of a plaza of stores. Elric pulls Ava against a brick wall before slumping down to the ground and holding his head in his hands while Ava crouches down next to him, leaning her head back against the brick.

"Well, she's really sweet," she says breathlessly.

XIII

T RIORA, LIGURIA ITALY 1588

Multiple women were congregated around him.

"Why would you want to help me?" Elric asked as he took a step back from the woman with the scar across her throat.

She looked at the other woman with the strip of cloth covering her eyes, but no one would speak.

"Who are you?" Elric asked, reaching for a dagger hidden beneath his cloak.

The one with covered eyes took a step forward and tilted her face towards Elric as his hand subtly shifted beneath his cloak.

"*Caevos Ipsumas*," she whispered.

Before Elric knew what was happening the dagger vanished from his grip and appeared in the woman's hand. She held the dagger in front of her blinded eyes. "Your dagger can do nothing to u*ssss*." She said, throwing the weapon to the floor. "I am Livia."

The woman with the scar across her throat nodded and looked down before speaking. "Iseppa."

The twins spoke after them. The one with the scar on the right was Osana, and the one with the scar on the left was Orsa.

The last woman, with her hand pressed against her throat, gasped. "Catterina."

"I'll ask you once more then. Why would you want to aid me?" Elric asked again, splaying both of his hands to show he meant no harm, hoping the gesture would protect him.

Iseppa spoke up. "We are forbidden from speaking our truth."

"By whom?" He ran his hand over his face. "We are forbidden from *ss*speaking *our* truth," Livia repeated.

"Do you want to hurt me?"

Catterina shook her head.

"Someone is forbidding you from speaking your truth? How?"

Catterina nodded. Iseppa walked up to her, resting her hand on her shoulder. To Elric, it looked like a sign of comfort.

"A bond," Iseppa said.

Elric looked at the markings on the wall. "Do you know Faye then? Your walls bear the same marks."

The women went silent and exchanged glances with one another. Elric balled up his fist in anger and looked around at the dozens of candles.

"I do not know how you expect me to figure out your mysteries with nothing to go on!"

Osana and Orsa silently walked over to the table with the single candle. They let go of each other's scarred hands for the first time that night. Osana's eyes clouded before they became completely black. Slowly she moved her hand in a circle over the table until a piece of parchment and charcoal were conjured. When Orsa's eyes matched her sister's, she turned to her twin to whisper in her ear. Without looking down, Osana's hand moved rapidly across the paper. The scratching sounds of charcoal were the only thing disturbing the silence in the room.

Elric watched intently as he walked up to the table. No one in the room stopped him from doing so, but all eyes were on him except for the twins, engaged in their magic. He laid his hands on the table, leaning over and studying the image coming to life. His heart stopped as he saw long curls strewn across the ground. Ava lay on the ground, reaching out. Her head had a gaping wound, and her face was covered in blood.

Anger spread like a shadow inside Elric, and before he knew it, he had Osana pinned to the wall by her throat.

"How do you know how she died last?" He spat through clenched teeth.

Osana coughed, and her eyes went back to normal as she snapped her head to look at her twin in terror. Orsa reached for her sister, but Elric held Osana tightly in place.

"*How do you know?*" He repeated.

"P-p-please," Osana whispered.

He tightened his hold before releasing her and returning to the picture. Orsa grabbed onto her twin, smoothing out her hair and whispering to her in the foreign language to calm her. He took the parchment and held it tightly until the edges of it crumpled in his fist.

Without looking up he spoke. "I am tortured enough for many lifetimes. I do not need aid in that with demented images. If this is all you have brought me down here for, then I implore you to let me leave."

Catterina walked up and gently touched the drawing to pull it down from Elric's view. His eyes followed the paper until it was no longer visible. He looked into Catterina's eyes and saw a brokenness in them. She reached out and rested her hand on his cheek. Instinctively, he wanted to pull back, but he remained where he was.

"What is it you can offer me then?" he asked, finally pulling away.

Catterina pressed on the old wound. "A possible solution to break yours and your beloved's soul free."

"Soul offerings," the twins whispered in unison.

Elric stared back and forth between the women in confusion before Iseppa took a few steps forward.

"We hunt. We go through the villages and look for people as desperate as you once were. We have access to the books with souls in them," Iseppa spoke.

Elric watched her intently, nodding his head to confirm his understanding and ask her to continue.

Iseppa went on. "You could swap souls for yours. If you were able to find a soul to make a deal like yours, they could seal their handprint over yours in the book. A soul for a soul."

Elric stared at the drawing in his hand, his heart palpitating beneath his ribs. He had gone through enough deaths of Ava's already and assumed there would be more to come. The madness and despair he faced was a wildfire that burned away a little more of his sanity every time it blew through. He had no idea what it was like for Ava and wondered if she had the phantom pains of death every time the fire came raging through.

"I know it," Osana began.

"Feels impossible," Orsa finished.

"She would be free?" Elric's voice cracked.

Catterina silently nodded.

"There isss a condition," Livia said. She gestured at Iseppa to fill him in.

Iseppa sighed. "It must be a very pure soul. Like no others. To the book, the swap is not worth it if it is not a greater trade."

Elric looked questioningly at Iseppa. "Go on."

"We know of two souls with great value. A mother whose child dies as we speak. A sickness invades his body. She would willingly make the trade."

"No," Elric sternly responded.

"You would be free."

"No," he straightened his posture as his voice grew with authority and force.

"But Ava–" Iseppa argued.

"I said no!" he shouted, his certainty tangibly strong. "I will never damn some-one else to *this*. Much less an innocent mother and her child... She would watch her child die over and over again. I could never live my life with that in my conscience. Why is my life of greater value than theirs?"

The women stared at him in silence, afraid to object.

Elric took a deep breath. "Do you have another way?"

Iseppa remained silent, eyes shifting to the women around her.

"Then I will take my leave. I appreciate you offering any sort of help, but I am unwilling to do that," he said matter of fact.

Catterina walked up to Livia to take the stolen dagger from her hand. The cusp of death and the pain of torture didn't scare him anymore, so he braced himself for the worst. But as soon as she had it in her hand, she ran the blade across her palm. No pain registered on her face, as if she didn't feel any at all. Catterina passed the knife to Iseppa, who stood to her right. Iseppa did the same and passed it to Livia, who passed it on to the twins. The cutting was finished with Orsa, who laid the knife in the center of the room. The women circled around the knife and linked arms, blood spilling over one another, creating a perfect circle below them. A unified groaning filled the room. The candles flickered, and a strange wind whipped Elric's cloak and hair around him, although there was no entryway for this wind to exist. The iron blade began to glow a burning hot red, but there was no fire to cause this.

The women's groaning turned into loud chanting,

"*Auxiib era examalolium*

Celconsili umtemp riosare

Incanfortis telum."

Elric understood nothing, but the chanting continued. The wind grew stronger, extinguishing the candles that were no longer needed. The iron was so bright it illuminated the entire room on its own.

The women abruptly went silent and released their hold on one another; the room went black, and everything was eerily quiet. The dark felt tangible. Elric dared not make a move. Slowly, one by one, the flames of the candles spontaneously lit until all the candles were as before.

Catterina was the first to break the circle. She grabbed the knife, and Elric watched it burn the skin of her palm, smoking as she walked it across to Elric. The smell of seared skin made Elric's stomach churn.

She placed it back in the sheath and beckoned for his hand.

Elric shook his head, "I cannot hold that without burning myself."

Catterina smiled at him, "I have cooled the metal, I assure you."

He reluctantly opened his hand to her, and she gingerly placed it in his grasp. He braced himself for heat but felt no sting. He closed his fingers around it, and she held his hand tightly in place.

The other four women walked up to him, surrounding Catterina. The women, barring Orsa and Osana, may not have been blood, but he could sense they were sisters, nonetheless.

The sheath was warm in Elric's hand.

"What did you do?" he questioned.

Catterina released her hold on him, pressed her throat, and smiled. "You will see."

MODERN-DAY ARCATA, CALIFORNIA

After waiting what seemed to be a safe amount of time, Ava mentioned that her apartment wasn't too far from their location. They could cut through part of Redwood Park to get there, keeping them covered a little longer.

Sensing the trouble may be behind them physically, Elric can't help but feel a lingering trepidation. They walk through the forest quietly, and the smell of the greenery and soil comforts both of them. Their footsteps are mostly silent as they step into the soft dirt. Ava brushes a fern with her fingertips as she passes by the plants around them. Wind rustles the leaves, sounding like whispered secrets, and the leaves murmur in reply. A few birds sing, adding to nature's conversations. Elric and Ava's hands find each other and interlock. With each step forward, their bodies come closer together until no space is left between them.

"What was it that the witches in Triora told you?" Ava asks, breaking the silence.

Elric sighs. "We will talk about that. I promise. Can we just take a moment to just be? I don't know what is going to become of our life after this, but just a few moments where we can pretend none of that exists."

"I will let you have your moment. I understand you can take your *time* when digesting things. But time is not a luxury we have anymore." She squeezes his hand before letting go to point up ahead. "We continue on this trail for about a mile or so and then just about another mile after that."

Elric stoically nods in response.

Although there are so many outside factors and tribulations on their doorstep, he can't feel anything but complete peace in this moment. His love on his arm, her completely whole while they walk through one of the most magnificent forests he's ever been in. The redwoods tower overhead, feeling like their personal guardians. The trees shelter and protect those below with their stature while remaining unmoved by the elements of the world. Elric wishes that these sturdy warriors could fight this battle for him.

"Oh, my god, Elric. This is one of the reasons I picked the apartment I did. A fairy ring!" Ava delightfully shrieks.

Ava releases Elric's arm, runs to a large, perfectly flat redwood stump, and climbs up to stand on top of it. He stays where he is and watches her, drinking in her every move as if it may be her last. Standing in the middle of the stump, she opens her arms wide and tilts her head back, closing her eyes. The wind gently brushes the hair around her shoulders, stirring it slightly. Six redwood trees, smaller than the stump, surround Ava in a perfect circle. Rays of sunshine weave through the other trees to create a perfect highlight that rests across her face.

"Try not to move." Elric quickly pulls out his moleskin and his stub of a pencil out of his back pocket.

Opening her eyes, she looks down at him. "Wait. We have a literal demon trying to get at us, and you still grabbed your sketchbook," she laughs.

He gives a quick smile, but his lips become a tight line of concentration as he begins to draw.

"It's habit. I can't help it. Keys, wallet, sketchbook, and pencil. Don't move." His pencil continues to move across the small page, little scratching noises filling the air.

"I know how to pose for you. I've been doing it for hundreds of years." Ava tilts her head back toward the sky.

"Right," he says, pulling up his brows.

"Do you know why this is called a fairy ring?" Ava asks.

"Tell me."

"The stump I'm standing on is the mother tree, and when she was cut down, a new generation of trees sprouted from her roots, creating this perfect circle. Most of them are genetically the same as the mother tree, too." She smiles and looks at the trees around her. "The fairy ring."

He grunts. "Do you not see the irony?"

"What?" Ava drops her arms and looks at him, puzzled.

"Your whole existence is a fairy ring. Original Ava at the center. Other Ava's sprouting up," he says, eyes darting back and forth between muse and sketch.

"Ha, well, look at that," she giggles. "Do you want to know the magic behind a fairy ring?"

"Of course."

Her face brightens. "It's the dwelling for fairies and elves. They dance here and create the ring. There's a lot of magic here, ya know. Some legends say if humans enter the fairy ring, they have to dance until they go mad. Another legend says you have to run nine times under the full moon before entering."

Elric laughs. "Did you run under the full moon nine times before entering?"

"I just think I have a pure enough soul, so the fairies don't mind if I come inside," she wiggles her shoulders in a confident dance.

"I think so, too."

Elric closes his notebook and steps onto the stump with Ava, closing his arms around her waist.

"Let me see the drawing," she says.

"Not yet. Let me bring your full beauty to life with color," Elric responds while kissing her neck.

"Fine. I'll trust the artist."

They walk on the trail hand in hand until they reach the trailhead, spitting them out into a parking lot with only a few scattered cars. Ava leans against the fallen tree on the edge of the lot, a bright orange tie on the end of it. She quickly grabs Elric by the jacket and pulls him in close to her body, brushing her lips against his, and then smiles. He looks deep into those emerald green eyes, and for once, he feels as though she's seeing all of him because she is truly all of her. Tenderly, he slips his hand behind her neck, pulling her in closer, leaving a small distance between them.

"I will love you beyond this life and any thereafter." He closes the gap with a kiss balanced with delicate yearning and fierce passion, but the emotions are covered in gratitude as well. Grateful that no matter where their course has been set, he has been able to keep his promise.

They arrive at a small studio apartment neatly tucked away in a quadplex not far from the forest.

"Oh, shoot. I left my clutch at your studio. My keys are in there." Ava scratches her head. "Oh! Thank god my mom made me get a hidey key!"

She reaches into the pot of a hanging fern and pulls out a faux stone, turning it over to reveal a key hidden under a latch. She opens the door and throws the key and stone back in its hidden spot. Ava walks in and tosses her phone on the bed before rifling through drawers of clothes and stuffing them into a duffle.

Elric looks around and takes in her apartment. It is nearly bare and mainly unorganized. A small kitchen with moving boxes full of half-packed items sits on the counter next to empty to-go boxes of delivered food. He walks past a tiny bathroom barely big enough for the standing shower and toilet it holds, yet she has found room for a pile of clothes in between. He walks over to the bed and sees that each side is lined with large wooden bookshelves filled to the brim with books, but he wouldn't expect anything less. Her bed is messy. Gray sheets are thrown about with nothing tucked in. A large, fuzzy navy-blue blanket is balled up by the six pillows piled at the headboard. In the middle of the mess, lying on the bed wide open, is her book, and Elric smiles.

"Don't ask me how many times I've read it because now I *really* don't know." Ava picks up *The Iliad* and gently sets the book on a shelf.

She falls across the bed, wrapping herself in the top sheet. "How has it only been a couple days since the mural unveiling? I feel like it's been six years. I'm so tired." She yawns.

Elric crawls onto the mattress behind her, wrapping himself around her. "I know, it's been a long couple of days."

She groans and slaps her forehead. "I forgot to call my mom. Hang on. Please don't move. I would really like to just lay here with you."

He smiles into the back of her hair. "I'll be here."

As she talks to her mother on the phone, assuring her that she is safe and home, Elric looks at the bookshelf, scanning her collection. A mix of classic and modern novels mostly fills the cases, and a few art books are on the bottom shelf.

Elric picks up one of the few art books and thumbs through it, landing on a page with *18th-century Art* as its header.

"What a great century," he says to himself.

Scanning down the page, he sees six canvases, and on the opposite page, he sees a self-portrait of the artist. Before he can study the book more, Ava comes back.

"I go missing for a couple days and the whole world loses it." She laughs as she resumes her position next to him.

He sets the book down on the floor so his arms are available to her.

"It's sweet," Elric says, enveloping her again.

"I know. I'm glad she cares. I guess Robyn was really losing it, questioning where I was."

Her eyebrows gather together suddenly, concerned, almost in pain. "You've been so alone. For so long. I know there are temporary relationships, but how do you do it? No family, no ending."

He looks down, reassured by one constant, "My long, insignificant, torturous existence has been made bearable knowing you are never far off in my life."

His answer seems to settle her for the moment, but he can tell by the pursing of her lips there is more she wants to say. Instead, she moves on.

"Okay, Triora," she starts, "explain to me what happened there."

Elric goes on to retell the events of those nights, sparing no details.

"They were really tricked by Faye?"

"Yes, and she made sure they died soon after the deal was made so she could collect," he replies, "but the details of that, I have no idea."

"Why couldn't she collect with you, though? How did you become immortal?"

"I'm not completely sure. I think the deal or contract that was struck became void because you weren't saved. You got stuck in a sort of repeating limbo, and somehow I was, I guess—spared?" He takes a deep breath, "Spared from her being able to enslave me. I can't die, she can't collect," Elric explains, "but honestly, I haven't felt very spared."

Ava turns over onto her back and stares at the ceiling, biting her lip deep in thought. "The dagger? They couldn't tell you what it was for?"

"No. Faye had some sort of curse on them, forbidding them from speaking but they were trying to find loopholes to help me, to tell me as much as they could. A lot of good a knife will do us. I stabbed her today, and nothing happened," he says, frustrated.

Without looking, Ava finds Elric's hand, offering comfort between them.

"But you have no idea what they chanted?"

"Nope. I didn't know enough Latin then and I can't remember what it was that they said now."

Ava elbows his side. "You can't remember a Latin spell from nearly 500 years ago? Typical man."

"I know, right?" He jokes and pulls her in closer. "I don't even think it was Latin, though. I had never heard those words spoken before or again."

They grow quiet, settling into each other.

"You've never met anyone like you or like me? In all the years and travels? Not even another witch, demon, or horrible thing like Faye?"

"No. I didn't even know where to look, and when I found anyone who had some sort of magic, they were no help. Surprisingly, the modern age hasn't helped. Everyone is easily a witch nowadays, and the real ones are hiding their true selves." Elric takes a deep breath. "The last couple years or so, I became really involved in the non-profit, so I am ashamed to say I haven't really been looking."

Turning his head away from Ava, hoping to hide the guilt too evident on his face.

"Hey," Ava places her hand on his chin, but he refuses to turn. "Elric, look at me, please."

He turns toward her face slowly until their gazes connect. His eyes become glassy and the regret surfaces.

"I was just waiting to meet you, but I was so tired of reaching dead ends, and it feels like I've looked everywhere trying to break this. I've been across the world searching for answers. Besides you, my art is the one constant thing that makes me feel joy. And it is the only thing that can't be taken away. Not like you."

She moves her thumb gently back and forth across his cheek, just as she has always done.

"Elric, you don't have to apologize for doing something just for you. I don't ever expect you to live eternity centered around me."

Closing his eyes, he brings her palm to his lips. "It's not that easy."

"Your art can be for you. I don't hold that against you. I wouldn't have held it against you had you not tried to find me," she speaks to him gently. "I love that you've kept doing what you loved all this time. How many artists can say they've painted through the centuries?"

She leans down to try to catch his eye from his hanging head.

Elric looks at her as she kisses the end of his nose. A sudden realization makes his eyes grow wide.

"What is it?" Ava asks, her eyebrows narrowing.

He sits up and picks the art book off of the floor, quickly finding the page he had looked at before.

"Elric?" Ava asks worriedly.

"Everything is okay. I just, I swear…" Without finishing his sentence, he pulls his phone out of his pocket, tapping on the search engine.

Ava gets up on her knees, looks over his shoulder, and watches him type.

"Bloody hell."

"What?" She squints at the screen. "*Revolution of Joy and Pain*. Okay? Is that the photographer next to it? Oh, those were in the cafe! I'm still confused."

Elric lays the phone in the middle of the open book.

Ava gasps. "Wait. Is that… that is the same man?"

"Gabriel."

XIV

"Who?"

Elric lifts his hand, running it through his hair. His eyes are focused on Gabriel's face, looking back between the photo of him on his phone and the portrait in the book. His hair was slicked back in the photo, but the same dark curls at the base of his neck were easily recognizable.

"Spain, seventeen seventy-something, I believe. We met him in a tavern one night. I'd often see him in the city square painting. We became very close, especially after you died *that* time," he says to her.

She sits back down, crossing her legs underneath herself. She wouldn't take her eyes off the picture as memories began to flood in one by one.

"He had a son with red hair like his mother. Alejandra?" She looks up at Elric. "What happened to them?"

Elric lifts his shoulders. "Honestly, I don't know. I stayed a few years more after you died, but it was about time for me to move on without raising suspicions. I left without saying goodbye."

He laughs, not because of the humor but in sheer disbelief, his body reacting on instinct.

Bringing the phone to his face, he studies the picture intensely.

"What do we do now?" she asks.

"We have to find him. We have to talk to him. It helps that he didn't try very hard to cover up who he was, but I am assuming it's because he thought no one would ever question if someone is immortal or not. He did change his surname, though. *Patudo to Bello*. He did this series of paintings and these photographs centuries apart, each under a different name. He probably relied on people thinking he was just making an homage."

Elric stood up and grabbed his phone off the floor, texting Anita.

Can you meet me at the studio in about an hour?

Anita's response is immediate. *Already here. See you soon.*

He calls a cab from his phone as well.

"Elric, what's the plan? What are we doing?" Ava asks, standing up next to him. Drawing her near, he holds her.

"He has to know something. At least more than we do. If it really is him—I'm not sure how it's not him. So then maybe there is hope for us. I don't know what it looks like, but it seems like something."

He pulls back from her so he can see her face. "Wait for my call. I'm going to run to the studio and see if Anita and I can locate him. I have a lot of connections in the art world, so I'm sure it won't be too hard. Call your mom and ask her to take you to get your car from the library. It will calm her nerves after you went AWOL."

Ava lays her face on his chest and closes her eyes. "I really don't want to leave you."

He nestles in closer to her. "I know. I don't want to leave you, either, but you have people here, and we have to do our best not to raise cause for concern. And..." Elric pulls her back out and holds her face. "What we are dealing with in general is dangerous. We have to keep these two parts of your lives separate as best we can. Business as usual for today. Especially if Robyn was already upset. Okay?"

"I know you're right. None of this is easy to navigate."

Elric kisses her intently.

He closes his eyes. "No matter what, I do not want to forget you as you are right now. Whole."

She breathes deeply. "Believe me, I want the same."

The embrace between the two is delicate, but the emotions stir behind it like a tidal wave.

"Tell me not to go, and I won't," Elric says in a hushed tone.

Ava reluctantly backs away from him, groaning as she walks into the small kitchen space.

"Go. I love you."He hesitates but continues past the kitchen and reaches for the doorknob. At the last second, he hurdles the counter, wraps her in his arms, and kisses her deeply. The passion behind it is an unstoppable motivation for what needs to be done.

"Beyond *any* life," he says with a profound intensity. "Do you understand?"

Ava's eyes grow heavy with emotion, but her arms are stiff with resolve as she pushes him out of the kitchen and to the door. He walks to the sidewalk, and the cab is already there waiting for him. He looks back before getting into the back seat and sees Ava standing in the doorway of her studio, watching him. The corners of her mouth draw up, and he waves before closing the car door behind him.

Dread sits in the pit of his stomach as the car pulls away.

"Things are going to get worse," he says to himself.

As soon as she hears the door open, Anita looks up from behind her sketch pad, beaming at Elric.

She gives him an eyebrow wiggle.

"So, you two got along quite famously," she says, poorly imitating Elric's accent.

He rolls his eyes, "Anita."

She holds her hands in front of her in sarcastic defense. "I'm not asking for details."

He walks into his office, sits at his desk, and opens his laptop. "I wasn't going to give any."

She follows him in. "It's okay. I'll ask Ava."

"Please don't, you won't look at me the same..."

Anita winces. "Fair enough."

She sits on the couch by Elric's desk. "So, what did you need me to do?"

He swivels his computer screen toward her. Getting off the couch, she bends over the computer to inspect what he is showing her.

She inhales excitedly, "Gabriel Bello! Did you see his exhibit in New York this year? *Flor de Roja*?! It was beautiful. All these magnificent photos of this woman with this dark red gorgeous hair. She held a giant white flower in front of her face at different locations around the world. Paris, India, Scotland, Tahiti... oh man, so many more. It was a series with at least over twenty photos. You never saw the woman's face, but I swear if I saw that hair walk by me, I would know it was her."

Elric is always grateful for her love of art. "Well, that's good for me that you know his work. I need to get in touch with him about a project."

Her jaw drops. "You might get to work with Gabriel Bello? I swear if you don't bring me with you—"

"It's not that kind of project. Could you look into some contacts? I need to go check something out in my room."

Elric stands up to leave, and Anita's face grows with disdain.

"What is it?" he asks.

"I know exactly who to call. He's the one who funded the exhibit in New York—to put himself on the map as an art collector," Anita tells him.

Elric's face lights up. "Great, let's go ahead and get him on the phone."

"It's Peter Kershaw," she replies grimly, plopping into her chair.

"Perfect," he groans. "Get him on the phone anyway. Ask him if we can talk."

She pulls out her phone. "I'll do my best. If he won't talk to you, I'll call around."

"Thank you, Anita."

As he walks to his private room, he hears Anita at her desk. "Hey, Olivia! How are you doing, girl? You know me, same ole, same ole. Is your boss available? Of course. Is he getting his weekly facial?"

He closes the door behind him, walking into the mess he and Ava had left a couple of nights ago. His eyes twinkle as he stares at the drop cloth. His senses are flooded as he thinks about how her skin smells like cinnamon and honey. How the curve of her body fits so perfectly against his own. The husky sound of her voice...

Elric shakes himself out of his thoughts before leaving everything he is supposed to do and runs back to her.

Quickly and carefully, he gathers dozens of paintings, making sure they stay protected as he stows them away. He leaves the most recent painting of her out since he hasn't had a chance to seal it yet. Elric leans it against the wall, lightly running his fingers across the red mark on her face before he notices the red mishap had dripped onto the center of her chest.

"Need to fix that later," he says making a mental note.

He looks around the room and searches for the paintings from Madrid, hoping something in them would jog his memory about Gabriel. Finding the few pieces, he lays them out on the worktable. Crossing his arms, he studies the art, hoping memories frozen in time will warm the engines in his mind.

Abruptly, he hears Anita yelling. "Hey! I said I would see if he was available– No! You can't just go wherever you want!"

Quickly, he emerges from his room to see what the commotion is.

"Ma'am, could you please chill out? I said I would talk to him," Anita yells at someone in the supply room in the back of the building.

"Anita, what–"

A frazzled-looking Robyn emerges from the stockroom. Her hair is thrown into a haphazard ponytail, her makeup smudged underneath her eyes from messy application but also seemingly days of wear. Her clothing looks disheveled, yet there's an obvious but unsuccessful effort to look put together. She wears a wrinkled white button-up, halfway tucked into a pair of biker shorts with sandals. The only thing that is applied well is the ruby red lipstick perfectly filling her lips.

"There you are!" Robyn cries out, elated to see him, running up and throwing her arms around his neck.

He recoils at the embrace, confusion and distress rattling his mind.

She looks over her shoulder at Anita. Without releasing her hold on Elric, Robyn raises her brow in disapproval. "See. I told you he'd be happy to see me."

Anita wrinkles her nose, and her top lip curls up. "Elric, do you want me to do something?"

Blindsided, Eric stutters. "N-n-no. That's quite alright, Anita. How about you use my office to make those phone calls?"

Anita gives Robyn a brief scan before collecting her things.

"If you need anything, I'll have the door open. *Anything*," she says, glaring at Robyn before she turns her back.

"Thank you," he responds, too stunned to know what to do next.

Robyn smugly watches Anita walk away before turning her attention back to him.

"I can't believe you never brought me here before," she says, her eyes wandering around the room.

Reaching up, he unlocks her grip from his neck and places her arms firmly at her side.

He takes a step back, his eyes narrowing at her. "How did you even find my studio?" Shaking his head after thinking through his question. "Never mind. It doesn't even matter. You need to leave."

His tone is hard, all traces of politeness and manners vanishing from his demeanor.

"Sweetie, I came to surprise you!" Robyn reaches up to touch his face.

Cringing at the pet name, he evades her touch.

Raising an eyebrow, he studies her. Her physical application looks just as off as the energy she puts into the atmosphere. Moving toward the door, he tries to escort her out as tactfully as he can.

The goal: avoid disturbing the obviously disturbed as much as possible.

He begins to worry that this whole encounter will cause much more trouble for Ava, especially after their recent conversation about her sister.

"Robyn, I am sorry. I know it's been hard…" Elric says as he opens the front door, assuming she has been trailing behind him.

"What's in here?"

As he turns around at the question, Robyn walks into his private room.

His heart stops for a moment. During the ruckus he didn't think about closing and locking it behind him.

He gives himself a mental kick, *I have GOT to shut that door.*

"Robyn!" Shouting as he rushes over, but it is too late.

"What is this?" Walking over, she picks up the latest painting of Ava.

She stares at it menacingly, holding the painting so tightly her index finger rips through the canvas.

"Have you been cheating on me?" She asks through gritted teeth.

Elric walks up to her, slowly turning her so she faces away from the wall with more hanging works of her sister. When he has her facing the door again, he slightly tugs at the canvas to remove it from her grasp, too bewildered to catch the phrasing of her question.

"Robyn. No. I did not cheat on you," he says, talking calmly as if he is coaxing a wild animal from his home.

He places the canvas on the worktable, slyly covering up the painting of Ava in Madrid beneath it.

"Then why would you have this?" She bursts into dramatic tears, pointing at the damaged painting.

Elric continues to try to usher her out the door, lightly touching her back.

She covers her eyes with her hands, the sobs growing stronger as she shuffles along. "We have a wonderful night together…"

Finally able to maneuver her out the door, it firmly shuts behind him, locking. He silently thanks God.

She continues to cry. "We say *I love you* to each other and then I can't even get a hold of you for a month? And then I find a painting of my sister? Who does that to their girlfriend?"

He stops dead in his tracks, her words finally registering. "What?"

"You've been avoiding me. My best friend said I should just give you space. You needed time. 'Men have such a hard time with commitment nowadays.' She told me, 'If you love someone, set them free, and then they come back.' So, I did. I gave you space. But don't you think it's been enough time? Isn't it time to come back? And then to find out you've been thinking of Ava." Her face goes twisted into a series of harsher sobs. "You never even painted me!"

He shakes his head in utter disbelief, "We broke up—over a month ago now. After your parents' dinner, we met at the beach, and we broke up. *I broke up with you.*"

She abruptly stops crying in a manner that makes his skin prickle. She looks dead into his eyes and tilts her head slightly, her face conveying exactly how confused Elric feels.

"No, we didn't," she states in a monotone voice.

He stares at her, running through the conversation in his mind from that evening.

"I am sorry. But I did break up with you. And I never told you I loved you. You were going to tell me, and I stopped it. We haven't talked because we are not together, and I've refused to answer your calls," Elric reminds her, his voice low but firm.

He needs to make her understand that they are not together, no matter how abrasive it seems.

Robyn begins to smile broadly; her eyes grow wide. A stream of tears falls steadily down her cheeks.

"You love me. You just need time," she lets the tears continue to flow. "I get it. Ava is just a distraction. Pledging your love to someone is a big step. I understand why you got scared and why you feel like you would need a distraction." She moves forward slowly, resting her hand on Elric's chest over his heart. "But you and I know what's in here, and it's real, and it's forever."

Robyn closes her eyes, leaning in to kiss him. He quickly sidesteps her, removing himself from underneath her hand.

Her eyes fly open, and a scowl replaces the look of yearning from seconds before.

"I don't understand why you're being like this," she says.

He holds his hands up. "Listen, the reason I never said *I love you* is because I never loved you. I was never going to love you." His tone is firm as he desperately hopes she'll snap back to sanity.

The scowl disappears, and tears almost instantly dry from her eyes. Robyn smooths out her shirt and fixes her ponytail.

"I don't believe you," she shrugs. "I think my sister poisoned you. I'll give you your fling, but you'll come back to me. And I'll forgive you. You know why? That's what love does."

Robyn turns around and walks out the door of the studio, getting into the passenger seat of a car he doesn't recognize. He stands there dumbfounded as it drives away.

"Holy crap, she is psycho."

Elric turns to his office and sees Anita standing in the doorframe.

"How much did you hear?" Frustrated, he rubs his hands down his face.

"Uhm, the parts where she sounded insane. All of it," Anita says.

"Perfect."

"What are you going to tell Ava?"

"The truth, of course. Nothing matters but the truth."

Anita jokingly bats her eyelashes at Elric. "What a man."

"Ha. Yeah..." He groans, trying to process.

"I do have good news, though."

"Please tell me."

"Peter Kershaw said he'll meet with you. Says he'll fly down tomorrow and meet with you the day after."

"Great, easier than I expected."

"No, sorry," she snorts. "He wants us to book the hotel, five stars only, of course, a room facing the west. Then, the day he flies in, schedule him a white caviar facial at some ooh-la-la spa. Then, he wants dinner reservations for the night and the next night and lunch reservations for the day he leaves. He'll have a lunch meeting with you the second day, but his assistant says that Kershaw better not walk into a restaurant that has prices on the menu or a menu at all," Anita rolls her eyes.

"Oh, that's all?" He rubs his forehead and lets out a deep exhale. "Could you please book all that for me?"

Anita nods her head. "Absolutely."

He pulls out his wallet, handing her a credit card. "I really appreciate you."

Elric takes out his phone to text Ava and smacks his forehead.

"Anita, I don't have Ava's number. Could you send it to me?"

Anita laughs. "How do you not have her number yet? You haven't talked to her since the morning after the gala?"

"I haven't left her since then," he says, grinning.

"Oooo, okay, I see you." She shimmies while pulling out her phone, "Alright, I sent it over!"

He pulls up a new text thread:

It's Elric. Grab enough clothes for a while. Maybe all your clothes and whatever else you want or need. Meet me at my house ASAP. Can you feed Geoffrey when you get there?

"I'm heading out. I'll call you in the morning, and we can go over Kershaw's schedule," he says, giving Anita's shoulder a gentle squeeze and handing her forty dollars in cash.

"Buy yourself dinner. Don't say no."

Before he walks out the door, he turns around to look at Anita. "If I had called you in for help, what would you have done?"

"Beat. Her. Ass," she says, throwing a punch in her palm at the emphasis of each word.

"Naturally."

"Night! Tell Ava I said hi.'" She waves as he walks out the door.

Elric's phone dings as he makes his way to the library to pick up his car. He looks at the screen, and Ava's number lights up the screen.

Gotcha. I just got back to my place. See you soon.

The events of the last hour have his mind swimming in different directions, but reading Ava's words brings calm into the madness. Breaking into a jog, he makes it to his car quickly, given that he is eager to make it back home to the woman who gives him peace and meaning.

XV

ISLA MUJERES, MEXICO 1954
They walked hand in hand on the beach, which was mostly empty except for the few who sat on the sand around bonfires. The sound of the waves overlapped as they each hit the shore. Elric took a deep breath, soaking in the smooth smell of salt. Just then, a wave barreled up the shore, drenching Elric and Ava from the waist down.

Ava laughed and ran away from the wave, but Elric chased after her. As soon as she was within reach, he grabbed her around the waist from behind, running into the ocean at full speed with her in his arms.

"No!" She begged flirtatiously.

He crashed into the water, taking her with him. She jumped up and laughed hysterically. Matted, wet hair masked her face as she tried to keep her skirt up; the water-soaked fabric greatly weighed down.

"I can't believe you," she said, looking at him as he laid back, propped up on his elbows in the water.

"What are you going to do about it?" He asked with teasing eyebrows raised, challenging her .

A look of determination spread across her face as she leapt full force at him, dragging him under the next wave.

They both sat up, unable to contain their joy. He scooped her up, placing her on his lap. She, in turn, wrapped her arms around his neck. Reaching up, he drew their faces together, kissing her underneath the moonlight.

"I feel like I've known you forever," Ava said once she pulled back.

He tugged her towards him, the truth on the cusp.

She coyly pushed him off.

"I'm serious! I met you, what—ten days ago? I don't do this kind of thing. Oh my gosh, my brother would be so mad," she said.

Her face suddenly grew grim, and she looked away. Elric tucked a finger under her chin, picking it up.

"What's wrong?" He asked, sweeping the wet hair off of her face.

"I leave in two days. I go back home to my life, and you go back to yours," she sadly replied.

"Unless you don't."

She stood up while he stayed seated in the ocean. "I can't just not go home."

"Why not?"

She placed her hands on her hips, making her way to shore.

"Hey! Wait!" He called, running after her.

She stopped walking and turned back toward him. "Elric, that's literally insane. I don't even know you."

"Untrue. You just said you felt like you've known me forever."

"Oh, okay. I *feel* like I have, but I haven't," she argued.

"That's what you think..." He mumbled.

"What did you say?" She asked

"I said, what's the worst that could happen?" He quickly replied.

"You could be a murderer."

"Well, ma'am, you have very slow and poor judgment then, considering what we did last night, and the night before, and this morning..." He counted his fingers as he spoke.

Ava batted his hand away and glared at him. "Hush. I know you're not a murderer. I don't have a good reason besides the fact that it's crazy."

Elric grabbed her swatting hand. "Crazy is the only way I've learned to survive."

She covered a smile. "That is the dumbest thing I've ever heard."

He gasped exaggeratingly. "It is not. It's deep."

"No, it's really not."

"Doesn't change the fact it's true."

"Doesn't change the fact I can't stay here with you. I don't even have money to do that."

"I'm rich. It's fine," he said to her pointedly.

She shook her head at him. "Oh, okay, and I'm Helen of Troy."

She pushed him away, continuing on the path along the beach's edge. Elric followed behind her, tracing the water-dripped marks on the sand from her body with his own.

"I'm serious. You would never have to worry about money."

"You've been sleeping in a tent on the beach!" She huffed.

"Not out of necessity! Have you thought I was a hobo this whole time? Again, very poor judgment on your part. You fell in love with a hobo, Miss Ordell," Elric laughed, amused at his own joke.

Ava turned to him. A streetlamp lit her face enough for him to notice the blush that crept up her cheeks at the statement they both knew to be true.

His voice went delicately affectionate. "Come here."

She stood rooted to the ground. "No."

"Come here, please," he said sweetly, holding out his hand to her. "I love you, too."

Her shoulders relaxed a bit, and she inched toward him. "It's insane, you know."

They closed the gap, and their hands found each other.

"It's not. I promise."

She sighed heavily into his neck. "Oh, but it is."

Elric whispered into her ear. "Okay then, it's insane. Who cares? Will you stay with the man you love, who loves you back?"

She picked her head up and looked at him with those eyes forever etched into his mind.

"Fine." She tried to keep her smile stowed away.

His face beamed before picking her up and running into the street, cheering.

"Oh my gosh, you are an insane hobo! Put me down!" She laughed.

He gently set her back down and wrapped his arm around her as they walked. As they made their way back to her hotel, they talked about canceling cars, missing flights, and they wondered aloud if the hotel would let her extend her stay a few more nights so they could enjoy Mexico together for a few more days before moving on to new ventures. Soon, they found themselves at a long street of vendors. Different stalls were set up with food, clothes, jewelry, and trinkets lining the streets.

Ava grabbed his hand, dragging him over to a table of jewelry. Rings with large turquoise stones and earrings made from seashells were what initially caught her eye.

As she looked, Elric nodded to the woman who sat behind the table. She was dressed in a simple white long-sleeve dress with a large ornate necklace covering her entire collar.

"*Holá. ¿Como está?*" he said to the woman.

She quickly averted her eyes, nodding her head to him. Before Elric could say anything else, Ava shrieked.

"Look how beautiful!"

Elric turned his attention to Ava, holding a golden chain with a hand-blown glass teardrop-shaped bottle no bigger than a couple of inches. He took the small glass vial in his hand, examining it. Inside was a small red poppy, sealed at the top with a metal cap and lavender wax. His gaze was fixed on the poppy, and the entire world around him seemed to buzz with electrifying energy.

"Isn't it gorgeous?" she said, snapping Elric back to reality.

He looked at her and smiled. "Would you like it?"

"No, it's just beautiful," Ava said, taking it back and placing it on the table.

Elric picked it back up and turned to the old woman. "*¿Cuanto?*"

The woman held up five fingers, never making eye contact with him.

He took a couple hundred pesos out of his pocket, all his cash soaked.

"*Lo siento. Todo por ti. Gracias.*" Awkwardly putting the waterlogged money into her open palm.

The woman took the money, nodding her head again, never looking up at him.

He turned to Ava, and she was giddy with excitement.

"You didn't have to, but thank you."

Reaching around her neck, he clasped the necklace for her, kissing her before he released the jewelry. She rubbed the glass between her forefinger and thumb and looked at Elric gratefully.

As they kept on down the street, they continued to talk about plans. He turned around to look at the woman once more, but the place where her table stood was vacant. The old woman gone with it.

MODERN-DAY ARCATA, CALIFORNIA

Elric walks into the front door of his home and, for the first time in a long time, is not met by his four-legged companion.

"Hello?" He calls out in confusion.

"In here!" Ava shouts.

He sets his belongings in the silver bowl at the entryway door. Above it sits a painting of a beach scene. Two people entangled in the ocean under the glow of the moon.

He makes his way to the living room and sees Ava curled up on the couch with a book and a blanket over her.

Bending down to kiss her in greeting, he scans the room, "Where's Geoffrey?"

She closes her book and flips over the blanket, revealing Geoffrey curled up in the crook of her body.

"What a traitor," Elric pats the dog's head lovingly.

Geoffrey raises his head to yawn, barely wagging his tail.

"Geoffrey, the first, loved me more, too," she says as she bats his hand away, taking on the role of scratching Geoffrey's head.

"I won't argue with you," he chuckles, making his way over to the couch.

Lifting up her legs, he places them over his lap, sitting close and squishing the pup. He didn't seem to mind, minorly readjusting before burying his head. Ava leans forward to set her book down on the coffee table.

"Oh, those look great," he says, tipping his chin in the direction of the doors.

"Yeah, I don't really know what your other ones looked like. I saw them once before you destroyed them."

"Yeah... How'd things go with your mom?" He asks, laying his head back and closing his eyes.

"Good. She had a lot of questions, but I think I covered myself really well. Thank god she doesn't know Anita."

Yawning, Ava stretches and crosses her arms behind her head. "What about you? Any luck tracking down Gabriel?"

"Yes and no," Elric says, never lifting his head. "Great news, there's only one degree of separation between Gabriel and myself. Bad news, the man who can get me to him is... what was it Anita called him? Right, an ass hat."

"Oh," Ava sighs, ready to return to square one to find Gabriel.

He pats her legs in comforting reassurance. "It's not a problem. He's motivated by money and thinking he can outsmart people. I'll give one and let him think he did the other."

He opens his eyes and sits up straight, making eye contact with Ava. "But there is something else."

"What is it?" She sits up, sensing his energy.

"Robyn came to the studio. I've never even taken her there, so she researched enough to find it."

She stares at him, distressed. "And what happened?"

"Ava," he says, rubbing his eyes. "She walked in and acted like we were still together. Hugging me, trying to kiss me. Going on about how we are in love."

"I'm sorry, what?" She pulls her legs off of Elric, sitting up straighter. "You were clear when you broke up with her, right?"

"Very clear. That's not even as bad as it got. She saw the painting of you from the first time we met. This time. She was angry, saying you poisoned me, and I could have a fling with you, but ultimately, I'm going to go back to her. She was so unhinged during the whole encounter, from beginning to end. I've never seen her like that."

Ava stands up off the couch and begins to pace between the living room and the kitchen. "That doesn't even sound like something she would do."

"I know."

"Where's my phone?" She stops mid-pace.

"It's right here." Reaching forward, picking up the phone off the coffee table, Elric holds it out to her.

She takes it, unlocks it, and begins to type out a message.

"Ava," he calls.

She stares at her phone, typing without acknowledging him.

"Ava..." He leans forward.

"What?" She looks up, her thumbs still moving across the screen.

"What are you doing?"

"I'm texting my sister."

He stands up and moves over to her, gently tugging the phone out of her hands and placing it on the coffee table.

"To say what?"

Grabbing her hair, she twists it to the side. "Well, it started off with 'What the hell are you doing,' then it went to 'Leave Elric alone,' then it went to 'Hey, we need to talk.'"

He stares at her, just waiting for her to process her feelings out loud.

She looks at him and sighs. "You know this sort of thing seems very trivial considering we are dealing with death and demons on the doorstep."

Placing his hand on her cheek, he slowly runs his thumb over her cheek.

"Listen. I am confused and concerned by the interaction with your sister. Something wasn't right, But you are right. It is trivial considering everything else. I just needed to tell you."

"It's so confusing. Everything else, I mean. My death, finding Gabriel, Faye... they are all today's problems. But Robyn feels like a *right-now* problem. This was already complicated because of our relationship and because of your relationship with her."

She walks away from Elric and into the middle of the living room, crossing her arms, obviously angry.

"You know, if you could have kept it in your pants, maybe this wouldn't have been a problem," Ava snaps.

Elric raises his eyebrows in disbelief. "You think that was the issue?"

"I mean, a little bit, yeah. You say that you wait for me, but I never asked you to give up your whole eternity to do that. *You* decide that. But what happens while you wait for me? You get bored? Find someone to bang it out with or fall in love with? How long do you string these women along, Elric? How many have there been? How many have there been just in *this* cycle as you waited for me?" She throws her arms up in irritation. Her words come out fast and with a searing bite to them.

He shakes his head and rakes his fingers through his hair.

"You're upset. Understandably so. You've had to process a lot in the last couple of days, and I'm certain it hasn't all been fleshed out yet. The Robyn thing throws a pain in it I didn't intend."

Walking to the fridge, Elric opens the door and pulls out a drink.

Leaving the door open to block Ava from view, he stares into the fridge. "This cycle, it's only been Robyn. But for complete transparency, yes, there have been other women."

Elric wants Ava to think he doesn't want to see her, but truly, Elric doesn't want her to see *him*. He takes a moment to try and regain control of the little bits of anger seething beneath the surface before making eye contact again. But anger continues to seep out from the roots of shame he carries, struggling with whether or not he has been unfaithful to Ava or not. Although he tries, the anger he has kept under lock and key for decades begins to beat at the door of his emotions. He shuts his eyes tightly and breathes deeply.

Bang.

How many years have I been alone? He thinks.

Bang.

How often have I beat myself up over how I have spent my time?

Bang.

How many times have I regretted this curse I have put on our semblance of a so-called life?

Bang.

"You just spend your time sleeping across the globe as I die every so often?" Ava spits out, immediately covering her mouth with her hands.

The door holding in his anger explodes into a thousand fragments, unable to contain it any longer.

Closing the fridge, he slams the drink down. Standing behind the countertop, he stares at Ava still rooted in the middle of the living room behind the coffee table. The furniture divide between them feels more like miles than the mere few feet it actually is.

"I don't keep a log of who, when, and how many there have been if that's what you're asking for," he retorts, "there is no little black book I can give you."

She scoffs. "Ha. Nice to know there's enough to have a whole log."

"Do you want to hear about the more memorable ones?" He badgered.

Moving over to the couch, she throws herself onto it with her back now towards Elric.

"Brigitte in Germany—she sure was dominant. Oh, Malee, this beautiful woman I met on the beach in Koh Phi Phi. She was probably the most flexible." His words fired out in anger quicker than he could stop them.

He walks to the center of the living room so he can face her, all reservations of causing hurt gone.

Ava looks directly into Elric's eyes.

Her stare is hard, and her expression cold. "Please continue."

"Delphine, this beautiful French woman. She definitely showed me a thing or two. Don't even get me started on my time in Ibiza, a drunk blur of women. If I painted that time it would be my Bokeh Era of art. All just blurred spots of women. Can't tell where one ends and one begins." Elric forces a dry laugh.

Ava's eyes well up and she quickly presses the palms of her hands to her eyes, extinguishing the tears threatening to spill.

She throws her hands out in front of her. "What a life you've lived then, Elric. It must be nice to keep me on the hook. Knowing that when you need something easy and not quite so elusive, here I am, waiting for you to trick me back into a relationship with you. You know me so well, so it has to be effortless. You must have perfected it over the years," Ava accuses.

He scoffs. "You figured it out, Ava."

Walking past her, he refuses to make eye contact, moving down the hallway and into his room.

He changes into a pair of running shorts and shoes and grabs a light sweatshirt from his closet. Slamming the doors shut, the closet hinges rattle.

"Be here or don't when I get back. That's your decision. I am not going to keep you anywhere you don't want to be. Especially with someone who has *tricked* you!" Elric yells into the living room.

There is no response, and the house is dead silent. Reaching the front door, he stops. His hand freezes on the doorknob before turning it. He rests his forehead against the wood, wishing he could erase every word that just escaped.

"Ava–" Elric murmurs, unsure where any reparations could even begin at this moment.

As he opens the door, he hears a muffled, stifled sob. He closes the door, sealing the emotion behind it, before taking off and jogging into the forest.

XVI

H "Don't come back!" The madame yelled at Elric as she pushed him out of the doors of the brothel.

He stumbled out onto the dirt road, his face hitting the ground with a loud smack. Elric rolled over onto his side and spat out a mixture of blood and dust. He reached up and touched his lip before holding up blood-stained fingers in front of his eyes. Flopping onto his back, he laughed loudly in his drunken stupor. His shirt lay across him untucked, and the leather tie closures on the front of his pants sat completely undone. The madame walked back into the brothel, shutting off all the noise and activity from the outside world.

Elric briefly propped himself up on his elbows, staring at the darkened entrance of the building, and shouted. "One of your whores said she could make me forget! I swear to you, they made me remember my pain more! I should get my money back!"

He began to laugh again and laid back down, staring up into the sky. Dawn had just started to hit the crest of the fjord, the reflection of light against the water

179

brightening up the streets.

He stood up and wobbled before finding his footing, patting around his body and looking for his coin purse.

"If you could be so kind," he bellowed out, "to return my coin, which is rightfully mine!"

A window up above him opened up, and a woman with long blonde hair stuck her head outside.

"Johanna! Has the fair maiden come to help me?" he asked in his drunken charm.

He reached up, and the woman sneered, turning her back to grab something off the table.

"Finally, someone with a mind."

As soon as Elric finished his sentence, Johanna poured out a tankard on the top of his head.

He spit whatever had made it into his mouth out and wiped his eyes.

"Is that your mead or your piss! Because I am certain it is the same thing!" He screamed.

Johanna blew a kiss before shutting the window closed again.

He wiped off what he could as he made his way down the street. The small village stirred with the creeping sun.

Elric had been traveling for years after his second encounter with an Ava reincarnate. Without Geoffrey to help sort it out, he still felt he was going insane. How could any of this really be reality? When he had met Ava in Skryne, Geoffrey swore it was an act of God to reunite the two. Ava died, and then Geoffrey soon after. He had assumed that would be the end of seeing another Ava—until it happened again. But Elric couldn't stay away from her even if it was all a delusion. He pursued her, and she died again. After that he no longer wanted to try and find her or a way to break whatever he was. He decided he was just going to live until he didn't live any longer, if it was possible.

Tripping over an upturned stone in the road, he fell squarely into a bush, flat on his back. He struggled for a moment to try and stand upright but instead thought it better to succumb to the alcohol-induced sleep.

"Hello?" A gentle voice called out.

Elric came to with the sun shining directly over him, making it difficult to open his eyes more than slits.

"Hello?" The voice repeated a little louder, this time accompanied by the poking of a staff in his side.

He sat up, covered in sweat, smelling the stale, dirty mead on himself.

"What is the time?" He asked, crawling out of the bush and coming face to face with a brown and white spotted cow.

Startled, Elric fell backward, ending up in the same position as before.

"Bloody hell," he cried out, pushing himself up again.

"Let me help," the voice said, reaching out and grabbing his hand. This assistance finally got him out of the bush into an upright position.

He covered his not-yet-adjusted eyes and squinted at the figure next to the cow. Elric rubbed at his eyes furiously, willing them to focus.

"Gratitude, mate. I would have been stuck in that bush until the next rising of the sun."

That well-known laugh rang out, and Elric froze in place, quickly sobering up, and refusing to open his eyes and look at her.

"Ava."

"Apologies, have we met? I would have remembered it, I'm sure." Ava asked.

Opening his eyes, a mix of elation and doom sat in the pit of his stomach.

"Uh, no. You and your kin have been mentioned. A fine farm to purchase milk." Promptly making up the lie based on her cow.

She laughed once more. "I did not think our presence was that well known, but it is a small town."

"Aye, it is a small town," he sighed, "Sometimes you never know how small."

"You look like you have had a bit of a rough go. I was just walking the herd back. Come with me. I can fill your belly with food and water. It looks like you need it." She smiled all too graciously.

He looked up into the sky, cursing fate. "'Tis a cruel joke you play."

Ava looked at him curiously. "What?"

Finally, he looked into the eyes he had avoided the entire conversation and smiled. "It would be the day I look like a fool, and a beautiful woman would find and aid me."

Finding solace in those emerald green eyes; Elric's heart fluttered, following the madness in the form of true love.

MODERN-DAY ARCATA, CALIFORNIA

Elric runs until his heart pounds in his ears. He runs until his body shakes with exhaustion. He runs until his head is clear, and he rebuilds the cage that keeps his anger at bay.

He rounds the corner to his block, shame and dread latching onto him. The heavy reality hits him that she may not be there.

"Ava and I finally have a chance to maybe end this curse, and I screw it up," Elric chastises himself as he jogs the final stretch to his house. His lungs burn, and he takes it as punishment, and so he pushes harder.

He keeps his eyes trained on his feet, not wanting to look up in fear that her car won't be parked in the driveway. He gets to his mailbox and throws his arm over it, breathing heavily.

"When you catch your breath, you can look up," he says.

Elric's chest returns to normal as his breathing slows. He lets out one final slow breath and looks up into his driveway, seeing her car parked in the same place as before.

He sprints up the walkway, swinging the door wide open and leaving it that way.

"Ava?!" He yells.

He doesn't see her on the sofa and runs into his bedroom, finding it empty as well.

"Ava?!" He calls for her again, and this time, he hears the doors to the backyard slide open.

Running into the living room, he sees Ava walking in, Geoffrey trotting in behind her. Her eyes are swollen, and the tip of her nose is red.

"Ava-"

"Elric-"

"Go ahead-"

"Go-"

They shift uncomfortably at the awkward interruptions, both unclear of who needs to start.

He clears his throat. "Please let me go first."

She closes the door, gathering her oversized cardigan around her tightly.

"I am so sorry for anything I said before to intentionally hurt you. I feel like I made everything so much worse because of Robyn. It's an insane complication that is not even just '*too close to home*,'" he says, holding his fingers up in air quotes, "It *is* actually home– your family right now in this life. But everything about the women... I am sorry I said any of that. This existence is hard and lonely, and it's not an excuse. But sometimes, it's easier to drown in people than to let my emotions swallow me whole, especially while I wait for you. Which I know you didn't ask me to do."

Elric approaches Ava, extending his arm toward her, wanting to touch her but he drops his hand at the last moment.

He takes a step back, placing his hands in the pockets of his sweatshirt. "I'll never not wait for you. It's not out of obligation, and it isn't out of a need. I could run into you one life and keep going. Never engage with you and go to another country. But I don't because my desire is to be with you. My desire is you."

They let the silence settle in for a few minutes as Elric sways back and forth, and Ava moves to a wingback chair in front of the window. She sits down cross-legged in the chair and holds the sweater around her body like a safety blanket.

"I provoked you because I'm overwhelmed," she says, swiping her hands over her eyes. "I'm me, but I don't feel like me. I feel like a hundred different versions of myself, and I guess it's because I am?"

He stops swaying, setting his posture to let her know he has her full attention.

"My brain is very full," she dryly laughs, leaning back into the chair and picking at the skin around her thumbnail. "I don't care that there were other women. I care, but I don't. Do I love the idea? Absolutely not. But this isn't exactly normal circumstances, and I don't expect you to live on a mountaintop alone until I'm around."

She looks up, clasping her hands in front of her. "I am so sorry, though, for the things I said. I didn't mean any of it; this is just a lot."

He walks toward her tentatively, hoping that his presence will be received. Ava stands up and meets him in the middle of the room. Still, neither one of them touches the other.

"No one has ever meant anything. Nowhere on the same plane of existence as what you are to me," he says to her.

Ava closes the gap between them, laying her head on his chest. He wraps her in his arms, and they just stand there, their hearts soon beating in rhythm. A steady rate of ease increases between them.

"By the way, the flexible woman in Thailand is you. You just haven't seen that picture yet."

Ava punches him. "Shut up."

Elric shrugs. "I keep that one in a secret place. *That* one is only for me."

She rolls her eyes and picks her head up off his chest. "I was in your little workshop, art studio shed thingy in the back before you got home."

"Oh yeah? What did you find? Hopefully not the Thailand painting," Elric jokes.

"A painting of me with cows. I didn't remember that one yet. And then I touched it, and I did." She looks at him with a raised eyebrow.

He chuckles uncomfortably as his face grows red. "Did you know when you met me?"

Ava laughs, washing away any of the tension left between them. "Did I know that in our small town in Hallstatt of a couple hundred people, you were the drunkard thrown out of the brothel? Yes, I knew."

He clears his throat. "Not my finest moment, I'll admit. But you still ran away with me."

"But I still ran away with you," she smiles, "I'll do it every single time."

Light gradually pours into the room, landing on the couple entangled in bed. Elric slowly begins to wake, stretching out his legs, careful not to wake Ava, who is lying on his arm. His foot nudges Geoffrey, and the small pup wakes up startled, growling before circling under the covers and finding sleep once again. Elric turns his head to face Ava and can't help but be entranced by her. Their bond has never wavered over the centuries, and his love for her never faltered. He delicately brushes hair off her cheek and holds his hand in place, simply grateful to be touching her again. He never wants to forget the feeling of her skin.

Slowly, he pulls his arm out from underneath her head, trying not to rouse her. He kisses her lightly on the forehead before fully departing from their bed. He stands, stretching out his arms high above his head, before making his way to the bathroom.

"Where are you going?"

Elric turns to the groggy voice in bed. Ava is lying on her stomach, her knee bent and tucked up. Her eyes are still closed, but a restful expression sits easily on her face.

He walks to her side of the bed and kneels down next to her. Ava turns on her side towards him, opening only one eye.

He holds her hand in both of his.

"I have to go meet the man who may have a connection to Gabriel," he says into her hand.

She opens both of her eyes, and a mischievous smile spreads across her face. Suddenly, she grabs him around the neck and grunts as she pulls him on top of her.

Ava closes her eyes and keeps the hold around his neck while wrapping her legs around his waist. Elric lays his head on her chest.

"Or you could stay here and cuddle me," she suggests.

"If you don't let go of me, I probably will."

"Alright, then. I won't let go," Ava says as she squeezes him tighter with her thighs.

He sighs. "But I have to. If this one meeting brings us closer to spending every morning like this, then I have to leave this bed today."

She drops her legs and grabs his face, lifting it to hers.

"Fine," she groans.

"I'll be back as soon as I can."

He kisses her before lifting himself off of her. Geoffrey swiftly replaces Elric on Ava's chest.

She nuzzles the top of the dog's head and pulls the blanket up over them.

Walking into the bathroom, he flips the switch to bring the lights to life.

While still lying in bed, gently stroking Geoffrey, Ava yells, "I'm going to the library. There's an event planning meeting for a children's reading week. But I'm going to resign for the foreseeable future. I'm just not sure what our future looks like, and work seems very…"

"Mundane?" he finishes as he turns on the shower.

"Basically. A little pointless, honestly. We have immortal issues and a crazy demon after us. I'm just supposed to go plan rainbow reading circles right now?" Ava sighs. "I have a few grand saved up, and that'll float me until we figure this out."

Elric pops his head out the bathroom door, laughing, with a toothbrush and mouth full of foam.

"Why are you laughing?" she asks.

"To put it plainly, I am still very rich. Disgustingly so," Elric says nonchalantly.

He disappears back into the bathroom to spit and rinse his mouth out.

"How? How does no one catch onto you?" She asks, slightly sitting up.

He shrugs. "I put it in a trust. I have an accountant I work with, and it's much easier now that everything can be done over the phone and on the Internet. No one really has to see my face except every so often. It's something that I can feign has been passed down to the next generation, with a family trust I set up so long ago. I have it tied up in properties, different investments, and selling art as assorted anonymous artists."

"I guess if you're going to be alive forever, you may as well have it work for you," she says.

Elric winks. "Exactly."

As he steps into the shower, she comes into the bathroom, pulling out her toothbrush and toothpaste from a bag on the counter.

"How are you feeling about the Robyn situation?" He asks, lathering his hair with shampoo.

"Weird," she says before putting her toothbrush in her mouth.

"I'm sorry."

"It's fine, not your fault. Well, kind of," she says, waving her toothbrush and spitting into the sink.

Pulling her hair to the side, she begins to braid it over her shoulder.

"Like we said, it's a trivial thing right now compared to everything else we are trying to figure out. A sister losing it over a man is literally so inconsequential when faced with death from a supernatural entity who has it out for us."

He bends his head under the falling water and grunts in agreement, letting the water run over his face.

"Do you want coffee?" She asks as she opens the shower door.

Elric lifts his head out of the stream of water and looks into that emerald green.

"Yes, thank you. I'll be out in a minute."

Ava places her hand under his chin, beckoning him closer. He leans in, briefly meeting her for a kiss before she walks away.

They enjoy cups of coffee with their legs intertwined on the couch, and their life feels normal for a moment. Just like any other couple, getting ready for the day. Elric takes a deep breath and lets his mind wander briefly, letting himself be hopeful for a future.

As Elric watches her car disappear around the corner of the block, his phone chimes off with a text from Anita.

Ass hat texted. Said he wants to do brunch instead of lunch. I called my friend, the maître d' at The Northern Markey. Res @ 11. Sorry for late notice. His assistant JUST called me. My friend's name is Benny. Ask for him at the front he said he would give you the hook up.

Elric groaned in annoyance when he saw the current time. 10:30.

On my way now. Thank you so much, Anita. You're getting a raise. You deserve it. Is there a dress code for this place?

Anita texts back instantaneously.

LOL Yes. Business casual, at least. Please leave paint-stained clothes at home.

Elric looks down at his shirt, which is covered in blue and green oil paint stains, and his jeans, which are torn at the knees.

"Agh!" He shouts, irritated.

Running back inside the house, he quickly opens his closet, scanning for the very few clothes he has that aren't ruined with paint. A pair of olive slacks hidden far back in the recesses of his closet seems to be the winner. He pulls a black t-shirt off a hanger, accidentally breaking off the hook, causing the t-shirt to drop to the floor.

"Damn it," he says, picking the t-shirt up and carefully grabbing a hanger holding a gray tweed jacket.

Elric throws on his clothes and the first pair of non-sneakers he can find in his closet. He takes a quick look at himself in the mirror and shakes his head, pushing his hair off his forehead.

"That'll do, I guess," he says to Geoffrey, sitting at his feet, wagging his tail.

Hurriedly he makes his way through the house, gathering his keys and wallet along the way, praying he makes it to the restaurant before Peter does. He doesn't need this man in any more of an entitled mood than he was born with.

XVII

E lric rushes through the doors of The Northern Market, tapping the screen of his phone to check the time. He sighs a breath of relief as he reads 10:52.

Waiting at the empty hostess stand, willing someone to hurry back, he looks around the room, wondering why he has never been here before. The restaurant is all atrium with large window panels from top to bottom. Plants and flowers of all varieties hang from the ceilings and walls. Green leaves contrast with bright purple and orange petals. Dark square mahogany pillars covered in ferns and pothos tower over the tables, reaching the ceiling of matching wooden beams. He stares at a table that has a pillar of dark and neon green colored leaves hanging on one side and, on the other, a large bird of paradise with orange flowers in full bloom. He makes a mental note to bring Ava back here so he can make a painting of her in this specific setting.

"Good morning, sir. Do you have a reservation?"

Elric drew his attention back to the hostess booth and the small blonde woman, dressed all in black, standing behind it.

"Good morning. Hope your day is going well," he politely smiles. "I was told to ask for Benny."

"One moment please," the woman says and walks away.

Within a minute, a young, tall, dark-skinned man with a clean-shaven face and head greets Elric.

"Benny," he says, holding out his hand for Elric. "You must be Anita's friend. Mr. Ferron?" he asks, his voice a smooth baritone.

Elric grips his hand firmly. "Yes. Thank you so much for doing this on such short notice. I really appreciate it. Mr. Kershaw isn't here yet, is he?"

"No sir, your guest hasn't arrived yet. And it's no problem! I'd do anything I can for Anita. If you'd follow me."

Benny leads him through the restaurant towards the back and into a private room. He slides open stained glass French doors, revealing a long white marbled twelve-person table. The wall opposite the door features a gentle waterfall cascading down the entire glass surface. The falling water distorts the view of the rest of the restaurant beyond that barrier.

"The chef owes me a favor and is creating a selective menu for this brunch," Benny tells Elric as he pulls out the chair at the head of the table.

"This is too much on such short notice. I appreciate the lengths you're going to," he says, completely grateful.

Benny chuckles. "Like I said, I'd do anything for Anita."

He watched Benny's face light up as he said her name.

"How do you two know each other?" He asks as he sits down.

Benny clears his throat. "We met in art school, in a human forms class."

Elric's mouth grows into a wide smile. "You're an artist?" He asks eagerly.

"The stereotypical starving artist," Benny replies.

Elric stands up, taking his wallet out of his back pocket and pulling out folded bills. He holds them out for Benny to take.

Benny shakes his head. "I don't take handouts, sir. But thank you."

"It's not a handout. This is for setting this all up on such short notice. Your restaurant was busy, so I know this wasn't an easy thing to pull off. So, please take this as a tip and for the copious amount of alcohol I need you to serve my guest."

Benny takes the money without looking at it and nods his head. "Thank you, sir. I appreciate it. And I'll get your guest as drunk as you need him. You just tell me when to stop."

He turns to walk out the door when Elric stops him. "Benny."

Benny stands at the door and waits.

"Next time you're off, let Anita know you're coming to the studio, and I'll meet you there. If there's one person who can create art, it's a starved artist. But an artist who yearns for someone, that's when genius happens."

He smirks at Elric and shakes his head. "I'll be there, and thank you," he says with genuine earnest.

He walks out and returns with a golden beverage cart that carries a pitcher of water, clean glasses filled with ice, and a bucket of the same with a bottle of champagne and a glass vase of red poppies. Elric doesn't notice.

"Would you like any other cocktails?" He asks.

"You can bring a Bloody Mary in here when Mr. Kershaw arrives. Thank you," Elric replies.

Benny walks out of the room, closes the restaurant chatter behind him, and leaves Elric to wait for Peter alone.

Elric takes out his phone to place it on silent and sees he has a few missed text messages. The first is from Anita, letting him know Peter's assistant said his massage would make him late.

Great... Elric replies.

He moves on to see the next text message is from Ava, and his eyes light up.

Wish we were together.

His face flushes as he responds.

As soon as I finish this up. Hopefully, it won't take more than an hour.

As Elric waits for a response, the sliding doors open, and Benny stands in the doorway.

He promptly moves to the side, "Mr. Ferron, your guest."

Peter stands at the threshold, scanning the room. He tilts down his blue-tinted sunglasses that match his powder blue slacks and matching suit jacket. Under his unbuttoned jacket is an oversized white silk shirt only buttoned to the middle of his bare chest. Elric gets up from the table to greet Peter and gives a nod in thanks to Benny.

Peter walks in, completely ignoring everyone, assuming the seat that had been occupied. Elric keeps his back to Peter as his lips press into a tight line.

A brief glimpse of irritation crosses Benny's face before he reins it back and replaces it with customer service courtesy. "I'll be right back with that Bloody Mary."

The doors slide behind them, and Elric takes a page from Benny's book and does his best to bring forth his courteous side. He assumes the seat to the left of his guest and pours them both glasses of water.

"Peter, I am really so appreciative that you would take time out of your busy schedule to come meet with me," he says, placing a glass of water in front of him.

"The champagne, please, and this *is* brunch correct? Then I should have a *brunch* cocktail right?" Peter berated.

Elric starts to pour a glass just as soon as a server walks in with a Bloody Mary and sets it down in front of Peter.

"Gentlemen, your first course will be out shor-"

"What the hell is this? Do I look like someone who would drink a tomato juice cocktail? This shirt is silk Dolce and Gabbana. Spill one drop of that you'll be paying for this shirt with months of wages."

The server stumbled over his words. "I-I-I am so sorry. What can I get you instead?"

Peter leans back in his chair and crosses his legs, staring at Elric. "French Martini." His tone more demanding than normal.

The server nods and quickly heads to the bar to get his new drink order started.

"Serving a Bloody Mary is like putting lipstick on a pig. Doesn't make you look refined," Peter quips.

Elric clears his throat. "Yes, good point. As I was saying, I'm appreciative. Anita says you hosted the gallery for Gabriel Bello. He's an old acquaintance I've been eager to get in contact with again. If you would be so kind as to give me his contact information-"

"This champagne is not great," he says, cutting Elric off.

"I'm sorry about that. Your drink should be coming soon," Elric dryly responds. "Gabriel is an old acquaint-"

Interrupted again, four servers come marching in with plates and drinks as the first course is served. Elric clenches his fist and slowly releases the tension from his hands.

"Fresh oysters," one of the waiters calls out as they all exit the room and shut the doors once more.

"Hm," Peter grunts as he examines the small plate in front of him. "At least the presentation is refined."

"Yes, quite." Try as he might, it proves harder than Elric thought to keep the annoyance out of his tone. "Peter, I am on a tight schedule and need that contact info."

"Nothing is too tight to ignore a good meal. Please. Eat," Peter says in that same demanding tone.

Feeling at his mercy, Elric does all he can do and eats. He indulges Peter by asking about his ventures. He knows one way to butter him up is to let him hear the sound of his own voice.

The second and third courses of lobster Benedict and matcha French toast came and went. Peter speaks of his newest additions to his art collections, his latest business conquests and what he refers to as various "triumphs" in the bedroom. Elric listens to him drone on and on and politely nods every so often, giving the pretense of actively listening, with an, *Oh yeah?* or *Really*.

Servers walk in, announcing the final course. "Dragon fruit panna cotta parfait and sorbet mimosas. Enjoy."

They finally finish the last course in silence, but as soon as the last drop of mimosa is gone, Elric starts to press.

"Peter, Gabriel's contact info-"

Peter waves him off. "Yes, yes, I heard you the first few times."

He wipes his mouth with the cloth napkin resting next to his plate and throws it back on the table. Leaning back in his chair, he rests folded hands on his crossed legs.

"I get what I can do for you. But what can you do for me? My time and presence are not free."

"I would never mean to take advantage of your time or... presence," Elric clears his throat, trying to swallow a laugh, "but I do believe I paid for your way here, your stay, your food, and your extracurriculars."

"You're correct, but none of this is tangible beyond a moment. I want something lasting from my new *friend*," Peter says the last word with a hint of mockery.

Elric grits his teeth. "I have a feeling you came here with something tangible in mind."

Peter smiles and runs his hand over his jacket, smoothing out the lapels. "Of course I did. I always have a goal in mind. I set my eyes on what I want, and I manifest it. And I always get it. You'll do well to remember that, Elric."

"What do you want?" All reservations about faking kindness are gone.

Elric knew he wouldn't come out of this without having to all but physically kiss Peter's ass, but he didn't anticipate Kershaw being able to get under his skin this much. Elric had also never been in the predicament he was currently in with Ava, so his fuse may have been shorter than normal.

Peter's smile broadens. "You told me last time none of your pieces were for sale. Not for me anyway." He takes off his glasses, setting them down on the table. "It seems you were right. None of them are for sale for me because I won't be buying anything. You'll be gifting them to me."

He leans forward with his elbows propped on the table, resting his chin on his clasped hands. Elric slides his tongue over the front of his teeth and shifts his jaw until it cracks. He sits up straighter in his chair and pulls his phone out, placing it on top of the table. The phone screen lights up, showing an unread text from Ava. Elric leans forward to read it.

We are doing what we need to do now to finally spend our lives together. Nothing else matters. Beyond this life.

A calm washes over Elric, and the corners of his mouth lift.

"Excuse me? Do you not want to hear what it is that you're giving me?" Peter asks, clearly irritated.

Elric brings up a closed hand, tucking it under his chin, a slight smile still dancing on his lips. "Of course. What will I be bestowing upon you?"

Peter fidgets with the hem of his shirt for a moment, annoyed that it seems he is no longer getting under Elric's skin.

"*Sea of Red*. And one of the dream girl."

Pushing his chair back, Elric stands up, moving past Peter and towards the door. "Fine. Let's go. Your driver can follow me to the studio."

Peter's jaw drops at the ease of the ask and he shuffles his seat backward, no sarcastic comment coming to mind quickly enough.

Elric sends out two texts from his phone.

One goes to Anita: *I'll be at the studio in 20. Could you call Benny and pay, tip 50%. And could you wrap up Sea of Red?*

The second text to Ava: *And any thereafter. Meet me at the studio in 20?*

Both texts receive immediate responses: Anita with a double thumbs up and Ava saying, *Of course.*

Peter swiftly stands and collects his things, following him out the door.

They pass Benny on the way out, and Elric stops to talk to him.

He extends his hand to Benny for a shake. "Sir, thank you so much for your service today. This was more than extraordinary. Anita should be calling to pay for everything. And I expect to see you at the studio sometime soon?"

"Absolutely," Benny replies brightly.

Elric smiles but quickly loses it as he turns back to Peter. "Alright, let's get this done."

Arriving at the studio, Elric pulls into a spot along the street with Peter's driver right behind him. He holds open the door to the studio, letting Peter walk in with an air of arrogance over a premature win.

Anita stands behind her desk, waiting for Elric to tell her what to do next.

"Mr. Kershaw," Anita says in a reluctant greeting.

Peter ignores her and looks around the studio. "Take me to your room and let me take my spoil. Maybe something else will pique my interest."

He walks ahead of Elric to the locked door, and Elric stays a couple steps behind. He leans over the desk to Anita, and she grimaces.

"Who talks like that?" She asks with her nose wrinkled like she smells something bad.

"Men who have nothing good to offer the world." He rubs his eyes. "Is she here yet?"

"Yes, would you like me to get her?"

"Elric!" Peter yells louder than necessary, standing only a few feet away.

"Can you tell her to come in there in like five minutes?" He whispers.

Anita tries to cover her abhorrence toward Peter but doesn't do well. "Sure thing."

"Thank you." He pats her hand before walking away. Elric puts his thumbprint on the deadbolt lock, opening the door. But before he can even move aside for Peter, he gets shouldered out of the way by the man.

Kershaw walks directly to the wall filled with the hanging portraits of Ava, brazenly shopping through the lot, rubbing his hands together in wicked glee. Elric holds his hands behind his back and follows him in.

"As you can see here, Anita has prepared the *Sea of Red* for you." Motioning his head towards the worktable where the painting lays covered in layers of tissue paper, foam, bubble wrap, and plastic.

Peter doesn't even turn to look and gives him a simple wave of his hand behind his back as he continues to shop the wall.

Elric hears light footsteps behind him, and he turns to see Ava standing in the doorway, her hair down and wearing a light blue sundress. His whole body fills with an ethereal feeling and it takes everything in him not to run to her. Ava raises her hand in greeting, opening her mouth to speak. Elric quickly puts a finger to his lips and gestures for her to come to him. She walks over to him, her subtle, captivating smile putting one on his face, too. He wraps his arm around her waist, bringing her in close. She, in turn, slides her arm around his shoulders, placing a kiss lightly on his cheek.

"I want the parchment, too," Peter speaks after a few silent minutes.

Before Elric can respond, Ava speaks up. "You can't have that one."

Peter laughs dryly, his focus still on the artwork.

"Elric, why is your assistant speaking for you and telling me what I can't do?"

"Peter," he calls, trying to shift his attention.

"She'll wrap this one for me as well. See to it please, *assistant*," he speaks with disdain as if any word not describing or naming himself was foul.

"Peter. This is not my assistant."

Peter turns around, blatant annoyance on his face. When he opens his eyes, and they land on Ava, his jaw drops. He turns to the art behind him and then back to Ava.

"The dream girl," he says in a low voice.

Elric's hold on Ava tightens as the satisfaction settles in. Peter could have all the copies he wants, but the tangible woman in Elric's arms will never be his.

"All those paintings were commissioned by me, so technically, they aren't anyone's but mine to give." Ava's eyes narrow, and her jaw is set. Her voice is steady and smooth as she puts Peter in his place.

Elric, although shocked at her candor, reins it in, letting her take the lead—even though that wasn't in *his* plans to do so. He merely wants to rub "The Dream Girl" in Peter's face.

Whether or not he figures out that the statement she gave is a lie is tomorrow's problem.

Peter, still shocked to see the living artwork before him, gives a haphazard attempt at sounding seductive. "You are stunning. To think if I had a woman on my arm half as beautiful as you, I'd let her commission as many portraits as she wanted." Instead, he comes across as a little inebriated, which he most likely is.

"The contact information for Gabriel Bello, please." Ava reaches into Elric's back pocket and pulls out his phone. Taking a step forward out of Elric's arm she holds the phone out for Peter to enter the information they've requested. Elric keeps his hand on the small of her back as she moves, letting his muse take the reins.

"One painting isn't worth my time or knowledge." Peter smiles wryly.

She crosses her arms. "That's fine. Leave empty-handed. We can find other resources. Someone not so needy." She looks over her shoulder. "Elric?"

"Sounds good to me."

She looks back at Peter. "Thanks for coming. You can leave the *Sea of Red*. I hope you enjoyed your stay in Arcata."

They stand to the side, waiting for Peter to make his way out of the room. Peter looks at the wrapped painting, at the couple, and then back to the painting. He digs into his too-tight slacks aggressively to get to his phone. He does some work on it and shoves it back in his pocket.

Furious at his obvious defeat, Peter speaks quickly. "I've sent you the number of the curator for his current exhibit in Montreal. Very exclusive. The opening is this weekend, actually."

"Wait," Ava stops him as Peter moves towards the painting. "You don't even have Gabriel's direct contact information?"

Peter rolls his eyes with great disdain. "He changed his number after the exhibit I promoted in New York. He said I was difficult to work with."

She laughs unapologetically in his face. "Sounds about right."

"Great. Now, if you wouldn't mind," Elric says, pointing to the door, "Take my painting and get the hell out of my studio."

Peter huffs, roughly grabbing the painting and tearing off a protective foam block on the corner in the process. As he walks by Elric, he turns his nose up and makes his way out the door—and out of their lives, Elric hopes.

Ava hears the outside door slam shut, and she turns to Elric, giggling, her cheeks rosy. "Did I sound legit? Like I knew what I was talking about?"

He places his hand on her cheek, kissing her triumphantly.

"Yes, you sounded very legit." He looks at her proudly as she pulls back.

"I'm sorry about your painting," Ava says, her tone thick with sympathy.

"It's fine. Bigger picture. Changing our future. I could always paint another one," he responds while rubbing the back of her hand with his thumb.

Suddenly, a throat clearing draws both of their attention behind them.

"You won't have to," Anita says, slightly bouncing up and down, wringing her hands.

"I won't have to what?" Elric asks.

"I just knew that's what Peter would ask for as soon as we set up the meeting. So, remember when that Saint John's Holy, whatever it is church wanted a copy of the *Sea of Red?* I called the church as soon as all the plans with Peter were confirmed. I asked if I could have it and told them it was an artistic emergency. I let them know that I would get them another copy ASAP. So..." Anita clapped her hands together, her smile reaching her eyes as they crinkled at the corners.

She disappeared momentarily, and Elric could see her rustling behind her desk. Anita walked back, dancing with the *Sea of Red* in her hands.

"Peter won't know unless he removes the glass in the frame or if a real artist actually looks at the painting. But let's hope that doesn't happen. He doesn't deserve to own any of your art," Anita explains, proud of her scheme.

Elric lets go of Ava and shakily takes the painting out of Anita's hands, setting it down on the table. Taking Anita by surprise, he wraps her in a full embrace. She puts her arms around Elric as well and must sense the tremble of his shoulders. She peeks around him, as much as possible, given how much he towers over her, and meets Ava's gaze. Standing there with her hand covering her mouth, Ava's eyes glisten.

She mouths, "Thank you," and Anita nods back, unsure where this wave of gratitude is coming from.

He pulls back and holds Anita by her shoulders, his eyes red and wet. "That is a painting of my best friend. The first painting of my best friend. I was willing to give it up, but it would have caused me pain to do so. But you, *my friend*, you saved me some pain. Which I often don't get to evade. Thank you."

Anita looks back and forth between the two, and the realization of something bigger going on hits her.

"Of course." She speaks reverently, trying to respect the delicate moment.

Anita watches Ava as she walks up to Elric, and he takes a step back toward her without even looking. Their hands find each other like a magnetic force only the two of them can feel.

"Can someone tell me what's going on? You two obviously know each other, like really *know* each other. And, as a matter of fact, I've never been in this room until right now, and tell me why your face..." she trails off, pointing aggressively at Ava. "Are all over these walls?"

They look at each other, having a conversation without words.

"I will tell you. Actually, we will tell you, but first, we have to take care of something incredibly important and time-sensitive," Elric says.

Turning, he opens his arms, moving about the room.

"Everything in here is dated. This is us. This is our story. Our *true* story. Look at all of it, spend as much time as you want in here. Write down questions. There will be many questions. As soon as we get back, I promise we will answer them."

Anita's eyes grow wide as she takes in the room and just nods.

He stares at the room, filled with canvases that span centuries, and then looks back at Ava. She watches him, her smile gentle and full of affection. Two lives spanning centuries, and neither one of them knows or even understands how much farther they have to go. Elric takes her hand and kisses it, leading her out of the room. Anita stays behind and immediately starts pulling out all the canvases within reach, using care as she lays each one out.

"Anita," he calls.

She looks up at him as she holds a painting from a wedding in Savannah that took place over a century ago.

"You're amazing."

"I know." She quips, turning her attention back to the painting in her hands.

Elric wouldn't have accepted any other kind of response from Anita.

They get into Elric's car, and he immediately pulls out his phone, uses the search engine, and hits the call button on a number.

"What are you doing?" Ava asks as she clicks her seat belt into place.

He starts the car and looks at Ava. "I'm calling—"

The call is answered on the other end, and Elric holds a finger up to her.

"Yes? Hello? What's your soonest flight to Montreal? Tonight at 8:40? One stop in San Francisco. Perfect... I am going to hand the phone over to my wi- fian- to my Ava... Yes. She's going to complete the booking."

He hands the phone and his wallet to Ava. "Just book one-way tickets. We will deal with the return when we've found Gabriel."

Ava nods and continues the call.

She briefly holds the phone away from her mouth and whispers. "They actually have an earlier flight in two hours. I can be packed and ready to go if you can. The 8:40 one is full. If not, the next flight isn't until tomorrow evening."

He gives her a thumbs up, and she turns her attention back to the phone to complete the reservation. They drive back home to pack their bags, and Elric feels the claws of anxiety sink into the back of his mind.

Ava snaps her fingers at him, bringing him back into the moment. He looks over at her, still on the phone, and she mouths, *"your speed."*

He looks down at the speedometer, immediately easing his foot off the gas. Just because he could pay for a speeding ticket doesn't mean he wants to. He takes a deep breath, trying to release the tension from his body. Focusing more on the numbers on the screen in his car than the thoughts rattling in his mind. Every step they take, moving closer to the hope of finding a solution, makes everything seem more volatile.

XVIII

KYOTO, JAPAN 1998

He sat at the end of the Fushimi Inari Shrine, dipping his head at the two geishas walking out from under the torii. Elric focused his attention back to his sketch adding the two geishas and their elaborate silk kimonos.

"*Konnichiwa*," he greeted them, nodding as they passed.

They bowed their heads in return and kept on their way. He sat up straight, stretching out his back. He glanced at the Casio digital watch on his wrist. 6:42 p.m.

"Goodness," he said as he stood up, taking a deep breath of the crisp spring air. He didn't realize he had been there in the same spot for nearly two hours.

Dusting the back of his pants off, he made his trek back to the main road to hail a taxi.

The car came to an abrupt stop and waited for him.

The man spoke in a rushed Japanese that Elric's minimal knowledge of the language couldn't pick up on. He pulled a little black leather booklet out of his maroon windbreaker's pocket and flipped through it until he found what he was looking for.

He spoke very slowly and was embarrassed by how he was butchering the language, "*Ichiban*." He flipped through more pages, "*Rōkaru*," and flipped through the book again, "*Resutoran*."

The driver laughed without care. Elric laughed with him, fully aware he sounded ridiculous.

"*Gomen*," Elric said when the driver's laughter finally died down.

God I hope I said that right. Elric thought.

"You did a good job for an Englishman," the driver responded in clear English.

Elric laughed, genuinely this time. "I didn't need to demonstrate my horrific Japanese?"

"No," the driver said, grinning and wiping his eyes, "but it was entertaining."

"Good, I can pay you in entertainment instead of yen," Elric joked.

The driver chuckled. "You can try, but you will only get that far," he said, pointing to a streetlamp no more than 20 feet up the road.

"Noted. I'll pay with yen now and work on my comedic skills in the meantime."

The driver snorted. "Deal. I will take you to my favorite restaurant—only ten-minute's drive up the road."

"Much obliged."

On the short drive, Elric learned that the man's name was Unmei. He told Elric the best and least crowded places to go and receive a real Kyoto experience.

They arrived at a small restaurant and exchanged money and goodbyes as Elric exited the cab.

Unmei drove off, leaving him to examine the front of the small unknown restaurant. A short string of five light bulbs hung low around the front of a white building. The light's soft luminescence barely emitted enough of a glow to see properly what was on the sign that hung overhead. Opening the heavy wooden door, he looked up at the sign hanging overhead before heading in. A bright red poppy was painted on the circular sign.

Before Elric fully made it into the building, he was greeted by the hostess. As she led him to an empty table, he looked around the small room, which consisted of only five tables in total. His eyes were drawn to the bright pink Cherry Blossom tree in full bloom sitting outside the window of the restaurant. He looked down at the table in front of the window and saw a single red poppy sitting in a clear vase in front of a lone patron. Her head was buried in a book, and her long black hair was draped over her face, concealing her from anyone who walked by.

But Elric knew.

He laughed out loud. "Of course."

The waitress turned to him, startled by his outburst.

"Sorry. Do you mind if I sit at that empty table across from the window?"

The hostess bowed her head and changed directions, waiting until he was seated to ask for his drink order.

Settling into the empty table, he set his things down in the chair beside him. "Matcha, please."

The hostess nodded her head and left to prepare his drink.

Elric ran a hand through his hair and leaned over. *"Everything is more beautiful because we are doomed."*

After living through it numerous times, he felt half the fun was the anticipation that came along with meeting her for the first time. He held his breath as she lifted her head and smiled, losing himself in seas of emerald green.

MODERN-DAY MONTREAL, CANADA

Ava yawns and stretches with a small yelp as she waits for Elric to unlock the hotel room with his key card. The hotel hallway smells of a freshly-ran vacuum as maids shuffle in and out of rooms down the hall.

"Tired?" he asks as the beep of the card reader goes off.

He lifts the strap of his duffel higher on his shoulder and grabs the suitcase out of her hand.

"Super," she says, her eyes widening as she enters the suite.

Dark herringbone patterned hardwood floors stretch across the foyer and living room—a stark comparison to the ivory furniture and cream-colored rug. A black marble wet bar and matching fireplace sit across from the sofa.

Ava drops her purse on the entryway table and marches through the hotel room, examining what lies behind every door and drawer.

"Elric!" She excitedly calls from the other side of the wall.

He sets the bags next to the fireplace and enters a minimalist, modern bedroom with a golden bed frame across from floor-to-ceiling windows. In between the bed and windows is a sitting area with rose-colored velvet sofas and a small white marble coffee table. A bottle of champagne and a box of chocolates sit on the coffee table beside a bouquet of red poppies. Elric reaches out to touch one of the poppy petals when Ava calls for him again.

He follows the sound of her giggling and finds her lying in an empty freestanding tub in the bathroom with white marble floors.

She sinks down lower and pops her feet out of the tub, pointing a toe at him. "Do not ever make me leave this tub."

He sits on the edge of the tub and rubs her foot. "If that's what you want. I'll find Gabriel and deal with Faye, and you just turn into a raisin."

"My dream," she says, closing her eyes and smirking. "Just bring me snacks."

"Alright. Done," he watches her devotedly.

He stands up and stretches, retrieving their bags and shuffling them around in the closet. He lays his wallet on the desk. Unlocking his phone, his fingers move rapidly across the screen.

Ava walks into the bedroom, readjusting the messy bun on top of her head. "Are you texting that person throwing the exhibit? What time do we even need to be at that? Where is it?"

Elric hits send on his phone, keeping hold of it and patiently waiting for a reply. "Now, that's probably what I should be doing, but I'm texting Anita, asking how Geoffrey is," he smiles.

A new message appears on his screen, and when he opens it, he laughs, turning the screen toward Ava so she can see. On the screen is a picture of Anita sitting cross-legged, smiling wide, and flashing a peace sign to the camera. On the floor in Elric's private room, rows of artworks are lined up behind Anita, but in her lap lies a perfectly curled-up ball of black and brown fur.

"Of course he would love her," she coos. "That was kind of her to watch him on such short notice."

"I know. She is a gem. I'm going to call the curator for the exhibit, see what we can work out." Elric dials the number Peter gave him and puts the phone to his ear.

The phone rings a few times and then goes to voicemail.

He leaves a quick message. "Jacqueline Wéi. This is Elric Ferron. I was given your number by an acquaintance. I was hoping you could get me in touch with a friend I've lost contact with. Gabriel Bello? I know you're curating his current exhibit, so if you could call me back, I'd appreciate it. Thank you." He hangs up the phone, tossing it on the bed.

"Now we wait."

Throwing open the doors to their private balcony, he welcomes the breeze that envelopes him. The city's lights come to life as the sun disappears behind the horizon. He leans against the railing, watching its pulse. Watching the cars move through the roads in fluidity, the city lights hitting the dark recesses of the streets. A college-aged group of boys pushes each other and laughs as they move down the street in tandem. A pair of lovers entangled beneath a tree strung with lights. A woman quickly crosses the street with a small black poodle on a leash, talking loudly on her phone.

"What are you thinking?" Ava asks, joining Elric and resting her head on his shoulder.

"Nothing," he replies, turning his head to kiss the top of hers.

Ava lifts her head off him and turns her back to the rail. Interlocking her fingers over her stomach, she leans back, resting on her elbows, and call his bluff. "Oh, okay."

"What? I'm not thinking about anything," he responds.

"I know you, Elric Ferron. I can see your little gears turning. What are you thinking about?" she presses.

He laughs at how well she knows him.

"I'd give anything for us to live a mundane life," he says, motioning toward the people below. "Live. Grow old. Die. Together."

Ava looks up into the sky and focuses on a hazy mist of clouds settling above. "I don't negate the fact that you've been trying to figure out for centuries what the hell you're supposed to do. And do I relish the fact I've died countless times? Obviously not. But what I do know," she stands up straight, placing her hands on the sides of his face and looking into his eyes, "Is that I have gotten to love you, and you've gotten to love me numerous times–each one deeper than before. A depth some do not get to experience. Not even once."

His gaze softens, and the corner of his mouth lifts. "Always the romantic."

"I try." She lifts her shoulders and winks.

"Fate must have a soft spot in her heart for us."

"Hm," she looks back up at the mist, "'Our fate, I tell you, stands on a razor's edge.'"

Elric's phone starts to ring before he can respond. He runs inside quickly, grabs his phone, and answers it.

"Hello? Yes, this is. Thank you for calling me back!"

Utterly enamored, Ava watches him from the balcony through the open door, completely unaware that she is being watched from the ground below.

Elric hangs up the phone and puts it back on the bed and she heads inside, waiting for him to divulge.

"Alright, we have to be ready in a couple hours. She said we have great timing. Gabriel was only showing face tonight for the opening. He flies out tomorrow morning."

"Awesome, let's go grab a bite to eat and then go."

He grimaces.

"Black tie. I didn't bring a tux. Did you pack a gown in that?" He asks, pointing to her small suitcase.

Ava shakes her head and sticks her bottom lip out. "I'm starving."

"I'm sorry, we have to go shopping. I saw a few stores as we were driving into the hotel."

She dramatically stomps her feet and throws her arms down at her side. "I just want to wear yoga pants and a t-shirt."

Elric smiles. "I know. I'm going to call the front desk and have a driver for us in 30 minutes."

"Alright. I have to shower. Travel stink."

He picks up the hotel room phone and lets the other end ring for the concierge. Ava pulls her hair down from her bun, her curls draping her shoulders softly. The phone keeps ringing, and he keeps his eyes steadily trained on her. She walks by him, and her eyes darken as seductive smile grows. She keeps walking with her back now to him, pulling her shirt over her head and dropping it at her feet.

The phone stops ringing, and someone answers, barely pulling Elric's attention.

He tries to speak, and a croak comes out instead. He clears his throat and begins again.

"I need a car."

The woman on the other end asks a question at the same time Ava slowly slides out of her pants, leaving them next to her shirt.

"Sir? Mr. Ferron?" The sound of someone loudly calling out his name gave him enough to spit out the next few words.

"Can you get me a driver?"

Ava turns and looks over her shoulder, her eyelids heavy with enticement as she unclasps her bra and adds it to the pile of dropped clothes.

She slowly turns around, baring herself to him. The heat stirring in his chest finally bursts and flows through his whole body, igniting every sense.

"Mr. Ferron. I can't help you if you don't give me any information." The concierge nearly shouts, partly out of frustration the other part unsure if Elric can hear her or not.

He speaks in a rush. "I need a driver in 30 minutes, actually, make it 45, please. Thanks. Bye. Love you."

Hanging up the phone, he barely puts it on the receiver, the dial tone ringing loudly.

Ava burst out laughing. "Did you just tell the front desk you love her?"

Elric's eyes hungrily search her body. "I don't know. Did I?"

He takes a step forward, letting out a husky moan. In response, Ava takes a step backward, covering her mouth as she giggles at the game.

Lunging forward, he captures her body in his hands and takes her into the bathroom.

His lips find hers, her body responding to his calling. Each of them finds steady ground in each other. Each of them rests in bliss.

XIX

Elric hands the driver outside of the store a hundred-dollar bill.

"Thank you for waiting. I need you to hurry and get us over to the gallery on Penrose Avenue."

The driver tilts his head acknowledging as he holds the backseat door open for Ava. She steps into the back of the car wearing a newly purchased gown. Since spending more time in the hotel room than anticipated, there wasn't much time to spare for shopping.

They had split apart in the boutique—Elric quickly finding a black tux and Ava grabbing the first dress in her size, which happened to be a floor-length, strapless, deep indigo blue with a corset fitted to her body that was adorned with black boning. The back opening dropped to her tailbone, laced in loose golden chains.

"Do I look okay? I feel like this dress is too much. My whole back is out. What if no one else is dressed like this? Jesus, I was just trying to hurry, and this fit. Now I think this is not a good idea," she fidgets at the fabric around her legs.

She pulls a small compact mirror out of a newly purchased clutch and starts to quickly apply eyeliner.

Elric hooks his finger under her chin to get her to look at him.

He kisses the top of her bare shoulder and grins.

"You look stunning. More than stunning, but my brain isn't functioning properly when I look at you, so stunning will have to suffice for the moment. You are perfection."

She laughs lightly and moves her shoulder away from him. "Stop it. It's not like I can do anything about it now," she says before turning her attention back to her make-up.

"There's something else I can't do anything about right now," he says, grabbing her hand and placing it between his legs.

"Elric!" She yelps as she snatches her hand back, looking in the rear-view mirror to see if the driver is watching.

Elric throws his head back and roars with mirth.

Sitting back up, he whispers in her ear. "The sooner we talk to Gabriel, the sooner we can go back to the room."

She narrows her eyes at him as her cheeks turn pink. He kisses that same area of pink and smiles.

"Leave me alone now. I have like five minutes to put on some sort of make-up."

She swaps out her eyeliner for the mascara that's rolling around in the bottom of her clutch.

They arrive at the gallery, and the driver jumps out of the car to open the back door for them. Stepping out, Elric hands the driver more folded bills. "Could you just hang around? We shouldn't be long."

The driver takes the money and tucks it away inside his coat pocket in agreement.

Elric holds out his hand for Ava as she maneuvers herself out of the car in the lengthy gown. She takes his arm as they make their way up the stone steps to the gallery entrance. A crowd of people walk into the exhibit, all dressed elegantly, and Ava sighs a breath of relief, knowing she didn't overdress. At the entrance, a man dressed in all black stands behind a podium, greeting each guest and checking them in.

Elric leans in and close, "Let's do this as quickly as possible. These events are full of the stuffiest and rudest people you could imagine."

Ava snickers as they approach the podium.

"Good evening. Name?" The man asks without looking up from his clipboard.

"I don't think we are going to be on the list, but Ferron," he tells him.

The man scans his list and lifts a second page.

"I'm so sorry, sir. I don't see your name and I can't let anyone in who's not on the list. You know this is a private event, right? Exclusive," he adds, lifting his head to look past them, smiling at the couple standing behind them.

"Mr. and Mrs. Elsher! Such a pleasure to see you again. Please enjoy yourselves!"

The host places himself in front of Elric and Ava, subtly pushing them back with his own body and extending his arm for the entrance of the Elshers.

Suddenly, a woman from within the building shouts Elric's name from afar. The man quickly turns towards the person calling and stands up straighter as Elric and Ava search for the owner of the unfamiliar voice.

"Elric Ferron!" A petite woman approaches them in a loud yellow tulle-layered dress, hitting people with the gown as she walks by. Her dark hair hangs to her waist in a sleek, thick braid. Elric thought she was what most would call classically beautiful with her high cheekbones, cinnamon-colored almond-shaped eyes, and full lips.

"Miss Wéi! I'm sorry, I had no idea this was your guest."

Jacqueline Wéi doesn't reply to the man as she swiftly pushes him aside. She walks up to Elric, the top of her stature barely to the middle of his chest and leaving a few inches in between them. She beckons him with her finger.

Elric bends down for her to kiss him on both cheeks, and she squeals with joy and an unknown accent. "Elric Ferron! Elric Ferron," she repeats to the host, peeved and in chastisement. "How the hell do you not know who Elric Ferron is? I don't know how much longer you'll be my assistant, honestly."

"Miss Wéi I—" the host tries to backtrack his rudeness.

Jacqueline holds up her hand and shoots him daggers with her eyes. "I didn't ask for your excuses. Hand me that small gift bag. Now, go."

Shamefully, the assistant walks back over to the booth to deal with the pooling line of guests.

"Elric! I am so delighted you are here. I have a gift for you, to thank you for coming to our event!" Jacqueline places the gift in Elric's hands.

"This is unnecessary. We are grateful to be here on such short notice." He says trying to hand the gift back.

"Nonsense." She pulls out a small black box opening it for him, revealing a thin metal bracelet.

Elric tries to get a closer look at the small etchings on the piece of jewelry but before he can Jacqueline has slipped it onto his wrist.

"Oh that looks stunning with your outfit. Come, come now." Jacqueline grabs Elric's hand and leads him inside.

He quickly grabs onto Ava's before she gets lost in the crowd. They make their way to the middle of the room, and Jacqueline links arms with him, leaving no room for Ava in the chain. Ava gives Elric's hand a tight squeeze of reassurance and falls into step behind them. The room is large and round, with high vaulted ceilings that cause echoes of conversations to bounce off the walls. Around the perimeter of the room are large canvases eight feet tall and six feet wide, completely covered in live flowers. The first canvas, Elric notices, is a wall of pink peonies. A woman with loosely draped matching pink silk around her body stands in front of the wall. She holds a large handmade fabric peony covering the entirety of her face. Her dark red hair is made voluminous around the flower. The next display is the same but traded for white Dahlias and drapery. The hair color is a perfect copy of the one before.

"The infamous incognito painter. Do you know how long I've been wanting to get my hands on you? You prove difficult to get a hold of, though," she says, patting him gently on the arm as they walk.

"Incognito for a reason," Elric looks back at Ava, making sure she is okay. She gives him a comforting nod.

"Which begs the question," he continues, "How do you know who I am?"

A waiter walks by with a platter of drinks and stops at the trio. Jacqueline takes one and offers it to Elric. He takes it just to hand it off to Ava before grabbing a second drink off the tray and pulling Ava into the enclave of his body.

Jacqueline lifts an eyebrow at Ava, assessing her gown, hair, and face before smiling at her. She throws her head back and finishes her drink in one fell swoop. Ava smiles, amused and impressed, as she sips on her own.

"Some of us sell our souls for knowledge and success, others for love," Jacqueline stares at Ava, the knowing smile still playing at the corners of her lips.

Ava hesitates mid-sip and her eyes move anxiously to Elric.

He inconspicuously runs his fingers down the back of her arm for reassurance as he smiles at Jacqueline and takes a drink.

He scans the room. "Did you make a deal with the devil? Because this is quite an event. Look at the turnout. You're notorious for your curations. This is an exquisite showcase of Gabriel's work. You two made his photographs come to life."

Jacqueline laughs. "Why, thank you. His work is beautiful. His obsession with the red hair is working. Would you like to see the display of his photographs? It's right down here."

Jacqueline begins to make her way in another direction when Elric lightly touches her elbow.

"Actually, I would love to see an old friend first. Where is Gabriel?" Elric smiles politely.

She looks around the room and stops a young girl dressed the same as the host up front to whisper to her. After they exchange words, the girl is sent on her way.

"It seems Gabriel is in the garden. Follow me."

Elric dips his head and smiles. "Please Miss Wéi, enjoy your incredible event and give attention to your other guests who, by the looks of it, are starving for it."

They both laugh, Elric out of flattery and Jacqueline out of the love of praise.

"Do not leave without coming to see me first. I'd love to set something up with you," Jacqueline says before taking her leave to another group of guests.

Elric looks at Ava and blows out an exasperated sigh.

"Does it sound like she knew something?"

He takes her arm, walking with her to the door leading outside.

"I don't know how she could. She's just the eccentric type. Don't overthink it."

They walk outside into the cool air, Ava's skin prickling down her arms in the chill. The garden is a wondrous sight; it is well-lit and surrounded by large draping purple Japanese Wisterias and various marble statues. The outside of the venue is not as busy as the inside, but it is still bustling, given the amount of people. Small groups of people converge around golden-clothed pub tables, circling the inside of the garden with drinks and appetizers.

"Do you see him anywhere?" Her eyes shift around.

Elric scans the tables, searching for the man in the photograph from the book.

"I don't see– wait."

A woman moves away from a crowded table, exposing a stout, tan-skinned man. His dark hair is much longer than in the photo, now pulled into a messy bun at the nape of his neck, contrasting sharply with his finely kept thick handlebar mustache that curls loosely at the ends.

"Ava, right there." Elric tilts his chin up at the group ahead.

They move slowly towards the table, waiting for another opening to give way. Gabriel stands in the center, being showered in praise from fans and artists alike. A server holding a platter of baked brie and figs walks by, giving Gabriel pause as he waves him down. The server crosses in front of Elric and Ava, making his way to the group. Gabriel's gaze flickers quickly over the couple and then back to the conversation in front of him. Within a couple of seconds, Gabriel abruptly stops mid-sentence and looks back over to Elric. His brow tightens in confusion before the realization of who is standing before him hits him. His eyebrows rise, and he blatantly gapes, looking back and forth between Ava and Elric. A guest continues conversing with Gabriel, knowing he has lost the man's attention. The guest follows Gabriel's pointed stare, trying to figure out who he is staring at.

Gabriel begins to grin from ear to ear, walking away from the poor admirer whose sentence trailed off without a proper ending.

"Elric!" He shouts, confused as he approaches, his accent still heavy from his Spanish roots.

Gabriel grabs Elric in a bear hug, holding him tight and energetically patting him on the back. Elric hugs him back, moved by his boisterous greeting. Being able to claim someone from his own past leaves a profound healing in his heart. Gabriel pulls away and holds him by the shoulders, his brows coming together. "How?"

Elric shakes his head.

"Do you have somewhere private we could talk?" He asks so others around may not hear.

Gabriel nods and turns his attention to Ava, tears hitting his eyes. He delicately reaches for her and brings her into a much gentler embrace.

He whispers to her with a quivering voice. "You are not dead."

They release each other, and Ava smiles, raising her shoulders. "Not this time."

Gabriel leans over to a man Elric hadn't noticed, who was standing a few feet from Gabriel the entire time. He didn't hear the conversation but got the gist once the man stood in between Gabriel and the group of people trying to reach him.

"*Vamos*," Gabriel says to Elric and Ava as he navigates the crowd, ignoring the people vying for his attention.

They walk through the great room adjacent to a smaller area with Gabriel's photos on display. Large and intricate chandeliers made of the flowers from the photos hang from the ceiling, matching the flowers depicted in each photo below them. Finally, he leads them into a back office, very plainly decorated but rich in taste. A solid wooden desk sits in front of wide windows overlooking the back garden.

Gabriel closes the door behind him. "Please! Sit, sit!" He says joyfully, pointing to a white loveseat positioned across from a set of matching wingback chairs.

"Elric, Ava. How is this possible?" Gabriel asks, clasping his hands together as he sits in one of the empty chairs.

"Gabriel, that's why we've come. To ask you the same thing. To see if you have information we don't that can break this," Elric says to him, holding onto Ava's hand.

Gabriel leans back in the chair and waving them off. "Tell me, why would you want to break this? We are *inmortal*. Gods among humans. We learn to play the game of life, and we win. I could never even begin to tell you how much money, fame, and power I have. It's *increíble*."

"Gabriel, I'm going to die," Ava says flatly, knowing they don't have the time to waste on the bragging of fortunes.

He scoffs and looks at Elric, whose eyes are fixed on Ava.

Gabriel stands up, picking up a rose gold letter opener. He runs it across his hand, causing a wound to immediately pool with blood that drips onto his white slacks.

"*Imposible*," He says, holding his palm out. The wound stops bleeding and stitches itself together slowly in front of their eyes.

He runs his hand over the front of his suit jacket, smearing blood across the fabric. He shows his palm to Ava, the cut looking like it had happened yesterday instead of a few seconds ago.

"We heal. We cannot die."

He removes his jacket and throws it down at his feet, returning to his seat.

"No, Gabriel. You and I, yes, but that's not how it's worked for Ava. When she died in Spain, that wasn't the first time or the last." Elric sighs heavily, leaning forward on his knees as he tries to explain to Gabriel. "Ava *reincarnates*—that's the best way I can put it. She dies, and then she lives again, another life, another location with no memories of the life before until now. She dies the year she turns twenty-eight. The age she was when she first died in 1348. But this time, for the first time, she touched a painting of herself by accident, and she remembered. Any painting she touches that I've done of her, all the memories of that life come flooding back."

"You made a deal with a *bruja*. To save her, yes?" Gabriel asks.

"Yes."

"It did not go according to plan. Or at least your plan."

"Correct."

Gabriel sits back and studies the two when Ava speaks up, "Why are you immortal, too? Elric recognized you in a book, so we came looking for you."

Stroking his mustache, Gabriel runs his fingers down his chin and clears his throat.

"I fell in love with my *bruja*. And then I had to kill her."

They stared at him, unsure of what to ask next.

"Eliana. *Mi flor*." he gives a grim smile. "She is my muse. Forever."

"The red hair, I remember it. Your son had the same." Elric's expression sobers, understanding his pain.

Gabriel keeps his smile, but his eyes grow sorrowful. "I knew the, *cómo se dice, trascendencia.*"

"Implications," Elric translates for him.

"Ah, *Sí*, the implications of being with my *bruja*. I loved her and she loved me. Together, our love made Ignacio. He was born with fiery red hair *como su madre*. I thought her intentions would change because of *amor*." Gabriel wipes a stray tear that escapes.

He clenches his fist tightly. "She promised me she would no longer do dark magic. I knew of her book of souls—I knew that's how she lived forever. But she promised me no more. She was going to make me *inmortal* and we agreed to wait for Ignacio, until he was older, truly until he could decide for himself. But who wouldn't want to live forever with their *familia*?" Gabriel took a deep, shuddering breath, letting his head fall to his chest. "Then Ignacio was murdered. We found his little body in a field. The man who did it was found and said he did it just because. He was *perturbado,* disturbed. He was executed. It wasn't enough for Eliana or I. *Nunca*. But Eliana changed when she realized there was no magic powerful enough to bring our *hijo* back. Eliana told me no one would ever take what's hers again. She would be more powerful than anyone."

Gabriel picks his head back up, his eyes red. "I no longer wanted the magic, but she begged me to still go through with it. That she didn't want to be alone. And I couldn't resist *mi flor*. She found a way to make me *inmortal* with her without having to trade my soul, but soon after, many people started disappearing. And Eliana's spirit, which was once bright and happy, turned dark *y malvada*."

"What does that mean?" Ava asks, turning to Elric.

He keeps his eyes on Gabriel and answers stoically. "Evil."

Gabriel nods, his grief palpable like a layer of fog no one can seem to get through.

"I found her book, which was supposed to have been buried, hidden for no one to ever find, under our floorboard. Fresh handprints on the pages. She was no longer my Eliana, no longer *mi flor*. She could not see past her pain. She was unwilling to learn to live with it. She wanted to crush it."

Elric anxiously sits on the edge of the sofa. "Gabriel. How did you do it?"

The tears begin to roll down the man's cheeks, and his voice becomes tight. "It was *mi hijo's* birthday. And she broke when I gave her a painting of him. A glimpse of her came through. She said she was done and needed me to end *su vida*. She told me how and made me promise I would do it. She told me how to end my life as well so that I could join her. I kept my promise and ended her life. But I did not want to join her. I could not forgive her. I still cannot. How many lives did she ruin for power? For vengeance? I love her but cannot forgive her. You cannot help who you fall in love with, isn't that right, *amigo*?"

Gabriel reached under his shirt collar, hooking his index finger around a small gold chain and revealing a hand-blown glass vial with a single red poppy and lavender wax sealing the top of it.

"This is what broke through her magic. She made one for her and one for me. She put an enchantment on it."

Elric's eyes widened as he stared at the necklace, holding out his hand for it. Gabriel took it off his neck and laid it in the palm of Elric's hand.

"Obviously, I have never used mine." Gabriel laughs with no humor in his tone.

"*Isle de Mujeres*," Ava murmurs.

"*¿Que?*" Gabriel asks.

"I bought one of these for Ava in the 50s, in Mexico. This same exact thing," Elric says, staring at the vial while turning it in his fingers.

"Gabriel, could you make us one? Do you know the spell she used for it? Could we have yours?" Ava stands up, anxious.

"*Lo siento,* I am sorry. It is a specific spell for each person cast on it. It would have to be made for your *bruja*. Someone who shares their blood magic."

Ava wrings her hands together and turns to Elric. "What are we supposed to do then? We aren't witches. We wouldn't know how to do that!" Her voice gets louder as she grows more anxious with defeat.

Elric stands up and hands the necklace back to Gabriel, who strings it back onto his neck.

"I still have yours," Elric tells her.

"What?" She asks, dropping her hands.

"Any jewelry that you've had over our time, I've kept it if I have been able to. You didn't wear that necklace all the time, and when you died, you weren't wearing it. It was at our home in Mexico. I have it now, at home."

Ava presses the palms of her hands together and holds them to her lips. "You have it."

Elric smiles. "I have it."

Gabriel claps his hands together and stands up with them. "*¡Muy bien!*"

She turns back to Gabriel. "What is it that we need to do?"

"Eliana and I traveled to the Irati River, deep within the forest. She said it had to be a great source of magic. And the *Anjanas*," he waves his hand, trying to think of the English translation, clapping loudly when it comes to him, "Fairies! Are sort of fairies, rumored to help those who are in need in that forest."

Gabriel faintly smiles. "Had it not been under such gruesome circumstances, it would have been a beautiful place to be with her," shaking his head, he continues. "She told me to gather the branches of the Rowan tree and create a circle around her with the branches. She could not cross the ring. A magic circle that cannot be broken. She gave me a spell to say and then to throw her vial necklace into the circle."

"That's all we have to do?" Ava asks him, urgency in her voice.

Gabriel turns his head away, hides his face, and shakes his head. "There is a spell I had to say once the vial was broken, *pero* I cannot remember it. But once I spoke it, she was mortal for only *pocos momentos*."

He pauses, placing his palm over his heart, thrumming his fingers in place. "I had to strike her in the heart before time was up. With a dagger."

"Jesus, Elric. Could we stab someone?" she tugs on his fingers, pulling him in closer to her.

Elric's fingers curl around hers. "The Faye you met in the cafe is one-tenth of the demon she actually is. So yes, I can absolutely stab her. Especially if that means saving you."

He quickly rubs his thumb over the top of her hand before looking back to Gabriel.

"We need to find the spell?"

"*Sí*," Gabriel replies

Elric runs his hands through his hair. "Great."

"And you need to find her marking and etch it into the blade," Gabriel adds.

"Her marking? She has markings all over her body. Which one?" Elric asks in frustration.

Gabriel reaches up and touches the back of his neck. "Every *bruja* has their mark right here. You need to have a *bruja* who is bound to her. Etch it into the blade to enchant it. They are of the same blood magic."

Elric presses his eyes. "This just keeps getting easier."

Gabriel reaches out to lay a hand on his shoulder. "*Amigo*. I am here to help any way I can." He grows solemn, "But the spell—that necklace—is not the key to breaking your immortal *vida*. But unless a necklace was made for you or you can destroy the book, I suppose you remain. *Y* Ava, I truly do not know, but at least you will be rid of your *bruja*."

Ava grips his shoulders, "Getting rid of Faye may be exactly what we need."

"Thank you, Gabriel. You gave us more than we had before, so I am most grateful," Elric says, embracing his friend once more.

Ava follows suit, hugging Gabriel before they depart. They exchange numbers as Gabriel walks them back out into the main room. Giving each other proper goodbyes, Elric releases him back to his exhibit.

Ava holds onto Elric's hand and puts her forehead on his shoulder, overwhelmed.

"How the hell are we going to do this?" Her shoulders sag, exhausted from the slew of information that was launched at them.

He lifts her head, and he can feel the broken hope radiating off of her. "Hey, look at me... Ava."

She meets his gaze, tears threatening to spill. "You'll see me again if I die. Make me touch the paintings, and we can figure it out again. I just don't see how finding a spell and the mark and anything else is going to happen."

"My love, we will figure this out without you dying and starting over. I don't know how, but we will. I'll never stop. Beyond this life." he says, stroking her cheek when their moment is abruptly interrupted.

"Elric! I told you to come find me!"

Elric purses his lips and fakes a smile before turning around to Jacqueline. "Jacqueline, amazing event, but we must go. I'll leave my number with your assistant."

"Tsk, tsk, Elric. You think I have nothing to offer you?" Jacqueline says. A smirk graces her lips as she raises an eyebrow in mild disapproval.

Reaching out, he searches for Ava's hand, interlocking once he finds it.

"Jacqueline, I'm tied up at the moment. I don't have time for a new project. Maybe at a later date."

He starts to move when Jacqueline puts a hand on his chest, throws her head back, and laughs. She holds up a finger, gesturing for him to wait. He stops impatiently, willing her to move faster so he can leave. Turning around, she lifts the thick braid off the nape of her neck, revealing a bright red rune.

E lric moves Ava behind him, blocking her body with his own. His heart races, his body responding to the adrenaline surging.

"Calm down," Jacqueline says, grabbing another drink from a passing waiter. "I'm not here to cause harm. I'm here to reunite you with an ally."

With a drink in her hand, she points behind Elric. He turns but keeps himself between Ava and Jacqueline. In the corner stands a floral display he hadn't noticed before. A woman with a large red poppy stands in front of a matching eight-foot display. Off to the right, a figure wears a sheer, black veil over her face. Golden head chains are layered on top, dropping into golden necklaces, not looking out of place in the high fashion art scene.

"Who is that?" Elric asks, uneasy.

"Go find out," Jacqueline replies, sipping her fresh drink.

He holds onto Ava's hand as he moves towards the veiled woman.

"Ava needs to stay here with me," Jacqueline says, removing Ava's hand from Elric's.

"Absolutely not," he snaps while reaching for her again. Sensing that he's so close to resolution, he feels too vulnerable without Ava.

Jacqueline quickly snags Elric's wrist, gripping it tightly, her expression menacing.

"Boy," she says through clenched teeth. "You have no idea the implications of this meeting tonight with her." Jacqueline moves her head in the direction of the mystery ally. "The danger it puts us *all* in. The less interaction I have to remove from her mind, the better."

She releases Elric. "Trust someone other than yourself."

"It's okay. I'll be fine," Ava says, looking at him with earnest reassurance. "I'm starving anyway. I'll grab some food."

He raises his eyebrows. "Are you sure?"

She nods, smiling, putting ease to his anxieties. He swiftly kisses her on the cheek and heads to his mystery meeting.

He pushes through the pulsing crowd, glancing behind him at Ava. He sees the back of her head disappear outside toward the plethora of appetizers and drinks.

He reaches the woman and notices that the area around her is surprisingly quiet and empty. When he gets close enough to see through the fabric of the veil, Elric observes a large scar down the woman's face.

"Iseppa."

The witch bows her head.

"Why are you here?"

"There is so much I am still unable to say," Iseppa says, never lifting her gaze.

"So why have you come here if you can't tell me anything?" Elric breathes heavily, vexed at what he assumes is a waste of his time.

"Do you have what was given to you long ago?" Her gaze quickly flickers to Elric and then to the floor again.

"What? I've been given a lot of stuff over the span of centuries. I don't have time for riddles. Could you say what you mean?" he asks angrily.

Iseppa shakes her head and then gently touches her index finger to his temple for a moment.

A succession of rapid images flash in Elric's mind. Italy, the stench of a dark alley, a room filled with candles, a group of women, and a silver blade hot to the touch.

He feels an electrifying jolt go through his body as Iseppa pulls away. His eyes grow wide as relief washes over him, realizing he already has one of the final pieces of the puzzle.

"The kn-"

She cuts him off, placing that same index finger over his lips.

"You could save us all." She tenderly places her hand on his cheek and smiles, the scar on her lip baring her teeth even more.

He starts to ask her if she knows the words to the incantation, but Iseppa disappears in a light mist before the question ever leaves his mouth. As soon as she is gone, the space around him that had remained empty during the interaction suddenly fills with people as if a barrier was removed. They all flood toward the previously unnoticed poppy display.

Elric politely pushes through the people before finally laying his eyes on Jacqueline and making a beeline for her.

Aggressively, he grabs her by the shoulder and pulls her face within inches of his. A brawny man who stands behind Jacqueline instantly steps in between them, balling Elric's lapel in his fist. Jacqueline holds up her hand, easing the man off of him. He releases Elric's jacket, but not before shoving him with his fist.

"What is it?" Jacqueline asks, her voice low.

"Who the hell are you?" he demands, his jaw tight.

"I am just a woman who wants to see others free. I mean you no harm, Elric Ferron." She smiles softly, but her eyes do not hide the heartbreak.

"You're a witch, too," Elric lets go of her and takes a step back. "Why do you care? Iseppa I can understand, she is trapped, but you, you aren't like her. You are like Faye, aren't you?" He whispers, spitting out the harsh accusation.

Jacqueline bites her bottom lip, stifling emotion from seeping out.

"I was. There are more of us than you think. I had my own book. And no matter how many souls I got, how long I lived, I was never really alive. I would never have love like Gabriel, like you. I could feel the darkness rotting me from the inside out, and the power wasn't worth it. I fight darkness within myself every day. And maybe I can try to right some of that rot in the world."

Elric hears Ava's laugh ring through the air out in the courtyard, his head turning to track the sound.

"I will never love like that," she says as she watches Elric's eyes light up at the sound.

He turns back to Jacqueline. "I'm sorry I accused you of ill intent."

"Nothing to forgive," she pats him gently on the chest, repeating the phrase. "Nothing to forgive."

She lightly dabs under her eyes. "I must go meet Iseppa. She still is bound to Faye, so I need to wipe her memories of you and tonight before Faye pulls the memories from her mind. Our paths are crossing again soon. Too much has been said and done tonight. And Elric, do not take off that bracelet."

Elric looks a the jewelry encompassing his wrist as Jacqueline begins to move into the crowd. Before she disappears completely Elric calls out to her.

"Jacqueline. How is it that we are all involved in the art world?" he asks.

She smiles. "It makes sense for us to grasp onto something that can make an immortal's memories come to life, does it not?"

Jacqueline winks at Elric before disappearing into the masses.

Elric walks toward Ava's laugh and finds her talking to an eccentrically dressed pair in matching feathered neon robes. He stands back and watches her interactions. Her smile is wide as she laughs in pure joy at some witty joke. The pair seem enchanted by her, and Elric knows the feeling all too well. He crosses his arms, watching Ava reach out and stroke the feathers of the collar on the woman's robe. The woman twirls her finger, gesturing for Ava to turn around so that she can admire the chain detailing on Ava's back.

For a moment, Elric places the problems they face by the wayside and lets himself marvel at the woman that is and always has been Ava Ferron. As Ava spins, she laughs, her eyes connecting with Elric's watchful gaze. She waves him over as she comes to a stop, but he hangs back for a minute more, fiercely protective of this moment before it disappears. How he wishes he had canvases to capture this on—this image of Ava laughing in the glow of hanging lights underneath the wisterias. She waves him over in earnest once more, and he breaks from the spell and makes his way across the room to her.

"You have to meet Noxolo," Ava says, reaching towards the woman, the smile never leaving her face.

Elric reaches out to delicately shake the woman's hand.

"And this is Jabu. They are sculptors from Lagos!"

Elric shifts over to Jabu, taking his hand firmly.

"I know your work. *Twin Souls.*" Elric grins. "I thought the way you incorporated glass into your sculpting was genius, truly mesmerizing. You and your sister are incredibly talented. Amazing work."

"Oh, my god, I didn't even notice you guys were twins. But now I see it!" Ava exclaims, laughing at her own faux pas.

The twins laugh in return, Noxolo speaking up first. "No worries. Most don't recognize if they don't know our work."

"Thank you for your kind words," Jabu replies to Elric. "And what was your name? Would I know any of your work?"

"James Marsh. And no, sadly, I am just an admirer. I'm sorry to cut the conversation short but we must be leaving. It was remarkable to meet you."

Ava gives Noxolo a quick hug and waves to Jabu as she follows behind Elric.

"Why did you give them a fake name?" Ava asks.

"Because, for the most part, I do not want people to know Elric Ferron exists, and for some reason, too many this year alone have heard my name."

"Okay then." Ava doesn't give another thought to his response. "They were so kind. You'll have to show me their work when we get back to the hotel," she says, thinking fondly over the encounter. "Who was the woman in the veil?"

"Once we get back to the hotel, I'll tell you everything, but I truly think we can break this curse," Elric tells Ava, sounding and feeling genuinely hopeful for the first time in centuries.

"Jacqueline's a witch?" Ava sits on the edge of the bed, taking off her shoes and tossing them into the corner of the room.

"A non-dark practicing one, I guess. I don't know. The details on that still really aren't entirely clear, but she set up the meeting with Iseppa." Elric shrugs off his jacket and throws himself on the bed beside her, causing her to gently bounce up from the bed.

"While you're back there, unhook all the chains."

He sits up and begins working at the chains laced throughout the back of the dress.

"How do we know Jacqueline isn't in on it? And if Iseppa is in Faye's little coven, how can we trust her?"

Elric shakes his head as he fumbles over the dress. "I have no way to be certain, but don't you think if they could have done anything to us, they already would have?"

Pulling aggressively, the chains refuse to come out of the eyelets.

"Elric, what is taking so long?" Ava asks, turning around as she pretends to be annoyed but smiles.

"My fingers are too big, and these chains are small!" he defends.

She furrows her brow and puffs out her lips. "Hand too big. Chain too small. Me caveman."

He laughs, gently inching her off the bed. "Then do it yourself, Miss Sophisticated."

"Just rip it off."

Elric's eyes spark as he looks her over. "Rip. It. Off."

She stands up and crosses her arms over her body, rolling her eyes.

"No, not like that. Listen, there are some real outside issues we have to figure out. We can't just constantly be going at it."

"I mean I think we could..." He suggests as she sits back down on the bed, pulling her hair back to the front to uncover the back of the dress.

"Are we just going to trust them? These women we don't know?"

Elric rubs at his face and then goes back to loosening the chains from the dress.

"When I first met Iseppa in Triora, she could have done something then. I mean, it was a whole group of them that could have attacked me, could have called Faye. But they didn't. This is the only chance we have."

"The spell to turn Faye mortal? How are we supposed to find that?"

"Honestly, I'm at a loss for that. Hopefully, we do see Jacqueline again soon and she can somehow help us."

They sit in silence for a while as Elric finally loosens the chains and Ava trades the gown for a big t-shirt, crawling under the covers while Elric changes out of his suit.

"Oh!" She exclaims.

She grabs for her phone, lying on the nightstand. "Jabu and Noxolo! I want to see their work!"

"*Twin Souls*..." she mutters aloud as she types it into the search engine on her phone. "Oh my god. That's beautiful. Elric! You've seen this?!" She asks.

Elric lays on top of the covers in his underwear and an unbuttoned shirt. He props himself up, looking at the screen Ava holds up for him. He stares at a picture of metal sculptures depicting a pair of identical statues standing side by side, their hands interlocked. The entirety of their bodies are made up of an intricate system of thousands of weaved metal strands. In the center of their chests, glass with gold veins runs through the sculpture, making it possible to see straight through them. The same glass with gold veins makes up their eyes, absent of pupils, staring out ominously at the onlooker.

He lays back on the pillow. "Did you know those sculptures are ten feet tall? They're huge. So much detailing in the faces. I can't imagine how long it took. Beautiful work."

Ava continues to stare at the picture on her phone.

"I wonder what the inspiration is. Why did they choose to scar their arms?" She resigns herself to stay in wonder. "Oh, to be in an artist's mind."

Elric sits up and snatches the phone out of her hand. "Sorry. Scarring? What scars?"

Positioning herself over him, she points to the interlocked hands.

"There. The empty spaces on their arms look like scarring. Like burn scars."

"Oh, my god. I haven't seen these witches in hundreds of years, and now they're coming out of the woodwork. The twins, Orsa and Osana."

"Are they a part of Faye's coven?"

He runs his hands through his hair. "Yes. They drew you, drew how you had died. Whatever power they have lets them see things they weren't there for."

Ava puts her hand over the phone, drawing his eyes to her.

"Elric, if we found them, could they see Gabriel when he said the spell to Eliana?"

"Possibly? I don't even know where they are. And Jacqueline made it seem like it was dangerous enough to talk to Iseppa."

"What about Jabu and Noxolo? I mean, these sculptures look just like those twins, so they must know them to sculpt them?"

"They are positively the twins, the scarring is too identical and the eyes, but I don't have contact information for Noxolo and Jabu," Elric says, leaning back on the headboard, his mind and body exhausted from the constant exertion this last week has brought on.

Ava kneels and beams at him, "I have Noxolo's number. They asked me how long I'd be in Montreal, and I told them we were leaving soon but if they were ever in NorCal to hit me up."

Elric looks at his social butterfly and draws her face to his, kissing her with smiling lips. She pulls away, taking her phone back.

"I'm going to text her. Maybe we can meet first thing in the morning."

"The sooner the better. I want to get back home," Elric says, standing up to take off his shirt and put on gym shorts.

Her thumbs fly across the screen as she texts Noxolo. Before she can even lie back down, she gets a reply.

She smiles at her phone. "Perfect. They said they'll meet us tomorrow for breakfast at *le Rosisignol*. 8:30 a.m."

"Good, nice, and early. After the meeting, hopefully, we can find a quick flight home. God, I hope they can help us." Elric crawls into bed and lays his forearm over his eyes, hoping to block out the room's light. Ava quickly replies and sets her phone down. Laying her head in the crook of Elric's arm, she buries herself in his neck.

"What if Jabu and Noxolo can't help us like we think? What if that sculpture is just a coincidence in looking like the twins?" Ava asks, concerned.

He lifts his arm from his eyes and lays it over Ava's waist. Turning to his side, he pulls her in closer to his body.

"If they can't help, then we keep looking. We exhaust every resource we can. I won't ever stop looking for a way for us to be together. Either forever or a permanent end."

Ava tries to move in closer to him although there is no physical space left between them. She overlaps her feet onto his and threads her fingers through the back of his hair.

"Beyond this life," she whispers.

"And any thereafter," he responds.

Their breathing soon syncs into a slow rhythm as they settle in, letting slumber consume them.

Elric is roused from sleep by a light, lyrical humming. He looks at Ava, who is still sleeping. He kisses her on the cheek, and she instinctively nestles into him. He lays back down, closes his eyes, and waits for sleep to claim him, but the humming grows louder. Sliding his arm out from beneath Ava, he sits up and looks at the hotel alarm clock. 3:33 a.m. The humming turns into discernible words, taking on the body of a song. Aware of the source after enduring different forms of torment for centuries, this one feels different. This time, it sets a panic loose in him.

The song continues to grow, the light, eerie voice seeming to carry with the wind right into his room.

I have loved all this past year
So that I may love no more;
I have sighed many a sigh,

Beloved, for thy pity,

Elric sits up, wild with fear, as the hauntingly familiar song grips him with contempt. Ava wakes from his sudden movement and places a hand on his chest.

"What's wrong?" She asks.

"The song. That damned song," he indignantly replies.

Ava becomes still, listening.

My love is never thee nearer,
And that me grieveth sore;
Sweet loved-one, think on me,
I have loved thee long.

"Did we leave a TV on?"

"No." Elric jumps out of bed and runs over to the balcony doors. "No. Faye sings that song as a taunt."

Kicking off the blanket her eyes go wide with fear. "She's here? How does she know where we are?"

She stands beside Elric as he looks through the windows. "There are instances where she knows where I am. Maybe because my soul is tied up in her book, but I've never been able to figure out how. There!"

He points at the street as he swings open the doors. He leans over the balcony as a figure wearing a sheer, white, soiled nightgown sways down the street, singing.

Sweet loved-one, I pray thee,
For one loving speech;
While I live in this wide world
None other will I seek.

Elric runs back into the room and slides into his sneakers. Ava follows and hurriedly puts on her sandals by the door. They take off, running through the hallways and down the few flights of stairs to make it onto the street. They hear the song louder than ever, echoing through the streets, but cannot find its source. Streetlights burn out one by one, moving away from them.

With thy love, my sweet beloved,

My bliss though mightest increase;
A sweet kiss of thy mouth
Might be my cure.

All at once hundreds of voices fill the street like a mass choir appearing in the middle of the night. The song, once melodic, turns into clamoring echoes of screams, disorienting Ava and Elric until all they can do is cover their ears and wait for the noise to stop. Physical pressure builds on their bodies, pushing them down to the pavement. Elric crawls closer to Ava, trying to protect her from the attack on their senses, barely able to move through the invisible force. He catches a glimpse of bright white hair in the distance, but his vision is warped, and he has a hard time focusing. For a moment, the image of Faye flickers, white hair flashing to a darker color. The nightgown, suddenly a red dress, and then back to the dingy cloth.

In unison, the voices stop, and the pressure releases, causing Ava and Elric to collapse onto their knees. Their breathing comes out hard and heavy, as if their lungs have been deprived of oxygen. He looks at Ava, placing his palm on her back. She nods her head, letting him know she's okay. Looking off into the distance to see if he can still spot Faye, he rests both his hands on the pavement, dizzy, his mind feeling hungover from the manipulation. The streets remain dark and empty, and the slight wind coming through the leaves is the only sound disrupting the silence. Elric helps Ava stand up on shaky legs.

The tears pooling in her eyes threaten to spill over. "Elric, what the hell was that?"

He wraps her in his arms and ushers them toward the hotel, shaken to his core. "That was Faye telling us she knows something."

XXI

They spend the rest of the early morning hours uneasy, unable to go back to sleep. Ava turns on the TV and flips through the channels, never settling on anything. Elric paces the room, keeping a constant lookout through a small opening in the now-drawn drapes. He remains unsettled, knowing full well a locked and covered room won't keep her out. He looks at his phone, 6:04 a.m.

He tosses his phone onto the bed. "I'm going to take a shower, and then we can pack up and leave. I don't care if we get to the restaurant early. I texted Anita, asking her to find a flight for early this afternoon. Whether we use the tickets or not, I want a guarantee we have a way out of here as soon as possible."

He couldn't shake the trepidation that settled into the atmosphere of their room. The sooner he could leave the city, the safer he would feel.

Ava stands up and follows him into the bathroom. "I don't want to be alone in that room." She buries her face in her hands. "But then I think that if we are in the bathroom, we can't see the rest of the room. She could be in here, but we wouldn't know it. But then you could be in the shower, I could be in the room, she could come in, and you wouldn't know she killed me."

Ava trembles as she speaks, different scenarios running through her head. Grabbing onto her, he holds her tightly. Waiting for her to become steady again, hoping she doesn't feel his own nerves.

"Faye could come in here, but I know one thing for sure. Killing us doesn't do anything for her, especially since I can't die, and you'll just return. Terrorizing us is what entertains her. She's a cruel child, and we are her butterflies. She's just trying to rip off our wings."

Ava pulls her hair into a high bun and nods her head, trying to trust in his reassurance.

"Come in the shower. You'll feel better." He lifts her face so he can look into her eyes.

The corners of her lips inch up a bit, forming the semblance of a smile, but her eyes remain worried. He cradles her face, tenderly running his thumb over her cheek. Elric kisses the top of her head and starts the shower.

They arrive at *le Rosisignol* a quarter after eight, deciding they'd rather wait on the siblings than spend another moment on that street. A host places them in a corner of the empty cafe, barring a lone man sitting at one of the tables. Placing their duffle and suitcase against the wall out of the way, they sit at a small table. Ava's eyes rapidly search for any source of danger. Elric rests his hand on top of her bouncing leg.

She looks at him and grimaces. "Sorry. I know we are fine."

"We are fine," he repeats, unsure if he believes it himself.

A server comes by with fresh coffee, cream, and sugar. Ava dresses up her coffee with the extras while Elric leaves his black. They sit in silence, waiting for the time to pass and their acquaintances to arrive, unsure of what to talk about after last night. What sort of casual conversation can be kept amid such uneasy circumstances? Their nerves are shot, and they know the caffeine won't help, but they drink it anyway to keep busy. Finally, the host brings Jabu and Noxolo to the table, and they breathe a sigh of relief. Ava stands to hug them in greeting while Eric offers a handshake to both. While they exchange pleasantries, Ava's and Elric's are half-hearted. Jabu pulls Noxolo's chair out for her as the waiter returns with fresh coffee for the table.

"James Marsh," Jabu smirks as he takes his seat.

Elric laughs out of exhaustion. "You know who I am."

"Yes." Noxolo smiles. "We were made aware of your situation many years ago."

"By whom?" Ava asks.

"The twins who had us make that sculpture. They said that it would cross your path when the time was right, leading you back to them," answered Noxolo.

"I'm glad we aren't beating around the bush," Elric sighs. "How do we find them then?"

"We did that sculpture fifteen years ago. It put our name out there as artists and set us up for success. It was very fortunate," Jabu tells them.

Noxolo continues. "When *Twin Souls* debuted fifteen years ago, Orsa and Osana came to the unveiling and said they wanted to work with us again. We were more than happy to accommodate."

She looks at her twin for confirmation. He dips his head, urging her to keep going.

"We thought that they would want to start next week, next month even, but we were confused when they scheduled something fifteen years out. I thought he was an idiot for putting it on our books. Barely recognized artists," she scoffs.

Jabu picks up the conversation, never leaving a lull where the other left off. "They kept in contact with us over the years and started to reveal things to us. Telling us things from our past no one could have known."

"And they told us things in our future that came to pass." Noxolo smiles into her cup as she raises it to her lips.

"Our scheduled date to meet with them is tomorrow."

"Okay, perfect! Where at?" Ava asks eagerly.

"Arcata," Jabu chuckles.

"You're joking." Elric runs his hands through his hair, bewildered that the witches had planned so well in advance or that they even had the ability to do so.

"I assure you we are not," Noxolo says, thrumming the side of her cup. "But this meeting in Arcata was never meant for us."

"We were prepared to meet Ava last night and for the information we needed to relay." Jabu looks to his twin so she can confirm his story.

"I do wish we were going to Northern California. But you will find the answers you seek."

"Maybe one day we will go to Arcata, but tomorrow is not that day." Jabu pulls his phone out of his pocket, tapping on the screen while he looks at Noxolo.

She nods her head, scooting her chair back as she stands, Jabu doing the same.

"Sorry to cut this meeting so short, but you know the less time we spend creating memories, the better," says Jabu.

Ava and Elric stand with them, leaving folded bills on the table to cover their tab and grabbing their luggage. They follow the twins outside, and Ava hugs them both in gratitude.

Elric hugs Noxolo. "Hopefully, someday we can show you Arcata."

"Hopefully." Noxolo smiles in return.

"Jabu, how are we supposed to know where to meet?" Elric asks, holding out his hand for Jabu.

"Someone is supposed to find you. That is all I know. The less information floating out there, the better." He waves his free hand around. "It's harder for witches to see decisions you've made the day of." He releases Elric's hand. "We are safe because of witches like Jacqueline. She fortifies our minds," Jabu taps his temple, "and covers us with her own magic."

Pulling up his sleeve he reveals a bracelet identical to Elric's.

Elric looks at his own wrist as Jabu turns around and leaves with Noxolo by his side.

Ava turns to Elric as the twins walk away. "Cool. Did you know about Faye's little trick? Tracking our decisions?" She asks, wringing her hair in her hands.

"I knew she could see things; she could always just show up where I was. But I didn't know there was a weakness to it."

He adjusts his duffle bag strap and grabs Ava's hand as he starts down the sidewalk.

"Let's go to the airport. See if there is an earlier flight because what I do know is that I want to get the hell out of Montreal."

Ava settles into her seat and looks out the window as the stewardess down the aisle gives her routine spiel on airline safety and protocol.

"Aren't you eager to hear from the twins?" She asks, turning her head to Elric. He stretches his legs out and fiddles with the screen before him.

"One thing I've learned over the centuries is patience." He smiles, leaning back in his seat. "Waiting for you is the hardest thing of my life. Words from someone else cannot hold a candle to you."

Leaning over, she kisses him before settling back into her seat, pulling her sweater around her.

"I am exhausted," she yawns.

Resting her head on Elric's shoulder, she closes her eyes and waits for the NyQuil they found at the terminal kiosk to kick in so that her mind can finally rest.

Elric pulls out his sketchbook, trying to capture the images from the gala. Giant wisterias drape over Ava as she talks to the twins, her smile captivating and her body language engaging. The plane starts to take off, and at the same time, he feels Ava's head drop. His worries about her ease a bit as she finds some rest.

A stewardess comes by asking him if he'd like a drink. He politely declines and then returns to the small sketch. He fills in vague outlines of people just for reference to add more detail later on a larger scale. Nodding off in the middle of drawing, his pencil drifts across the page, creating a line by mistake. He closes his notebook, leaving it on the small tray in front of him. He presses his eyelids tight and then brings his fingers to the bridge of his nose, pinching it and yawning. Without disturbing Ava, he slowly leans back and crosses his arms. She moves slightly to accommodate the movement while wrapping her arm around his, and he quickly drifts off beside her.

"Sir! Sir! Please wake up! Sir!"

"Ma'am! Oh, my god. Becky, where the hell is Kent? Ma'am!"

Elric wakes up panicked with a flight crew in his face. Covered in a cold sweat, his face is wet from his own tears. He looks over to his left at Ava; she mirrors his own state of mind.

"Sir! Are you alright?"

He places his hand on Ava's face, searching it. "Are you okay?"

She nods, biting her lip, trying to hold back a sob.

He runs his hand through his hair, pushing it back while he tries to compose himself.

"I am so sorry for the..." he says, not finishing the sentence, unsure of what even happened.

"You two were screaming in your sleep." The stewardess's eyes are wide with fear. She turns to a man coming up on her right.

She pulls on the bottom of her shirt, straightening it out. "This is Kent, our on-board medic. He's going to check you guys out, make sure everything is okay."

An unassuming-looking man stands behind Kent, and Elric can only guess it's the air marshal.

Elric nods. "Of course, I am so sorry for the disturbance. We haven't gotten a lot of sleep and took some sleep aids before the flight. Probably wasn't a good idea." He nervously laughs and reaches for Ava's hand, holding it tightly.

He knows they must think they are some kind of drug addicts.

Regaining himself, he smiles at Kent. "What do you need us to do, sir?"

The man kneels down and opens a black duffle bag. "Just a routine check, nothing crazy. Blood pressure, eyes, heart rate. Run of the mill. Just want to make sure you two are okay. Would you like to go first or the missus?"

Elric looks at Ava as she can no longer hold back the emotion in her eyes.

239

"I'll go first. Give her a minute."

The medic gives Ava a genuinely kind look before wrapping a cuff around Elric's arm. "Were you guys in Montreal or just a layover?"

"Just a quick trip to Montreal to visit a friend."

Kent keeps the small talk going as he continues the exam. Elric replies, trying not to do it curtly but wanting to get through the pointless exam so he can do his own checkup on Ava.

"Alright, chief! You're looking good." Kent lightly slaps Elric on the shoulder and leaves his hand there. "I have to ask; did you take anything besides the sleep aid?"

Elric shakes his head. "No, sir. We are just really sensitive to medicine. Our honest mistake."

Kent gives a small smile and looks at Ava. "Okay, ma'am, are you ready?"

She gives a quiet yes, taking her sweater off so that Kent can finish the exam quickly and go on his way. The air marshal behind them gives them one last look before leaving with the rest of the staff.

Ava turns to Elric and begins to sob, covering her mouth to stifle the sounds. Elric responds by quickly pulling her into his arms.

"Shhhh. It's okay. It wasn't real. You're safe," he whispers to her.

Her shoulders shudder in his arms. "Elric, what the hell was that? Did we have the same nightmare? You were there in mine."

She pulls back to look into his face, her cheeks blotchy and her eyes red.

"We were in the same nightmare," he responds grimly.

She lowers her voice to a whisper. "It was all my deaths. All of them. But you..." she shakes her head, choking out her words.

"I know," he says, looking away.

Ava pulls her sweater back over her shoulders and wipes her face with her sleeves, "I know it wasn't you. I know you never killed me in any of those past lives. I know that."

Elric looks at her, his eyes filled with despair, tears falling in stride.

"I felt it, Ava." He looks at his hands and balls his fist. "I felt myself doing it."

The plane's speaker crackles on, and the pilot's voice is heard overhead. "Ladies and gentlemen, we are beginning our descent. Welcome to Arcata."

Ava holds onto Elric's hand and sits back in her seat, the tears still not stopping. "She's taunting us more."

He looks at her, their sorrow and fear evident.

His desires are resolved. "I cannot wait to drive a blade through her heart."

XXII

E lric sighs deeply as he scoots into the back of a cab next to Ava. Still shaken up by the nightmare, Ava picks at the skin around her fingers.

"Can we stop by my place first? I left *The Iliad* and a blanket my mom made for me there. It would just be nice to have a few comfort items."

"Of course." He gives her hand a quick squeeze.

Ava rattles off the address, and the cab takes them to her studio. The ride is silent. The busy little town carries on with business, and the envy makes Elric sick.

To only need to take the trash out and go to work, he thinks.

The cab stops, and he asks the driver to hang back while they run inside. Walking up to her door, the distinct feeling of fear settles into them as they see that it has been left slightly ajar, and the flickering of a light can be seen going off inside.

Ava stutters over her words. "May-maybe my mom stopped by?"

Elric rubs her back and forces a smile. "Probably."

He pulls her back behind him by her hand and enters the studio first. Opening the door, a foul stench hits his nostrils. His gag reflex takes over, threatening to empty the bile in his stomach. Swallowing hard to keep it down, he enters and covers his nose. The room is completely destroyed. What little furniture Ava has is either flipped over or broken into pieces. Her books have been thrown off the shelves and ripped into shreds, pages strewn across the floor. Black feathers haphazardly lay around the room. Pictures on the walls with slash marks through them are marred with splatters of red. Ava walks in and gags, the smell overwhelming.

"Oh, my god." She looks around in horror.

She looks at her bed and screams. Elric searches for what is causing such a visceral reaction and sees a blackbird cut open from neck to belly. Its entrails lie around it in a circle on the bed, staining the pages of *The Iliad*, left on her sheets, red. In what can only be the bird's blood, a message is written on the wall above the bed in a red scrawl. Its dripping stream lands on her headboard. The lights flicker, showing the message in increments.

you can't take him from me

"Let's go now." He pushes her out the door and closes it behind him.

"What is this?" Ava asks as they hastened down the walkway, her breathing quick and shallow.

Elric, at a loss, takes her back to the street. "I don't know. Let's get back to my place."

They get back in the cab and do exactly that. Ava counts backward quietly from a thousand, trying to distract her mind. They thank the driver once they arrive and stand on the sidewalk, watching him drive away.

Ava tugs at Elric's arm. "How do we know there is nothing in there?"

He sets his bag down in the driveway. "Do you want to wait out here while I check, or do you want to come with me?"

"Neither." She sets her bag down next to his, shaking her head. "I'd rather come with."

They approach the closed door slowly and are on high alert. He reaches for the doorknob and turns. It's locked.

Elric sighs with relief. "That's a good sign." He pulls out his keys and unlocks the door. As he walks in, he is ready to fight if he has to but finds nothing.

"Ava, it's fine," he calls out behind him.

He hears her let out her breath in one steady stream of relief. "Okay, I'm going to go grab the bags."

He carefully searches all the rooms in his home but finds nothing amiss. She finds him in the bedroom, finishing the last of his inspections.

"I hate this," she says.

Standing behind him, she wraps her arms around him, burying her face between his shoulder blades. He overlaps her hands with his own and stands there silently, knowing no calming words exist to quell the current emotional chaos.

"It'll be over soon," she murmurs into his back, "I hope."

"Ava," he turns in her arms so they are face to face. His voice is tight as he speaks. "I'm so sorry this is our life."

A mere few days have stretched into feeling like a dark few months. For a moment, Elric regrets finding her, and this becoming their life.

He squeezes his eyes shut and shakes his head as if trying to clear bad memories from his mind. "I was so afraid of losing you."

She reaches up and touches his cheek. "Do not apologize. I would have done the same for you." The sincerity of her statement shows true in her soft smile.

A knock on the door startles them, and Ava's eyebrows raise. "Was Anita bringing Geoffrey back tonight?"

Elric's eyes narrowed. "No, I asked her to keep him for a few more days. Stay here."

"Absolutely freaking not." She scans the room, looking for some defensive weapon. "Baseball bat, gun, golf club? Anything to protect ourselves?" she asks, throwing her hands in the air, frustrated at the lack of objects in the simple, uncluttered house.

The rap at the door repeats itself.

"I have a fire stoker. Would you like me to grab that?"

"Please."

Elric jogs out of the room and returns quickly with the stoker in hand. "Come on."

The succession of knocks continues in a count of three with a break in between.

He walks out of the room, Ava following closely behind him. Another round of knocks sounds off throughout the house. He opens the door, barely enough to stick his head out, keeping Ava completely out of view.

A young girl in a soccer uniform stands on the porch, staring down at the ground. Elric, thinking she can't be much older than sixteen, feels no imminent danger from the stranger.

"Hello, can I help you?" he asks politely. Inconspicuously handing the stoker off to Ava, he opens the door wider so he can stand in the doorway.

She doesn't respond and keeps her focus on the ground with her hands held together. Ava nudges Elric over so she can stand beside him. She watches the girl for a moment, waiting for her to respond.

"Sweetie? Do you need something?" Ava takes a step forward, concern for the girl outweighing the worries from before.

She stretches out her arm and hesitates for a moment before deciding to lightly rest her hand on the girl's shoulder. As soon as contact is made, the girl's head snaps up, startling Ava and causing her to jump back reactively. The girl still doesn't move but now stares straight ahead past Ava.

"Ava, her eyes." Elric places his hand on her arm and begins to pull her back.

She responds slowly to his touch, mesmerized by the girl's eyes. The entirety of her sockets are filled with gray swirling clouds as if they were plucked from the sky on a rainy day.

"Who are you?" Ava asks, her voice barely audible.

The girl's head tilts to the side, like a dog listening for a whistle.

She inhales sharply and then lets out a rattled breath. "Meet in the avenue of Titans, at the feet of the fallen giant."

The girl sounds as if there are two voices in her throat speaking in unison.

"What?" Elric's eyes narrow. He waves his hand in front of her face in an attempt to bring her to.

The girl lurches forward, looking up into his face with her unnerving clouded eyes, and gives a wry smile.

"Meet us in the avenue. At the feet of the fallen giant in the last bathing of the sun."

Then, without warning, the girl's eyes flush and light brown eyes stare back at Elric, dazed.

She moves backward, her eyebrows furrowing. "Uhm, how did- uh," she stammers over her words, trying to gather her wits about her.

"Honey, are you headed to soccer practice?" Ava peers over Elric's shoulder.

She nods her head. "Yeah, I was walking there and then... I don't know."

"It's okay." Ava smiles compassionately. "It happens! Oh, look, I see your bag right there on the sidewalk! Is soccer practice at Sun Valley Park?"

The young girl nods again, pursing her lips in an effort to not cry.

"Hey! How about I walk you? It's right up the street. We can call your Mom and Dad, okay?" Ava steps around Elric as the girl sniffles.

"Okay," she says, her voice cracking.

"Elric, I'll be right back. If I'm not back in ten minutes, call me." She raises an eyebrow at him that really says *Please make sure I don't get murdered.*

He slowly nods. "Are you sure you don't want me to go?"

Ava grins at him, and he can see it all—she's spooked, but the kind woman in her is still worried about the innocent girl. "I'm good. Be right back."

He watches Ava pick up the duffle bag and carry it for the girl as they continue down the street. As soon as he can't see them anymore, he runs inside and grabs a sketch pad and pen off the counter. Writing down the cryptic message, he assumes and hopes it is from Orsa and Osana.

Meet at the avenue

Titans

Fallen giant

Bathing sun

Staring at the page, he scratches his head, saying the written words over and over again, hoping it'll make sense.

"Oh! The knife. Necklace." Elric reminds himself aloud.

He runs back into his room, still repeating the riddle and pushes aside clothes hanging in the closet, revealing a large antique walnut chest. He shuffles through different items from over the centuries until he finds what he is looking for. As he is pulling out an old black leather sheath and a purple velvet drawstring pouch, he hears the front door open and shut, followed by footsteps coming into the bedroom.

"Is she okay?" Elric asks, looking over his shoulder at Ava.

She wraps her sweater around herself and crosses her arms. "Very shaken up. Obviously. I got her in touch with her parents, and they're coming to pick her up. She doesn't remember what she said to us either."

Ava shakes her head and kneels beside him. "It's very terrifying to think about how much power these witches have. In our dreams, in my house, in that girl. And we've only found out about a small portion of them."

Elric stands up and holds Ava close, her arms still tucked into her body.

"I know, but," he holds up the items for Ava to see, "we are closer to being rid of the one who torments us."

She takes the velvet bag from his hand, opens it, and turns the contents into her hand. "The necklace. The night I found out you weren't a hobo." She says gently nudging him.

"I still could be a hobo. You'll never know."

She laughs and he unsheathes the knife, turning it over in his hand to study the mark that had gone unnoticed for so long. He runs his fingers into the deep etching of a rune at the base. His index finger follows an elongated V that is curved at the ends with two lines that cut across the base of the letter. Along both sides, there are two notches that mimic three more down the center of the V.

"I can't believe I never gave this mark a second look." Elric shakes his head at his own ignorance. "Now, to figure out that riddle. I'm so sick of this cryptic speech."

"Oh, I know exactly what it means," Ava says, turning the small glass bottle in her hand.

"No, you do not," he scoffs.

Placing her hands on her hips, she raises a brow.

Elric Ferron, do you forget that not only am I the funniest person you know, but I am also the smartest?"

Elric laughs and takes her to the notepad on the countertop in the kitchen. "Alright, what is it?"

She points to the pad of paper. "The Dyersville Giant. In the Avenue of the Giants. Pretty sure that last one is just a sunset thing."

He glares at the piece of paper. "No way."

"Yes," Ava nods her head. "Titan is giant. The feet of the fallen has to be the Dyersville Giant. This area is literally known for the Avenue of the Giants. And if they were trying to be secretive but make sure we still understood, then this is absolutely it." She smiles victoriously. "I grew up here. Well, this time, I grew up here, so I know it. It's about an hour south, and sunset is in about 90 minutes, so we need to go *now*. The sunset thing, I am absolutely taking a chance on, but if they are trying to give as little time as possible to make sure Faye doesn't know but also enough time, so we do know, then this has to be it."

Elric winces as he opens the hallway closet and grabs a jacket for Ava and himself. "Next time we fight witches, can everything be more local?"

Ava insists on driving Elric's car, hoping that he try to get some sleep. Reluctantly, he agrees, but not before giving some pushback. He backs the Aston Martin out of the garage, not wanting to subject Ava to driving a manual in the Mustang for the next hour. After stashing the knife and necklace into the glove compartment, she turns on music, and he pulls his hood over his head and nestles it into his seat. Quicker than he anticipates, sleep claims him, revealing the exhaustion of the past few days. Elric begins to dream of his home in Arcata, Ava sitting on the back patio wrapped in blankets with her head buried in *The Iliad* for the ten-thousandth time over the centuries. He sits out back with an easel and paints his muse. He smiles broadly, and everything feels just as it should. A breeze rolls through and brushes her hair across her face. She is looking up at Elric and laughing—his favorite sound. Thunder rolls in over their heads and he looks up while Ava still laughs. She continues to do so, and soon, it becomes an indiscernible noise. He looks back at her, and tears of blood fall on her cheeks. She touches her face and looks at her wet, crimson fingertips, still making the disturbing noise.

She reaches out, perfectly calm, and calls to him. "Elric."

He hurriedly stands and bumps into the easel with his shoulder, knocking it down to the ground with a loud crash. The painting he had been working on suddenly mirrors the scene before them. He reaches for her hand, and right before his fingertips reach hers, she vanishes. Grasping at the blanket that was wrapped around her, he throws it to the side. Turning around frantically in the yard, he hears a voice,

My love is never thee nearer,
And that me grieveth sore;

In the middle of the grass, Ava stands with her back to him, wearing a white linen tunic covered from head to toe in a black oil-like liquid.

"Ava?" Elric runs to her and clutches onto her shoulders.

Her eyes are focused on him as she continues to sing with a wide smile plastered on her face. She reaches up and caresses Elric's cheek leaving a black mark on him.

Sweet loved-one, think on me,
I have loved thee long.

Her eyes are wide and dazed as she continues to sing, pulling him in closer.

Sweet loved-one, I pray thee,
For one loving speech;

Ava threads her fingers through the back of his hair and brings her lips to his, closing her eyes. He puts his arms around her waist and lets her grab onto him tighter. Her nails dig into his back. She bites his bottom lip and draws blood. Giving a small shout from the pain, he pulls back to touch his lip. As he brings his hand into view, he realizes it's no longer Ava standing in front of him, but

Robyn, smiling wickedly.

Robyn pulls his hair aggressively and holds his head back.

Bringing her lips to his ear, she whispers seductively, "What? Don't like it rough? That's not how I remember it," she cackles. "Maybe it's not rough enough. Let's see if this helps?"

Robyn's form shifts before Elric, and in the next instant, Faye's fingers are pulling his hair, her arms around him. He jerks away, causing Faye's grip to constrict and pull his head back farther.

Elric tries to shout but can't. His lips pull at the skin, but he can't make his mouth open. Reaching up to feel his lips, he fingers thick stitches in a seam. His heart beats out of control, and his breathing is ragged.

Faye pouts. "Aw, what's wrong? Let's see if you can say the spell now."

She licks at the stitches on his lips, maliciously laughing as she steps back.

"You think you can defeat me? You won't be free, Elric. Ever."

Elric wakes up, jolting straight up in the seat of the car, ripping the hood off his head. Hyperventilating, he clutches at the dashboard, his hands cold and clammy.

"Elric?!" Ava quickly pulls the car off to the shoulder and throws the shift into park.

She reaches out for him, and he recoils, his eyes wide with fright.

She tugs her hands back and speaks softly. "Hey..."

Shaking his head, he gingerly touches his fingers to his lips, half expecting to feel seams still. He takes a deep breath, grounding himself back to reality when he feels his normal skin. Ava sits patiently, waiting, letting him take his time.

"Faye is stuck on tormenting us."

Ava reaches for Elric again to lovingly place her hand on the back of his neck. He leans into it, dropping his head.

"What was it?" Ava moves her thumb back and forth against his neck.

"It was us just being us, and then it wasn't." He looks up at her, the worry clear on her face.

"That bloody, stupid song was being sung, and you went to kiss me, and then you were Robyn. Then Robyn was Faye."

Elric forcefully presses his palms into his eyes. "My lips were sewn together. I couldn't speak, couldn't scream. Faye..." he shakes his head and looks back to Ava, "she absolutely knows we are trying to find the spell."

Dread twists inside Ava. "What do we do? Do we keep going?"

An icy wave washes over him, the fear threatening to invade his resolve. He looks into those green eyes, and the warmth breaks through.

Resting his hand on her cheek. "I will always keep going."

The corner of her mouth lifts in a pitiful attempt at reassurance, but it doesn't reach her eyes.

"Beyond this life and any thereafter," she says, using his coined phrase.

They sit in the car without speaking until Elric breaks the silence, "We have about forty minutes before sunset. How far out are we from the trail to the Dyersville Giant?"

Ava leans forward and points straight ahead. "The trailhead is up here to the right, but we have to go around and park the car in the woods. I'm not positive, but a park ranger may not let us go past a certain point. It's not worth losing time so I think we should just take the rest up by foot."

"Sounds like a plan," Elric says, rolling down his window and looking out.

As he takes in the wonder of the Redwoods towering over them hundreds of feet in the air, Ava carefully pulls the car off the shoulder and back onto the road, moving forward down the way until finding a suitable place to hide the vehicle. After covering the car with the appropriate amount of shrub, they find each other's hands as she leads the way to the fallen giant.

As they continue to walk deeper into the forest, the sun quietly dips below the tops of the trees. Elric stares straight up at the Redwoods, tripping over a large root in the process.

Ava helps keep him upright. "You have to watch the ground, there's too much that's going to trip you up."

I can't help it. Even in the middle of this utter chaos, I can't not be enamored by this place," Elric tells her.

"Okay, let's be enamored later. We are burning daylight, and we can't afford it," she says seriously.

They move through the woods faster. The sun seems to keep up with them. Advancing without speaking, the crunching of the leaves and the groaning of the trees fill the absence of their words.

Elric peers through the woods and sees that the sun is almost completely out of sight.

Slightly panicked, he pulls her to a halt. "Ava, where is it? Where's this tree?"

Ava points to the right. "It's around this bend, but maybe another quarter of a mile." She looks at the disappearing light, and his panic registers for her. "We are going to miss our window. We have to run."

"Go! I'll follow you. Just go!" He yells.

Running through the woods, their feet carry them through years of decayed earth. A tall shrub branch strikes Ava in the face, causing a bleeding cut on her cheek. She flinches but doesn't stop running, trying to beat the vanishing of the day.

"Elric!" She shouts, keeping her eyes forward. "I see it!"

"Go! I'm righ-" his words are cut off as he falls to the ground, the wind knocked out of him.

He turns onto his side, gasping for breath, looking down at his feet to see what tripped him. A large root unwraps itself from his ankle and slithers back into the recesses of the forest.

"What the f-"

"Elric!" Ava hooks him underneath his arm, trying to drag him up. "Are you okay?! Come on!"

He scrambles to his feet, kicking the earth up behind him and watching the root disappear from sight. The Dyersville Giant now looms above them, and the shadows continue to invade the forest as the sun sets. Adrenaline pushes them forward, blood pulsing in their ears. The tree lays with the underside of the stump fully exposed. Small roots hang, and bushes of moss have grown over the dormant giant. In the limited light that remains, Elric can see two figures in black-hooded cloaks. He and Ava reach the shrinking sunlight simultaneously, and before they can say a word to the twins, a black plume of smoke swallows them up, making the world around them disappear.

"Ava!" Elric yells, desperately reaching out for her, suddenly terrified that they ran into a trap.

He waits for a moment and hears nothing except a roaring wind in his ears before he starts screaming incessantly for Ava as the black smoke twists around him.

"Ava! Ava!" His throat is raw, and he can feel the blood vessels around his eyes beginning to strain.

He trips and starts crawling on the ground, still searching for her. The smoke around him finally begins to dissipate. As his sight clears, he no longer sees Ava anywhere nearby. He claws at the ground, and his hands fill with sand. Confused, he picks up a pile and drops it in front of him.

He looks up to see a long white gown in front of him.

"Hello, Elric."

XXIII

Ava

"Elric! Where are you?" Ava screams through loud winds, receiving no reply.

She tries to move, but the terror flowing through her makes it impossible, keeping her frozen in place. The winds die, and a location different from the one she and Elric had arrived in comes into view.

Ava spins around and finds herself on a building rooftop, a twinkling city skyline illuminating the concrete jungle in the distance.

"I am so sorry we had to do that."

Ava whips around at the voice behind her and sees two young girls standing side by side. One with scarring on her left side wears a white smock dress, and the other with scarring on her right wears the same but in gray. They take a step forward in unison, causing Ava to take a step back and hit the railing of the building's edge.

"Please."

"This was to ensure she couldn't find out."

Both speak in the same hushed tone.

Ava grips the railing tighter, her fright mounting. "Are you Orsa and Osana?"

"We are," they say simultaneously, nodding their heads.

The twin in white speaks first. "I am Orsa."

"I am Osana," says the one in gray.

"Are you here to help? Or kill me?" Ava trembles, wishing she could control it.

"We are here to help," Orsa says.

"*She* has no link to you. It is to Elric. You were just a..." Osana looks at her sister "By-product," Orsa finishes.

Ava releases her grip on the railing and stands straight, relaxing only slightly. She moves away from the edge, and the twins watch her intently.

"We need the spell from you that Eliana gave Gabriel. Can you look into the past and get it? Elric said you might be able to." Her voice is still shaky.

The twins smile at each other, speaking at the same time. "It was the plan all along."

They drop to their knees, and as soon as they hit the ground, their eyes go black. Osana claps, pressing her hands together and slowly pulling them back apart, conjuring a paper and pencil. Orsa covers her mouth and whispers in her sister's ear. Ava cannot hear what she is saying but notices the rapidly spoken whispers. Osana's hand moves across the page to make an image come to life on the paper. Ava moves forward cautiously, her eyes narrowing at the paper. Gabriel's pain-stricken face plainly comes into view in the middle of a forest. Leafless, large, moss-covered trees canopy over Gabriel, who is sitting in a circle of branches. Osana draws his arms empty in a cradling position until, finally, a woman's lifeless body is placed in the crook of them. A dark mark on the center of the woman's chest contrasts against her dress. A dagger stands straight up from where her heart would be. Osana begins to scribble across the whole page, covering the picture. Finally, the twins collapse into one another, both stopping the other from completely falling onto the ground. They look up at Ava, their eyes clear once more. Orsa, breathing heavily, picks up the paper and hands it to Ava.

She holds the paper out in front of her and reads, "*Morcreom Ortalisantus.*"

"Elric cannot know," Orsa tells her

Osana nods in agreement. "She will see."

"She will know," Orsa follows.

Ava folds the paper and places it in her pants. "Okay. Okay, okay," she repeats to herself, looking around apprehensively while still waiting for some mysterious force to come out and slit her throat.

"Okay." She runs her hands down her face, hoping it will snap her into a stable mental space. "Alright, so that's it? Everything Gabriel told us to do, and then this?"

The twins shake their heads no. Osana pats the ground, beckoning Ava to take a seat across from them.

Elric

"Where am I? Why are you here?"

Elric scrambles to his feet and backs away, looking for some weapon on this deserted island, but all he sees his broken driftwood at a distance.

"I told you before, I mean you no harm, Elric Ferron." Jacqueline smiles at him and extends her hand. "I'm here to help."

She stands on the sand, her feet in the crawling waves of water. Her black hair is completely loose around her body, and it flutters in the ocean's breeze. The dress, cross-wrapped around her neck, moves with her hair and clings to her.

He looks around the shoreline. "Where's-"

Jacqueline quickly puts a finger onto his lips and shakes her head earnestly.

"Safe," she says quickly and under her breath. "Come take my arm, walk with me."

Elric reluctantly takes her arm and oddly feels at ease with her.

"Why am I here? Where am I? Why are you here?" He repeats himself.

"It's an in-between of sorts. It makes those who can see someone's mind's eye receive muddied, distorted images. Sometimes, they're completely broken memories." Jacqueline strokes Elric's arm linked in hers. "It's safer here. But still, try not to speak so plainly if you can help it. She cannot see me and my side of the conversation, but she can still receive bits of yours. The bracelet I have given you," she says tilting her head towards the jewelry on his arm, "has helped distort as well since Montreal. It's not a complete sever from you, but as I said, it helps."

"What about everyone else I have come into contact with in discussions over this particular subject?" He asks.

"Everyone since Montreal has been shielded from her as well. That I can extend to them. But I don't quite understand how Faye has such a grasp on your soul, so here we are in an in-between, or limbo."

"Great... Well, I need to find the incantation," Elric says, releasing her arm and turning towards her. The inshore waves lap at his feet, soaking the hem of his pants.

"Okay, try *not* to speak plainly, is what I said." Jacqueline laughs, shaking her head. "Not to worry. It'll find you."

"What am I supposed to do while I wait? Are we just shooting the breeze? Setting up another exhibit? I don't have time for this." He turns to walk away but remembers he has nowhere to go.

She lets out a soft chuckle, closing her eyes and lifts her face toward the sunlight.

"Who put it in that pretty little head of yours that this was only *your* issue to rectify? Hm?"

She turns her head to him and opens one eye. "You may have been the one to mark the book, Elric, but there are two souls wrapped in this plague."

"But it was my doing that put us here." He throws his hands into the air in frustration. "And here you are bathing in the sunlight, seemingly not a care in the world."

Marching up to her, he stops only a couple of inches from her face and glares. "Tell me Jacqueline, why are you in this? You have no skin in the game."

She turns and meets his gaze, challenging what he calls into question.

Her eyes go dark, and the skies go with it. The ocean's breeze turns into harsh winds. Waves begin to grow in height, the crashing of the waters forceful. "You act as though you are the only one who has lost a loved one to these circumstances."

Elric's eyes soften a bit, but his voice has not lost its harsh tone. "Who?"

Jacqueline takes a deep breath, and her eyes are calm, the elements calming with her. She steps further out into the ocean until she is knee-deep and stares at the horizon. He watches her wade for a moment before walking out beside her. He gently takes her hand, fully understanding the pain of losing a piece of your heart. With his irritation dissolved and his fight at bay, he approaches the woman who has helped him with empathy. In those few quiet moments in the water, Elric reflects on how his life has been nothing but fight and turbulent emotion. But he is not the only one who is lost in the waves of chaos and pain.

"She is my sister."

He looks at Jacqueline. The dipping sun softly reflects off the tears rolling down her face. Her eyes move toward their linked hands and then to his face. Her smile is soft yet so broken, the fragility of her emotions apparent in her gaze.

"Not by blood but by every other right, Faye is my sister." Jacqueline gently dabs at her tears. "We were not raised in dark magic, but the power of it was alluring to us both. We traveled the world for years, and both our collections of souls were growing. Until finally, one day, I watched her take a child's soul and then kill him immediately without a second thought. No remorse. It showed me where the darkness of that magic could take you, and in that moment, it showed me how terrifying it was."

She releases Elric's hand and crosses her arms over herself tightly as if she is trying to comfort herself.

"Why was that? What snapped you out of it?" He asks.

Jacqueline's face twists in pain. "It was her own son."

Elric runs his hands through his hair and looks back out at the ocean. "Is it revenge you seek?"

Shaking her head slightly, Jacqueline reaches up and brushes his hair behind his ear. "Oh no. It's release."

"For you?"

"For her."

Elric looks at her questioningly.

"I will never escape what I've done, seen, or been complicit in. Her only escape from that kind of evil is a *true* end. When you take the life of someone you love, there's no way to reclaim your soul. Never."

A light chiming rings through the air around the pair, and Jacqueline gives a watery-eyed smile, "It's time. Ignorance is your best friend right now."

Before Elric can ask any more, the same billowing black smoke swallows him whole, distorting any vision into the world. The next moment, he finds himself at the foot of the Dyersville Giant, staring at the back of Ava's head.

His anxiety eases as he finally places his hands on her. She turns around, startled by his touch.

"Oh, my god." She throws herself onto him, wrapping her arms tightly around his neck.

"Are you okay?" He asks desperately, smoothing down the back of her hair.

"Yes, I'm completely fine. Are you?" She pulls back, looking over his face for any sign of distress or injury.

"Your cheek!" He says, gently touching the laceration.

She winces and pulls back. "I forgot. I'm fine. That happened when we were running."

"Where were you?" He asks.

Ava shakes her head. "I can't—"

Recalling what Jacqueline had told him moments before, he nods but lacks the resolve to avoid discussing it with Ava.

Elric looks around, surrounded by the looming titans of the forest in complete darkness. The hair stands on the back of his neck as a warning or a precursor for the fight yet to come.

"Come on, let's get going. Right now, being here feels unnerving." She takes his hand, leading the way back through the trail, eager to get back to the car.

He lets her lead and follows in silence. His mind races, thinking of all Jacqueline told him and wonders where Ava has been all this time and with whom. The trip back to the car seemed shorter than the trek out, but they were thankful to be out of the canopy of darkness the forest offered. He opens the door for Ava and waits until she is buckled before he shuts the door. He just needs the peace of mind to see her be safe. It feels as though darkness now lurks, and it sets him on edge.

He gets into the driver's seat and sets course back to home.

Ava pulls out her phone, typing out a text as she speaks. "Don't head home."

Quickly glancing at her sideways, Elric tries to go with the flow. "Okay, where to?"

"I'll let you know in a few. Just keep driving."

She keeps her eyes down on her phone, and Elric can see the text bubbles moving up the screen as the conversation goes back and forth.

"Who is that?"

"I'll let you know in a few."

Her thumbs keep moving across the screen. Pulling a worn paper from her back pocket she begins to take pictures of it. Anytime Elric tries to look over, she flips the page up before he can get a glance.

"Quit it. I'm serious." She says sternly, keeping her eyes focused on what she's doing.

Elric's grip tightens on the steering wheel, and his knuckles turn white. Relinquishing control is not his forte, and for him to not know the situation doesn't bode well either.

Ava turns the phone screen down onto her lap, tucking the paper away, and looks at Elric. Leaning forward, she makes an obvious motion, trying to make eye contact.

"Hey," she says tenderly.

"Hmph," he grunts in return, still not turning her way.

"Elric, I know this isn't easy. Especially when you feel like it's your responsibility. But it isn't just yours. And you not knowing is to protect us all."

"Okay."

"Elric–"

"Ava, I said okay."

She leans back in her seat and stares out the window, the forest now just a constant blur. He glances at her and his hold on the wheel loosens.

He places his hand over her knee, gently squeezing. "Ava."

She turns her head back towards him, and he takes a deep breath, letting it out slowly.

"This is not easy for me. I've spent hundreds of years trying to find out how to fix what I have done to us. This is *my* mistake. *My* error to fix. And now, to find the only way to fix it is to essentially keep me out of it. It's not easy."

She places her hands over his, entwining their fingers. "Do you trust me?"

"Absolutely."

"Do you trust what you were told tonight?" She asks, raising an eyebrow.

"I don't know."

"That's okay. This is *our* curse to break. Let me do my part so you can do yours."

He strokes the underside of her palm. "Okay."

He picks up her hand and kisses it, leaving her hand at his lips as he drives.

Ava's phone chimes off, and she pulls her hand from Elric's to open the text. She exhales with relief and responds to the incoming text. "Okay, head to the studio."

Elric lets her lead without question.

Pulling into an empty parking spot in front of the studio, Elric shuts off the car and runs around to open Ava's door. No matter the immediate threat they are in, he will always be the gentleman. As he approaches the door, his eyebrows knit together at the collection of white symbols marking the walkway in front of the door and the door frame itself. Ava steps out of the car, putting a finger to her lips and shaking her head. She takes him by the hand and leads him inside the studio. He quickly closes the door behind him, following her without saying a word. Inside, he looks around, noticing the same unfamiliar markings on the walls. Anita walks out of his office, white dust across her forehead and Geoffrey in her hands. Benny, with unused pieces of chalk in his hand, follows closely behind Anita. Geoffrey begins furiously wagging his tail, squirming out of Anita's arms until she puts him down. He runs to Ava and Elric, barking and jumping at their feet. Elric picks up Geoffrey and scratches him behind the ears, smiling.

Anita smiles at them, embracing the two together. "You guys are safe."

Ava pulls back and squeezes her shoulder.

"Thank you for doing this so quickly. You have no idea." She peeks around Anita's shoulder at Benny. "Benny? I know we've never formally met, but I have heard so much about you. Thank you for coming to help."

Ava walks over and hugs him, the gratitude behind it making the act more familiar.

"Of course. Anita called, and you guys are important to her. So it was important." Benny says.

Elric, still holding Geoffrey, looks around bewildered, from Anita to Ava, to the walls, to Benny, and back to Ava.

XXIV

"I texted Anita pictures of the runes needed to protect us in here. Faye can't access you while you're in here. Everything we say is completely blocked off from her," Ava excitedly tells Elric, taking him into his study.

"How?"

"Orsa and Osana!" She reaches into her pocket and pulls out the tattered paper with rushed charcoal markings covering the front and back.

Throughout his existence, Elric had never been one for prayer, but he prayed those women became as free as he hoped for Ava and himself, knowing the risk they put themselves at.

"I feel like it's safer in this room, honestly. The ones outside feel shoddy. These enchantments seem more authentic, so we are actually blocking people out instead of like conjuring a Lo Mein dinner from Imperial Garden," Anita says, staring at the handiwork on the ceiling.

Benny laughs and folds a ladder standing in the middle of the room, putting it off to the side.

"I could have never done it without him, though, can't reach those really high spots." Anita's smitten gaze settles on the young man.

"So, how much do you two know?" Elric asks, setting Geoffrey down.

The dog runs over to a small fluffy dog bed set in the corner behind Elric's desk. Quickly curling in on himself, he goes to sleep almost on the spot.

"Not a lot," Anita tells him, flopping down on one of the sofas. She tilts her head to the side, gesturing for Benny to sit next to her.

Elric sits behind his desk, and Ava sits on the corner of it cross-legged in front of him.

"I know you have questions," she says looking at Elric, "but Anita did all this for us without hesitation. I feel like we owe her, and now Benny, an explanation."

Elric crosses his arms and rests his chin on his hand. "There is no way in hell they'll believe it."

There is no fear about telling these people his truth, the only worry is wasting time trying to get them to *believe* the absurdity of his world.

Ava raises her shoulders, shrugging out of her sweater. "It's not up to us to make sure they believe us, just our job to be truthful."

He sits back, signaling Ava to proceed.

Ava lets out a heavy breath and turns to the sofa. "Okay, well. I guess." She looks over her shoulder back to Elric. "Where the hell do I even start?"

"The paintings," Anita interjects before Elric can speak.

She turns back toward Anita and Benny and smiles. "Alright, all the paintings of me. Those date back literally hundreds of years. The one from Spain was done in the 1700s. France, 1800s. They were actually painted at that *time.*"

"The charcoal parchment?" Anita asks, her brows puckered.

Elric clears his throat and sits up. He looks at Ava, searching for his calm in that green. He has never willingly told his secret to anyone, and to speak it aloud with seemingly no forbearance makes his uneasiness obvious. She reaches over and cups his chin, her smile warm and full of comfort. Ava mouths, *It's okay,* before releasing him.

"Spring, 1348. Ava told me she was pregnant. I was a blacksmith in Bristol, and when I could spare a penny for a piece of parchment, I would make way for my love of art."

Elric pauses, waiting for looks of skepticism, and all he can see is his friend literally on the edge of her seat, giving him her full attention. Whether or not she believes him is still in question, but there is no doubt that she has the grace to hear him out.

Closing his eyes, he pinches the bridge of his nose and continues. "She contracted the Plague, and I was unwilling to lose her without trying every single thing on Earth that I could."

Elric shifts in his seat. "My best friend, Geoffrey," at the sound of the name, the pup perks his head and softly wags his tail, "whom I named that gentleman after," he reaches over and gives Geoffrey a quick scratch on his head before continuing. "He knew how desperate I was, and he let me know a sort of witchcraft he kept hidden so that no one could make the trade I did that day. I called forth a witch named Faye, and I thought she would help me, but Ava died anyway, and then I couldn't die at all. I tried to kill myself, and I could not die."

The two sit on the couch listening fervently as Elric continues to recant the story to Anita and Benny, from the first reincarnation of Ava, to the present Ava getting her memories back, and to this very moment. They all sit together in silence, Elric and Ava letting Anita and Barry digest the information.

After a few minutes, Anita finally speaks up. "I want to believe you because I don't believe either one of you to be liars. I took a leap putting up these... spells?" she says, waving her hand around, questioning the words coming out of her mouth, "Because Ava said it was important, and you were in trouble. But this is insane. Like what other proof do we have besides paintings that literally could have been doctored up to look old?"

Ava and Elric look at each other, never having been put in this position for proof before.

"Oh!" Ava exclaims. "Do the Gabriel thing!"

Elric's shoulders move as he laughs, confused. "The Gabriel thing? What is that?"

"Oh, good lord," Ava says, looking around the desk until her eyes settle on a retractable box cutter, covered in paint and tape, sitting beside a coffee cup of brushes and pencils.

Without a second thought, she leans over and pulls out the blade, knocking over the cup and its contents in the process. She quickly grabs Elric's hand, pulls it onto her lap, and aims the blade. Anita and Benny both jump from the sofa, lunging towards Ava.

"Ava, the hell!" Anita yells.

Before Anita reaches her, Ava slices open his palm, spilling blood onto her leg. Benny wraps his arms around Ava, dragging her away from Elric. Elric immediately bolts up from his seat with a deep protective growl in his throat.

Anita cuts Elric's path off. "Oh, my god, are you okay?" she asks.

"I'm okay," he says without looking at her.

He glares at Benny and clenches his hand, unintentionally squeezing the blood from his palm in a neat puddle, onto the floor. "Benny, let her go. *Now*." Elric threatens in a low voice.

"Hey, she just cut you open. You want me to let her loose on you?" Benny asks, his hold on Ava tightening. "I don't know what kind of toxic relationship crap this is, but it's not putting Anita in danger."

Ava turns to Elric, "He didn't do anything wrong. He thinks I'm dangerous, which we obviously can see why. Now, can you just show him your freaking hand," she says nonchalantly.

Elric looks down at his fist hanging above a neat pool of red below on the floor. The streaming has already ceased. He holds his palm open for Anita and Benny to see, showing the wound neatly healing itself, a tender pink line in the wake of an open injury.

Their eyes both grow wide in astonishment, a dumbstruck Benny releasing Ava without thought.

"Is it magic?" Benny asks in utter shock.

Ava walks over to Elric and holds the healing hand in her palms. "I think? That's the best way to describe it."

She rubs the healed cut, "Sorry, I just went for it."

"It's fine," he says, holding her close.

"Okay." Anita takes a deep breath, letting it balloon in her cheeks and holding it.

"Anita? Are you okay?" Ava asks, concerned.

She slowly lets out her breath and stares at the two. "Okay. You are like a thousand years old."

"Somewhere closer to seven hundred," Elric interrupts, and she shoots him daggers.

He holds his hand up in defense. "Right, semantics."

"*You're* like a thousand years old." She glares at Elric one more time, and he smiles sheepishly in return. "And Ava is on her like billionth life."

"Basically," Ava replies.

Anita sits back down on the couch and leans her head back, staring at the ceiling. Benny sits beside her only leaving a couple of inches of space between them. He rests his arm on the back of the couch, and Anita lifts her head, waiting for him to drape his arm around her shoulders. He scoots in closer and does as she asks without words.

But she quickly sits back up, Benny's arm falling behind her, and directs her stare at Elric. "You are super rich?"

Elric throws his head back and laughs at the random afterthought. "Yes."

"I am never feeling bad for you paying for anything ever again." She waves off Elric and Ava. "I know you two have things to discuss. Go ahead while I let this settle in my brain."

Anita takes Benny by the hand and yells over her shoulder on the way out. "I'm going to go look at these apparently priceless ancient artifacts you have in your room over here."

They walk out hand in hand, shutting the door behind them. Ava takes their empty spots on the sofa, pulling her legs up underneath her.

Elric sits next to her, glad that their understanding of him as a person led them to trust the truth about his life so easily.

"Alright, so who gave you these markings to put all over the place? Where were you when we were separated?"

"The twins! I don't know. I was on a rooftop in a city I'd never been to before. They told me everything I needed to do in order to defeat this. I got the spell from them."

"Perfect. What is it?" He asks.

"I can't tell you."

"Okay..." Elric says, puzzled. "What else did you all talk about?"

"I can't tell you," Ava says, looking away.

"What do I get to know?"

"That there is a plan."

Standing, he rakes his healed hand through his hair, "And I get to know none of that plan?"

She leans forward. "Elric, have you ever wondered how Faye always knows where you are? How she knew to come find us when I was whole? How she knew where my apartment was to write that message?"

"She's a witch. I assumed it just came with the territory." He walks over to the desk to lean against it. "Obviously it's more than that."

"She has a link to your soul. Whatever the hell happened with her curse still left a tie to you. A very intimate knowing of your mind. Didn't Jacqueline explain that to you?"

"Sort of. I don't know. We discussed a lot."

Ava twirls the ends of her hair in her fingers as she talks. "Anything you may talk about outside this building, anything you might even *think* about, she could have access to. We can't risk it."

"Ava. I'm just supposed to let you take the brunt of *my* mistake and not lift a finger?"

He sits in his office chair and folds his arms behind his head. "I'll sit here and relax. Oh, could you grab me dinner before you go out? Thanks."

"Elric..."

Sitting up, he brings his fists down upon the wood in a hard crash.

"No, Ava. You're sitting here telling me that not only are we in this curse because of me, but the reason we can't get ahead of it is also because of me."

Ava runs her hands over her face in frustration. "God, Elric. If we break it, why does it matter who knows the plan?"

"Because I need to be the one to break it!" He yells.

"Why does that matter?"

"It just does."

Raising her voice, she crosses her arms. "Are you kidding me? Is this just a pride thing? Because honestly, I don't have time for that." She walks to him and puts her hand on his shoulder, softening her tone. "We can defeat her together, but you have to just follow my lead. For you to know anything else is a liability right now."

He moves his shoulder back out of her hand. "It's not good enough. And frankly, I don't want you anywhere near it. You're staying here while I take care of it."

"Oh, okay," she dryly laughs. "Is your ego so damn fragile? You don't own me, Elric. I'm going to go do what I need to do."

Elric stands up, slamming the chair into the wall behind him. "I am your husband; I am protecting you."

"You aren't in this lifetime, baby. And even if you were, I am not cattle to herd around. Like I said, I am doing what needs to be done," she snaps.

"No!" He barks.

"No?" Defiance darkens her eyes.

"Ava, I cannot lose you." The anguish in his gaze doesn't match the hardness of his tone.

Walking back over to the desk, she tightly grips her sweater, but she pauses and closes her eyes, leaving her hand frozen on the fabric. Taking a deep breath, she opens her eyes and searches his face before staring into his gaze, calculating the next words to come out of her mouth.

She looks away before she speaks. "Elric, you can't do this. You are a liability. You've got us in this curse, and now it's my job to clean it up."

Ava can't look at his face. She knows the brokenness across it will unravel the plan and her determination. She'll run back in his arms, and they'll hold each other's broken pieces, making it better again. Turning her back to him, she puts on her sweater and clears her throat, hoping to smother the sobs threatening to work their way up her throat.

As she begins to walk out the door, Elric somberly calls out, "Ava, I never meant-"

The door slams shut before he can say another word, leaving him in a swirl of anger and hurt. He can hear the commotion of Anita and Benny chasing Ava as she runs out the front door of the studio. He sits back down, his mind stubborn enough not to follow. But his heart screams, begging him to run after her.

Empty minutes go by, and the grandfather clock rings out. Elric looks up and reads ten o'clock. He hears the front door open and rushes out to meet Ava in front. As he gets to the door, he sees only Anita and Benny whispering to each other on the threshold.

"Where is she?" He asks.

His worry quickly churns the tides of rage within him.

The thought of her not returning to work out their argument never occurred to him, and the fact that she isn't standing in front of him makes his nightmare a reality. She is going to go face Faye alone.

The pair stare at Elric in silence.

"Where is she?!" He screams, punching his fist through the wall. The drywall gives way easily beneath his fury.

Anita jumps and Benny instinctively steps in closer to her.

Benny speaks first. "She said she was going to the fairy ring. That she needed to deal with it, end it all."

"Elric," Anita's eyes start to well, "I tried stopping her. I didn't want her going without you."

He rushes past Anita to where he had parked his car and sees his vehicle is gone. He pulls his phone out and calls Ava. He immediately hears a ringing inside the studio and runs inside, seeing her phone sitting on Anita's desk. The sound of it echoes.

"Damn it!" He yells, worrying for Ava and remembering the necklace and knife in the glove compartment. Rushing to his office, he grabs the blade Ava had used to cut his hand and stuffs it in the pocket of his jacket.

Taking a deep breath to calm himself down, he approaches the two, watching him worriedly from the front.

"Anita, Benny."

He reaches out, gently placing a hand on Anita's shoulder. "I need to go to her now, and I don't want you anywhere near it. It's dangerous in a way you couldn't even begin to understand. But I need your car."

Without a word, Anita nods her head and digs into her pocket until she finds a single car key to place in Elric's hand.

XXV

Elric frantically drives Anita's Subaru to the closest opening of the trail leading to the fairy ring. They had only been to that one together, and he prayed it was the one Ava chose. The night is silent, and the roads are empty, allowing Elric to run red lights and stop signs. The last thing he needs is a cop pulling him over, but he has no time to pretend like the laws of man apply to him, especially not tonight. He furiously bangs his hands on the steering wheel as he speeds through the streets, hoping to lure Faye to himself rather than Ava facing her alone. He blows through an intersection and narrowly misses a pickup truck coming in from the left. The truck turns harshly, trying to avoid the Subaru, and runs over a sidewalk, stopping safely in a parking lot. The truck driver lays on his horn, hanging out his window and flipping Elric the bird.

"Come on!" He shouts to himself as he looks for the street he needs to turn on. Finally spotting the entrance of the park, he takes a sharp turn into the vacant lot and quickly turns it off, leaving the keys in the ignition.

He sees the fallen tree with the bright orange tie on it and spots the trailhead to the fairy ring. Elric sprints down the path, hoping the luminescence of the moon is enough to light the way. The forest is covered in a dense, low fog. The mist rises up from the ground in tendrils, swaying with the kiss of the breeze. He arrives at the ring of trees and finds the mother stump in the middle completely unoccupied by Ava or any other living creature. He steps up onto the stump and stands directly in the middle of it, looking out into the forest to see if he is truly alone. The dark patches of space between the trees are unsettling. Thresholds of the forest are too dark to see through. A breeze floats by, calling his attention behind him, but again, he sees nothing except the scattering of birds leaving one tree for another. Maybe this isn't the fairy ring Ava was going to try to summon Faye to, which means Elric is entirely in the wrong spot and has no way of finding where Ava will be in hundreds of acres of forest.

He pulls the blade from his pocket and pushes out the gleaming silver before pressing it to his left wrist and dragging it down the center. He sucks in his breath as he makes sure the bite of the blade is deep so that he won't heal too soon. The warm sensation of blood flows down his fingers and onto the stump below. He switches the blade to his blood-soaked hand, preparing to do it to his right wrist. The handle becomes slippery and hard to grip. A cold sweat breaks over his brow. Quickly, without thinking about it much longer, he drags the blade again, opening the skin and giving way to the seeping of his blood. His vision begins to go fuzzy at the edges the quicker the blood flows and pools down below. With a hard thud, he lands on his knees at the edge of the stump and falls off. Sweat runs down his back, pooling underneath his arms and down the backs of them. His breathing is shallow and ragged. The wind begins to build, causing the tree branches to groan loudly. The sound is menacing and almost taunts him.

"Come on, Elric," he says.

The smell of earth and copper makes his stomach churn, causing him to want to vomit. He realizes now he may have cut too deep. In an effort to lure Faye to him, he may not have given himself a fighting chance if he passes out before he realizes she's there.

With a shaky breath, he tries to push himself up with his hands, but his wrists collapse, the skin splitting open more. His face takes a hard dive into the dirt onto a root, causing a small gash on his temple. With as much momentum as he can gain, he rolls himself onto his back. The blood from the new wound on his head starts to trickle down his face, and he grows dizzy. He raises a hand to wipe his face, but with the blood soaking his skin, he knows it'll do no good. Giving up on the action, Elric lays his arms at his sides once again.

Looking up at the sky with the perfect clearing above him, he stares at the brush-stroked stars across the sky and weeps.

If only he weren't so stubborn, he thinks, then he and Ava would be together, and he would be assured of her safety. It never needed to be him specifically to put an end to the curse. The curse just needs to end no matter who the hand is that deals the final blow.

His mind runs over each Ava he has known, the Ava she has always been. His true north for his most lost days.

When the world stops becoming such a dizzy haze, he slightly lifts his head off the ground to look down at his wrists. The blood has stopped flowing, and little tissue fibers slowly link themselves back together. He smiles and puts his arms back down, finally feeling a morsel of sureness in his plan.

As he looks back up, a silhouette is in his sight, bending over him with its long hair hanging down like a curtain.

"Ava?" He asks hopefully.

The face comes closer into view, the moonlight glinting off of white hair. "Oh, no. You and wifey had a fight?"

A malevolent giggle sounds off into the empty forest, and it seems as though the trees moan in reply.

"Faye," Elric groans in agony.

"Of course." Faye lies next to him as if they are partners in bed, sharing pillow talk.

The blood from his wounds quickly seeps into her red dress, darkening the shade. Picking up his arm, she examines it and pokes at the open flesh. Elric grits his teeth at the pain. She throws his arm over him. It softly bounces against his chest and back to his side.

"You know, Elric, the connection over the last couple days has been *fuzzy*. Then you were missing for a while tonight. Twice. That's never happened to me before, let alone twice." Faye turns over on her side, propping herself up on her arm. "And every time I tried to see you, it was nothingness. It gave me a headache actually."

Taking her free arm, she digs her nails into his wound, causing him to cry out.

"It's like the connection was static when I could see you. I could feel your anger, and then I saw you passing the welcome sign into this place. Then..."

Faye releases his arm, and her eyes light up.

She licks her lips and grabs at her chest. "I could feel you doing that delicious little thing you do when you pretend like you can kill yourself. And it drew me here."

Suddenly, she sits up and straddles his hips, leaning down and placing her hands on the ground beside his head. Setting her face beside his, she licks at his ear and clenches down on it forcefully, drawing blood. Subtly, he moves his hand as slyly as he can to his pocket.

Faye sits back up, licking his blood from her lips.

"You don't have to do this to call me here. If you're bored with Ava, just say so. I'm happy to throw you a bone."

With a quick pull, Elric takes out the ejected blade and thrusts it into the center of her chest. The contact is met with a resounding smack, causing Faye to slide back off of his body. He quickly scrambles to his feet as fast as his healing wounds will let him, trying to prepare to strike again when she gets up. She sits there silently, slumped over, not making a single move. Elric watches her and thinks of striking her again for good measure. He didn't think the first stab would do anything but hinder her a bit since he didn't have the spell, but at least she wasn't with Ava. As he steps forward, he hears a deep, throaty cackle erupt. Faye straightens her back and rolls her neck, a cracking noise following each roll. She looks down at her chest and dabs at the black, oily substance leaking from the wound.

"Ouch," she says with cold sarcasm. "You know, Elric, that really hurts my feelings."

"I'd believe that if there were any feelings other than hatred," he replies.

She neatly rises onto her knees, dusting the earth off her blood and oil-stained dress as if removing dirt would help. In the next moment, Faye appears directly next to Elric. With a wicked smile, she viciously grabs him by the throat, lifting him off of the ground. He claws at her hand as his airway is crushed. His grip tightens on the blade still in his hand as he swings his arm as hard as he can, making contact with her eye. He hits her skull hard enough that his hand swells instantly as he hears bones shatter.

Faye hisses, dropping him to the ground. She pulls away with the blade still embedded in her eye socket. He chokes at the intake of air as he dizzily finds his way back upright on his feet. She buckles over and reaches up to clasp the handle sticking out of her eye and cuts through the night with a shrill and agonizing scream as she rips the knife out of the delicate tissue. That dark substance and a clear liquid oozes from what is left of the mangled eye. Elric rushes her, hoping to catch her off guard, but before he can reach her, she holds an open hand towards him.

"*Duraad Prohatus,*" she shrieks.

He stops mid-stride, unable to move. His mind wills his body, but his body can't follow the command. He tries to yell, but only muffled sounds escape with his lips sealed in place.

Faye cocks her head to the side. "Oh, you need to say something?"

She slowly walks closer to him, her hand never wavering, the spell keeping him in place.

Her eyes narrow as she whispers, the bitterness in her voice transparent. "*Nuosec Laminere.*"

Elric tries to scream as the skin over his chest bursts open as if it were only held together by thread. Two identical lacerations slowly travel from his shoulder to the bottom of his rib cage. The wounds weep, soiling his shirt.

"You know what's the nice thing about you not being able to die?" Faye snickers as she circles him.

She stands behind him, never loosening the spell that holds him frozen in place. "*Nuosec Laminere,*" she repeats, causing another set of cuts down the center of his back.

"I can torture you over and over and over again, and I'll never be at risk of losing you. The best relationship I've ever had, if I'm being honest."

She laughs a dark, evil laugh as she makes her way back to Elric's line of sight, close enough to touch him. His body trembles, and sweat drips down his forehead.

She moves her finger gently over her mouth, following the shape of his lips. "*Demoteom Orisumas.*"

Elric feels the freedom of his jaw muscles, and pries open his mouth, screaming in pain as he does so.

Through gritted teeth, he snarls. "You are going to die tonight."

Faye places her hand over her heart, feigning a look of worry. "Oh, I'm scared."

She raises her hand high in the air and rapidly draws it downward. Elric's body mimics the motion, slamming to the ground as a resounding crack rings through the air. He immediately knows his ribs have broken. The wind is knocked out of him, sending him into another fit, gasping for breath. He tries to crawl to the stump to attempt to somehow trap her inside this ring that is supposed to have power. As he drags his body to the base, she strides over to him and delivers a powerful kick to his face. Immediately, he sputters out the air he had caught, blood spraying the side of the tree.

He turns over, leans back on the stump, and smiles up at Faye, his teeth crimson.

"It must kill you," he coughs out.

Faye squats down next to him in an animalistic manner and clutches his chin aggressively, glaring at him with the unmutilated eye.

Her voice comes out sickeningly sweet, "What kills me?" She broods.

Elric laughs in between fits of coughing, "That no matter what life I find her in, we still get to love each other. That our souls are not a complete tortuous ode to your power. You thought you were robbing me when you've given me hundreds of lifetimes of loving her instead."

She backhands him and points his face back at hers.

"The fact that I can ensure her death is enough satisfaction for me."

She stands up and spits in his face, circling his beaten body. Elric tries once more to get himself to the top of the stump. He turns and sees a notch in the tree to secure his grip and hoists himself up with the last of his strength. His wrists have almost completely closed, but the wounds on his back and chest are still leeching him of his strength. Faye stands back and crosses her arms, watching the display in amusement. He pushes his feet at the tree and finally drags himself to the center of it. Lying on his side, the only thing he thinks about is how grateful he is she is away from Ava.

Faye leaps up onto the stump with ease and sings in an eerily melodious tone, circling Elric like a wolf with its prey.

I have loved all this past year
So that I may love no more;
I have sighed many a sigh.

Abruptly, her song is cut short by the sound of breaking glass, and a mist of crimson haze explodes in the fairy ring. As if there are walls in between the trees of the fairy ring, the mist hits the invisible barrier and stays in the confines of the circle. Faye sniffs the air as the scent of poppies settles around her. Her eye swims with fear, frantically moving back and forth, trying to place the source. She dashes towards an opening in between the trees, looking for escape. Her body flies backward as if she hit an electric fence, and she lands on her back. Elric looks around to see where this magic has come from. Only a few inches from his face is a gold chain lying in the middle of a broken glass vial. A single small red poppy lays on top, emitting a soft glow. He squints beyond the invisible barrier, and behind one of the shorter trees, Ava emerges with the blade from Triora in her hand. She silently steps into the circle, not looking at Elric. Her focus is zeroed in on Faye's twitching body, balled up on the ground. Ava takes another step forward, snapping a branch beneath her step. Faye's head snaps to Ava at the sound of the crack, and she screeches in anger. She rushes toward Ava, her hand outstretched, her mouth agape, but before sound can come out, Ava cries out, "*Morcreom Ortalisantus!*"

Faye's body jerks, but it doesn't stop her momentum.

As she's about to reach Ava, she calls out, "*Duurad Prohatus!*"

But Ava takes another step forward. And another. Leaving no distance between them.

Faye freezes in place as she realizes Ava still has full autonomy over her body, the spell doing nothing to her. She bares her teeth, threatening to say the spell again, but before she can, Ava plunges the knife deep into Faye's heart. Ava's breathing quickens, and she clenches her jaw as she feels the flesh making way for the blade. Faye's breath catches, and she looks down at the weapon. A red, seeping stain of blood pools around the knife. Faye sees the rune on the base of the knife as it glows bright red. She reaches up and touches the matching symbol on the back of her neck and moans. As the red mortal blood continues to waterfall down the front of her dress, she drops heavily to her knees. Faye begins to cackle but immediately starts to choke and gurgle on the blood bubbling in her throat.

Ava runs to Elric, gently laying his head in her lap, the tears pouring down her face.

"Elric, I am so sorry. This is the only way they said it would work. I couldn't let Faye see anything. I'm so sorry." She tenderly moves the hair stuck to the blood on his forehead to the side. Her eyes search him all over in a panic, and the remorse is heavy on her face.

He reaches up, doing his best to smile. "It's okay, I get it."

"God, you're so hurt." Her breath comes out in shudders, and her tears won't stop.

Faye wheezes from behind them. "You don't... even know... if... it will break... the curse..." she says, gasping in between words.

Elric pushes himself upward, wincing as he does so. Ava gently helps him sit upright. He reaches to Ava's face and pulls her close, their foreheads resting against one another.

"I'll be okay. I'm already better."

Ava pulls back, her worry and relief filled eyes scanning over every inch of him. She releases Elric and turns towards Faye, who is still gasping for breath. Ava crawls over to her, placing her hands on the hilt of the blade.

"Your... daughter," Faye sneers, "Would have looked... just like Elric... with pretty green... eyes," she rasps.

Ava clenches her teeth and twists the blade, driving it in as far it will go.

With one final spasm, Faye's shoulders collapse and her breathing stops. Ava gives the knife a final push, knocking Faye onto her back. Her lifeless eye stares up at the night sky, a gruesome smile still spread across her lips. Her body steadily begins to dissipate into a black smoke, seeping into the mother tree trunk of the fairy ring. Ava returns to Elric and embraces him as tightly as she can without causing him pain. He wraps his arms around her waist, finally letting his lungs fill to capacity as he holds her safe. After a few moments, they pull apart but do not release each other. She lifts his arm, examining the now almost sealed self-inflicted wounds.

Sticking a finger in the collar of his shirt, pulling it open to examine his chest. "I can't tell if you're healing or not. Everything is so bloody."

Ava releases the tension on his shirt. "How do we know if it's broken or not? If killing her broke part of the curse?"

Elric looks over at where his centuries-long personal demon had laid moments before. Whatever semblance of a being she was no longer existed. He hoped.

"I don't know," he says, looking back at Ava. "Will you help me up?"

She hooks her arms under his, following his lead on how quickly he can move. Elric gets to his feet and tightly clutches the back of Ava's jacket, unsure of his footing.

"It's okay. We can take our time," says Ava.

The calm of the forest does not match the calamity of the night, making them both feel unsettled with their nerves shot.

"No, we need to go."

Elric takes a heavy step forward. Slowly limping the trail with Ava by his side, his battered body makes it difficult to move at a normal pace.

"I didn't mean anything I said back at the studio. I just had to make sure Faye couldn't see the plan. I am so sorry." Ava begins to cry again as they continue forward.

"I understand, my love. It's okay." He kisses the top of her head.

He laughs and winces in pain. "Had I not been so stubborn, maybe I wouldn't have maimed myself."

The side of her mouth lifts, but her expression remains troubled at the sight. "I was counting on you being stubborn for this to work, actually."

"Well, glad I could play my part."

"You took so long to get into the ring. I couldn't waste the chance we had. Watching what she was doing to you was," she covers her mouth and sniffles, "horrible," she says, her lips tight.

"It's done now, though. Truly, I understand," he vows hoarsely.

Elric knows nothing could have worked had he known. The connection with Faye was too deep and twisted, always keeping her steps ahead of them.

He gently rubs Ava's back and prays she is not plagued by the guilt of decisions made from this night.

They finally reach the parking lot, where the Subaru sits untouched.

Elric looks around the empty lot. "Where did you park without me seeing?"

"There's another lot up the way, with a path funneling into the other trail."

Walking over to the car, he opens the passenger side door, grimacing as he does so. He holds his side tightly where his ribs have broken, afraid if he lets go, he will fall apart.

"Get in and rest. I'll drive," Ava says, taking his arm and leading him into the seat.

"If you say so." He smiles, cringing at the pain the gesture causes his face.

She leans over and kisses him before running around the car to the driver's side. Ava starts the car and heads down the road back to the studio.

"We can deal with the other car later. Let's just go back. I'm sure Anita is worried," Elric says.

Ava nods and backs out of the parking lot. He reaches over and places his hand on her knee, looking over and smiling at her. She lovingly returns his smile. He settles back in his seat, keeping his hand on Ava. He waits for the claws of dread he has felt embedded in his being for centuries to loosen, but the feeling doesn't subside.

Nerves. He thinks, trying to convince himself.

XXVI

THIRTEEN MONTHS LATER BRISTOL, ENGLAND

His arms are tightly wrapped around her waist as they stand at the edge of a field, staring across an expansive sea of red. The full moon gives a soft glow, lighting a still-standing monastery untouched by people but not time. An oak tree that has been bound to the earth for centuries past and will be for centuries to come sits on the west side. Elric glances at it, knowing who is buried beneath that tree. His grip tightens around her waist, thinking of all the nights they have had to endure since then.

He raises his watch in plain view for both of them, and they watch the minute hand silently tick across the face. The time strikes midnight, giving way to a new day. Ava turns to him, beaming, a light glistening of fresh tears in her eyes.

"Happy twenty-ninth birthday, my love." The corners of his mouth lift as he pulls her in close for a soft kiss.

She draws back, and he can feel the moisture on his cheeks from her tears.

"I am twenty-nine." She smiles, grateful for the hour, symbolizing a year of life she's never experienced.

Ava opens her arms wide and throws her head back, laughing joyfully into the night air. She buries her face into Elric's chest, crying joyful sobs without restraint. He holds her tightly, kissing the top of her head, grateful to see the end of the curse in the same place it began.

Elric locks the door of their hostel behind them as Ava crawls onto the bed.

"I feel like I have an entire year of sleep to catch up on. Just waiting to see if I was going to die was exhausting," she says as she grabs a pillow, curling around it.

He shrugs out of his jacket, placing it on a small table in the corner before jumping on the bed. She laughs as her body bounces from the attack. She turns over on her back to look up at her love.

"Do you think it's really over?" Ava asks as she glances down at the place scars should be on his forearms.

Running her finger tenderly down the imaginary line, she continues. "I'm twenty-nine. What does that mean? Are we normal?"

Elric's eyes follow her finger as she traces his arm and laughs.

"No. We will never be normal. Maybe mortal, maybe immortal. Who knows. Only time will tell, but never normal."

She sits up on her elbows and smiles, stretching her neck to meet his lips. His eyes darken, and he submits, falling into her. Elric buries himself in her neck, and her hands go over the ever-familiar territory that is his body. She slides her hands up his shirt, pulling it over his shoulders. His back and chest are just as unmarred as his wrists. Only the scars in his mind remain from that horrific night. Ava's hand grazes over him, focused on her desire, not on the trauma of the past. Soon, nothing stands between them. He presses his body into her delicate skin, offering everything he is.

Ava turns over with Elric still wrapped around her from behind and picks her phone up off the nightstand. The screen reads 8:36 a.m. with a string of unread text notifications below it. She flips over onto her back, and Elric nuzzles into her neck, softly moaning. She smiles as she opens the first text message: a picture from Anita, Benny, and Geoffrey smiling brightly and wishing her a happy birthday.

Opening one eye, he looks at the picture and chuckles. "When we get back, Geoffrey is going to be a hundred pounds. She spoils him."

She laughs and nudges him. "No, he's a good boy. He gets all the treats."

"Hmm." He closes his eyes, beckoning Ava to lie closer.

Scooting in closer she opens the next set of text messages, a group text from her mom and dad.

Happy birthday, baby girl! Can't believe you've been gone for six months already! Can't wait to celebrate when you get back next week!

She responds with, "*Miss you so much and can't wait to see you and dad. Love you!*" and opens separate text messages from Kylie and Kiera. Kylie tells her happy birthday and asks for her to bring her back something cool. Kiera sends her a gif of a cat in front of a birthday cake. Ava laughs, unsurprised by their texts, and sends them both a heart emoji in reply. She finishes reading and replying to a slew of birthday texts from friends and family. When she lays down her phone on the nightstand, Elric sits up, resting on his hand, studying her face.

"She didn't text you, did she?"

Ava purses her lips. "No, she didn't. I mean, I didn't expect it. We haven't talked in almost a year."

"I'm sorry," he says, feeling responsible for the divide.

She turns over and lays on her side.

"Not your fault. We knew Robyn wasn't okay. What were we supposed to do? Especially after she started stalking you, showing up at our place multiple times in the middle of the night, the studio during the day." Ava sighs heavily. "I'm fortunate Mom and Dad have been gracious since we told them we were together. God, after everything we've been through, family drama seems so inconsequential. After Faye, it seemed like there could be nothing else wrong in the world, but Robyn just lost it when she found out we were together." She rubs her face in frustration. "Like, stop being petty—we've been together hundreds of years. We can't help it." Ava jokes and throws her leg over Elric's hip.

"I know," he chuckles, adjusting himself to comfort her body.

Humor laces her voice, but he can hear the sorrow behind it.

"We've just been trying to live a not harrowing life over the last year. And it's been hard not waking up every day looking over my shoulder, ready to see death. But I'm here. I'm alive. I'm twenty-nine. I'm with you."

"It's okay that you worry for her," he says, stroking her cheek, "That you miss her."

"Last time my mom said she checked out of the facility, I just knew that was the downfall. She's not even Robyn anymore."

Ava draws in close to Elric as he continues to stroke her hair. Eventually, she falls back asleep, and he remains awake by her side. The world outside them stirs. People are coming in and out of the building, exchanging pleasantries and goods, and car engines sputter down narrow streets.

Laying back, Elric raises his arm to lay it over his forehead. His thoughts swirl with the past, present, and future.

He's happy to be here with Ava by his side, her curse seemingly broken.

Elric looks around the room of the simple hostel, but something still doesn't feel right. Every night for the past year, he still feels the threat of losing Ava looming over them. He tries to put on a confident facade not to worry her, but he knows she can see right through it. After the night in the forest with Faye, they discussed a plan if it didn't work. How Elric would find her and bring her back to the paintings, and hopefully, it would restore her memories again. Expectations that Jacqueline and the others could still help if this all didn't go according to plan. But after that night, they never spoke of it again, steadfastly hoping that night was the end of it. They made plans to travel, and off they went, enjoying these last few months, both unwilling to bring up the possibility that they are working on borrowed time.

But as Ava said, the last year was spent full of unknowns, and now they made it past the marker. Maybe now this is where pure, unadulterated peace reigns. He runs his hands through his hair, the habitual move never ceasing.

"What are you thinking?"

Elric looks down at his anchor in those green eyes, unaware she was awake. He slides down into the bed so they are face to face, only an inch or so between them.

"Nothing." He grins.

She rolls her eyes. "Elric Ferron, I can hear those brain cells rubbing together, I swear."

He rolls onto his back and laughs loudly, slapping his chest.

"Sorry, I didn't know they were so loud," he says, rubbing his eyes.

Elric turns back over so they are facing each other, and she lays her hand on his cheek.

"What are you thinking about so hard?" She asks again.

She smiles at him, but her eyes are full of concern.

He stays silent for a moment, gazing at the face he knows so well. The one he has painted hundreds of times and will paint a thousand more. His one constant that has never changed and never will. His grounding in a storm of uncertainties.

"I love you." He wraps his hand around the back of her neck, kissing her with passion fueled by the centuries. Elric pulls his lips away but keeps hold of her.

"Genuinely, as much as I can mean it. Beyond this life, this plane of existence. I will love you until there is no more breath left in me. Every day, I love you more. Through the changing of the seasons and lands, I will love you. I will love you longer than the sun and moon continue to spin around the earth, and I will love you beyond the death of any star. Through our most blissful moments and our darkest, desolate ones, I love you. I have kissed you in your final moments, and I have cried with you when life was given, and each time I loved you more. But I promise you, Ava, I will love you beyond this life and any thereafter."

His throat became tight as he searched over the face he had memorized over centuries.

Her eyes well, "That promise you have kept."

They sit there silently regarding each other and reveling in the moment that is their love.

After a moment, Ava clears her throat. "I think. We should get married today. That's what I want to do today for my birthday. I don't need an official ceremony. I want to go into Micheldever Woods and, just in front of the trees and flowers, become one in this new life. This new life we can actually live. That's what I want."

The joy on her face leaves a permanent mark in his memory, and any feelings of worry dissipate.

"Let's go."

In a few hours' time, Elric and Ava walk hand in hand into a carpeted forest of blue and purple hues. Ava wears a dusty blue floral dress with capped sleeves—something she said she was saving for a special occasion. True to his personality, Elric wears a tan henley shirt and jeans. He decided against holes in the pants, wanting to dress more "elegant" for the occasion, he joked.

In full bloom, the bluebells take over, transforming the forest into an untouched haven amidst the growing cities. They walk into the woods until they are completely alone, with just the sun peeking through the canopy above.

Elric gently bumps into her. "You look beautiful."

Her cheeks grow pink. "How you always make me blush, I'll never know."

His smile is wide and full of pride. "I hope I never stop."

They find a narrow clearing where they don't have to worry about stepping on the carpet of delicate flowers and taking each other's hands. The breeze swirls the fresh scent of bluebells in the air all around them. The sun's rays form a halo behind them, and the cascading shadows settle on Ava and Elric's chests.

Standing there for a moment in the quiet solitude, staring intently at one another, Ava begins to giggle. Confused, he watches her as she bursts into loud belly laughter. He can't help but smile at her when she exudes pure, unadulterated joy.

"What is it?" He asks, infatuated with her. She catches her breath and speaks between failed, stifling chuckles. "I don't know, I didn't think this through. I don't know what to do now that we are here."

She breaks out into another round of laughter, and Elric grabs her, bringing her in tight and laughing as well. Their chuckles turn into cackles, their sides ache, and any animals in the glen have now wandered off for more peaceful territory. Soon, they regain control. Ava finds a clearing in the meadow and sits, gracefully smelling the flowers. Elric sits down by her side, cradling her in his arms. She presses her back into his chest, resting into the easiness of their physicality.

"I feel like I already said what would be vows back in bed," he says.

They sit silently for a moment longer before Ava turns her face towards him.

"Any moment might be our last. Everything is more beautiful because we are doomed. You will never be lovelier than you are right now. We will never be here again." She kisses him and leans back into him. "I love you, Elric Ferron."

Elric wraps his arms around her and holds her tight. Sitting in the solace of the meadow with the sun beginning to set, he never wants to lose sight of this moment—a moment they have worked so hard for. He stares out at the flowers, grateful for blue instead of red.

He brings his lips to her ear, whispering his promise. "Beyond this life. And any thereafter."

XXVII

ONE WEEK LATER ARCATA, CALIFORNIA
"It seems like too much. Maybe I shouldn't wear it in."

Ava fiddles with her new wedding ring, twisting it around her finger. She stares at the oval blue sandstone, set in a sunburst halo of diamonds. The sandstone reminds her of the night sky with all of its twinkling flecks, expansive and limitless—just as she hopes their future will be.

"You don't have to wear it." Elric pats her fidgeting hand as he drives.

"But I want to wear it."

"Okay, wear it." He smiles over at her as he releases her hand, placing both of his back on the steering wheel.

"I'm going to wear it. It's my birthday party." She readjusts her loose white blouse tucked into her jeans. "I just don't know if she is going to show. I doubt she will. Mom said she talked to her and said Robyn was in a really good place and knew she acted crazy with you. But I don't know. I think she is still mad."

Elric drums on the steering wheel with his thumbs. "I understand why you are feeling the way you are. But right now, we can't do anything about Robyn.

You haven't seen your family and friends in months. I know you can't just completely put your sister out of your mind, and I don't expect you to, but enjoy it as much as *you* can. Everyone will be excited to see you and be happy for you. Does that sound like a good deal?"

She smiles and nods, continuing to mess with the new piece of jewelry around her finger.

He parks the car down the street from Ava's parent's house in the only available parking space. Cars are packed bumper to bumper along the street.

"Jesus, did they invite everyone I've ever met?"

"Maybe just from 5th grade on?" He jokes.

Ava takes a deep breath and looks at him. "Alright, let's do this."

Elric puts the car into park and hops out, running over to her side to open the door. She gets out, straightening out her shirt once more. He offers her his hand, and she clasps onto it like she never plans on letting go.

Ava opens the door to her childhood home and walks into a festive atmosphere; people are mingling in all corners of the household. A large pink Happy Birthday banner hangs from the ceiling in greeting. Accompanying streamers of pink and gold hang throughout the house, and bright balloons filled with confetti sit in bunches in corners of the rooms. A loud shriek cuts across the room, and Ava's mother, Brooke, comes rushing to the doorway. The home's chatter abruptly stops at the startling noise but soon erupts into happy birthdays and cheers. Brooke brings Ava into a tight embrace, pinning her arms to her side.

"My baby!!! I've missed you so much! James! James!" Brooke cries.

James and her two younger sisters all run up to Ava, joining in on the greetings and embraces.

Brooke releases Ava, letting her dad have a turn for a solo hug, and turns her attention to Elric, opening up her arms to him. "Get over here!"

Elric laughs, embracing her family as if they really were his own.

"Oh my god, Ava, are you engaged?" Kiera yells out, astonished.

Ava gives an awkward smile, her cheeks bright red. "Well..."

Elric steps in next to Ava and loops his arm around her waist. "Actually, we got married. It was just so romantic and how often do you get the chance to get married in another country on a whim?"

Everyone stares at the couple, shocked, until from the back of the room, someone shouts, "Congratulations!"

The guests in the house turn toward the voice, and Anita stands up from the couch, Benny standing up with her.

She raises her drink in a toast to Elric and Ava. "Congratulations to Mr. and Mrs. Ferron!" She yells out, a wide smile spread across her face.

The house breaks out in noise again of congratulatory cheers and well wishes. Ava's family joins in with genuine delight at the news as soon as the shock wears off.

Everyone settles in after a while, and Ava finally relaxes and lets herself enjoy the night. She makes her rounds to different guests, introducing Elric to each. She gets stuck talking to an aunt who insists on discussing how soft and entitled the new generation is. Elric stands behind Ava, who quickly turns trying to save him from the conversation.

"How about you go find Anita and Benny? I'll join you shortly." She forces a pleasant tone.

Kissing her forehead, he goes off to find his friends. He walks into the kitchen, the countertops filled with an immense spread of food, where he finds Anita in the corner of the kitchen indulging in bite-size tiramisu. Benny watches her as if she is the only person in the house.

"Elric!" Anita calls, her mouth full.

He embraces each of them warmly. "I've missed you!"

"Eh," she shrugs.

She laughs, and they talk about the trip, with Ava joining them shortly.

The party continues; the indulgence of food, drink, and laughter is the theme of the night, and eventually, people start to trickle out.

When it's just Elric, Ava, Anita, and Benny left, Ava's parents bid the four goodnight, telling them to stay as long as they want. Elric sits on the couch with his feet on an ottoman and his arm around Ava's shoulders.

Anita looks at the time. "Three in the morning! God, Benny, we have to get home to let Geoffrey out. Ava, your parents throw a rager!"

"Don't I know it," she replies, blowing out a long stream of air.

"Thank you so much for looking after him, Anita," Elric says.

"Of course. I'm probably not giving him back," Anita laughs. "But if you guys do want him, I'll be at home all day tomorrow if you want to come pick him up."

"That sounds good. Love you," Ava says, reaching her hand towards Anita.

Anita takes her hand and examines Ava's ring, her eyebrows raising. "Shewwww, that is pretty. Good job, Elric."

Benny shakes Elric's hand on the way out, and soon, Ava and Elric are alone on the sofa.

"Did you have a good time?" He asks.

"I really did," she answers, laying her head on Elric's shoulder and smiling sleepily.

"You ready to head home?"

"Yes. I'm exhausted."

Elric stands and takes her by the hand, bringing her in for a long, fiery kiss.

"But I'm not *too* exhausted. Let's hurry," she says, the hoods of her eyes becoming heavily seductive.

They quickly make their way back, hands and lips still engaged the entire time. She giggles as they stumble up the walkway to the front door. He tries to get his keys and get the door unlocked quickly, but it proves difficult with his mouth still on Ava's.

He laughs. "Hang on."

He gets the lock undone, and he swings open the door, haphazardly closing it with his foot as they begin to undress each other. Elric throws the keys into his bowl in the entryway, where his newest artwork hangs. Dark greens and redwood trees circle Ava in guardianship, her arms spread wide, and the warm rays of sunshine highlight a blissful smile.

Elric hears something familiar and abruptly stops what he is doing, holding his hands over Ava's, causing her to be still.

"What is it?" she asks.

An intimate fear rests heavily on both of them, embracing them like an old friend as the familiar song is sung.

While I live in this wide world
None other will I seek.
With thy love, my sweet beloved,
My bliss though mightest increase;
A sweet kiss of thy mouth
Might be my cure.

Elric puts Ava behind him and walks to where the sound is coming from. The French doors to his backyard are wide open, and he can see a woman in a backless, floor-length red dress in the middle of the yard. They walk up to the doorway and stop.

"Rob?" Ava says, confused.

Robyn turns around with a malevolent and unhinged smile, "Happy Birthday, sissy."

"Robyn, what are you doing? This has to stop. Please," Ava cries, holding her hand out to her sister.

She takes a step towards her, but Elric holds her back.

Robyn yells furiously. "Stop what?! Stop fighting for what you stole?! You tricked him!"

"Where did you hear that song?" Elric asks, his voice hard.

Her gaze softens as she looks at him. "I thought you would like it, my love. My friend taught it to me."

"Robyn. This doesn't have to be this way. Please." Ava breaks out of Elric's hold and walks up to her.

Ava grabs onto her arms, with tears rolling down her face. "Rob, I miss you so much. Nothing has to be this way. It's not worth it."

"You took him from me." Robyn's eyes narrow. "I tried to scare you off. I tried to let you know whose territory you were coming for, but you were *incessant*.

Surely, I thought the bird gutted on your bed would have nipped it in the bud."

"Why would you- You did that to my home? It doesn't even matter." The desperation in Ava's voice is thick as she tries to break through to her sister.

"There is so much you don't know, and maybe one day I can tell you, but I want you to be okay first."

Ava brushes a hair out of Robyn's face.

An icy, fear-laden urgency grips Elric's heart as an overwhelming sense of doom consumes him. His breathing is shallow and rapid, each second feeling like an eternity before he moves. The dread is almost paralyzing, clouding every single coherent thought before something inside him screams, *Move!*

He quickly reaches Ava, yelling, "Ava! Get back from her now!"

Robyn leans in and responds to Ava through clenched teeth. "*I will be.*"

Robyn pulls out a knife, driving it deep into Ava's chest. Elric roars with an insurmountable grief, and catches her before she falls to the ground, but by the time he makes contact, her body is already lifeless. A loud guttural cry erupts from Elric, emitting nothing but the pure chaos inside him. Falling to his knees, he gently cradles her body. A crimson stain is seeping through her shirt, and his tears add to the layers of loss.

As he stares at his beloved's face, trying to memorize the tangible version of her one more time, he can hear soft steps approaching.

"Elric, we can be together now. She's not in the way anymore." Robyn says softly.

She kneels down next to him and tries to hold his hand, but he violently rips it away from her, tenderly placing it back on Ava's face.

He glares at Robyn and screams. "Get away from me! I will *never* love you."

He looks back down at Ava, kissing her cheek softly. "Beyond any life... and any... thereafter." His sobs break apart the words.

For the first time, he doesn't know what this death will mean, and fear fills him like never before.

Robyn sits back on her feet, puzzled. "This isn't how I thought it would go. I did what Faye said."

Elric's head snaps up. "What did you say?"

"Faye!" She laughs. "You know Faye. I met her after the night at the beach when you tried breaking up with me. She offered me things a lot more valuable than friendship."

Robyn turns around to show a marking branded on the back of her neck.

"She showed me power. She *gave* me power, power to make everything how it should be. Elric, you and I are supposed to be together. It can happen now. The spell Ava had you under should be broken. That's what Faye said."

Staring down at Ava's face, love in the form of his tears continues to fall on her cheeks.

Elric's voice is as broken as his spirit. "It was never a spell with her. Ava is my true love, my best friend, my muse." He runs his thumb delicately over her lips, the fear of never feeling them again flooding his body. "My soul mate."

Robyn tries to reach for him again, a wild look in her eyes. "You say that because you were tricked. Elric, I am your *everything*. There is nothing in the way now. We can spend forever together."

Rage churns a tide in Elric's chest, his resolve leaving him unwilling to be toyed with any longer.

"Never!" He yells as he takes the dagger from Ava's heart and savagely stabs it into Robyn's chest.

Robyn watches him, her eyes wide in amusement as he pushes the cold steel farther in, waiting for it all to be over. Throwing her head back, she begins to laugh maniacally. Reaching forward, she swiftly pulls the dagger from her chest. Looking down, she studies her chest, thoroughly amused. He follows her gaze and sees her open wound slowly healing itself, the flesh knitting together. His eyes grow wide, swimming with terror and confusion.

She turns her hand in a dramatic circle and conjures Faye's book of souls out of thin air. Robyn's eyes go completely white, and she gives a depraved smile. "I won't let you go that easily, my love."

She affectionately runs her hand down the side of his face, "*Esbris Igdade.*"

The edges of Elric's world start to close in and he begins to lose sight of Ava lying limp in his arms.

"Beyond this life," he whispers as his senses dull and the relentless pain in his soul continues to pulse.

Just before an unconscious darkness could overtake him, he feels the faint rise and fall of her breath...

TIME'S ABANDONED

READ AN EXCERPT FROM BOOK TWO:

He wakes with a jolt sitting up straight in bed, his breathing labored. Covered in a cold sweat, beads of perspiration travel down his spine. His eyes wander around the dark room, willing his mind to calm. A soft warm hand reaches from the other side of the bed and delicately rests it on his chest.

"Elric, what's wrong?"

Placing his hand over the top of hers, Elric swallows his anxieties to not worry her. It's already been a tough couple months.

"I'm fine." He smiles in the dark even though she can't see it.

"Is it the nightmares again?" She asks.

Flashes of blood and screaming rattle Elric's mind, he doesn't want to lie again. She always knows when he is lying anyway.

"Yes, every time I think things are better the nightmares and headaches come back." He reluctantly but truthfully answers.

She pulls him down as she lays back. He wraps his arms around her, burying his face in the back of her neck.

"We will call the doctor tomorrow. She said that should have been getting better by now." He can hear the worry in her voice.

His hold on her briefly tightens in reassurance, "It's okay. It's much better than it was even a few months ago." He kisses her behind her ear, "I'm so lucky to have you."

"You're right. We will see what the doctor says tomorrow." She nestles deeper to him, "I love you."

He tenderly kisses the back of her neck, "I love you too, Robyn."

ACKNOWLEDGEMENTS

To my forever muse, whom I could not have wrote a love story as great as this one, without having ours first. Isaiah you have championed me from day one and there are not enough "Thank yous" or "I love yous" in the world to show my gratitude in this journey of my book or in our life. I will love you beyond this life. To my four babies who put up with mommy on the computer and who always cheered me on even though they didn't truly know what was going on. I love you four so much and you gave me the courage to put myself out there so you can learn to never let fear stop you. Mom, thanks for being a pain in my butt. But thank you for pushing me even though you knew I was scared and for encouraging a passion, I had hidden, every step of the way. Life surely gave us lemons, but look at this lemonade. Precious Baby Angel, Hannah, you knew of this before I could even talk about it to anyone else. You are my precious little angel whom I love so much. You were such a huge part of the push that made this a reality. Kayla, you were my sounding board for the years it took me to make this happen. From storyline to font types to multiple designs. I'm so grateful for you, so much of this wouldn't have happened if you hadn't been so supportive. Vanessa, thank you for coming in. You did so much more for me than you realize, your love for reading has always matched mine and your marketing strategies and just overall encouragement over the last leg of the race will never be taken for granted. Anna, I don't have the words to say what you came in and did for me. I would have been a dumpster fire without. Grateful doesn't cover it. Thank you so much

ABOUT THE AUTHOR

Dreana is a passionate novelist whose love for storytelling started in her hometown of San Diego, CA. Soon trading the sunny coast for the enchanting woods of the south, she now lives in Tennessee. Married to her first love, Isaiah, they share in each others creative pursuits, while also sharing in the joy and chaos of raising four spirited children.

Dreana is a devoted fan of fantasy literature and is influenced by timeless tales and epic love stories.

When she's not writing she's watching a quarterly marathon of "Lord of the Rings" or spending time in nature with her family.

Whether her head is buried in a book or she's lost in the woods, her life is on the constant pursuit for creative expression.

Keep up with Dreana and her books here:
Tiktok: **@dreana.ellis**
Instagram: **@dreana.ellis**